THE STORIES AND FABLES
OF AMBROSE BIERCE

CONTENTS

FABLES

NOTE ON SOURCES

The material in this book has been taken from the following volumes of *The Collected Works of Ambrose Bierce*, 12 vols. (New York and Washington, D.C.: The Neale Publishing Company, 1909–12), with some alteration in orthography and punctuation:

Volume 2, *In the Midst of Life (Tales of Soldiers and Civilians)* (1909): "A Horseman in the Sky," "An Occurrence at Owl Creek Bridge," "Chickamauga," "One of the Missing," "Killed at Resaca," "The Coup de Grâce," "One Kind of Officer," "One Officer, One Man" from the section "Soldiers"; "The Man and the Snake" from "Civilians."

Volume 3, *Can Such Things Be?* (1910): "The Death of Halpin Frayser," "The Secret of Macarger's Gulch," "One Summer Night," "Moxon's Master," "Staley Fleming's Hallucination," "A Resumed Identity," "A Psychological Shipwreck," "John Bartine's Watch," "The Damned Thing," "Haïta the Shepherd," "An Inhabitant of Carcosa," "The Stranger" from the section "Can Such Things Be?"; "Present at a Hanging," "A Wireless Message," "An Arrest" from "The Ways of Ghosts"; "Three and One Are One" from "Soldier-Folk"; "The Difficulty of Crossing a Field" from "Some Haunted Houses."

Volume 6, *The Monk and the Hangman's Daughter / Fantastic Fables* (1911): "The Monk and the Hangman's Daughter" and the fables. The fables here entitled "A Little Learning," "A Plucked Goose," "A Matter of Taste," "The Seeker for Simplicity" and "No Irregularity" were originally published, without titles, in *Fun* magazine in London in 1872–73 and are taken from the section "Fables from 'Fun.'"

Volume 8, *Negligible Tales / On with the Dance / Epigrams* (1911): "Curried Cow" from the section "Negligible Tales"; "Oil of Dog" and "The Hypnotist" from "The Parenticide Club."

INTRODUCTION

LIKE Robert Ingersoll and H. L. Mencken, Bierce is allied
to the minor American tradition of the Village Atheist.
He also stands with Brockden Brown, Poe, Hawthorne,
Fitz James O'Brien, Melville, Mark Twain, Stephen Crane,
Hemingway, Faulkner and others among the "dark" writers,
though it is not here asserted either that this label wholly
covers the work of any or all of these nor yet that they were
at all alike in other respects. Franklin Walker tried to undercut
Bierce's cynicism by placing it in the tradition of San Francisco journalism. His facts are both indisputable and invalu-
able, but it is impossible to see Bierce's tone as wholly the
product of external influences. Nor can one quite go along with
his brother Alfred's notion that he changed after having been
wounded in the head, for he was only sixteen when he dreamed
that God and Man were both dead and that he came upon the
"dreadfully decomposed" but still sentient corpse of himself.
He downgraded almost all institutions and professions and
most human activities. Like W. C. Fields, he even hated, or
professed to hate, both dogs and children, at least boys, though
he was kind to other animals and seems to have had a certain
magnetism for them.

From one point of view, however, Bierce may be said to
sport an unmatchable title as one of the "immortals" of
American literature: he is the only writer of reputation who

has left us with no record of his death. He simply disappeared in revolutionary Mexico at the end of 1913, and if the present existence of a man born in 1842 were not among the things which cannot be (yet surely not more so than some that he solemnly recorded), one might even argue that he never died at all, or even, to carry the fantasy further, that he never lived. For he himself wrote:

> My how my fame rings out in every zone
> A thousand critics shouting, "He's unknown!"

Perhaps, after all, it was suitable that a respected historian of American literature, whom Christian charity here leaves nameless, should have written, in a generally disparaging notice of him, that "a few of his novels may be studied with profit as models of their kind," a sweet tribute by which Bierce, who never wrote a novel, would surely have been charmed.

Coming back from Cloud Cuckoo Land, however, one may record prosaically that Bierce is reported to have been born, on June 24, 1842, in Meigs County, Ohio, the tenth of thirteen children, all of whose names began with *A*. The family was of old New England stock, going back, on the mother's side, to William Bradford. Bierce's father was a farmer who loved literature, not the "unwashed savage" his son called him, and his uncle became mayor of Akron and a local hero.

At fifteen the boy left home and became a printer's devil. Two years later he was sent to a military academy for a year, from which he returned to do odd jobs in Warsaw. Four days after Lincoln issued his call for volunteers, he became the second man in his county to enlist. He was at Shiloh, Murfreesboro, Nashville, Chickamauga and Franklin, and was wounded at Kennesaw Mountain. He was captured by the enemy and cited for bravery. He became a second lieutenant and a brevet-major, and after the war served the Treasury Department in confiscating rebel property, in which capacity he acquired considerable sympathy for the old enemy and was outraged by the conduct of the army of occupation in New Orleans.

From here he went as an "engineer officer" with an army surveying expedition in the West. Late in 1866 he reached

San Francisco, where he first worked as night watchman in the Mint, then began writing for such publications as *The Californian*, *The Golden Era* and *The Alta California*. His reputation for stinging wit began with the publication of satirical paragraphs about local figures in the "Town Crier" department of *The News-Letter*.

On Christmas Day, 1871, he married Mollie Day; his father-in-law financed a trip to England, where Bierce remained until September 1875, becoming an habitué of the Fleet Street Bohemia and an intimate of lesser English literary lights and journalists. The piratical publisher John Camden Hotten, whom Mark Twain loathed, brought out his first, unimportant book, *The Fiend's Delight*, in 1872.

After his return to San Francisco, he wrote for *The Argonaut*, *The Call* and *The Wasp*, and in 1880 he was general agent for a mining company in Dakota. From 1887 until 1908 he wrote for the San Francisco *Examiner* and other publications controlled by William Randolph Hearst, who showed the patience of a saint in refusing to accept his numerous resignations when his copy had been tampered with and even failed to register resentment over the outrageous quatrain Bierce published after the assassination of the governor-elect of Kentucky, which gave Hearst's enemies the chance to accuse him of having inspired the killing of President McKinley:

> The bullet that pierced Goebel's breast
> Can not be found in all the West;
> Good reason, it is speeding here
> To stretch McKinley on his bier.

In the winter of 1895–96 Bierce had gone to Washington to represent the Hearst papers, campaigning against the Southern Pacific–inspired Funding Bill, and in 1905 he began writing "The Passing Show" for *Cosmopolitan*.

His reputation as a writer of short stories rests upon two volumes, *In the Midst of Life* or *Tales of Soldiers and Civilians* (1891) and *Can Such Things Be?* (1893). Doubleday, Page published *The Cynic's Word Book*, later *The Devil's Dictionary*, in 1906, and in 1909–12 Walter Neale brought out a twelve-volume, limited collected edition of his writings. In June 1913

Bierce was again in California, but he left in October and crossed the Mexican border in November. His last-known letter was written from Chihuahua City on December 26. He had always championed a human being's right to die, and some of the things he said and did before leaving for Mexico strongly suggest that he did not intend to come back.

Bierce was a tall, handsome, blue-eyed blond, of military bearing and of great vitality and magnetism. In the narrower sense of the term, his immoderate drinking seems to have been his only serious moral transgression. He professed a determination to preserve "the ancient, primitive distinction between right and wrong," had an almost quixotic sense of honor, and nobody has ever suspected him of "selling out." There is some rather vague, doubtful testimony to wide sexual contacts, but it is also clear that he was a prude. Juliet's conduct in the Balcony Scene shocked him, and he boasted that not even his wife had ever seen him naked. Except for *The Dance of Death*, in which he collaborated with others in 1877 in attacking the waltz and other manifestations of sexuality, and which sold 18,000 copies and was judged by many to be more offensive than its targets, he was as timid about using sexual excitation in literature as he was bold in glutting his readers with physical horrors. He held misogynist views, and the only women for whom he ever seems to have expressed admiration were the Empress Eugénie, George Eliot, Mrs. Phoebe Apperson Hearst, Gertrude Atherton and Agnes Repplier—surely a strangely assorted list. He left his wife, who apparently adored him, when he discovered that she had received a love letter, though she seems to have been altogether innocent. His children he for the most part ignored; the girl survived, but both the boys came to bad ends. The elder, Day, committed murder and suicide in his mid-teens; when the girl he thought he was in love with married somebody else, he killed both her husband and himself (wounding her for good measure). The younger, Leigh, less spectacularly drank himself to death. Bierce's parting words to Day, when he visited him on his deathbed, may well be the maddest parental blessing on record: "You are a noble soul, Day—you did just right."

His political philosophy, like his literary theories, was in

line with his temperament. Jack London thought that, if he
had been born a generation later, he might have been a revolutionary socialist, and it is true that he advocated the abolition
of private ownership of land and a heavy inheritance tax and
maintained the obligation of society to provide employment
for every man. When a writer declares that the best elements
in the American melting pot are, in order, the Jews, the
Chinese and the Mormons, he does not seem to have been
tarred with the usual WASP brush. Bierce always wrote "£eland
$tanford," and he was a brave soldier in Hearst's war against
the Southern Pacific; if it is true that when Huntington offered
him to name his price, he named $75,000,000, or his estimate
of the railroad's tax indebtedness, to be paid to the United
States Treasurer, this was certainly his finest hour. On the
whole, however, he came much closer to fascism than to anything we now regard as revolutionary. He supported the Boer
War and, with some reservations, the Spanish-American War.
He disliked labor unions and labor leaders and had no tenderness for immigrants. He favored harsh prison discipline and
the death penalty, which he even wished to inflict in advance
upon those judged likely to commit murder in the future. He
wanted to establish a censorship over the press, the church
and the stage ("a violation of good taste . . . outrages me more
than does many a crime of murder committed under the stress
of some powerful and justifiable emotion"), and his advocacy
of governmental control over railroad and telegraph was in
the interest of authority, for all his sympathies were with an
aristocracy of brains or a kind of aristocratic and paternalistic
feudalism. "It is the despotisms of the world that have been
the conservators of civilization."

Yet, though his habitual stance as a journalist was that of
attack, Bierce was not a reformer, for he concerned himself
only with particularities, not principles. When the *Examiner*
published Edwin Markham's poem "The Man with the Hoe,"
which swept like a prairie fire over America, Bierce thought
it lacked even "the vitality of a sick fish." To be sure, he had
his defense ready here: "I care nothing for principles—they
are lumber and rubbish. What concerns our happiness and
welfare, as affectable by our fellow men, is conduct. 'Prin-

ciples, not men,' is a rogue's cry. . . ." As a rebuke to those
who only oppose "sin" but never attack the evildoer, this is
excellent, but the uncomfortable suspicion persists that he
had only a temperamental basis for his attacks rather than a
philosophical or intellectual one.

On the subject of religion, however, Bierce's apostasy has
often been overstressed. Though he thought of himself as
antireligious, he has enough conventional religious references
(as "one of God's mysterious messengers" in "The Death of
Halpin Frayser" and "victory or defeat, as God might will" in
"One Officer, One Man") to make it clear that his imagination,
like Mark Twain's, was haunted by the thought of God, angels
and the Judgment. It is perhaps not without significance that
even his childish disillusionment over Santa Claus demanded
a difficult adjustment and was long brooded over. On a deeper
level, his conviction of the profound evil in mankind may well
owe something to the Calvinism in his background; see, for
example, the interesting passage on foreordination (very
similar to Mark Twain's chain philosophy) in "One of the
Missing." Whether they "believe" or not, writers who find
an important part of their inspiration in the supernatural are
not materialists by temperament, and Bierce's stories are not
free of metaphysical speculation, sometimes in the form of
quotations from occult lore or what purports to be such. There
can be no question about his sincerity when he writes that
"the virtues of Socrates, the wisdom of Aristotle, the example
of Marcus Aurelius, the selflessness of Jesus Christ engage
my admiration and rebuke my life," but he does not stop with
this. He believed that the application of the Golden Rule was
the only cure for industrial disputes, and he comes amazingly
close to Charles M. Sheldon's best-selling novel, *In His Steps*,
when he declares: "This is my ultimate and determining test
of right—'What, in the circumstances, would Jesus have
done?'" Indeed, many of his jibes against the church are
inspired by its failure to live up to Jesus' teaching, and in the
remarkable letter he wrote Mrs. McCracken, shortly before
he disappeared, though reaffirming his dislike of religion, he
authorized her to pray for him: "Why, yes, dear—that will
not harm either of us."

Like Poe, Bierce believed that poems must be short, for otherwise the poetic quality cannot be sustained (a poem for him was essentially imagery), and that a novel was only "a short story padded." His style, even in his fiction, has something of the baldness and directness of journalism, but he combines this with a military or aristocratic formality and reserve. The eighteenth-century "serenity, fortitude and reasonableness" he professed to admire shows not in his subject matter, which is often highly sensational, but only in his passion for correctness and his emotional reserve; the last book published during his lifetime was a literary manual called *Write It Right* (1909). Like Aristotle and James Branch Cabell, he wanted a writer to "represent life, not as it is, but as it might be; character, not as he finds it, but as he wants it to be." In his own stories there is little character, as the psychological realists understand it, the whole emphasis being upon situation. He hated local color, and slang was for him "the grunt of the human hog," and he also hated realism, at least as it was practiced by "Miss Nancy Howells" and "Miss Nancy James, Jr."

These principles he imposed upon both himself and his literary protégés, of whom the most important was George Sterling. Mary Austin, who thought Bierce "something of a *poseur*, tending to overweight a slender inspiration with apocalyptic gestures," and saw him as "a man secretly embittered by failure to achieve direct creative power, a man of immense provocative capacity, always secretly, perhaps even to himself, seeking to make good in some other's gift what he himself had missed," felt that the value of his guidance was doubtful, leaving "as many aspirants sticking in the bog of unrealized aspirations as he drew out on firm ground." This may be too severe. Bierce certainly did fail to "achieve direct creative power" in poetry, but this he was himself the first to perceive and proclaim. It is certainly true, however, that he was a picayunish and dictatorial mentor and that anybody who wished to retain his interest must dot every *i* and cross every *t* according to his own highly specialized standards.

Bierce's sardonicism, often bitter, sometimes not unmixed with a grim kind of amusement, appears in its most undiluted form in *The Devil's Dictionary*, which, not being a work of fiction, has not been drawn upon for this collection, and in his fables (the principal collection of which, *Fantastic Fables*, was published in New York in 1899), which have been liberally represented. *The Monk and the Hangman's Daughter*, an interesting variation of the *Thaïs* situation, or the conflict between eros and agape (though the girl is certainly no courtesan), is something else again, for though it is in a sense our *pièce de résistance*, it can be called Bierce's work only in a somewhat Pickwickian sense, and it has often been warmly admired by those who do not care much for his more characteristic work. According to his preface to the story, Bierce substantially rewrote G. A. Danziger's attempted translation of a German tale. After its initial serial publication in the San Francisco *Examiner*, beginning on September 13, 1891, and its first book publication, the next year, by the F. J. Schulte Company of Chicago, which promptly went bankrupt, Bierce and his collaborator, Danziger (also known as Adolphe de Castro), quarreled violently concerning the extent and value of their respective contributions, and the controversy was not resolved during Bierce's lifetime. Within ten days in 1893, Bierce claimed, in his "Prattle" column in the *Examiner*, both that it made no difference whether he or Danziger had had the larger share "in spoiling the work of a better man than either" and that he had written "every word of the story" as published. Publishers and critics have shared in the resultant confusion. In 1928 Albert and Charles Boni agreed to pay Danziger a share of the royalties on their edition. In 1929 C. Hartley Grattan conjecturally credited Bierce not only with stylistic improvement but also with heightening the dramatic conflict and perceiving "the essentials of the sexual-psychological conflict" in the monk, and entered a high claim for the work as an American religious novel, and as late as 1967 Richard O'Connor thought he discerned in the monk's feeling of exaltation upon his first sight of the mountains an echo of "Bierce's experience as a youthful soldier marching into the Appalachians of West Virginia" and in the treatment of "the role of sexuality in religious fervor" a reminiscence of his "unwilling attendance at backwoods revival meetings when a boy."

The "better man than either" Danziger or himself to whom Bierce referred was the German writer Richard Voss, whose tale, "Der Mönch von Berchtesgaden," appeared originally in a German magazine, *Vom Fels zum Meer*. In 1924 he would republish it at Stuttgart in a book called *Der Mönch von Berchtesgaden und andere Geschichten*. Danziger read the magazine version late in 1890 and translated it, and two other writers had a hand at "improving" his version before he brought it to Bierce, who knew little or no German, for the same purpose.

O'Connor apparently had not read Frank Monaghan's article, "Ambrose Bierce and the Authorship of *The Monk and the Hangman's Daughter*," which appeared in *American Literature* 2 (1930–31) : 338–49, for it was Monaghan who moved toward settling the dispute by making a careful comparative study of "Der Mönch" and *The Monk*, the result of which was to show that no significant changes appeared in the English version. About fifty lines of small deletions were made, while about seventy lines comprised small, numerous amplifications by Bierce, Danziger or another (since Danziger's manuscript is not extant, it is impossible to be sure which). The only important change occurs at the very end, where the addition of a dozen lines, bastardizing Benedicta, makes the tale more ironic (Monaghan assigned this to Bierce). All the rest is "either close paraphrasing or literal translation." Naturally these findings do not impugn the stylistic excellence of the English version, which, Danziger's limitations as a stylist being what they were, it seems safe to credit to Bierce.

The principal themes of the short stories upon which Bierce's claim as a writer must rest primarily are war, death, horror, madness, ghosts, and fear, and, as we might expect, his presentation of all of them is shot through with bitter irony. Thus "One of the Missing" is an almost sadistic study of a trapped, immobilized soldier, frightened to death by his own rifle pointed at his head—but the gun is not loaded; in "One Officer, One Man," Captain Graffenreid falls upon his own

sword when "the strain upon his nervous organism" grows
"insupportable." Nor are such terrors confined to the battlefield; in "The Man and the Snake," Harker Brayton, spending
the night in a herpetologist's house, is frightened to death by
a stuffed reptile in his bedroom.

In the "Parenticide" stories, Bierce treats death whimsi-
cally, but this seems even less "wholesome" to many of his
readers than his reveling in its horrors. Historically he ranks
with J. W. DeForest and Stephen Crane as having pioneered
in the realistic portrayal of war in fiction. To him a soldier
is an assassin for his country, a "hardened and impenitent
man-killer." In his pages son kills father and troops fire on
their own men and shell their own homes; in "One Kind of
Officer" he offers a bleak picture of the mindlessness of military discipline. Yet he has none of the moral revulsion against
war that characterized the war novels published after World
War I; although he is free of "patriotics," one often finds it
difficult to decide whether his emphasis upon war's horrors
has been inspired by what he calls its "criminal insanity" or
by his love of sensation. He himself carried the military
temperament in some aspects into civil life, where he packed
a gun, and he might well have stayed in the army had he
received the commission he thought he deserved. Sometimes
he gives the impression of preferring the horrors of war to
the corruptions of peace, and he revisited Civil War battle-
fields (one fancies nostalgically) before disappearing into
Mexico.

It has been objected to Bierce's stories of the supernatural
that they lack atmosphere and that the entrance of the other-
worldly element into the tale, being unprepared for, is therefore unimpressive and unconvincing. None of this is true, I
think, except in such brief, bald tales as "Present at a Hanging" and "The Difficulty of Crossing a Field," where the
absence of atmosphere is very much the point of the yarn.
These stories deal with just such inexplicable phenomena as
have come without preparation into the experience of innumerable human beings from time to time, which seem to
admit of no rational explanation, yet cannot be explained
away, so that we are left helplessly ejaculating Bierce's ques-

tion, "Can such things be?" But when atmosphere serves Bierce's purpose, he can supply it to burn, as in "One Kind of Officer": "The gray fog, thickening every moment, closed in about him like a visible doom." The menacing setting in "The Secret of Macarger's Gulch" combines natural and super-natural threats, and "An Inhabitant of Carcosa" ("In all this there were a menace and a portent—a hint of evil, an intima-tion of doom") could hardly have been bettered by Poe himself.

Bierce's concentration upon particularities is perhaps seen most strikingly in his Civil War stories, which, so far from dealing with issues or large movements, generally present solitary soldiers facing individual dilemmas. The dull run-of-the-mill of day-by-day life in the military is not for this author; indeed, his preoccupation with the sensational and the unusual and his passion for smashing climaxes tempts the reader of contemporary short stories to regard his as arti-ficially contrived or old-fashioned. Nevertheless, the best of his tales, both in this area and elsewhere, are much more varied in their technical expertise than some commentators have been willing to grant.

To be sure, such items as the "Negligible Tales" and the pieces in "The Parenticide Club" are essentially tall tales or burlesques, dedicated to achieving the broadest effects of what we now call "black humor." ("Having murdered my mother under circumstances of singular atrocity, I was arrested and put upon my trial"—"My Favorite Murder." "Early one June morning in 1872 I murdered my father—an act which made a deep impression on me at the time"—"An Imperfect Con-flagration.") Some are ineffective. Those that succeed owe their success to a masterly use of incongruity or inversion of values, murderers being referred to as saints, et cetera. But Bierce's reputation does not rest upon such work as this.

Although he is best known for his ghost stories and Civil War tales, not all his work comes under these heads. The Western stories suggest a grim Bret Harte. "Moxon's Master" is science fiction, clearly allied to the Poe who wrote "Maelzel's Chess Player," and "Haïta the Shepherd" is straightforward allegory in the Cupid and Psyche tradition. But the variations and modifications of technique are more impressive than those that appear in subject matter. In one of the "Negligible Tales," Bierce remarks parenthetically that "a story once begun should not suffer impedition." This is not in accord with his own practice, however, for he weaves forward and backward with great skill, a master of every device the narrator knows to enlist interest and build up suspense.

Look, for example, at "A Horseman in the Sky," certainly one of the finest tales. It begins with an elaborate description of the setting. Then, in Section II, we get a long flashback, giving us the background of the leading character, so that we may understand the situation in which he finds himself. Next, the confrontation that is the essence of the tale is introduced, the father's own authority is invoked to sanction his killing, and the shot fired by Carter Druse at the end of the section is the only positive action in the story. In Section III the scene shifts to a Federal officer who sees the horseman fall. Section IV returns to the end of III and, at last, to Druse's specific admission that he knew the man he shot was his father.

In "An Occurrence at Owl Creek Bridge," on the other hand, the situation in which Peyton Farquhar finds himself is set forth at the very beginning. There follows a precise description of scene and surroundings, creating suspense through a long paragraph, before we come back to "the man who was engaged in being hanged." Next comes further description of the setting and of the persons involved in the imminent action, some of it from the point of view of an omniscient narrator, some from Farquhar's own, and including such effective use of the irrelevant, faithful to the workings of the mind under stress, as his observation of the "piece of dancing driftwood" moving down the sluggish stream. His pondering how he might act if he could free his hands and throw off the noose is preparation; it misleads the reader into accepting what follows and makes the surprise ending more of a shock when it comes. The last sentence in Section I—"The sergeant stepped aside"—is really the end of the story, but we do not know that until we have read through two more sections. Section II gives us Farquhar's background and history, and Section III deals with what goes on in his mind before his fall at the end of the rope breaks his neck. This piece, which Howells chose for his anthology of great American stories, is probably Bierce's most brilliant achievement, but it is essentially a tour de force, much trickier than the "Horseman" and to that extent not quite so convincing.

Perhaps Bierce's most masterly use of the surprise ending is at the close of "The Coup de Grâce," which is only an anecdote in itself but which requires every word of the elaborate build-up Bierce supplies for the full comprehension of its irony. Sometimes, as at the end of "The Man and the Snake," Bierce carefully spells out what has happened, but sometimes he leaves the solution to the ingenuity of the reader: was Staley Fleming killed by the ghost of his victim's dog or by his own guilty fear? Both "One Kind of Officer" and "The Coup de Grâce" have an "open" ending; the climactic action comes after the story is over, but Bierce does not tell us what it was. As for "impedition," even the editorializing about euthanasia in "The Coup de Grâce" is necessary to the final effect: everybody recognizes the right of the hopelessly injured horse to be helped out of his misery, but Captain Madwell may well pay with his life for having been generous enough to grant the same to his friend. The revelation at the end of the terrible "Chickamauga" that the child is a deaf mute helps us to accept what we might have questioned before, for only complete incomprehension can justify complete indifference to suffering. "Chickamauga" has a disarmingly gentle beginning for so grim a tale, and the description of the horribly mangled soldiers approaches the bounds of the bearable, yet even the resemblance between the blood-bedaubed men and the make-up of the painted clowns the child has seen in the circus is at least partially true to the workings of the child mind. The turn of the screw comes, of course, with the realization that the pretty light that had so pleased him comes from his own burning house, where his mother lies horribly dead.

If "The Death of Halpin Frayser" seems more rambling and casual in its organization than these other tales, the numerous elements contained in it have still been fitted together with great ingenuity. "John Bartine's Watch" uses narrative within a narrative, and Ernest Hemingway could not have set down the expert notation of detail at the beginning of "The Damned Thing" any better. Both "One of the Missing" and "Killed at Resaca" make skillful use of an epilogue, but each in a different way. "Resaca" is a first-person narrative, but the narrator is not the principal character. There is a straightforward expositional introduction, which is followed by character analysis and generalizations about battle that run on for several pages before the action begins. This story is a character study, but the figure in the carpet does not emerge until the final epilogue records the narrator's visit to the dead hero's sinister sweetheart in San Francisco a year after the war, when we learn it was her taunt that inspired the foolhardiness which cost his life. Again the last sentence cracks the whip, and since the girl herself surely takes it literally, the irony is perfect and complete.

Benedetto Croce once remarked that in literature technique either did not exist at all or else it was synonymous with art itself. I have never been quite sure that this was not an overstatement, but there can be no question that, in the case of Ambrose Bierce at least, both subject matter and method were perfect mirrors of his own mind and soul. This is the measure of both his success and his failure, and it may well be that the same thing is quite as true of other writers.

West Newton, Massachusetts   EDWARD WAGENKNECHT

STORIES

A PSYCHOLOGICAL
SHIPWRECK

IN the summer of 1874, I was in Liverpool, whither I had gone on business for the mercantile house of Bronson & Jarrett, New York. I am William Jarrett. My partner was Zenas Bronson. The firm failed last year, and unable to endure the fall from affluence to poverty, he died.

Having finished my business, and feeling the lassitude and exhaustion incident to its dispatch, I felt that a protracted sea voyage would be both agreeable and beneficial, so instead of embarking for my return on one of the many fine passenger steamers I booked for New York on the sailing vessel *Morrow*, upon which I had shipped a large and valuable invoice of the goods I had bought. The *Morrow* was an English ship with, of course, but little accommodation for passengers, of whom there were only myself, a young woman and her servant, who was a middle-aged Negress. I thought it singular that a traveling English girl should be so attended, but she afterward explained to me that the woman had been left with her family by a man and his wife from South Carolina, both of whom had died on the same day at the house of the young lady's father in Devonshire—a circumstance in itself sufficiently uncommon to remain rather distinctly in my memory, even had it not afterward transpired in conversation with the young lady that the name of the man was William Jarrett, the same as my own. I knew that a branch of my family had settled in South Carolina, but of them and their history I was ignorant.

The *Morrow* sailed from the mouth of the Mersey on the fifteenth of June, and for several weeks we had fair breezes and unclouded skies. The skipper, an admirable seaman but nothing more, favored us with very little of his society, except at his table; and the young woman, Miss Janette Harford, and I became very well acquainted. We were, in truth, nearly always together, and being of an introspective turn of mind I often endeavored to analyze and define the novel feeling with which she inspired me—a secret, subtle, but powerful attraction which constantly impelled me to seek her; but the attempt was hopeless. I could only be sure that at least it was not love. Having assured myself of this and being certain that she was quite as wholehearted, I ventured one evening (I remember it was on the third of July) as we sat on deck to ask her, laughingly, if she could assist me to resolve my psychological doubt.

For a moment she was silent, with averted face, and I began to fear I had been extremely rude and indelicate; then she fixed her eyes gravely on my own. In an instant my mind was dominated by as strange a fancy as ever entered human consciousness. It seemed as if she were looking at me, not *with*, but *through*, those eyes—from an immeasurable distance behind them—and that a number of other persons, men, women and children, upon whose faces I caught strangely familiar evanescent expressions, clustered about her, struggling with gentle eagerness to look at me through the same orbs. Ship, ocean, sky—all had vanished. I was conscious of nothing but the figures in this extraordinary and fantastic scene. Then all at once darkness fell upon me, and anon from out of it, as to one who grows accustomed by degrees to a dimmer light, my former surroundings of deck and mast and cordage slowly resolved themselves. Miss Harford had closed her eyes and was leaning back in her chair, apparently asleep, the book she had been reading open in her lap. Impelled by surely I cannot say what motive, I glanced at the top of the page; it was a copy of that rare and curious work, Denneker's *Meditations*, and the lady's index finger rested on this passage:

"To sundry it is given to be drawn away, and to be apart from the body for a season; for, as concerning rills which would flow across each other the weaker is borne along by the stronger, so there be certain of kin whose paths intersecting, their souls do bear company, the while their bodies go fore-appointed ways, unknowing."

Miss Harford arose, shuddering; the sun had sunk below the horizon, but it was not cold. There was not a breath of wind; there were no clouds in the sky, yet not a star was visible. A hurried tramping sounded on the deck; the captain, summoned from below, joined the first officer, who stood looking at the barometer. "Good God!" I heard him exclaim.

An hour later the form of Janette Harford, invisible in the darkness and spray, was torn from my grasp by the cruel vortex of the sinking ship, and I fainted in the cordage of the floating mast to which I had lashed myself.

It was by lamplight that I awoke. I lay in a berth amid the familiar surroundings of the stateroom of a steamer. On a couch opposite sat a man, half undressed for bed, reading a book. I recognized the face of my friend Gordon Doyle, whom I had met in Liverpool on the day of my embarkation, when he was himself about to sail on the steamer *City of Prague*, on which he had urged me to accompany him.

After some moments I now spoke his name. He simply said, "Well," and turned a leaf in his book without removing his eyes from the page.

"Doyle," I repeated, "did they save *her?*"

He now deigned to look at me and smiled as if amused. He evidently thought me but half awake.

"Her? Whom do you mean?"

"Janette Harford."

His amusement turned to amazement; he stared at me fixedly, saying nothing.

"You will tell me after a while," I continued. "I suppose you will tell me after a while."

A moment later I asked, "What ship is this?"

Doyle stared again. "The steamer *City of Prague*, bound from Liverpool to New York, three weeks out with a broken shaft. Principal passenger, Mr. Gordon Doyle; ditto lunatic, Mr. William Jarrett. These two distinguished travelers embarked together, but they are about to part, it being the resolute intention of the former to pitch the latter overboard."

I sat bolt upright. "Do you mean to say that I have been for three weeks a passenger on this steamer?"

"Yes, pretty nearly. This is the third of July."

"Have I been ill?"

"Right as a trivet all the time, and punctual at your meals."

"My God! Doyle, there is some mystery here. Do have the goodness to be serious. Was I not rescued from the wreck of the ship *Morrow!*"

Doyle changed color and, approaching me, laid his fingers on my wrist. A moment later, "What do you know of Janette Harford?" he asked very calmly.

"First tell me what *you* know of her?"

Mr. Doyle gazed at me for some moments as if thinking what to do, then seating himself again on the couch, said:

"Why should I not? I am engaged to marry Janette Harford,

whom I met a year ago in London. Her family, one of the wealthiest in Devonshire, cut up rough about it, and we eloped—are eloping, rather, for on the day that you and I walked to the landing stage to go aboard this steamer she and her faithful servant, a Negress, passed us, driving to the ship *Morrow.* She would not consent to go in the same vessel with me, and it had been deemed best that she take a sailing vessel in order to avoid observation and lessen the risk of detection. I am now alarmed lest this cursed breaking of our machinery may detain us so long that the *Morrow* will get to New York before us, and the poor girl will not know where to go."

I lay still in my berth—so still I hardly breathed. But the subject was evidently not displeasing to Doyle, and after a short pause he resumed:

"By the way, she is only an adopted daughter of the Harfords. Her mother was killed at their place by being thrown from a horse while hunting, and her father, mad with grief, made away with himself the same day. No one ever claimed the child, and after a reasonable time they adopted her. She has grown up in the belief that she is their daughter."

"Doyle, what book are you reading?"

"Oh, it's called Denneker's *Meditations.* It's a rum lot. Janette gave it to me. She happened to have two copies. Want to see it?"

He tossed me the volume, which opened as it fell. On one of the exposed pages was a marked passage:

"To sundry it is given to be drawn away, and to be apart from the body for a season; for, as concerning rills which would flow across each other the weaker is borne along by the stronger, so there be certain of kin whose paths intersecting, their souls do bear company, the while their bodies go foreappointed ways, unknowing."

"She had—she has—a singular taste in reading," I managed to say, mastering my agitation.

"Yes. And now perhaps you will have the kindness to explain how you knew her name and that of the ship she sailed in."

"You talked of her in your sleep," I said.

A week later we were towed into the port of New York. But the *Morrow* was never heard from.

CHICKAMAUGA

ONE sunny autumn afternoon a child strayed away from its rude home in a small field and entered a forest unobserved. It was happy in a new sense of freedom from control, happy in the opportunity of exploration and adventure; for this child's spirit, in bodies of its ancestors, had for thousands of years been trained to memorable feats of discovery and conquest—victories in battles whose critical moments were centuries, whose victors' camps were cities of hewn stone. From the cradle of its race it had conquered its way through two continents and passing a great sea had penetrated a third, there to be born to war and dominion as a heritage.

The child was a boy aged about six years, the son of a poor planter. In his younger manhood the father had been a soldier, had fought against naked savages and followed the flag of his country into the capital of a civilized race to the far South. In the peaceful life of a planter the warrior-fire survived; once kindled, it is never extinguished. The man loved military books and pictures, and the boy had understood enough to make himself a wooden sword, though even the eye of his father would hardly have known it for what it was. This weapon he now bore bravely, as became the son of a heroic race, and pausing now and again in the sunny space of the forest, assumed, with some exaggeration, the postures of aggression and defense that he had been taught by the engraver's art. Made reckless by the ease with which he overcame invisible foes attempting to stay his advance, he committed the common enough military error of pushing the pursuit to a dangerous extreme, until he found himself upon the margin of a wide but shallow brook, whose rapid waters barred his direct advance against the flying foe that had crossed with illogical ease. But the intrepid victor was not to be baffled; the spirit of the race which had passed the great sea burned unconquerable in that small breast and would not be denied. Finding a place where some boulders in the bed of the stream lay but a step or a leap apart, he made his way across and fell again upon the rear guard of his imaginary foe, putting all to the sword.

Now that the battle had been won, prudence required that he withdraw to his base of operations. Alas, like many a mightier conqueror, and like one, the mightiest, he could not

> curb the lust for war,
> Nor learn that tempted Fate will leave the loftiest star.

Advancing from the bank of the creek he suddenly found himself confronted with a new and more formidable enemy: in the path that he was following, sat, bolt upright, with ears erect and paws suspended before it, a rabbit! With a startled cry the child turned and fled, he knew not in what direction, calling with inarticulate cries for his mother, weeping, stumbling, his tender skin cruelly torn by brambles, his little heart beating hard with terror—breathless, blind with tears—lost in the forest! Then, for more than an hour, he wandered with erring feet through the tangled undergrowth, till at last, overcome by fatigue, he lay down in a narrow space between two rocks, within a few yards of the stream and still grasping his toy sword, no longer a weapon but a companion, sobbed himself to sleep. The wood birds sang merrily above his head; the squirrels, whisking their bravery of tail, ran barking from tree to tree, unconscious of the pity of it, and somewhere far away was a strange, muffled thunder, as if the partridges were drumming in celebration of nature's victory over the son of her immemorial enslavers. And back at the little plantation, where white men and black were hastily searching the fields and hedges in alarm, a mother's heart was breaking for her missing child.

Hours passed, and then the little sleeper rose to his feet. The chill of the evening was in his limbs, the fear of the gloom in his heart. But he had rested, and he no longer wept. With some blind instinct which impelled to action he struggled through the undergrowth about him and came to a more open ground—on his right the brook, to the left a gentle acclivity studded with infrequent trees; over all, the gathering gloom of twilight. A thin, ghostly mist rose along the water. It frightened and repelled him; instead of recrossing, in the direction whence he had come, he turned his back upon it, and went forward toward the dark enclosing wood. Suddenly he saw before him a strange moving object which he took to be some large animal—a dog, a pig—he could not name it; perhaps it was a bear. He had seen pictures of bears, but knew of nothing to their discredit and had vaguely wished to meet one. But something in form or movement of this object—something in the awkwardness of its approach—told him that it was not a bear, and curiosity was stayed by fear. He stood still and as it came slowly on gained courage every moment, for he saw that at least it had not the long, menacing ears of the rabbit. Possibly his impressionable mind was half conscious of something familiar in its shambling, awkward gait. Before it had approached near enough to resolve his doubts he saw that it was followed by another and another. To right and to left were many more; the whole open space about him was alive with them—all moving toward the brook.

They were men. They crept upon their hands and knees. They used their hands only, dragging their legs. They used their knees only, their arms hanging idle at their sides. They strove to rise to their feet, but fell prone in the attempt. They did nothing naturally, and nothing alike, save only to advance foot by foot in the same direction. Singly, in pairs and in little groups, they came on through the gloom, some halting now and again while others crept slowly past them, then resuming their movement. They came by dozens and by hundreds; as far on either hand as one could see in the deepening gloom they extended, and the black wood behind them appeared to be inexhaustible. The very ground seemed in motion toward the creek. Occasionally one who had paused did not again go on, but lay motionless. He was dead. Some, pausing, made strange gestures with their hands, erected their arms and lowered them again, clasped their heads; spread their palms upward, as men are sometimes seen to do in public prayer.

Not all of this did the child note; it is what would have been noted by an elder observer; he saw little but that these were men, yet crept like babes. Being men, they were not terrible, though unfamiliarly clad. He moved among them freely, going from one to another and peering into their faces with childish curiosity. All their faces were singularly white and many were streaked and gouted with red. Something in this— something, too, perhaps, in their grotesque attitudes and movements—reminded him of the painted clown whom he had seen last summer in the circus, and he laughed as he watched them. But on and ever on they crept, these maimed and bleeding men, as heedless as he of the dramatic contrast between his laughter and their own ghastly gravity. To him it was a merry spectacle. He had seen his father's Negroes creep upon their hands and knees for his amusement—had ridden them so, "making believe" they were his horses. He now approached one of these crawling figures from behind and with an agile movement mounted it astride. The man sank upon his breast, recovered, flung the small boy fiercely to the ground as an unbroken colt might have done, then turned upon him a face that lacked a lower jaw—from the upper teeth to the throat was a great red gap fringed with hanging shreds of flesh and splinters of bone. The unnatural prominence of nose, the absence of chin, the fierce eyes, gave this man the appearance of a great bird of prey crimsoned in throat and breast by the blood of its quarry. The man rose to his knees, the child to his feet. The man shook his fist at the child; the child, terrified at last, ran to a tree nearby, got upon the farther side of it, and took a more serious view of the situation. And so the clumsy multitude dragged itself slowly and painfully along

in hideous pantomime—moved forward down the slope like
a swarm of great black beetles, with never a sound of going—
in silence profound, absolute.

Instead of darkening, the haunted landscape began to
brighten. Through the belt of trees beyond the brook shone
a strange red light, the trunks and branches of the trees making a black lacework against it. It struck the creeping figures
and gave them monstrous shadows, which caricatured their
movements on the lit grass. It fell upon their faces, touching
their whiteness with a ruddy tinge, accentuating the stains
with which so many of them were freaked and maculated. It
sparkled on buttons and bits of metal in their clothing. Instinctively the child turned toward the growing splendor and
moved down the slope with his horrible companions; in a few
moments had passed the foremost of the throng—not much
of a feat, considering his advantages. He placed himself in
the lead, his wooden sword still in hand, and solemnly directed
the march, conforming his pace to theirs and occasionally
turning as if to see that his forces did not straggle. Surely
such a leader never before had such a following.

Scattered about upon the ground now slowly narrowing by
the encroachment of this awful march to water were certain
articles to which, in the leader's mind, were coupled no significant associations: an occasional blanket, tightly rolled length-
wise, doubled and the ends bound together with a string; a
heavy knapsack here, and there a broken rifle—such things,
in short, as are found in the rear of retreating troops, the
"spoor" of men flying from their hunters. Everywhere near
the creek, which here had a margin of lowland, the earth was
trodden into mud by the feet of men and horses. An observer
of better experience in the use of his eyes would have noticed
that these footprints pointed in both directions; the ground
had been twice passed over—in advance and in retreat. A few
hours before, these desperate, stricken men, with their more
fortunate and now distant comrades, had penetrated the forest
in thousands. Their successive battalions, breaking into swarms
and re-forming in lines, had passed the child on every side—
had almost trodden on him as he slept. The rustle and murmur

of their march had not awakened him. Almost within a stone's throw of where he lay they had fought a battle; but all unheard by him were the roar of the musketry, the shock of the cannon, "the thunder of the captains and the shouting." He had slept through it all, grasping his little wooden sword with perhaps a tighter clutch in unconscious sympathy with his martial environment, but as heedless of the grandeur of the struggle as the dead who had died to make the glory.

The fire beyond the belt of woods on the farther side of the creek, reflected to earth from the canopy of its own smoke, was now suffusing the whole landscape. It transformed the sinuous line of mist to the vapor of gold. The water gleamed with dashes of red, and red, too, were many of the stones protruding above the surface. But that was blood; the less desperately wounded had stained them in crossing. On them, too, the child now crossed with eager steps; he was going to the fire. As he stood upon the farther bank he turned about to look at the companions of his march. The advance was arriving at the creek. The stronger had already drawn themselves to the brink and plunged their faces into the flood. Three or four who lay without motion appeared to have no heads. At this the child's eyes expanded with wonder; even his hospitable understanding could not accept a phenomenon implying such vitality as that. After slaking their thirst these men had not had the strength to back away from the water, nor to keep their heads above it. They were drowned. In rear of these, the open spaces of the forest showed the leader as many formless figures of his grim command as at first; but not nearly so many were in motion. He waved his cap for their encouragement and smilingly pointed with his weapon in the direction of the guiding light—a pillar of fire to this strange exodus.

Confident of the fidelity of his forces, he now entered the belt of woods, passed through it easily in the red illumination, climbed a fence, ran across a field, turning now and again to coquet with his responsive shadow, and so approached the blazing ruin of a dwelling. Desolation everywhere! In all the wide glare not a living thing was visible. He cared nothing for that; the spectacle pleased, and he danced with glee in

imitation of the wavering flames. He ran about, collecting fuel, but every object that he found was too heavy for him to cast in from the distance to which the heat limited his approach. In despair he flung in his sword—a surrender to the superior forces of nature. His military career was at an end.

Shifting his position, his eyes fell upon some outbuildings which had an oddly familiar appearance, as if he had dreamed of them. He stood considering them with wonder, when suddenly the entire plantation, with its enclosing forest, seemed to turn as if upon a pivot. His little world swung half around; the points of the compass were reversed. He recognized the blazing building as his own home!

For a moment he stood stupefied by the power of the revelation, then ran with stumbling feet, making a half-circuit of the ruin. There, conspicuous in the light of the conflagration, lay the dead body of a woman—the white face turned upward, the hands thrown out and clutched full of grass, the clothing deranged, the long dark hair in tangles and full of clotted

16

blood. The greater part of the forehead was torn away, and from the jagged hole the brain protruded, overflowing the temple, a frothy mass of gray, crowned with clusters of crimson bubbles—the work of a shell.

The child moved his little hands, making wild, uncertain gestures. He uttered a series of inarticulate and indescribable cries—something between the chattering of an ape and the gobbling of a turkey—a startling, soulless, unholy sound, the language of a devil. The child was a deaf mute.

Then he stood motionless, with quivering lips, looking down upon the wreck.

AN OCCURRENCE AT OWL CREEK BRIDGE

I

A MAN stood upon a railroad bridge in northern Alabama, looking down into the swift water twenty feet below. The man's hands were behind his back, the wrists bound with a cord. A rope closely encircled his neck. It was attached to a stout cross-timber above his head and the slack fell to the level of his knees. Some loose boards laid upon the sleepers supporting the metals of the railway supplied a footing for him and his executioners—two private soldiers of the Federal army, directed by a sergeant who in civil life may have been a deputy sheriff. At a short remove upon the same temporary platform was an officer in the uniform of his rank, armed. He was a captain. A sentinel at each end of the bridge stood with his rifle in the position known as "support," that is to say, vertical in front of the left shoulder, the hammer resting on the forearm thrown straight across the chest—a formal and unnatural position, enforcing an erect carriage of the body. It did not appear to be the duty of these two men to know what was occurring at the center of the bridge; they merely blockaded the two ends of the foot planking that traversed it.

Beyond one of the sentinels nobody was in sight; the railroad ran straight away into a forest for a hundred yards, then, curving, was lost to view. Doubtless there was an outpost farther along. The other bank of the stream was open ground—a gentle acclivity topped with a stockade of vertical tree trunks, loopholed for rifles, with a single embrasure through which protruded the muzzle of a brass cannon commanding the bridge. Midway of the slope between bridge and fort were the spectators—a single company of infantry in line, at "parade rest," the butts of the rifles on the ground, the barrels inclining slightly backward against the right shoulder, the hands crossed upon the stock. A lieutenant stood at the right of the line, the point of his sword upon the ground, his left hand resting upon his right. Excepting the group of four at the center of the bridge, not a man moved. The company faced the bridge, staring stonily, motionless. The sentinels, facing the banks of the stream, might have been statues to adorn the bridge. The captain stood with folded arms, silent, observing the work of his subordinates, but making no sign. Death is a dignitary who when he comes announced is to be received with formal manifestations of respect, even by those most familiar with him. In the code of military etiquette silence and fixity are forms of deference.

The man who was engaged in being hanged was apparently about thirty-five years of age. He was a civilian, if one might judge from his habit, which was that of a planter. His features were good—a straight nose, firm mouth, broad forehead, from which his long, dark hair was combed straight back, falling behind his ears to the collar of his well-fitting frock coat. He wore a mustache and pointed beard, but no whiskers; his eyes were large and dark gray, and had a kindly expression which one would hardly have expected in one whose neck was in the hemp. Evidently this was no vulgar assassin. The liberal military code makes provision for hanging many kinds of persons, and gentlemen are not excluded.

The preparations being complete, the two private soldiers stepped aside and each drew away the plank upon which he had been standing. The sergeant turned to the captain, saluted, and placed himself immediately behind that officer, who in turn moved apart one pace. These movements left the condemned man and the sergeant standing on the two ends of the same plank, which spanned three of the cross-ties of the bridge. The end upon which the civilian stood almost, but not quite, reached a fourth. This plank had been held in place by the weight of the captain; it was now held by that of the sergeant. At a signal from the former the latter would step aside, the plank would tilt and the condemned man go down between two ties. The arrangement commended itself to his judgment as simple and effective. His face had not been covered nor his eyes bandaged. He looked a moment at his "unsteadfast footing," then let his gaze wander to the swirling water of the stream racing madly beneath his feet. A piece of dancing driftwood caught his attention and his eyes followed it down the current. How slowly it appeared to move! What a sluggish stream!

He closed his eyes in order to fix his last thoughts upon his wife and children. The water, touched to gold by the early sun, the brooding mists under the banks at some distance down the stream, the fort, the soldiers, the piece of drift—all had distracted him. And now he became conscious of a new disturbance. Striking through the thought of his dear ones was a sound which he could neither ignore nor understand, a sharp, distinct, metallic percussion like the stroke of a blacksmith's hammer upon the anvil; it had the same ringing quality. He wondered what it was, and whether immeasurably distant or nearby—it seemed both. Its recurrence was regular, but as slow as the tolling of a death knell. He awaited each stroke with impatience and—he knew not why—apprehension. The intervals of silence grew progressively longer; the delays became maddening. With their greater infrequency the sounds increased in strength and sharpness. They hurt his ear like the thrust of a knife; he feared he would shriek. What he heard was the ticking of his watch.

He unclosed his eyes and saw again the water below him. "If I could free my hands," he thought, "I might throw off the noose and spring into the stream. By diving I could evade the bullets and, swimming vigorously, reach the bank, take to the woods and get away home. My home, thank God, is as yet outside their lines; my wife and little ones are still beyond the invader's farthest advance."

As these thoughts, which have here to be set down in words,

were flashed into the doomed man's brain rather than evolved from it the captain nodded to the sergeant. The sergeant stepped aside.

II

Peyton Farquhar was a well-to-do planter, of an old and highly respected Alabama family. Being a slave owner and like other slave owners a politician he was naturally an original secessionist and ardently devoted to the Southern cause. Circumstances of an imperious nature, which it is unnecessary to relate here, had prevented him from taking service with the gallant army that had fought the disastrous campaigns ending with the fall of Corinth, and he chafed under the inglorious restraint, longing for the release of his energies, the larger life of the soldier, the opportunity for distinction. That opportunity, he felt, would come, as it comes to all in wartime. Meanwhile he did what he could. No service was too humble for him to perform in aid of the South, no adventure too perilous for him to undertake if consistent with the character of a civilian who was at heart a soldier, and who in good faith and without too much qualification assented to at least a part of the frankly villainous dictum that all is fair in love and war.

One evening while Farquhar and his wife were sitting on a rustic bench near the entrance to his grounds, a gray-clad soldier rode up to the gate and asked for a drink of water. Mrs. Farquhar was only too happy to serve him with her own white hands. While she was fetching the water her husband approached the dusty horseman and inquired eagerly for news from the front.

"The Yanks are repairing the railroads," said the man, "and are getting ready for another advance. They have reached the Owl Creek bridge, put it in order, and built a stockade on the north bank. The commandant has issued an order, which is posted everywhere, declaring that any civilian caught interfering with the railroad, its bridges, tunnels or trains will be summarily hanged. I saw the order."

"How far is it to the Owl Creek bridge?" Farquhar asked.

"About thirty miles."

"Is there no force on this side the creek?"

"Only a picket post half a mile out, on the railroad, and a single sentinel at this end of the bridge."

"Suppose a man—a civilian and student of hanging—should elude the picket post and perhaps get the better of the sentinel," said Farquhar, smiling, "what could he accomplish?"

The soldier reflected. "I was there a month ago," he replied. "I observed that the flood of last winter had lodged a great quantity of driftwood against the wooden pier at this end of the bridge. It is now dry and would burn like tow."

The lady had now brought the water, which the soldier drank. He thanked her ceremoniously, bowed to her husband, and rode away. An hour later, after nightfall, he repassed the plantation, going northward in the direction from which he had come. He was a Federal scout.

III

As Peyton Farquhar fell straight downward through the bridge he lost consciousness and was as one already dead. From this state he was awakened—ages later, it seemed to him—by the pain of a sharp pressure upon his throat, followed by a sense of suffocation. Keen, poignant agonies seemed to shoot from his neck downward through every fiber of his body and limbs. These pains appeared to flash along well-defined lines of ramification and to beat with an inconceivably rapid periodicity. They seemed like streams of pulsating fire heating him to an intolerable temperature. As to his head, he was conscious of nothing but a feeling of fullness—of congestion. These sensations were unaccompanied by thought. The intellectual part of his nature was already effaced; he had power only to feel, and feeling was torment. He was conscious of motion. Encompassed in a luminous cloud, of which he was now merely the fiery heart, without material substance, he swung through unthinkable arcs of oscillation, like a vast

pendulum. Then all at once, with terrible suddenness, the light about him shot upward with the noise of a loud plash; a frightful roaring was in his ears, and all was cold and dark. The power of thought was restored; he knew that the rope had broken and he had fallen into the stream. There was no additional strangulation; the noose about his neck was already

suffocating him and kept the water from his lungs. To die of
hanging at the bottom of a river!—the idea seemed to him
ludicrous. He opened his eyes in the darkness and saw above
him a gleam of light, but how distant, how inaccessible! He
was still sinking, for the light became fainter and fainter until
it was a mere glimmer. Then it began to grow and brighten,
and he knew that he was rising toward the surface—knew it
with reluctance, for he was now very comfortable. "To be
hanged and drowned," he thought, "that is not so bad, but I
do not wish to be shot. No, I will not be shot. That is not fair."

He was not conscious of an effort, but a sharp pain in his
wrist apprised him that he was trying to free his hands. He
gave the struggle his attention, as an idler might observe the
feat of a juggler, without interest in the outcome. What splendid effort! What magnificent, what superhuman strength! Ah,
that was a fine endeavor! Bravo! The cord fell away; his arms
parted and floated upward, the hands dimly seen on each side
in the growing light. He watched them with a new interest as
first one and then the other pounced upon the noose at his
neck. They tore it away and thrust it fiercely aside, its undulations resembling those of a water snake. "Put it back, put
it back!" He thought he shouted these words to his hands, for
the undoing of the noose had been succeeded by the direst
pang that he had yet experienced. His neck ached horribly;
his brain was on fire; his heart, which had been fluttering
faintly, gave a great leap, trying to force itself out at his
mouth. His whole body was racked and wrenched with an insupportable anguish! But his disobedient hands gave no heed
to the command. They beat the water vigorously with quick,
downward strokes, forcing him to the surface. He felt his
head emerge; his eyes were blinded by the sunlight; his chest
expanded convulsively, and with a supreme and crowning
agony his lungs engulfed a great draught of air, which instantly he expelled in a shriek!

He was now in full possession of his physical senses. They
were, indeed, preternaturally keen and alert. Something in the
awful disturbance of his organic system had so exalted and
refined them that they made record of things never before
perceived. He felt the ripples upon his face and heard their

separate sounds as they struck. He looked at the forest on the bank of the stream, saw the individual trees, the leaves and the veining of each leaf—saw the very insects upon them: the locusts, the brilliant-bodied flies, the gray spiders stretching their webs from twig to twig. He noted the prismatic colors in all the dewdrops upon a million blades of grass. The humming of the gnats that danced above the eddies of the stream, the beating of the dragonflies' wings, the strokes of the water spiders' legs, like oars which had lifted their boat—all these made audible music. A fish slid along beneath his eyes and he heard the rush of its body parting the water.

He had come to the surface facing down the stream; in a moment the visible world seemed to wheel slowly round, himself the pivotal point, and he saw the bridge, the fort, the soldiers upon the bridge, the captain, the sergeant, the two privates, his executioners. They were in silhouette against the blue sky. They shouted and gesticulated, pointing at him. The captain had drawn his pistol, but did not fire; the others were unarmed. Their movements were grotesque and horrible, their forms gigantic.

Suddenly he heard a sharp report and something struck the water smartly within a few inches of his head, spattering his face with spray. He heard a second report, and saw one of the sentinels with his rifle at his shoulder, a light cloud of blue smoke rising from the muzzle. The man in the water saw the eye of the man on the bridge gazing into his own through the sights of the rifle. He observed that it was a gray eye and remembered having read that gray eyes were keenest, and that all famous marksmen had them. Nevertheless, this one had missed.

A counterswirl had caught Farquhar and turned him half round; he was again looking into the forest on the bank opposite the fort. The sound of a clear, high voice in a monotonous singsong now rang out behind him and came across the water with a distinctness that pierced and subdued all other sounds, even the beating of the ripples in his ears. Although no soldier, he had frequented camps enough to know the dread significance of that deliberate, drawling aspirated chant; the lieutenant on shore was taking a part in the morning's work. How coldly and pitilessly—with what an even, calm intonation, pre-saging, and enforcing tranquillity in the men—with what accurately measured intervals fell those cruel words:

"Attention, company! . . . Shoulder arms! . . . Ready! . . . Aim! . . . Fire!"

Farquhar dived—dived as deeply as he could. The water roared in his ears like the voice of Niagara, yet he heard the dulled thunder of the volley and, rising again toward the sur-face, met shining bits of metal, singularly flattened, oscillating slowly downward. Some of them touched him on the face and hands, then fell away, continuing their descent. One lodged between his collar and neck; it was uncomfortably warm and he snatched it out.

As he rose to the surface, gasping for breath, he saw that he had been a long time under water; he was perceptibly farther downstream—nearer to safety. The soldiers had almost fin-ished reloading; the metal ramrods flashed all at once in the sunshine as they were drawn from the barrels, turned in the air, and thrust into their sockets. The two sentinels fired again, independently and ineffectually.

The hunted man saw all this over his shoulder; he was now swimming vigorously with the current. His brain was as ener-getic as his arms and legs; he thought with the rapidity of lightning.

"The officer," he reasoned, "will not make that martinet's error a second time. It is as easy to dodge a volley as a single shot. He has probably already given the command to fire at will. God help me, I cannot dodge them all!"

An appalling plash within two yards of him was followed by a loud, rushing sound, diminuendo, which seemed to travel back through the air to the fort and died in an explosion which stirred the very river to its deeps! A rising sheet of water curved over him, fell down upon him, blinded him, strangled him! The cannon had taken a hand in the game. As he shook his head free from the commotion of the smitten water he heard the deflected shot humming through the air ahead, and in an instant it was cracking and smashing the branches in the forest beyond.

"They will not do that again," he thought. "The next time

they will use a charge of grape. I must keep my eye upon the gun. The smoke will apprise me—the report arrives too late; it lags behind the missile. That is a good gun."

Suddenly he felt himself whirled round and round—spinning like a top. The water, the banks, the forests, the now distant bridge, fort and men—all were commingled and blurred. Objects were represented by their colors only; circular horizontal streaks of color—that was all he saw. He had been caught in a vortex and was being whirled on with a velocity of advance and gyration that made him giddy and sick. In a few moments he was flung upon the gravel at the foot of the left bank of the stream—the southern bank—and behind a projecting point which concealed him from his enemies. The sudden arrest of his motion, the abrasion of one of his hands on the gravel, restored him, and he wept with delight. He dug his fingers into the sand, threw it over himself in handfuls and audibly blessed it. It looked like diamonds, rubies, emeralds; he could think of nothing beautiful which it did not resemble. The trees upon the bank were giant garden plants; he noted a definite order in their arrangement, inhaled the fragrance of their blooms. A strange, roseate light shone through the spaces among their trunks and the wind made in their branches the music of aeolian harps. He had no wish to perfect his escape—was content to remain in that enchanting spot until retaken.

A whiz and rattle of grapeshot among the branches high above his head roused him from his dream. The baffled cannoneer had fired him a random farewell. He sprang to his feet, rushed up the sloping bank, and plunged into the forest.

All that day he traveled, laying his course by the rounding sun. The forest seemed interminable; nowhere did he discover a break in it, not even a woodman's road. He had not known that he lived in so wild a region. There was something uncanny in the revelation.

By nightfall he was fatigued, footsore, famishing. The thought of his wife and children urged him on. At last he found a road which led him in what he knew to be the right direction. It was as wide and straight as a city street, yet it seemed untraveled. No fields bordered it, no dwelling anywhere. Not so much as the barking of a dog suggested human habitation. The black bodies of the trees formed a straight wall on both sides, terminating on the horizon in a point, like a diagram in a lesson in perspective. Overhead, as he looked up through this rift in the wood, shone great golden stars looking unfamiliar and grouped in strange constellations. He was sure they were arranged in some order which had a secret and malign significance. The wood on either side was full of singular noises, among which—once, twice, and again—he distinctly heard whispers in an unknown tongue.

His neck was in pain and lifting his hand to it he found it horribly swollen. He knew that it had a circle of black where the rope had bruised it. His eyes felt congested; he could no longer close them. His tongue was swollen with thirst; he relieved its fever by thrusting it forward from between his teeth into the cold air. How softly the turf had carpeted the untraveled avenue—he could no longer feel the roadway beneath his feet!

Doubtless, despite his suffering, he had fallen asleep while walking, for now he sees another scene—perhaps he has merely recovered from a delirium. He stands at the gate of his own home. All is as he left it, and all bright and beautiful in the morning sunshine. He must have traveled the entire night. As he pushes open the gate and passes up the wide white walk, he sees a flutter of female garments; his wife, looking fresh and cool and sweet, steps down from the veranda to meet him. At the bottom of the steps she stands waiting, with a smile of ineffable joy, an attitude of matchless grace and dignity. Ah, how beautiful she is! He springs forward with extended arms. As he is about to clasp her he feels a stunning blow upon the back of the neck; a blinding white light blazes all about him with a sound like the shock of a cannon—then all is darkness and silence!

Peyton Farquhar was dead; his body, with a broken neck, swung gently from side to side beneath the timbers of the Owl Creek bridge.

A HORSEMAN IN THE SKY

I

ONE sunny afternoon in the autumn of the year 1861 a soldier lay in a clump of laurel by the side of a road in western Virginia. He lay at full length upon his stomach, his feet resting upon the toes, his head upon the left forearm. His extended right hand loosely grasped his rifle. But for the somewhat methodical disposition of his limbs and a slight rhythmic movement of the cartridge box at the back of his belt he might have been thought to be dead. He was asleep at his post of duty. But if detected he would be dead shortly afterward, death being the just and legal penalty of his crime.

The clump of laurel in which the criminal lay was in the angle of a road which after ascending southward a steep acclivity to that point turned sharply to the west, running along the summit for perhaps one hundred yards. There it turned southward again and went zigzagging downward through the forest. At the salient of that second angle was a large flat rock, jutting out northward, overlooking the deep valley from which the road ascended. The rock capped a high cliff; a stone dropped from its outer edge would have fallen sheer downward one thousand feet to the tops of the pines. The angle where the soldier lay was on another spur of the same cliff. Had he been awake he would have commanded a view, not only of the short arm of the road and the jutting rock, but of the entire profile of the cliff below it. It might well have made him giddy to look.

The country was wooded everywhere except at the bottom of the valley to the northward, where there was a small natural meadow, through which flowed a stream scarcely visible from the valley's rim. This open ground looked hardly larger than an ordinary dooryard, but was really several acres in extent. Its green was more vivid than that of the enclosing forest. Away beyond it rose a line of giant cliffs similar to those upon which we are supposed to stand in our survey of the savage scene, and through which the road had somehow made its climb to the summit. The configuration of the valley, indeed, was such that from this point of observation it seemed entirely shut in, and one could but have wondered how the road which found a way out of it had found a way into it, and whence came and whither went the waters of the stream that parted the meadow more than a thousand feet below.

No country is so wild and difficult but men will make it a theater of war; concealed in the forest at the bottom of that military rat-trap, in which half a hundred men in possession of the exits might have starved an army to submission, lay five regiments of Federal infantry. They had marched all the previous day and night, and were resting. At nightfall they would take to the road again, climb to the place where their unfaithful sentinel now slept, and descending the other slope of the ridge fall upon a camp of the enemy at about midnight. Their hope was to surprise it, for the road led to the rear of it. In case of failure, their position would be perilous in the extreme; and fail they surely would should accident or vigilance apprise the enemy of the movement.

II

The sleeping sentinel in the clump of laurel was a young Virginian named Carter Druse. He was the son of wealthy parents, an only child, and had known such ease and cultivation and high living as wealth and taste were able to command in the mountain country of western Virginia. His home was but a few miles from where he now lay. One morning he had risen from the breakfast table and said, quietly but gravely, "Father, a Union regiment has arrived at Grafton. I am going to join it."

The father lifted his leonine head, looked at the son a moment in silence, and replied, "Well, go, sir, and whatever may occur do what you conceive to be your duty. Virginia, to which you are a traitor, must get on without you. Should we both live to the end of the war, we will speak further of the matter. Your mother, as the physician has informed you, is in a most critical condition; at the best she cannot be with us longer than a few weeks, but that time is precious. It would be better not to disturb her."

So Carter Druse, bowing reverently to his father, who returned the salute with a stately courtesy that masked a breaking heart, left the home of his childhood to go soldiering. By conscience and courage, by deeds of devotion and daring, he soon commended himself to his fellows and his officers; and it was to these qualities and to some knowledge of the country that he owed his selection for his present perilous duty at the extreme outpost. Nevertheless, fatigue had been stronger than resolution, and he had fallen asleep. What good or bad angel came in a dream to rouse him from his state of crime, who shall say? Without a movement, without a sound, in the profound silence and the languor of the late afternoon, some invisible messenger of fate touched with unsealing finger the eyes of his consciousness—whispered into the ear of his spirit the mysterious awakening word which no human lips ever have spoken, no human memory ever has recalled. He quietly raised his forehead from his arm and looked between the masking stems of the laurels, instinctively closing his right hand about the stock of his rifle.

His first feeling was a keen artistic delight. On a colossal pedestal, the cliff—motionless at the extreme edge of the capping rock and sharply outlined against the sky—was an equestrian statue of impressive dignity. The figure of the man sat the figure of the horse, straight and soldierly, but with the repose of a Grecian god carved in the marble which limits the suggestion of activity. The gray costume harmonized with its aerial background; the metal of accouterment and caparison was softened and subdued by the shadow; the animal's skin had no points of highlight. A carbine strikingly foreshortened lay across the pommel of the saddle, kept in place by the right hand grasping it at the "grip"; the left hand, holding the bridle rein, was invisible. In silhouette against the sky the profile of the horse was cut with the sharpness of a cameo; it looked across the heights of air to the confronting cliffs beyond. The face of the rider, turned slightly away, showed only an outline of temple and beard; he was looking downward to the bottom of the valley. Magnified by its lift against the sky and by the soldier's testifying sense of the formidableness of a near enemy, the group appeared of heroic, almost colossal, size.

For an instant Druse had a strange, half-defined feeling that he had slept to the end of the war and was looking upon a noble work of art reared upon that eminence to commemorate the deeds of a heroic past of which he had been an inglorious part. The feeling was dispelled by a slight movement of the group: the horse, without moving its feet, had drawn its body slightly backward from the verge; the man remained immobile as before. Broad awake and keenly alive to the significance of the situation, Druse now brought the butt of his rifle against his cheek by cautiously pushing the barrel forward through the bushes, cocked the piece, and glancing through the sights covered a vital spot of the horseman's breast. A touch upon the trigger and all would have been well with Carter Druse. At that instant the horseman turned his head and looked in the direction of his concealed foeman— seemed to look into his very face, into his eyes, into his brave, compassionate heart.

Is it then so terrible to kill an enemy in war—an enemy who has surprised a secret vital to the safety of one's self and comrades—an enemy more formidable for his knowledge than all his army for its numbers? Carter Druse grew pale; he shook in every limb, turned faint, and saw the statuesque group before him as black figures, rising, falling, moving unsteadily in arcs of circles in a fiery sky. His hand fell away from his weapon, his head slowly dropped until his face rested on the leaves in which he lay. This courageous gentleman and hardy soldier was near swooning from intensity of emotion.

It was not for long; in another moment his face was raised from earth, his hands resumed their places on the rifle, his forefinger sought the trigger; mind, heart, and eyes were clear, conscience and reason sound. He could not hope to capture that enemy; to alarm him would but send him dashing to his camp with his fatal news. The duty of the soldier was plain: the man must be shot dead from ambush—without warning, without a moment's spiritual preparation, with never so much as an unspoken prayer, he must be sent to his account. But no —there is a hope; he may have discovered nothing—perhaps he is but admiring the sublimity of the landscape. If permitted, he may turn and ride carelessly away in the direction whence he came. Surely it will be possible to judge at the instant of his withdrawing whether he knows. It may well be that his fixity of attention—Druse turned his head and looked through the deeps of air downward, as from the surface to the bottom of a translucent sea. He saw creeping across the green meadow a sinuous line of figures of men and horses—some foolish commander was permitting the soldiers of his escort to water their beasts in the open, in plain view from a dozen summits!

Druse withdrew his eyes from the valley and fixed them again upon the group of man and horse in the sky, and again it was through the sights of his rifle. But this time his aim was at the horse. In his memory, as if they were a divine mandate, rang the words of his father at their parting: "Whatever may occur, do what you conceive to be your duty." He was calm now. His teeth were firmly but not rigidly closed; his nerves were as tranquil as a sleeping babe's—not a tremor affected any muscle of his body; his breathing, until suspended in the act of taking aim, was regular and slow. Duty had conquered; the spirit had said to the body: "Peace, be still." He fired.

III

An officer of the Federal force, who in a spirit of adventure or in quest of knowledge had left the hidden bivouac in the valley, and with aimless feet had made his way to the lower edge of a small open space near the foot of the cliff, was considering what he had to gain by pushing his exploration further. At a distance of a quarter-mile before him, but apparently at a stone's throw, rose from its fringe of pines the gigantic face of rock, towering to so great a height above him that it made him giddy to look up to where its edge cut a sharp, rugged line against the sky. It presented a clean, vertical profile against a background of blue sky to a point half the way down, and of distant hills, hardly less blue, thence to the tops of the trees at its base. Lifting his eyes to the dizzy altitude of its summit the officer saw an astonishing sight— a man on horseback riding down into the valley through the air!

Straight upright sat the rider, in military fashion, with a firm seat in the saddle, a strong clutch upon the rein to hold

his charger from too impetuous a plunge. From his bare head his long hair streamed upward, waving like a plume. His hands were concealed in the cloud of the horse's lifted mane. The animal's body was as level as if every hoof-stroke encountered the resistant earth. Its motions were those of a wild gallop, but even as the officer looked they ceased, with all the legs thrown sharply forward as in the act of alighting from a leap. But this was a flight!

Filled with amazement and terror by this apparition of a horseman in the sky—half believing himself the chosen scribe of some new Apocalypse, the officer was overcome by the intensity of his emotions; his legs failed him and he fell. Almost at the same instant he heard a crashing sound in the trees— a sound that died without an echo—and all was still.

The officer rose to his feet, trembling. The familiar sensation of an abraded shin recalled his dazed faculties. Pulling himself together he ran rapidly obliquely away from the cliff to a point distant from its foot; thereabout he expected to find his man; and thereabout he naturally failed. In the fleeting instant of his vision his imagination had been so wrought upon by the apparent grace and ease and intention of the marvelous performance that it did not occur to him that the line of march of aerial cavalry is directly downward, and that he could find the objects of his search at the very foot of the cliff. A half-hour later he returned to camp.

This officer was a wise man; he knew better than to tell an incredible truth. He said nothing of what he had seen. But when the commander asked him if in his scout he had learned anything of advantage to the expedition he answered:

"Yes, sir. There is no road leading down into this valley from the southward."

The commander, knowing better, smiled.

IV

After firing his shot, Private Carter Druse reloaded his rifle and resumed his watch. Ten minutes had hardly passed when a Federal sergeant crept cautiously to him on hands and knees. Druse neither turned his head nor looked at him, but lay without motion or sign of recognition.

"Did you fire?" the sergeant whispered.

"Yes."

"At what?"

"A horse. It was standing on yonder rock—pretty far out. You see it is no longer there. It went over the cliff."

The man's face was white, but he showed no other sign of emotion. Having answered, he turned away his eyes and said no more. The sergeant did not understand.

"See here, Druse," he said, after a moment's silence, "it's no use making a mystery. I order you to report. Was there anybody on the horse?"

"Yes."

"Well?"

"My father."

The sergeant rose to his feet and walked away. "Good God!" he said.

ONE OF THE MISSING

J EROME Searing, a private soldier of General Sherman's army, then confronting the enemy at and about Kennesaw Mountain, Georgia, turned his back upon a small group of officers with whom he had been talking in low tones, stepped across a light line of earthworks, and disappeared in a forest. None of the men in line behind the works had said a word to him, nor had he so much as nodded to them in passing, but all who saw understood that this brave man had been entrusted with some perilous duty. Jerome Searing, though a private, did not serve in the ranks; he was detailed for service at division headquarters, being borne upon the rolls as an orderly. "Orderly" is a word covering a multitude of duties. An orderly may be a messenger, a clerk, an officer's servant—anything. He may perform services for which no provision is made in orders and army regulations. Their nature may depend upon his aptitude, upon favor, upon accident. Private Searing, an incomparable marksman, young, hardy, intelligent and insensible to fear, was a scout. The general commanding his divison was not content to obey orders blindly without knowing what was in his front, even when his command was not on detached service, but formed a fraction of the line of the army; nor was he satisfied to receive his knowledge of his vis-à-vis through the customary channels; he wanted to know more than he was apprised of by the corps commander and the collisions of pickets and skirmishers. Hence

Jerome Searing, with his extraordinary daring, his woodcraft, his sharp eyes, and truthful tongue. On this occasion his instructions were simple: to get as near the enemy's lines as possible and learn all that he could.

In a few moments he had arrived at the picket line, the men on duty there lying in groups of two and four behind little banks of earth scooped out of the slight depression in which they lay, their rifles protruding from the green boughs with which they had masked their small defenses. The forest extended without a break toward the front, so solemn and silent that only by an effort of the imagination could it be conceived as populous with armed men, alert and vigilant—a forest formidable with possibilities of battle. Pausing a moment in one of these rifle-pits to apprise the men of his intention, Searing crept stealthily forward on his hands and knees and was soon lost to view in a dense thicket of underbrush.

"That is the last of him," said one of the men. "I wish I had his rifle. Those fellows will hurt some of us with it."

Searing crept on, taking advantage of every accident of ground and growth to give himself better cover. His eyes penetrated everywhere, his ears took note of every sound. He stilled his breathing, and at the cracking of a twig beneath his knee stopped his progress and hugged the earth. It was slow work, but not tedious; the danger made it exciting, but by no physical signs was the excitement manifest. His pulse was as regular, his nerves were as steady as if he were trying to trap a sparrow.

"It seems a long time," he thought, "but I cannot have come very far; I am still alive."

He smiled at his own method of estimating distance, and crept forward. A moment later he suddenly flattened himself upon the earth and lay motionless, minute after minute. Through a narrow opening in the bushes he had caught sight of a small mound of yellow clay—one of the enemy's rifle-pits. After some little time he cautiously raised his head, inch by inch, then his body upon his hands, spread out on each side of him, all the while intently regarding the hillock of clay. In another moment he was upon his feet, rifle in hand, striding rapidly forward with little attempt at concealment. He had rightly interpreted the signs, whatever they were; the enemy was gone.

To assure himself beyond a doubt before going back to report upon so important a matter, Searing pushed forward across the line of abandoned pits, running from cover to cover in the more open forest, his eyes vigilant to discover possible stragglers. He came to the edge of a plantation—one of those forlorn, deserted homesteads of the last years of the war, upgrown with brambles, ugly with broken fences, and desolate with vacant buildings having blank apertures in place of doors and windows. After a keen reconnoissance from the safe seclusion of a clump of young pines, Searing ran lightly across a field and through an orchard to a small structure which stood apart from the other farm buildings, on a slight elevation. This he thought would enable him to overlook a large scope of country in the direction that he supposed the enemy to have taken in withdrawing. This building, which had originally consisted of a single room elevated upon four posts about ten feet high, was now little more than a roof; the floor had fallen away, the joists and planks loosely piled on the ground below or resting on end at various angles, not wholly torn from their fastenings above. The supporting posts were themselves no longer vertical. It looked as if the whole edifice would go down at the touch of a finger.

Concealing himself in the debris of joists and flooring, Searing looked across the open ground between his point of view and a spur of Kennesaw Mountain, a half-mile away. A road leading up and across this spur was crowded with troops —the rear guard of the retiring enemy, their gun barrels gleaming in the morning sunlight.

Searing had now learned all that he could hope to know. It was his duty to return to his own command with all possible speed and report his discovery. But the gray column of Confederates toiling up the mountain road was singularly tempting. His rifle—an ordinary "Springfield," but fitted with a globe sight and hair-trigger—would easily send its ounce and a quarter of lead hissing into their midst. That would probably not affect the duration and result of the war, but it is the business of a soldier to kill. It is also his habit if he is a good soldier. Searing cocked his rifle and "set" the trigger.

But it was decreed from the beginning of time that Private Searing was not to murder anybody that bright summer morning, nor was the Confederate retreat to be announced by him. For countless ages events had been so matching themselves together in that wondrous mosaic to some parts of which, dimly discernible, we give the name of history, that the acts which he had in will would have marred the harmony of the pattern. Some twenty-five years previously the Power charged with the execution of the work according to the design had provided against that mischance by causing the birth of a certain male child in a little village at the foot of the Carpathian Mountains, had carefully reared it, supervised its education, directed its desires into a military channel, and in due time made it an officer of artillery. By the concurrence of an infinite number of favoring influences and their preponderance over an infinite number of opposing ones, this officer of artillery had been made to commit a breach of discipline and flee from his native country to avoid punishment. He had been directed to New Orleans (instead of New York), where a recruiting officer awaited him on the wharf. He was enlisted and promoted, and things were so ordered that he now commanded a Confederate battery some two miles along the line from where Jerome Searing, the Federal scout, stood cocking his rifle. Nothing had been neglected—at every step in the progress of both these men's lives, and in the lives of their contemporaries and ancestors, and in the lives of the contemporaries of their ancestors, the right thing had been done to bring about the desired result. Had anything in all this vast concatenation been overlooked Private Searing might have fired on the retreating Confederates that morning, and perhaps have missed. As it fell out, a Confederate captain of artillery, having nothing better to do while awaiting his turn to pull out and be off, amused himself by sighting a field-piece obliquely to his right at what he mistook for some Federal officers on the crest of a hill, and discharged it. The shot flew high of its mark.

As Jerome Searing drew back the hammer of his rifle and

with his eyes upon the distant Confederates considered where he could plant his shot with the best hope of making a widow or an orphan or a childless mother—perhaps all three, for Private Searing, although he had repeatedly refused promotion, was not without a certain kind of ambition—he heard a rushing sound in the air, like that made by the wings of a great bird swooping down upon its prey. More quickly than he could apprehend the gradation, it increased to a hoarse and horrible roar, as the missile that made it sprang at him out of the sky, striking with a deafening impact one of the posts supporting the confusion of timbers above him, smashing it into matchwood, and bringing down the crazy edifice with a loud clatter, in clouds of blinding dust!

When Jerome Searing recovered consciousness he did not at once understand what had occurred. It was, indeed, some time before he opened his eyes. For a while he believed that he had died and been buried, and he tried to recall some portions of the burial service. He thought that his wife was kneeling upon his grave, adding her weight to that of the earth upon his breast. The two of them, widow and earth, had crushed his coffin. Unless the children should persuade her to go home he would not much longer be able to breathe. He felt a sense of wrong. "I cannot speak to her," he thought. "The dead have no voice, and if I open my eyes I shall get them full of earth."

He opened his eyes. A great expanse of blue sky, rising from a fringe of the tops of trees. In the foreground, shutting out some of the trees, a high, dun mound, angular in outline and crossed by an intricate, patternless system of straight lines; the whole an immeasurable distance away—a distance so inconceivably great that it fatigued him, and he closed his eyes. The moment that he did so he was conscious of an insufferable light. A sound was in his ears like the low, rhythmic thunder of a distant sea breaking in successive waves upon the beach, and out of this noise, seeming a part of it, or possibly coming from beyond it, and intermingled with its ceaseless undertone, came the articulate words: "Jerome Searing, you are caught like a rat in a trap—in a trap, trap, trap."

Suddenly there fell a great silence, a black darkness, an

infinite tranquillity, and Jerome Searing, perfectly conscious of his rathood, and well assured of the trap that he was in, remembering all and nowise alarmed, again opened his eyes to reconnoiter, to note the strength of his enemy, to plan his defense.

He was caught in a reclining posture, his back firmly supported by a solid beam. Another lay across his breast, but he had been able to shrink a little away from it so that it no longer oppressed him, though it was immovable. A brace joining it at an angle had wedged him against a pile of boards on his left, fastening the arm on that side. His legs, slightly parted and straight along the ground, were covered upward to the knees with a mass of debris which towered above his narrow horizon. His head was as rigidly fixed as in a vise; he could move his eyes, his chin—no more. Only his right arm was partly free. "You must help us out of this," he said to it. But he could not get it from under the heavy timber athwart his chest, nor move it outward more than six inches at the elbow.

Searing was not seriously injured, nor did he suffer pain. A smart rap on the head from a flying fragment of the splintered post, incurred simultaneously with the frightfully sudden shock to the nervous system, had momentarily dazed him. His term of unconsciousness, including the period of recovery, during which he had had the strange fancies, had probably not exceeded a few seconds, for the dust of the wreck had not wholly cleared away as he began an intelligent survey of the situation.

With his partly free right hand he now tried to get hold of the beam that lay across, but not quite against, his breast. In no way could he do so. He was unable to depress the shoulder so as to push the elbow beyond that edge of the timber which was nearest his knees; failing in that, he could not raise the forearm and hand to grasp the beam. The brace that made an angle with it downward and backward prevented him from doing anything in that direction, and between it and his body the space was not half so wide as the length of his forearm. Obviously he could not get his hand under the beam nor over it; the hand could not, in fact, touch it at all. Having demonstrated his inability, he desisted, and began to think whether he could reach any of the debris piled upon his legs.

In surveying the mass with a view to determining that point, his attention was arrested by what seemed to be a ring of shining metal immediately in front of his eyes. It appeared to him at first to surround some perfectly black substance, and it was somewhat more than a half-inch in diameter. It suddenly occurred to his mind that the blackness was simply shadow and that the ring was in fact the muzzle of his rifle protruding from the pile of debris. He was not long in satisfying himself that this was so—if it was a satisfaction. By closing either eye he could look a little way along the barrel—to the point where it was hidden by the rubbish that held it. He could see the one side, with the corresponding eye, at apparently the same angle as the other side with the other eye. Looking with the right eye, the weapon seemed to be directed at a point to the left of his head, and vice versa. He was unable to see the upper surface of the barrel, but could see the under surface of the stock at a slight angle. The piece was, in fact, aimed at the exact center of his forehead.

In the perception of this circumstance, in the recollection that just previously to the mischance of which this uncomfortable situation was the result he had cocked the rifle and set the trigger so that a touch would discharge it, Private Searing was affected with a feeling of uneasiness. But that was as far as possible from fear; he was a brave man, somewhat familar with the aspect of rifles from that point of view, and of cannon, too. And now he recalled, with something like amusement, an incident of his experience at the storming of Missionary Ridge, where, walking up to one of the enemy's embrasures from which he had seen a heavy gun throw charge after charge of grape among the assailants, he had thought for a moment that the piece had been withdrawn; he could see nothing in the opening but a brazen circle. What that was he had understood just in time to step aside as it pitched another peck of iron down that swarming slope. To face firearms is one of the commonest incidents in a soldier's life— firearms, too, with malevolent eyes blazing behind them. That is what a soldier is for. Still, Private Searing did not altogether relish the situation, and turned away his eyes.

After groping, aimless, with his right hand for a time he made an ineffectual attempt to release his left. Then he tried to disengage his head, the fixity of which was the more annoying from his ignorance of what held it. Next he tried to free his feet, but while exerting the powerful muscles of his legs for that purpose it occurred to him that a disturbance of the rubbish which held them might discharge the rifle; how it could have endured what had already befallen it he could not understand, although memory assisted him with several instances in point. One in particular he recalled, in which in a moment of mental abstraction he had clubbed his rifle and beaten out another gentleman's brains, observing afterward that the weapon which he had been diligently swinging by the muzzle was loaded, capped, and at full cock—knowledge of which circumstances would doubtless have cheered his antagonist to longer endurance. He had always smiled in recalling that blunder of his "green and salad days" as a soldier, but now he did not smile. He turned his eyes again to the muzzle of the rifle and for a moment fancied that it had moved; it seemed somewhat nearer.

Again he looked away. The tops of the distant trees beyond the bounds of the plantation interested him: he had not before observed how light and feathery they were, nor how darkly blue the sky was, even among their branches, where they somewhat paled it with their green; above him it appeared almost black. "It will be uncomfortably hot here," he thought, "as the day advances. I wonder which way I am looking."

Judging by such shadows as he could see, he decided that his face was due north; he would at least not have the sun in his eyes, and north—well, that was toward his wife and children.

"Bah!" he exclaimed aloud, "what have they to do with it?"

He closed his eyes. "As I can't get out I may as well go to sleep. The rebels are gone and some of our fellows are sure to stray out here foraging. They'll find me."

But he did not sleep. Gradually he became sensible of a

pain in his forehead—a dull ache, hardly perceptible at first, but growing more and more uncomfortable. He opened his eyes and it was gone—closed them and it returned. "The devil!" he said, irrelevantly, and stared again at the sky. He heard the singing of birds, the strange metallic note of the meadow lark, suggesting the clash of vibrant blades. He fell into pleasant memories of his childhood, played again with his brother and sister, raced across the fields, shouting to alarm the sedentary larks, entered the somber forest beyond and with timid steps followed the faint path to Ghost Rock, standing at last with audible heartthrobs before the Dead Man's Cave and seeking to penetrate its awful mystery. For the first time he observed that the opening of the haunted cavern was encircled by a ring of metal. Then all else vanished and left him gazing into the barrel of his rifle as before. But whereas before it had seemed nearer, it now seemed an inconceivable distance away, and all the more sinister for that. He cried out and, startled by something in his own voice—the note of fear—lied to himself in denial: "If I don't sing out I may stay here till I die."

He now made no further attempt to evade the menacing stare of the gun barrel. If he turned away his eyes an instant it was to look for assistance (although he could not see the ground on either side of the ruin), and he permitted them to return, obedient to the imperative fascination. If he closed them it was from weariness, and instantly the poignant pain in his forehead—the prophecy and menace of the bullet— forced him to reopen them.

The tension of nerve and brain was too severe; nature came to his relief with intervals of unconsciousness. Reviving from one of these he became sensible of a sharp, smarting pain in his right hand, and when he worked his fingers together, or rubbed his palm with them, he could feel that they were wet and slippery. He could not see the hand, but he knew the sensation; it was running blood. In his delirium he had beaten it against the jagged fragments of the wreck, had clutched it full of splinters. He resolved that he would meet his fate more manly. He was a plain, common soldier, had no religion and not much philosophy; he could not die like a hero, with great and wise last words, even if there had been someone to hear them, but he could die "game," and he would. But if he could only know when to expect the shot!

Some rats which had probably inhabited the shed came sneaking and scampering about. One of them mounted the pile of debris that held the rifle; another followed and another. Searing regarded that at first with indifference, then with friendly interest; then, as the thought flashed into his bewildered mind that they might touch the trigger of his rifle, he cursed them and ordered them to go away. "It is no business of yours," he cried.

The creatures went away; they would return later, attack his face, gnaw away his nose, cut his throat—he knew that, but he hoped by that time to be dead.

Nothing could now unfix his gaze from the little ring of metal with its black interior. The pain in his forehead was fierce and incessant. He felt it gradually penetrating the brain more and more deeply, until at last its progress was arrested by the wood at the back of his head. It grew momentarily more insufferable: he began wantonly beating his lacerated hand against the splinters again to counteract that horrible ache. It seemed to throb with a slow, regular recurrence, each pulsation sharper than the preceding, and sometimes he cried out, thinking he felt the fatal bullet. No thoughts of home, of wife and children, of country, of glory. The whole record of memory was effaced. The world had passed away—not a vestige remained. Here in this confusion of timbers and boards is the sole universe. Here is immortality in time—each pain an everlasting life. The throbs tick off eternities.

Jerome Searing, the man of courage, the formidable enemy, the strong, resolute warrior, was as pale as a ghost. His jaw was fallen; his eyes protruded; he trembled in every fiber; a cold sweat bathed his entire body; he screamed with fear. He was not insane—he was terrified.

In groping about with his torn and bleeding hand he seized at last a strip of board, and, pulling, felt it give way. It lay parallel with his body, and by bending his elbow as much as the contracted space would permit, he could draw it a few inches at a time. Finally it was altogether loosened from the wreckage covering his legs; he could lift it clear of the ground its whole length. A great hope came into his mind: perhaps he could work it upward, that is to say backward, far enough to lift the end and push aside the rifle; or, if that were too tightly wedged, so place the strip of board as to deflect the bullet. With this object he passed it backward inch by inch, hardly daring to breathe lest that act somehow defeat his intent, and more than ever unable to remove his eyes from the rifle, which might perhaps now hasten to improve its waning opportunity. Something at least had been gained: in the occupation of his mind in this attempt at self-defense he was less sensible of the pain in his head and had ceased to wince. But he was still dreadfully frightened and his teeth rattled like castanets.

The strip of board ceased to move to the suasion of his hand. He tugged at it with all his strength, changed the direction of its length all he could, but it had met some extended obstruction behind him and the end in front was still too far away to clear the pile of debris and reach the muzzle of the gun. It extended, indeed, nearly as far as the trigger guard, which, uncovered by the rubbish, he could imperfectly see with his right eye. He tried to break the strip with his hand, but had no leverage. In his defeat, all his terror returned, augmented tenfold. The black aperture of the rifle appeared to threaten a sharper and more imminent death in punishment of his rebellion. The track of the bullet through his head ached with an intenser anguish. He began to tremble again.

Suddenly he became composed. His tremor subsided. He clenched his teeth and drew down his eyebrows. He had not exhausted his means of defense; a new design had shaped itself in his mind—another plan of battle. Raising the front end of the strip of board, he carefully pushed it forward through the wreckage at the side of the rifle until it pressed against the trigger guard. Then he moved the end slowly outward until he could feel that it had cleared it, then, closing his eyes, thrust it against the trigger with all his strength! There was no explosion; the rifle had been discharged as it dropped from his hand when the building fell. But it did its work.

Lieutenant Adrian Searing, in command of the picket guard on that part of the line through which his brother Jerome had passed on his mission, sat with attentive ears in his breastwork behind the line. Not the faintest sound escaped him; the cry of a bird, the barking of a squirrel, the noise of the wind among the pines—all were anxiously noted by his overstrained sense. Suddenly, directly in front of his line, he heard a faint, confused rumble, like the clatter of a falling building translated by distance. The lieutenant mechanically looked at his watch. Six o'clock and eighteen minutes. At the same moment an officer approached him on foot from the rear and saluted.

"Lieutenant," said the officer, "the colonel directs you to move forward your line and feel the enemy if you find him. If not, continue the advance until directed to halt. There is reason to think that the enemy has retreated."

The lieutenant nodded and said nothing; the other officer retired. In a moment the men, apprised of their duty by the noncommissioned officers in low tones, had deployed from their rifle-pits and were moving forward in skirmishing order, with set teeth and beating hearts.

This line of skirmishers sweeps across the plantation toward the mountain. They pass on both sides of the wrecked building, observing nothing. At a short distance in their rear their commander comes. He casts his eyes curiously upon the ruin and sees a dead body half buried in boards and timbers. It is so covered with dust that its clothing is Confederate gray. Its face is yellowish white; the cheeks are fallen in, the temples sunken, too, with sharp ridges about them, making the forehead forbiddingly narrow; the upper lip, slightly lifted, shows the white teeth, rigidly clenched. The hair is heavy with moisture, the face as wet as the dewy grass all about. From his point of view the officer does not observe the rifle; the man was apparently killed by the fall of the building.

"Dead a week," said the officer curtly, moving on and absently pulling out his watch as if to verify his estimate of time. Six o'clock and forty minutes.

A WIRELESS
MESSAGE

IN the summer of 1896 Mr. William Holt, a wealthy manufacturer of Chicago, was living temporarily in a little town of central New York, the name of which the writer's memory has not retained. Mr. Holt had had "trouble with his wife," from whom he had parted a year before. Whether the trouble was anything more serious than incompatibility of temper, he is probably the only living person that knows: he is not addicted to the vice of confidences. Yet he has related the incident herein set down to at least one person without exacting a pledge of secrecy. He is now living in Europe.

One evening he had left the house of a brother whom he was visiting, for a stroll in the country. It may be assumed—whatever the value of the assumption in connection with what is said to have occurred—that his mind was occupied with reflections on his domestic infelicities and the distressing changes that they had wrought in his life. Whatever may have been his thoughts, they so possessed him that he observed neither the lapse of time nor whither his feet were carrying him; he knew only that he had passed far beyond the town limits and was traversing a lonely region by a road that bore no resemblance to the one by which he had left the village. In brief, he was lost.

Realizing his mischance, he smiled; central New York is not a region of perils, nor does one long remain lost in it. He turned about and went back the way that he had come. Before he had gone far he observed that the landscape was growing more distinct—was brightening. Everything was suffused with a soft, red glow in which he saw his shadow projected in the road before him. "The moon is rising," he said to himself. Then he remembered that it was about the time of the new moon, and if that tricksy orb was in one of its stages of visibility it had set long before. He stopped and faced about, seeking the source of the rapidly broadening light. As he did so, his shadow turned and lay along the road in front of him as before. The light still came from behind him. That was surprising; he could not understand. Again he turned, and again, facing successively to every point of the horizon. Always the shadow was before—always the light behind, "a still and awful red."

Holt was astonished—"dumfounded" is the word that he used in telling it—yet seems to have retained a certain intelligent curiosity. To test the intensity of the light whose nature and cause he could not determine, he took out his watch to see if he could make out the figures on the dial. They were plainly visible, and the hands indicated the hour of eleven o'clock and twenty-five minutes. At that moment the mysterious illumination suddenly flared to an intense, an almost blinding splendor, flushing the entire sky, extinguishing the stars and throwing the monstrous shadow of himself athwart the landscape. In that unearthly illumination he saw near him, but apparently in the air at a considerable elevation, the figure of his wife, clad in her night clothing and holding to her breast the figure of his child. Her eyes were fixed upon his with an expression which he afterward professed himself unable to name or describe, further than that it was "not of this life."

The flare was momentary, followed by black darkness, in which, however, the apparition still showed white and motionless; then by insensible degrees it faded and vanished, like a bright image on the retina after the closing of the eyes. A peculiarity of the apparition, hardly noted at the time, but afterward recalled, was that it showed only the upper half of the woman's figure: nothing was seen below the waist.

The sudden darkness was comparative, not absolute, for gradually all objects of his environment became again visible.

In the dawn of the morning Holt found himself entering

the village at a point opposite to that at which he had left it.
He soon arrived at the house of his brother, who hardly knew
him. He was wild-eyed, haggard, and gray as a rat. Almost
incoherently, he related his night's experience.

"Go to bed, my poor fellow," said his brother, "and—wait.
We shall hear more of this."

An hour later came the predestined telegram. Holt's dwelling
in one of the suburbs of Chicago had been destroyed by fire.
Her escape cut off by the flames, his wife had appeared at an
upper window, her child in her arms. There she had stood,
motionless, apparently dazed. Just as the firemen had arrived
with a ladder, the floor had given way, and she was seen no
more.

The moment of this culminating horror was eleven o'clock
and twenty-five minutes, standard time.

THE STRANGER

MAN stepped out of the darkness into the little illuminated circle about our failing campfire and seated himself upon a rock.

"You are not the first to explore this region," he said, gravely.

Nobody controverted his statement; he was himself proof of its truth, for he was not of our party and must have been somewhere near when we camped. Moreover, he must have companions not far away; it was not a place where one would be living or traveling alone. For more than a week we had seen, besides ourselves and our animals, only such living things as rattlesnakes and horned toads. In an Arizona desert one does not coexist with only such creatures as these: one must have pack animals, supplies, arms—"an outfit." And all these imply comrades. It was perhaps a doubt as to what manner of men this unceremonious stranger's comrades might be, together with something in his words interpretable as a challenge, that caused every man of our half-dozen "gentlemen adventurers" to rise to a sitting posture and lay his hand upon a weapon—an act signifying, in that time and place, a policy of expectation. The stranger gave the matter no attention and began again to speak in the same deliberate, uninflected monotone in which he had delivered his first sentence.

"Thirty years ago Ramon Gallegos, William Shaw, George W. Kent and Berry Davis, all of Tucson, crossed the Santa

53

Catalina mountains and traveled due west, as nearly as the configuration of the country permitted. We were prospecting and it was our intention, if we found nothing, to push through to the Gila River at some point near Big Bend, where we understood there was a settlement. We had a good outfit but no guide—just Ramon Gallegos, William Shaw, George W. Kent and Berry Davis."

The man repeated the names slowly and distinctly, as if to fix them in the memories of his audience, every member of which was now attentively observing him, but with a slackened apprehension regarding his possible companions somewhere in the darkness that seemed to enclose us like a black wall; in the manner of this volunteer historian was no suggestion of an unfriendly purpose. His act was rather that of a harmless lunatic than an enemy. We were not so new to the country as not to know that the solitary life of many a plainsman had a tendency to develop eccentricities of conduct and character not always easily distinguishable from mental aberration. A man is like a tree: in a forest of his fellows he will grow as straight as his generic and individual nature permits; alone in the open, he yields to the deforming stresses and tortions that environ him. Some such thoughts were in my mind as I watched the man from the shadow of my hat, pulled low to shut out the firelight. A witless fellow, no doubt, but what could he be doing there in the heart of a desert?

Having undertaken to tell this story, I wish that I could describe the man's appearance; that would be a natural thing to do. Unfortunately, and somewhat strangely, I find myself unable to do so with any degree of confidence, for afterward no two of us agreed as to what he wore and how he looked; and when I try to set down my own impressions they elude me. Anyone can tell some kind of story; narration is one of the elemental powers of the race. But the talent for description is a gift.

Nobody having broken silence the visitor went on to say:

"This country was not then what it is now. There was not a ranch between the Gila and the Gulf. There was a little game here and there in the mountains, and near the infrequent water holes grass enough to keep our animals from starvation.

If we should be so fortunate as to encounter no Indians we might get through. But within a week the purpose of the expedition had altered from discovery of wealth to preservation of life. We had gone too far to go back, for what was ahead could be no worse than what was behind; so we pushed on, riding by night to avoid Indians and the intolerable heat, and concealing ourselves by day as best we could. Sometimes, having exhausted our supply of wild meat and emptied our casks, we were days without food or drink; then a water hole or a shallow pool in the bottom of an arroyo so restored our strength and sanity that we were able to shoot some of the wild animals that sought it also. Sometimes it was a bear, sometimes an antelope, a coyote, a cougar—that was as God pleased; all were food.

"One morning as we skirted a mountain range, seeking a practicable pass, we were attacked by a band of Apaches who had followed our trail up a gulch—it is not far from here. Knowing that they outnumbered us ten to one, they took none of their usual cowardly precautions, but dashed upon us at a gallop, firing and yelling. Fighting was out of the question. We urged our feeble animals up the gulch as far as there was footing for a hoof, then threw ourselves out of our saddles and took to the chaparral on one of the slopes, abandoning our entire outfit to the enemy. But we retained our rifles, every man—Ramon Gallegos, William Shaw, George W. Kent and Berry Davis."

"Same old crowd," said the humorist of our party. He was an Eastern man, unfamiliar with the decent observances of social intercourse. A gesture of disapproval from our leader silenced him and the stranger proceeded with his tale.

"The savages dismounted also, and some of them ran up the gulch beyond the point at which we had left it, cutting off further retreat in that direction and forcing us on up the side. Unfortunately the chaparral extended only a short distance up the slope, and as we came into the open ground above we took the fire of a dozen rifles; but Apaches shoot badly when in a hurry, and God so willed it that none of us fell. Twenty yards up the slope, beyond the edge of the brush, were vertical cliffs, in which, directly in front of us, was a narrow opening. Into that we ran, finding ourselves in a cavern about as large as an ordinary room in a house. Here for a time we were safe: a single man with a repeating rifle could defend the entrance against all the Apaches in the land. But against hunger and thirst we had no defense. Courage we still had, but hope was a memory.

"Not one of those Indians did we afterward see, but by the smoke and glare of their fires in the gulch we knew that by day and by night they watched with ready rifles in the edge of the bush—knew that if we made a sortie not a man of us would live to take three steps into the open. For three days, watching in turn, we held out before our suffering became insupportable. Then—it was the morning of the fourth day— Ramon Gallegos said:

" 'Señores, I know not well of the good God and what please him. I have live without religion, and I am not acquaint with that of you. Pardon, señores, if I shock you, but for me the time is come to beat the game of the Apache.'

"He knelt upon the rock floor of the cave and pressed his pistol against his temple. 'Madre de Dios,' he said, 'comes now the soul of Ramon Gallegos.'

"And so he left us—William Shaw, George W. Kent and Berry Davis.

"I was the leader. It was for me to speak.

" 'He was a brave man,' I said—'he knew when to die, and how. It is foolish to go mad from thirst and fall by Apache bullets, or be skinned alive—it is in bad taste. Let us join Ramon Gallegos.'

" 'That is right,' said William Shaw.

" 'That is right,' said George W. Kent.

"I straightened the limbs of Ramon Gallegos and put a handkerchief over his face. Then William Shaw said: 'I should like to look like that—a little while.'

"And George W. Kent said that he felt that way, too.

" 'It shall be so,' I said. 'The red devils will wait a week. William Shaw and George W. Kent, draw and kneel.'

"They did so and I stood before them.

" 'Almighty God, our Father,' said I.

" 'Almighty God, our Father,' said William Shaw.

" 'Almighty God, our Father,' said George W. Kent.

" 'Forgive us our sins,' said I.

" 'Forgive us our sins,' said they.

" 'And receive our souls.'

" 'And receive our souls.'

" 'Amen!'

" 'Amen!'

"I laid them beside Ramon Gallegos and covered their faces."

There was a quick commotion on the opposite side of the campfire. One of our party had sprung to his feet, pistol in hand.

"And you!" he shouted. "*You* dared to escape? You dare to be alive? You cowardly hound, I'll send you to join them if I hang for it!"

But with the leap of a panther the captain was upon him, grasping his wrist. "Hold it in, Sam Yountsey, hold it in!"

We were now all upon our feet—except the stranger, who sat motionless and apparently inattentive. Someone seized Yountsey's other arm.

"Captain," I said, "there is something wrong here. This fellow is either a lunatic or merely a liar—just a plain, every-day liar whom Yountsey has no call to kill. If this man was of that party it had five members, one of whom—probably himself—he has not named."

"Yes," said the captain, releasing the insurgent, who sat down, "there is something—unusual. Years ago four dead bodies of white men, scalped and shamefully mutilated, were found about the mouth of that cave. They are buried there. I have seen the graves—we shall all see them tomorrow."

The stranger rose, standing tall in the light of the expiring fire, which in our breathless attention to his story we had neglected to keep going.

"There were four," he said. "Ramon Gallegos, William Shaw, George W. Kent and Berry Davis."

With this reiterated roll call of the dead he walked into the darkness and we saw him no more.

At that moment one of our party, who had been on guard, strode in among us, rifle in hand and somewhat excited.

"Captain," he said, "for the last half-hour three men have

been standing out there on the mesa." He pointed in the direction taken by the stranger. "I could see them distinctly, for the moon is up, but as they had no guns and I had them covered with mine I thought it was their move. They have made none, but, damn it! they have got on to my nerves."

"Go back to your post, and stay till you see them again," said the captain. "The rest of you lie down again, or I'll kick you all into the fire."

The sentinel obediently withdrew, swearing, and did not return. As we were arranging our blankets the fiery Yountsey said, "I beg your pardon, Captain, but who the devil do you take them to be?"

"Ramon Gallegos, William Shaw and George W. Kent."

"But how about Berry Davis? I ought to have shot him."

"Quite needless. You couldn't have made him any deader. Go to sleep."

THE MAN AND
THE SNAKE

*It is of veritabyll report, and attested of so many that there
be nowe of wyse and learned none to gaynsaye it, that ye ser-
pente hys eye hath a magnetick propertie that whosoe falleth
into its suasion is drawn forwards in despyte of his wille, and
perisheth miserabyll by ye creature hys byte.*

STRETCHED at ease upon a sofa, in gown and slippers,
Harker Brayton smiled as he read the foregoing sentence in old Morryster's *Marvells of Science.* "The only
marvel in the matter," he said to himself, "is that the wise and
learned in Morryster's day should have believed such nonsense
as is rejected by most of even the ignorant in ours."

A train of reflection followed—for Brayton was a man of
thought—and he unconsciously lowered his book without altering the direction of his eyes. As soon as the volume had gone
below the line of sight, something in an obscure corner of the
room recalled his attention to his surroundings. What he saw,
in the shadow under his bed, was two small points of light,
apparently about an inch apart. They might have been reflections of the gas jet above him, in metal nailheads; he gave
them but little thought and resumed his reading. A moment
later something—some impulse which it did not occur to him
to analyze—impelled him to lower the book again and seek for
what he saw before. The points of light were still there. They
seemed to have become brighter than before, shining with a

59

greenish luster that he had not at first observed. He thought, too, that they might have moved a trifle—were somewhat nearer. They were still too much in shadow, however, to reveal their nature and origin to an indolent attention, and again he resumed his reading. Suddenly something in the text suggested a thought that made him start and drop the book for the third time to the side of the sofa, whence, escaping from his hand, it fell sprawling to the floor, back upward. Brayton, half-risen, was staring intently into the obscurity beneath the bed, where the points of light shone with, it

seemed to him, an added fire. His attention was now fully aroused, his gaze eager and imperative. It disclosed, almost directly under the foot rail of the bed, the coils of a large serpent—the points of light were its eyes! Its horrible head, thrust flatly forth from the innermost coil and resting upon the outermost, was directed straight toward him, the definition of the wide, brutal jaw and the idiotlike forehead serving to show the direction of its malevolent gaze. The eyes were no longer merely luminous points; they looked into his own with a meaning, a malign significance.

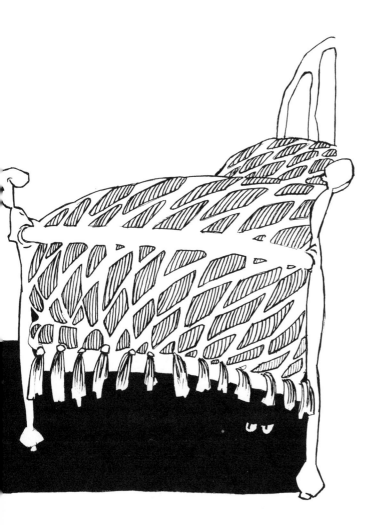

II

A snake in a bedroom of a modern city dwelling of the better sort is, happily, not so common a phenomenon as to make explanation altogether needless. Harker Brayton, a bachelor of thirty-five, a scholar, idler and something of an athlete, rich, popular and of sound health, had returned to San Francisco from all manner of remote and unfamiliar countries. His tastes, always a trifle luxurious, had taken on an added exuberance from long privation; and the resources of even the Castle Hotel being inadequate to their perfect gratification, he had gladly accepted the hospitality of his friend, Dr. Druring, the distinguished scientist. Dr. Druring's house, a large, old-fashioned one in what is now an obscure quarter of the city, had an outer and visible aspect of proud reserve. It plainly would not associate with the contiguous elements of its altered environment, and appeared to have developed some of the eccentricities which come of isolation. One of these was a wing, conspicuously irrelevant in point of architecture, and no less rebellious in matter of purpose; for it was a combination of laboratory, menagerie and museum. It was here that the doctor indulged the scientific side of his nature in the study of such forms of animal life as engaged his interest and comforted his taste—which, it must be confessed, ran rather to the lower types. For one of the higher nimbly and sweetly to recommend itself unto his gentle senses it had at least to retain certain rudimentary characteristics allying it to such "dragons of the prime" as toads and snakes. His scientific sympathies were distinctly reptilian; he loved nature's vulgarians and described himself as the Zola of zoology. His wife and daughters not having the advantage to share his enlightened curiosity regarding the works and ways of our ill-starred fellow creatures, were with needless austerity excluded from what he called the Snakery and doomed to companionship with their own kind, though to soften the rigors of their lot he had permitted them out of his great wealth to outdo the reptiles in the gorgeousness of their surroundings and to shine with a superior splendor.

Architecturally and in point of "furnishing" the Snakery had a severe simplicity befitting the humble circumstances of its occupants, many of whom, indeed, could not safely have been entrusted with the liberty that is necessary to the full enjoyment of luxury, for they had the troublesome peculiarity of being alive. In their own apartments, however, they were under as little personal restraint as was compatible with their protection from the baneful habit of swallowing one another; and, as Brayton had thoughtfully been apprised, it was more than a tradition that some of them had at divers times been found in parts of the premises where it would have embarrassed them to explain their presence. Despite the Snakery and its uncanny associations—to which, indeed, he gave little attention—Brayton found life at the Druring mansion very much to his mind.

III

Beyond a smart shock of surprise and a shudder of mere loathing Mr. Brayton was not greatly affected. His first thought was to ring the call bell and bring a servant, but although the bell cord dangled within easy reach he made no movement toward it; it had occurred to his mind that the act might subject him to the suspicion of fear, which he certainly did not feel. He was more keenly conscious of the incongruous nature of the situation than affected by its perils; it was revolting, but absurd.

The reptile was of a species with which Brayton was unfamiliar. Its length he could only conjecture; the body at the largest visible part seemed about as thick as his forearm. In what way was it dangerous, if in any way? Was it venomous? Was it a constrictor? His knowledge of nature's danger signals did not enable him to say; he had never deciphered the code.

If not dangerous the creature was at least offensive. It was *de trop*—"matter out of place"—an impertinence. The gem was unworthy of the setting. Even the barbarous taste of our time and country, which had loaded the walls of the room with pictures, the floor with furniture and the furniture with brica-brac, had not quite fitted the place for this bit of the savage life of the jungle. Besides—insupportable thought!—the exhalations of its breath mingled with the atmosphere which he himself was breathing.

These thoughts shaped themselves with greater or less definition in Brayton's mind and begot action. The process is what we call consideration and decision. It is thus that we are wise and unwise. It is thus that the withered leaf in an autumn breeze shows greater or less intelligence than its fellows, falling upon the land or upon the lake. The secret of human action is an open one: something contracts our muscles. Does it matter if we give to the preparatory molecular changes the name of will?

Brayton rose to his feet and prepared to back softly away from the snake, without disturbing it if possible, and through the door. Men retire so from the presence of the great, for greatness is power and power is a menace. He knew that he could walk backward without error. Should the monster follow, the taste which had plastered the walls with paintings had consistently supplied a rack of murderous Oriental weapons from which he could snatch one to suit the occasion. In the meantime the snake's eyes burned with a more pitiless malevolence than before.

Brayton lifted his right foot free of the floor to step backward. That moment he felt a strong aversion to doing so.

"I am accounted brave," he thought. "Is bravery, then, no more than pride? Because there are none to witness the shame shall I retreat?"

He was steadying himself with his right hand upon the back of a chair, his foot suspended.

"Nonsense!" he said aloud. "I am not so great a coward as to fear to seem to myself afraid."

He lifted the foot a little higher by slightly bending the knee and thrust it sharply to the floor—an inch in front of the other! He could not think how that occurred. A trial with the left foot had the same result; it was again in advance of the right. The hand upon the chair back was grasping it; the arm was straight, reaching somewhat backward. One might have said that he was reluctant to lose his hold. The snake's malignant head was still thrust forth from the inner coil as before, the neck level. It had not moved, but its eyes were now electric sparks, radiating an infinity of luminous needles.

The man had an ashy pallor. Again he took a step forward, and another, partly dragging the chair, which when finally released fell upon the floor with a crash. The man groaned; the snake made neither sound nor motion, but its eyes were two dazzling suns. The reptile itself was wholly concealed by them. They gave off enlarging rings of rich and vivid colors, which at their greatest expansion successively vanished like soap bubbles; they seemed to approach his very face, and anon were an immeasurable distance away. He heard, somewhere, the continuous throbbing of a great drum, with desultory bursts of far music, inconceivably sweet, like the tones of an aeolian harp. He knew it for the sunrise melody of Memnon's statue, and thought he stood in the Nileside reeds hearing with exalted sense that immortal anthem through the silence of the centuries.

The music ceased; rather, it became by insensible degrees the distant roll of a retreating thunderstorm. A landscape, glittering with sun and rain, stretched before him, arched with a vivid rainbow framing in its giant curve a hundred visible cities. In the middle distance a vast serpent, wearing a crown, reared its head out of its voluminous convolutions and looked at him with his dead mother's eyes. Suddenly this enchanting landscape seemed to rise swiftly upward like the drop scene at a theater, and vanished in a blank. Something struck him a hard blow upon the face and breast. He had fallen to the floor; the blood ran from his broken nose and his bruised lips. For a time he was dazed and stunned, and lay with closed eyes, his face against the floor. In a few moments he had recovered, and then knew that this fall, by withdrawing his eyes, had broken the spell that held him. He felt that now, by keeping his gaze averted, he would be able to retreat. But the thought of the serpent within a few feet of his head, yet unseen—perhaps in the very act of springing upon him and throwing its coils about his throat—was too horrible! He lifted his head, stared again into those baleful eyes, and was again in bondage.

The snake had not moved and appeared somewhat to have lost its power upon the imagination; the gorgeous illusions of a few moments before were not repeated. Beneath that flat and brainless brow its black, beady eyes simply glittered as at first with an expression unspeakably malignant. It was as if the creature, assured of its triumph, had determined to practice no more alluring wiles.

Now ensued a fearful scene. The man, prone upon the floor, within a yard of his enemy, raised the upper part of his body upon his elbows, his head thrown back, his legs extended to their full length. His face was white between its stains of blood; his eyes were strained open to their uttermost expansion. There was froth upon his lips; it dropped off in flakes. Strong convulsions ran through his body, making almost serpentile undulations. He bent himself at the waist, shifting his legs from side to side. And every movement left him a little nearer to the snake. He thrust his hands forward to brace himself back, yet constantly advanced upon his elbows.

IV

Dr. Druring and his wife sat in the library. The scientist was in rare good humor.

"I have just obtained by exchange with another collector," he said, "a splendid specimen of the *ophiophagus*."

"And what may that be?" the lady inquired with a somewhat languid interest.

"Why, bless my soul, what profound ignorance! My dear, a man who ascertains after marriage that his wife does not know Greek is entitled to a divorce. The *ophiophagus* is a snake that eats other snakes."

"I hope it will eat all yours," she said, absently shifting the lamp. "But how does it get the other snakes? By charming them, I suppose."

"That is just like you, dear," said the doctor, with an affectation of petulance. "You know how irritating to me is any allusion to that vulgar superstition about a snake's power of fascination."

The conversation was interrupted by a mighty cry, which rang through the silent house like the voice of a demon shouting in a tomb! Again and yet again it sounded, with terrible distinctness. They sprang to their feet, the man confused, the lady pale and speechless with fright. Almost before the echoes of the last cry had died away the doctor was out of the room, springing up the stairs two steps at a time. In the corridor in front of Brayton's chamber he met some servants who had come from the upper floor. Together they rushed at the door without knocking. It was unfastened and gave way. Brayton lay upon his stomach on the floor, dead. His head and arms were partly concealed under the foot rail of the bed. They pulled the body away, turning it upon the back. The face was daubed with blood and froth, the eyes were wide open, staring—a dreadful sight!

"Died in a fit," said the scientist, bending his knee and placing his hand upon the heart. While in that position, he chanced to look under the bed. "Good God!" he added, "how did this thing get in here?"

He reached under the bed, pulled out the snake and flung it, still coiled, to the center of the room, whence with a harsh, shuffling sound it slid across the polished floor till stopped by the wall, where it lay without motion. It was a stuffed snake; its eyes were two shoe buttons.

THE COUP DE GRÂCE

T HE fighting had been hard and continuous; that was attested by all the senses. The very taste of battle was in the air. All was now over; it remained only to succor the wounded and bury the dead—to "tidy up a bit," as the humorist of a burial squad put it. A good deal of "tidying up" was required. As far as one could see through the forests, among the splintered trees, lay wrecks of men and horses. Among them moved the stretcher-bearers, gathering and carrying away the few who showed signs of life. Most of the wounded had died of neglect while the right to minister to their wants was in dispute. It is an army regulation that the wounded must wait; the best way to care for them is to win the battle. It must be confessed that victory is a distinct advantage to a man requiring attention, but many do not live to avail themselves of it.

The dead were collected in groups of a dozen or a score and laid side by side in rows while the trenches were dug to receive them. Some, found at too great a distance from these rallying points, were buried where they lay. There was little attempt at identification, though in most cases, the burial parties being detailed to glean the same ground which they had assisted to reap, the names of the victorious dead were known and listed. The enemy's fallen had to be content with counting. But of that they got enough: many of them were counted several times, and the total, as given afterward in the official report of the victorious commander, denoted rather a hope than a result.

At some little distance from the spot where one of the burial parties had established its "bivouac of the dead," a man in the uniform of a Federal officer stood leaning against a tree. From his feet upward to his neck his attitude was that of weariness reposing; but he turned his head uneasily from side to side; his mind was apparently not at rest. He was perhaps uncertain in which direction to go; he was not likely to remain long where he was, for already the level rays of the setting sun straggled redly through the open spaces of the wood and the weary soldiers were quitting their task for the day. He would hardly make a night of it alone there among the dead. Nine men in ten whom you meet after a battle inquire the way to some fraction of the army—as if anyone could know. Doubtless this officer was lost. After resting himself a moment he would presumably follow one of the retiring burial squads.

When all were gone he walked straightaway into the forest toward the red west, its light staining his face like blood. The air of confidence with which he now strode along showed that he was on familiar ground; he had recovered his bearings. The dead on his right and on his left were unregarded as he passed. An occasional low moan from some sorely stricken wretch whom the relief parties had not reached, and who would have to pass a comfortless night beneath the stars with his thirst to keep him company, was equally unheeded. What, indeed, could the officer have done, being no surgeon and having no water?

At the head of a shallow ravine, a mere depression of the ground, lay a small group of bodies. He saw, and swerving suddenly from his course walked rapidly toward them. Scanning each one sharply as he passed, he stopped at last above one, which lay at a slight remove from the others, near a clump of small trees. He looked at it narrowly. It seemed to stir. He stooped and laid his hand upon its face. It screamed.

The officer was Captain Downing Madwell, of a Massachusetts regiment of infantry, a daring and intelligent soldier, an honorable man.

In the regiment were two brothers named Halcrow—Caffal

and Creede Halcrow. Caffal Halcrow was a sergeant in Captain Madwell's company, and these two men, the sergeant and the captain, were devoted friends. Insofar as disparity of rank, difference in duties and considerations of military discipline would permit they were commonly together. They had, indeed, grown up together from childhood. A habit of the heart is not easily broken off. Caffal Halcrow had nothing military in his taste nor disposition, but the thought of separation from his friend was disagreeable; he enlisted in the company in which Madwell was second lieutenant. Each had taken two steps upward in rank, but between the highest noncommissioned and the lowest commissioned officer the gulf is deep and wide, and the old relation was maintained with difficulty and a difference.

Creede Halcrow, the brother of Caffal, was the major of the regiment—a cynical, saturnine man, between whom and Captain Madwell there was a natural antipathy which circumstances had nourished and strengthened to an active animosity. But for the restraining influence of their mutual relation to Caffal these two patriots would doubtless have endeavored to deprive their country of each other's services.

At the opening of the battle that morning the regiment was performing outpost duty a mile away from the main army. It was attacked and nearly surrounded in the forest, but stubbornly held its ground. During a lull in the fighting, Major Halcrow came to Captain Madwell. The two exchanged formal salutes, and the major said, "Captain, the colonel directs that you push your company to the head of this ravine and hold your place there until recalled. I need hardly apprise you of the dangerous character of the movement, but if you wish, you can, I suppose, turn over the command to your first lieutenant. I was not, however, directed to authorize the substitution; it is merely a suggestion of my own, unofficially made."

To this deadly insult Captain Madwell coolly replied:

"Sir, I invite you to accompany the movement. A mounted officer would be a conspicuous mark, and I have long held the opinion that it would be better if you were dead."

The art of repartee was cultivated in military circles as early as 1862.

A half-hour later Captain Madwell's company was driven

from its position at the head of the ravine, with a loss of one-third its number. Among the fallen was Sergeant Halcrow. The regiment was soon afterward forced back to the main line, and at the close of the battle was miles away. The captain was now standing at the side of his subordinate and friend.

Sergeant Halcrow was mortally hurt. His clothing was deranged; it seemed to have been violently torn apart, exposing the abdomen. Some of the buttons of his jacket had been pulled off and lay on the ground beside him and fragments of his other garments were strewn about. His leather belt was parted and had apparently been dragged from beneath him as he lay. There had been no great effusion of blood. The only visible wound was a wide, ragged opening in the abdomen. It was defiled with earth and dead leaves. Protruding from it was a loop of small intestine. In all his experience Captain Madwell had not seen a wound like this. He could neither conjecture how it was made nor explain the attendant circumstances—the strangely torn clothing, the parted belt, the besmirching of the white skin. He knelt and made a closer examination. When he rose to his feet, he turned his eyes in different directions as if looking for an enemy. Fifty yards away, on the crest of a low, thinly wooded hill, he saw several dark objects moving about among the fallen men—a herd of swine. One stood with its back to him, its shoulders sharply elevated. Its forefeet were upon a human body, its head was depressed and invisible. The bristly ridge of its chin showed black against the red west. Captain Madwell drew away his eyes and fixed them again upon the thing which had been his friend.

The man who had suffered these monstrous mutilations was alive. At intervals he moved his limbs; he moaned at every breath. He stared blankly into the face of his friend and if touched screamed. In his giant agony he had torn up the ground on which he lay; his clenched hands were full of leaves and twigs and earth. Articulate speech was beyond his power; it was impossible to know if he were sensible to anything but pain. The expression of his face was an appeal; his eyes were full of prayer. For what?

There was no misreading that look; the captain had too fre-

quently seen it in eyes of those whose lips had still the power
to formulate it by an entreaty for death. Consciously or unconsciously, this writhing fragment of humanity, this type and
example of acute sensation, this handiwork of man and beast,
this humble, unheroic Prometheus, was imploring everything,
all, the whole non-ego, for the boon of oblivion. To the earth
and the sky alike, to the trees, to the man, to whatever took
form in sense or consciousness, this incarnate suffering addressed that silent plea.

For what, indeed? For that which we accord to even the
meanest creature without sense to demand it, denying it only
to the wretched of our own race: for the blessed release, the
rite of uttermost compassion, the coup de grâce.

Captain Madwell spoke the name of his friend. He repeated
it over and over without effect until emotion choked his utterance. His tears plashed upon the livid face beneath his own
and blinded himself. He saw nothing but a blurred and moving
object, but the moans were more distinct than ever, interrupted
at briefer intervals by sharper shrieks. He turned away, struck
his hand upon his forehead, and strode from the spot. The
swine, catching sight of him, threw up their crimson muzzles,

regarding him suspiciously a second, and then with a gruff, concerted grunt, raced away out of sight. A horse, its foreleg splintered by a cannon-shot, lifted its head sidewise from the ground and neighed piteously. Madwell stepped forward, drew his revolver and shot the poor beast between the eyes, narrowly observing its death struggle, which, contrary to his expectation, was violent and long; but at last it lay still. The tense muscles of its lips, which had uncovered the teeth in a horrible grin, relaxed; the sharp, clean-cut profile took on a look of profound peace and rest.

Along the distant, thinly wooded crest to westward the fringe of sunset fire had now nearly burned itself out. The light upon the trunks of the trees had faded to a tender gray; shadows were in their tops, like great dark birds aperch. Night was coming and there were miles of haunted forest between Captain Madwell and camp. Yet he stood there at the side of the dead animal, apparently lost to all sense of his surroundings. His eyes were bent upon the earth at his feet; his left hand hung loosely at his side, his right still held the pistol. Presently he lifted his face, turned it toward his dying friend and walked rapidly back to his side. He knelt upon one knee, cocked the weapon, placed the muzzle against the man's forehead, and turning away his eyes pulled the trigger. There was no report. He had used his last cartridge for the horse.

The sufferer moaned and his lips moved convulsively. The froth that ran from them had a tinge of blood.

Captain Madwell rose to his feet and drew his sword from the scabbard. He passed the fingers of his left hand along the edge from hilt to point. He held it out straight before him, as if to test his nerves. There was no visible tremor of the blade; the ray of bleak skylight that it reflected was steady and true. He stooped and with his left hand tore away the dying man's shirt, rose and placed the point of the sword just over the heart. This time he did not withdraw his eyes. Grasping the hilt with both hands, he thrust downward with all his strength and weight. The blade sank into the man's body—through his body into the earth; Captain Madwell came near falling forward upon his work. The dying man drew up his knees and at the same time threw his right arm across his breast and grasped the steel so tightly that the knuckles of the hand visibly whitened. By a violent but vain effort to withdraw the blade the wound was enlarged; a rill of blood escaped, running sinuously down into the deranged clothing. At that moment three men stepped silently forward from behind the clump of young trees which had concealed their approach. Two were hospital attendants and carried a stretcher.

The third was Major Creede Halcrow.

CURRIED COW

My Aunt Patience, who tilled a small farm in the state of Michigan, had a favorite cow. This creature was not a good cow, nor a profitable one, for instead of devoting a part of her leisure to secretion of milk and production of veal she concentrated all her faculties on the study of kicking. She would kick all day and get up in the middle of the night to kick. She would kick at anything—hens, pigs, posts, loose stones, birds in the air and fish leaping out of the water; to this impartial and catholic-minded beef, all were equal—all similarly undeserving. Like old Timotheus, who "raised a mortal to the skies," was my Aunt Patience's cow; though, in the words of a later poet than Dryden, she did it "more harder and more frequently." It was pleasing to see her open a passage for herself through a populous barnyard. She would flash out, right and left, first with one hind leg and then with the other, and would sometimes, under favoring conditions, have a considerable number of domestic animals in the air at once.

Her kicks, too, were as admirable in quality as inexhaustible in quantity. They were incomparably superior to those of the untutored kine that had not made the art a life study—mere amateurs that kicked "by ear," as they say in music. I saw her once standing in the road, professedly fast asleep, and mechanically munching her cud with a sort of Sunday morning lassitude, as one munches one's cud in a dream. Snouting about at her side, blissfully unconscious of impending danger and wrapped up in thoughts of his sweetheart, was a gigantic black hog—a hog of about the size and general appearance of a yearling rhinoceros. Suddenly, while I looked—without a visible movement on the part of the cow—with never a perceptible tremor of her frame, nor a lapse in the placid regularity of her chewing—that hog had gone away from there—had utterly taken his leave. But away toward the pale horizon a minute black speck was traversing the empyrean with the speed of a meteor, and in a moment had disappeared, without audible report, beyond the distant hills. It may have been that hog.

Currying cows is not, I think, a common practice, even in Michigan; but as this one had never needed milking, of course she had to be subjected to some equivalent form of persecution; and irritating her skin with a curry-comb was thought as disagreeable an attention as a thoughtful affection could devise. At least she thought it so; though I suspect her mistress really meant it for the good creature's temporal advantage. Anyhow my aunt always made it a condition to the employment of a farm servant that he should curry the cow every morning; but after just enough trials to convince himself that it was not a sudden spasm, nor a mere local disturbance, the man would always give notice of an intention to quit, by pounding the beast half-dead with some foreign body and then limping home to his couch. I don't know how many men the creature removed from my aunt's employ in this way, but judging from the number of lame persons in that part of the country, I should say a good many; though some of the lameness may have been taken at second hand from the original sufferers by their descendants, and some may have come by contagion.

I think my aunt's was a faulty system of agriculture. It is true her farm labor cost her nothing, for the laborers all left her service before any salary had accrued; but as the cow's fame spread abroad through the several states and territories, it became increasingly difficult to obtain hands; and, after all, the favorite was imperfectly curried. It was currently remarked that the cow had kicked the farm to pieces—a rude metaphor, implying that the land was not properly cultivated, nor the buildings and fences kept in adequate repair.

It was useless to remonstrate with my aunt: she would concede everything, amending nothing. Her late husband had attempted to reform the abuse in this manner, and had had the argument all his own way until he had remonstrated himself into an early grave; and the funeral was delayed all day, until a fresh undertaker could be procured, the one originally engaged having confidingly undertaken to curry the cow at the request of the widow.

Since that time my Aunt Patience had not been in the matrimonial market; the love of that cow had usurped in her heart the place of a more natural and profitable affection. But when she saw her seeds unsown, her harvests ungarnered, her fences overtopped with rank brambles and her meadows gorgeous with the towering Canada thistle, she thought it best to take a partner.

When it transpired that my Aunt Patience intended wedlock, there was intense popular excitement. Every adult single male became at once a marrying man. The criminal statistics of Badger County show that in that single year more marriages occurred than in any decade before or since. But none of them was my aunt's. Men married their cooks, their laundresses, their deceased wives' mothers, their enemies' sisters—married whomsoever would wed; and any man who, by fair means or courtship, could not obtain a wife went before a justice of the peace and made an affidavit that he had some wives in Indiana. Such was the fear of being married alive by my Aunt Patience.

Now, where my aunt's affection was concerned she was, as the reader will have already surmised, a rather determined woman; and the extraordinary marrying epidemic having left but one eligible male in all that county, she had set her heart upon that one eligible male; then she went and carted him to her home. He turned out to be a long Methodist parson, named Huggins.

Aside from his unconscionable length, the Reverend Berosus Huggins was not so bad a fellow, and was nobody's fool. He was, I suppose, the most ill-favored mortal, however, in the whole northern half of America—thin, angular, cadaverous of visage and solemn out of all reason. He commonly wore a

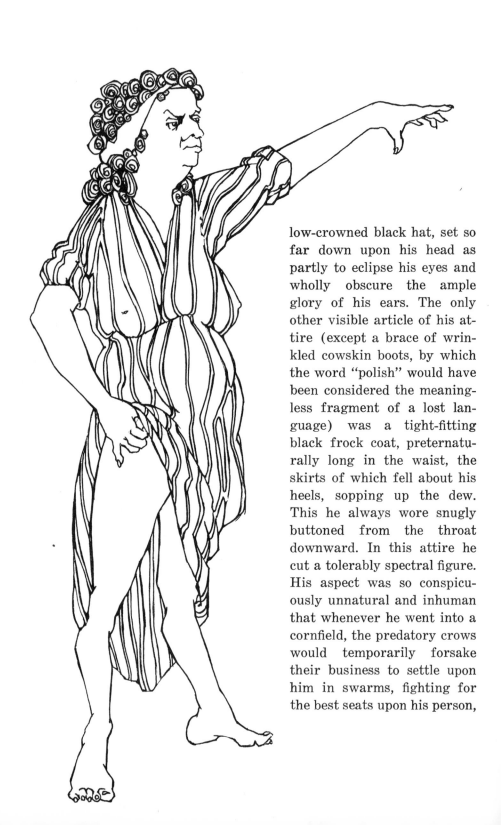

low-crowned black hat, set so far down upon his head as partly to eclipse his eyes and wholly obscure the ample glory of his ears. The only other visible article of his attire (except a brace of wrinkled cowskin boots, by which the word "polish" would have been considered the meaningless fragment of a lost language) was a tight-fitting black frock coat, preternaturally long in the waist, the skirts of which fell about his heels, sopping up the dew. This he always wore snugly buttoned from the throat downward. In this attire he cut a tolerably spectral figure. His aspect was so conspicuously unnatural and inhuman that whenever he went into a cornfield, the predatory crows would temporarily forsake their business to settle upon him in swarms, fighting for the best seats upon his person, by way of testifying their contempt for the weak inventions of the husbandman.

The day after the wedding my Aunt Patience summoned the Reverend Berosus to the council chamber, and uttered her mind to the following intent:

"Now, Huggy, dear, I'll tell you what there is to do about the place. First, you must repair all the fences, clearing out the weeds and repressing the brambles with a strong hand. Then you will have to exterminate the Canadian thistles, mend the wagon, rig up a plow or two, and get things into shipshape generally. This will keep you out of mischief for the better part of two years; of course you will have to give up preaching, for the present. As soon as you have—O! I forgot poor Phoebe. She—"

"Mrs. Huggins," interrupted her solemn spouse, "I shall hope to be the means, under Providence, of effecting all needful reforms in the husbandry of this farm. But the sister you mention (I trust she is not of the world's people)—have I the pleasure of knowing her? The name, indeed, sounds familiar, but—"

"Not know Phoebe!" cried my aunt, with unfeigned astonishment. "I thought everybody in Badger knew Phoebe. Why, you will have to scratch her legs, every blessed morning of your natural life!"

"I assure you, madam," rejoined the Reverend Berosus, with dignity, "it would yield me a hallowed pleasure to minister to the spiritual needs of sister Phoebe, to the extent of my feeble and unworthy ability; but, really, I fear the merely secular ministration of which you speak must be entrusted to abler and, I would respectfully suggest, female hands."

"Whyyy, youuu ooold foooool!" replied my aunt, spreading her eyes with unbounded amazement, "Phoebe is a *cow!*"

"In that case," said the husband, with unruffled composure, "it will, of course, devolve upon me to see that her carnal welfare is properly attended to, and I shall be happy to bestow upon her legs such time as I may, without sin, snatch from my strife with Satan and the Canadian thistles."

With that the Reverend Mr. Huggins crowded his hat upon

his shoulders, pronounced a brief benediction upon his bride, and betook himself to the barnyard.

Now, it is necessary to explain that he had known from the first who Phoebe was, and was familiar, from hearsay, with all her sinful traits. Moreover, he had already done himself the honor of making her a visit, remaining in the vicinity of her person, just out of range, for more than an hour and permitting her to survey him at her leisure from every point of the compass. In short, he and Phoebe had mutually reconnoitered and prepared for action.

Among the articles of comfort and luxury which went to make up the good parson's *dot*, and which his wife had already caused to be conveyed to his new home, was a patent cast-iron pump, about seven feet high. This had been deposited near the barnyard, preparatory to being set up on the planks above the barnyard well. Mr. Huggins now sought out this invention and conveying it to its destination put it into position, screwing it firmly to the planks. He next divested himself of his long gabardine and his hat, buttoning the former loosely about the pump, which it almost concealed, and hanging the latter upon the summit of the structure. The handle of the pump, when depressed, curved outwardly between the coat skirts, singularly like a tail, but with this inconspicuous exception, any unprejudiced observer would have pronounced the thing Mr. Huggins, looking uncommonly well.

The preliminaries completed, the good man carefully closed the gate of the barnyard, knowing that as soon as Phoebe, who was campaigning in the kitchen garden, should note the precaution she would come and jump in to frustrate it, which eventually she did. Her master, meanwhile, had laid himself, coatless and hatless, along the outside of the close board fence, where he put in the time pleasantly, catching his death of cold and peering through a knothole.

At first, and for some time, the animal pretended not to see the figure on the platform. Indeed, she had turned her back upon it directly she arrived, affecting a light sleep. Finding that this stratagem did not achieve the success that she had expected, she abandoned it and stood for several minutes irresolute, munching her cud in a half-hearted way, but ob-

viously thinking very hard. Then she began nosing along the ground as if wholly absorbed in a search for something that she had lost, tacking about hither and thither, but all the time drawing nearer to the object of her wicked intention. Arrived within speaking distance, she stood for a little while confronting the fraudful figure, then put out her nose toward it, as if to be caressed, trying to create the impression that fondling and dalliance were more to her than wealth, power and the plaudits of the populace—that she had been accustomed to them all her sweet young life and could not get on without them. Then she approached a little nearer, as if to shake hands, all the while maintaining the most amiable expression of countenance and executing all manner of seductive nods and winks and smiles. Suddenly she wheeled about and with the rapidity of lightning dealt out a terrible kick—a kick of inconceivable force and fury, comparable to nothing in nature but a stroke of paralysis out of a clear sky!

The effect was magical! Cows kick, not backward, but sideways. The impact which was intended to project the counterfeit theologian into the middle of the succeeding conference week reacted upon the animal herself, and it and the pain together set her spinning like a top. Such was the velocity of her revolution that she looked like a dim, circular cow, surrounded by a continuous ring like that of the planet Saturn —the white tuft at the extremity of her sweeping tail! Presently, as the sustaining centrifugal force lessened and failed, she began to sway and wobble from side to side, and finally, toppling over on her side, rolled convulsively on her back and lay motionless with all her feet in the air, honestly believing that the world had somehow got atop of her and she was supporting it at a great sacrifice of personal comfort. Then she fainted.

How long she lay unconscious she knew not, but at last she unclosed her eyes, and catching sight of the open door of her stall, "more sweet than all the landscape smiling near," she struggled up, stood wavering upon three legs, rubbed her eyes, and was visibly bewildered as to the points of the compass. Observing the iron clergyman standing fast by its faith, she threw it a look of grieved reproach and hobbled heartbroken into her humble habitation, a subjugated cow.

For several weeks Phoebe's right hind leg was swollen to a monstrous growth, but by a season of judicious nursing she was "brought round all right," as her sympathetic and puzzled mistress phrased it, or "made whole," as the reticent man of God preferred to say. She was now as tractable and inoffensive "in her daily walk and conversation" (Huggins) as a little child. Her new master used to take her ailing leg trustfully into his lap, and for that matter, might have taken in into his mouth if he had so desired. Her entire character appeared to be radically changed—so altered that one day my Aunt Patience, who, fondly as she loved her, had never before so much as ventured to touch the hem of her garment, as it were, went confidently up to her to soothe her with a pan of turnips. Gad! How thinly she spread out that good old lady upon the face of an adjacent stone wall! You could not have done it so evenly with a trowel.

THE SECRET
OF MACARGER'S GULCH

NORTHWESTWARDLY from Indian Hill, about nine miles as the crow flies, is Macarger's Gulch. It is not much of a gulch—a mere depression between two wooded ridges of inconsiderable height. From its mouth up to its head—for gulches, like rivers, have an anatomy of their own—the distance does not exceed two miles, and the width at bottom is at only one place more than a dozen yards; for most of the distance on either side of the little brook which drains it in winter, and goes dry in the early spring, there is no level ground at all; the steep slopes of the hills, covered with an almost impenetrable growth of manzanita and chamiso, are parted by nothing but the width of the watercourse. No one but an occasional enterprising hunter of the vicinity ever goes into Macarger's Gulch, and five miles away it is unknown, even by name. Within that distance in any direction are far more conspicuous topographical features without names, and one might try in vain to ascertain by local inquiry the origin of the name of this one.

About midway between the head and the mouth of Macarger's Gulch, the hill on the right as you ascend is cloven by another gulch, a short dry one, and at the junction of the two is a level space of two or three acres, and there a few years ago stood an old board house containing one small room. How the component parts of the house, few and simple as they were, had been assembled at that almost inaccessible point is a problem in the solution of which there would be greater satisfaction than advantage. Possibly the creek bed is a re-formed road. It is certain that the gulch was at one time pretty thoroughly prospected by miners, who must have had some means of getting in with at least pack animals carrying tools and supplies; their profits, apparently, were not such as would have justified any considerable outlay to connect Macarger's Gulch with any center of civilization enjoying the distinction of a sawmill. The house, however, was there, most of it. It lacked a door and a window frame, and the chimney of mud and stones had fallen into an unlovely heap, overgrown with rank weeds. Such humble furniture as there may once have been, and much of the lower weatherboarding, had served as fuel in the campfires of hunters; as had also, probably, the curbing of an old well, which at the time I write of existed in the form of a rather wide but not very deep depression nearby.

One afternoon in the summer of 1874, I passed up Macarger's Gulch from the narrow valley into which it opens, by following the dry bed of the brook. I was quail-shooting and had made a bag of about a dozen birds by the time I had reached the house described, of whose existence I was until then unaware. After rather carelessly inspecting the ruin I resumed my sport, and having fairly good success prolonged it until near sunset, when it occurred to me that I was a long way from any human habitation—too far to reach one by nightfall. But in my game bag was food, and the old house would afford shelter, if shelter were needed on a warm and dewless night in the foothills of the Sierra Nevada, where one may sleep in comfort on the pine needles, without covering. I am fond of solitude and love the night, so my resolution to "camp out" was soon taken, and by the time that it was dark I had made my bed of boughs and grasses in a corner of the room and was roasting a quail at a fire that I had kindled on the hearth. The smoke escaped out of the ruined chimney, the light illuminated the room with a kindly glow, and as I ate my simple meal of plain bird and drank the remains of a bottle of red wine which had served me all the afternoon in place of the water which the region did not supply, I experienced a sense of comfort which better fare and accommodations do not always give.

Nevertheless, there was something lacking. I had a sense of comfort, but not of security. I detected myself staring more frequently at the open doorway and blank window than I could find warrant for doing. Outside these apertures all was black, and I was unable to repress a certain feeling of apprehension as my fancy pictured the outer world and filled it with unfriendly entities, natural and supernatural—chief among which, in their respective classes, were the grizzly bear, which I knew was occasionally still seen in that region, and the ghost, which I had reason to think was not. Unfortunately, our feelings do not always respect the law of probabilities, and to me that evening, the possible and the impossible were equally disquieting.

Everyone who has had experience in the matter must have observed that one confronts the actual and imaginary perils of the night with far less apprehension in the open air than in a house with an open doorway. I felt this now as I lay on my leafy couch in a corner of the room next to the chimney and permitted my fire to die out. So strong became my sense of the presence of something malign and menacing in the place, that I found myself almost unable to withdraw my eyes from the opening, as in the deepening darkness it became more and more indistinct. And when the last little flame flickered and went out I grasped the shotgun which I had laid at my side and actually turned the muzzle in the direction of the now invisible entrance, my thumb on one of the hammers, ready to cock the piece, my breath suspended, my muscles rigid and tense. But later I laid down the weapon with a sense of shame and mortification. What did I fear, and why?—I, to whom the night had been

> a more familiar face
> Than that of man—

I, in whom that element of hereditary superstition from which none of us is altogether free had given to solitude and darkness and silence only a more alluring interest and charm! I was unable to comprehend my folly, and losing in the conjecture the thing conjectured of, I fell asleep. And then I dreamed.

I was in a great city in a foreign land—a city whose people were of my own race, with minor differences of speech and costume; yet precisely what these were I could not say; my sense of them was indistinct. The city was dominated by a great castle upon an overlooking height whose name I knew, but could not speak. I walked through many streets, some broad and straight with high, modern buildings, some narrow, gloomy, and tortuous, between the gables of quaint old houses whose overhanging stories, elaborately ornamented with carvings in wood and stone, almost met above my head.

I sought someone whom I had never seen, yet knew that I should recognize when found. My quest was not aimless and fortuitous; it had a definite method. I turned from one street into another without hesitation and threaded a maze of intricate passages, devoid of the fear of losing my way.

Presently I stopped before a low door in a plain stone house which might have been the dwelling of an artisan of the better sort, and without announcing myself, entered. The room, rather sparely furnished, and lighted by a single window with small diamond-shaped panes, had but two occupants: a man and a woman. They took no notice of my intrusion, a circumstance which, in the manner of dreams, appeared entirely natural. They were not conversing; they sat apart, unoccupied and sullen.

The woman was young and rather stout, with fine large eyes and a certain grave beauty; my memory of her expression is exceedingly vivid, but in dreams one does not observe the details of faces. About her shoulders was a plaid shawl. The man was older, dark, with an evil face made more forbidding by a long scar extending from near the left temple diagonally downward into the black mustache; though in my dreams it seemed rather to haunt the face as a thing apart—I can express it no otherwise—than to belong to it. The moment that I found the man and woman I knew them to be husband and wife.

What followed, I remember indistinctly; all was confused and inconsistent—made so, I think, by gleams of consciousness.

It was as if two pictures, the scene of my dream, and my actual surroundings, had been blended, one overlying the other, until the former, gradually fading, disappeared, and I was broad awake in the deserted cabin, entirely and tranquilly conscious of my situation.

My foolish fear was gone, and opening my eyes I saw that my fire, not altogether burned out, had revived by the falling of a stick and was again lighting the room. I had probably slept only a few minutes, but my commonplace dream had somehow so strongly impressed me that I was no longer drowsy; and after a little while I rose, pushed the embers of my fire together, and lighting my pipe proceeded in a rather ludicrously methodical way to meditate upon my vision.

It would have puzzled me then to say in what respect it was worth attention. In the first moment of serious thought that I gave to the matter I recognized the city of my dream as Edinburgh, where I had never been; so if the dream was a memory it was a memory of pictures and description. The recognition somehow deeply impressed me; it was as if something in my mind insisted rebelliously against will and reason on the importance of all this. And that faculty, whatever it was, asserted also a control of my speech. "Surely," I said aloud, quite involuntarily, "the MacGregors must have come here from Edinburgh."

At the moment, neither the substance of this remark, nor the fact of my making it, surprised me in the least; it seemed entirely natural that I should know the name of my dreamfolk and something of their history. But the absurdity of it all soon dawned upon me: I laughed aloud, knocked the ashes from my pipe, and again stretched myself upon my bed of boughs and grass, where I lay staring absently into my failing fire, with no further thought of either my dream or my surroundings. Suddenly the single remaining flame crouched for a moment, then, springing upward, lifted itself clear of its embers and expired in air. The darkness was absolute.

At that instant—almost, it seemed, before the gleam of the blaze had faded from my eyes—there was a dull, dead sound, as of some heavy body falling upon the floor, which shook beneath me as I lay. I sprang to a sitting posture and groped at my side for my gun; my notion was that some wild beast had leaped in through the open window. While the flimsy structure was still shaking from the impact I heard the sound of blows, the scuffling of feet upon the floor, and then—it seemed to come from almost within reach of my hand, the sharp shrieking of a woman in mortal agony. So horrible a cry I had never heard nor conceived; it utterly unnerved me; I was conscious for a moment of nothing but my own terror! Fortunately my hand now found the weapon of which it was in search, and the familiar touch somewhat restored me. I leaped to my feet, straining my eyes to pierce the darkness. The violent sounds had ceased, but more terrible than these, I heard, at what seemed long intervals, the faint intermittent gasping of some living, dying thing!

As my eyes grew accustomed to the dim light of the coals in the fireplace, I saw first the shapes of the door and window, looking blacker than the black of the walls. Next, the distinction between wall and floor became discernible, and at last I was sensible to the form and full expanse of the floor from end to end and side to side. Nothing was visible, and the silence was unbroken.

With a hand that shook a little, the other still grasping my gun, I restored my fire and made a critical examination of the place. There was nowhere any sign that the cabin had been entered. My own tracks were visible in the dust covering the floor, but there were no others. I relit my pipe, provided fresh fuel by ripping a thin board or two from the inside of the house—I did not care to go into the darkness out of doors— and passed the rest of the night smoking and thinking, and feeding my fire; not for added years of life would I have permitted that little flame to expire again.

Some years afterward I met in Sacramento a man named Morgan, to whom I had a note of introduction from a friend in San Francisco. Dining with him one evening at his home I observed various trophies upon the wall, indicating that he was fond of shooting. It turned out that he was, and in relating some of his feats he mentioned having been in the region of my adventure.

"Mr. Morgan," I asked abruptly, "do you know a place up there called Macarger's Gulch?"

"I have good reason to," he replied. "It was I who gave to the newspapers, last year, the accounts of the finding of the skeleton there."

I had not heard of it; the accounts had been published, it appeared, while I was absent in the East.

"By the way," said Morgan, "the name of the gulch is a corruption; it should have been called 'MacGregor's.' My dear," he added, speaking to his wife, "Mr. Elderson has upset his wine."

That was hardly accurate—I had simply dropped it, glass and all.

"There was an old shanty once in the gulch," Morgan resumed when the ruin wrought by my awkwardness had been repaired, "but just previously to my visit it had been blown down, or rather blown away, for its debris was scattered all about, the very floor being parted, plank from plank. Between two of the sleepers still in position I and my companion observed the remnant of a plaid shawl, and examining it found that it was wrapped about the shoulders of the body of a woman, of which but little remained besides the bones, partly covered with fragments of clothing, and brown dry skin. But we will spare Mrs. Morgan," he added with a smile. The lady had indeed exhibited signs of digust rather than sympathy.

"It is necessary to say, however," he went on, "that the skull was fractured in several places, as by blows of some blunt instrument; and that instrument itself—a pick-handle, still stained with blood—lay under the boards nearby."

Mr. Morgan turned to his wife. "Pardon me, my dear," he said with affected solemnity, "for mentioning these disagreeable particulars, the natural though regrettable incidents of a conjugal quarrel—resulting, doubtless, from the luckless wife's insubordination."

"I ought to be able to overlook it," the lady replied with composure. "You have so many times asked me to in those very words."

I thought he seemed rather glad to go on with his story.

"From these and other circumstances," he said, "the coroner's jury found that the deceased, Janet MacGregor, came to her death from blows inflicted by some person to the jury unknown; but it was added that the evidence pointed strongly to her husband, Thomas MacGregor, as the guilty person. But Thomas MacGregor has never been found nor heard of. It was learned that the couple came from Edinburgh, but not— my dear, do you not observe that Mr. Elderson's boneplate has water in it?"

I had deposited a chicken bone in my finger bowl.

"In a little cupboard I found a photograph of MacGregor, but it did not lead to his capture."

"Will you let me see it?" I said.

The picture showed a dark man with an evil face made more forbidding by a long scar extending from near the temple diagonally downward into the black mustache.

"By the way, Mr. Elderson," said my affable host, "may I know why you asked about Macarger's Gulch?"

"I lost a mule near there once," I replied, "and the mischance has—has quite—upset me."

"My dear," said Mr. Morgan, with the mechanical intonation of an interpreter translating, "the loss of Mr. Elderson's mule has peppered his coffee."

A RESUMED
IDENTITY

I
THE REVIEW AS A FORM OF WELCOME

ONE summer night a man stood on a low hill overlooking a wide expanse of forest and field. By the full moon hanging low in the west he knew what he might not have known otherwise: that it was near the hour of dawn. A light mist lay along the earth, partly veiling the lower features of the landscape, but above it the taller trees showed in well-defined masses against a clear sky. Two or three farmhouses were visible through the haze, but in none of them, naturally, was a light. Nowhere, indeed, was any sign or suggestion of life except the barking of a distant dog, which, repeated with mechanical iteration, served rather to accentuate than dispel the loneliness of the scene.

The man looked curiously about him on all sides, as one who among familiar surroundings is unable to determine his exact place and part in the scheme of things. It is so, perhaps, that we shall act when, risen from the dead, we await the call to judgment.

A hundred yards away was a straight road, showing white in the moonlight. Endeavoring to orient himself, as a surveyor or navigator might say, the man moved his eyes slowly along its visible length and at a distance of a quarter-mile to the south of his station saw, dim and gray in the haze, a group of horsemen riding to the north. Behind them were men afoot, marching in column, with dimly gleaming rifles aslant above their shoulders. They moved slowly and in silence. Another group of horsemen, another regiment of infantry, another and another—all in unceasing motion toward the man's point of view, past it, and beyond. A battery of artillery followed, the cannoneers riding with folded arms on limber and caisson. And still the interminable procession came out of the obscurity to south and passed into the obscurity to north, with never a sound of voice, nor hoof, nor wheel.

The man could not rightly understand: he thought himself deaf; said so, and heard his own voice, although it had an unfamiliar quality that almost alarmed him; it disappointed his ear's expectancy in the matter of timbre and resonance. But he was not deaf, and that for the moment sufficed.

Then he remembered that there are natural phenomena to which someone has given the name "acoustic shadows." If you stand in an acoustic shadow there is one direction from which you will hear nothing. At the battle of Gaines's Mill, one of the fiercest conflicts of the Civil War, with a hundred guns in play, spectators a mile and a half away on the opposite side of the Chickahominy Valley heard nothing of what they clearly saw. The bombardment of Port Royal, heard and felt at St. Augustine, a hundred and fifty miles to the south, was inaudible two miles to the north in a still atmosphere. A few days before the surrender at Appomattox a thunderous engagement between the commands of Sheridan and Pickett was unknown to the latter commander, a mile in the rear of his own line.

These instances were not known to the man of whom we write, but less striking ones of the same character had not escaped his observation. He was profoundly disquieted, but for another reason than the uncanny silence of that moonlight march.

"Good Lord!" he said to himself—and again it was as if another had spoken his thought—"if those people are what I take them to be we have lost the battle and they are moving on Nashville!"

Then came a thought of self—an apprehension—a strong sense of personal peril, such as in another we call fear. He stepped quickly into the shadow of a tree. And still the silent battalions moved slowly forward in the haze.

The chill of a sudden breeze upon the back of his neck drew his attention to the quarter whence it came, and turning to the east he saw a faint gray light along the horizon—the first sign of returning day. This increased his apprehension.

"I must get away from here," he thought, "or I shall be discovered and taken."

He moved out of the shadow, walking rapidly toward the graying east. From the safer seclusion of a clump of cedars he looked back. The entire column had passed out of sight: the straight white road lay bare and desolate in the moonlight!

Puzzled before, he was now inexpressibly astonished. So swift a passing of so slow an army!—he could not comprehend it. Minute after minute passed unnoted; he had lost his sense of time. He sought with a terrible earnestness a solution of the mystery, but sought in vain. When at last he roused himself from his abstraction the sun's rim was visible above the hills, but in the new conditions he found no other light than that of day; his understanding was involved as darkly in doubt as before.

On every side lay cultivated fields showing no sign of war and war's ravages. From the chimneys of the farmhouses thin ascensions of blue smoke signaled preparations for a day's peaceful toil. Having stilled its immemorial allocution to the moon, the watchdog was assisting a Negro who, prefixing a team of mules to the plow, was flatting and sharping contentedly at his task. The hero of this tale stared stupidly at the pastoral picture as if he had never seen such a thing in all his life; then he put his hand to his head, passed it through his hair and, withdrawing it, attentively considered the palm—a singular thing to do. Apparently reassured by the act, he walked confidently toward the road.

II
WHEN YOU HAVE LOST YOUR LIFE
CONSULT A PHYSICIAN

Dr. Stilling Malson, of Murfreesboro, having visited a patient six or seven miles away, on the Nashville road, had remained with him all night. At daybreak he set out for home on horseback, as was the custom of doctors of the time and region. He had passed into the neighborhood of Stone's River battlefield when a man approached him from the roadside and saluted in the military fashion, with a movement of the right hand to the hatbrim. But the hat was not a military hat, the man was not in uniform and had not a martial bearing. The doctor nodded civilly, half thinking that the stranger's uncommon greeting was perhaps in deference to the historic surroundings. As the stranger evidently desired speech with him, he courteously reined in his horse and waited.

"Sir," said the stranger, "although a civilian, you are perhaps an enemy."

"I am a physician," was the noncommittal reply.

"Thank you," said the other. "I am a lieutenant, of the staff of General Hazen." He paused a moment and looked sharply at the person whom he was addressing, then added, "Of the Federal army."

The physician merely nodded.

"Kindly tell me," continued the other, "what has happened here. Where are the armies? Which has won the battle?"

The physician regarded his questioner curiously with half-shut eyes. After a professional scrutiny, prolonged to the limit of politeness, "Pardon me," he said. "One asking information should be willing to impart it. Are you wounded?" he added, smiling.

"Not seriously—it seems."

The man removed the unmilitary hat, put his hand to his head, passed it through his hair and, withdrawing it, attentively considered the palm.

"I was struck by a bullet and have been unconscious. It must have been a light, glancing blow. I find no blood and feel no pain. I will not trouble you for treatment, but will you kindly direct me to my command—to any part of the Federal army—if you know?"

Again the doctor did not immediately reply: he was recalling much that is recorded in the books of his profession—something about lost identity and the effect of familiar scenes in restoring it. At length he looked the man in the face, smiled, and said:

"Lieutenant, you are not wearing the uniform of your rank and service."

At this the man glanced down at his civilian attire, lifted his eyes, and said with hesitation:

"That is true. I—I don't quite understand."

Still regarding him sharply but not unsympathetically the man of science bluntly inquired:

"How old are you?"

"Twenty-three—if that has anything to do with it."

"You don't look it. I should hardly have guessed you to be just that."

The man was growing impatient. "We need not discuss that," he said. "I want to know about the army. Not two hours ago I saw a column of troops moving northward on this road. You must have met them. Be good enough to tell me the color of their clothing, which I was unable to make out, and I'll trouble you no more."

"You are quite sure that you saw them?"

"Sure? My God, sir, I could have counted them!"

"Why, really," said the physician, with an amusing consciousness of his own resemblance to the loquacious barber of the Arabian Nights, "this is very interesting. I met no troops."

The man looked at him coldly, as if he had himself observed the likeness to the barber. "It is plain," he said, "that you do not care to assist me. Sir, you may go to the devil!"

He turned and strode away, very much at random, across the dewy fields, his half-penitent tormentor quietly watching him from his point of vantage in the saddle till he disappeared beyond an array of trees.

III
THE DANGER OF LOOKING INTO
A POOL OF WATER

After leaving the road the man slackened his pace, and now went forward, rather deviously, with a distinct feeling of fatigue. He could not account for this, though truly the interminable loquacity of that country doctor offered itself in explanation. Seating himself upon a rock, he laid one hand upon his knee, back upward, and casually looked at it. It was lean and withered. He lifted both hands to his face. It was seamed and furrowed; he could trace the lines with the tips of his fingers. How strange! A mere bullet stroke and a brief unconsciousness should not make one a physical wreck.

"I must have been a long time in hospital," he said aloud. "Why, what a fool I am! The battle was in December, and it is now summer!" He laughed. "No wonder that fellow thought me an escaped lunatic. He was wrong. I am only an escaped patient."

At a little distance a small plot of ground enclosed by a stone wall caught his attention. With no very definite intent he rose and went to it. In the center was a square, solid monument of hewn stone. It was brown with age, weather-worn at the angles, spotted with moss and lichen. Between the massive blocks were strips of grass the leverage of whose roots had pushed them apart. In answer to the challenge of this ambitious structure Time had laid his destroying hand upon it, and it would soon be "one with Nineveh and Tyre." In an inscription on one side his eye caught a familiar name. Shaking with excitement, he craned his body across the wall and read:

HAZEN'S BRIGADE
to
The Memory of Its Soldiers
who fell at
Stone River, Dec. 31, 1862.

The man fell back from the wall, faint and sick. Almost within an arm's length was a little depression in the earth;

it had been filled by a recent rain—a pool of clear water. He crept to it to revive himself, lifted the upper part of his body on his trembling arms, thrust forward his head and saw the reflection of his face, as in a mirror. He uttered a terrible cry. His arms gave way; he fell, face downward, into the pool and yielded up the life that had spanned another life.

ONE KIND OF OFFICER

I
OF THE USES OF CIVILITY

CAPTAIN Ransome, it is not permitted to you to know *anything*. It is sufficient that you obey my order— which permit me to repeat. If you perceive any movement of troops in your front you are to open fire, and if attacked hold this position as long as you can. Do I make myself understood, sir?"

"Nothing could be plainer. Lieutenant Price"—this to an officer of his own battery, who had ridden up in time to hear the order—"the general's meaning is clear, is it not?"

"Perfectly."

The lieutenant passed on to his post. For a moment General Cameron and the commander of the battery sat in their saddles, looking at each other in silence. There was no more to say; apparently too much had already been said. Then the superior officer nodded coldly and turned his horse to ride away. The artillerist saluted slowly, gravely, and with extreme formality. One acquainted with the niceties of military etiquette would have said that by his manner he attested a sense of the rebuke that he had incurred. It is one of the important uses of civility to signify resentment.

When the general had joined his staff and escort, awaiting him at a little distance, the whole cavalcade moved off toward

102

the right of the guns and vanished in the fog. Captain Ransome was alone, silent, motionless as an equestrian statue. The gray fog, thickening every moment, closed in about him like a visible doom.

II

UNDER WHAT CIRCUMSTANCES MEN DO NOT WISH TO BE SHOT

The fighting of the day before had been desultory and indecisive. At the points of collision the smoke of battle had hung in blue sheets among the branches of the trees till beaten into nothing by the falling rain. In the softened earth the wheels of cannon and ammunition wagons cut deep, ragged furrows, and movements of infantry seemed impeded by the mud that clung to the soldiers' feet as, with soaken garments and rifles imperfectly protected by capes of overcoats, they went dragging in sinuous lines hither and thither through dripping forest and flooded field. Mounted officers, their heads protruding from rubber ponchos that glittered like black armor, picked their way, singly and in loose groups, among the men, coming and going with apparent aimlessness and commanding attention from nobody but one another. Here and there a dead man, his clothing defiled with earth, his face covered with a blanket or showing yellow and claylike in the rain, added his dispiriting influence to that of the other dismal features of the scene and augmented the general discomfort with a particular dejection. Very repulsive these wrecks looked—not at all heroic, and nobody was accessible to the infection of their patriotic example. Dead upon the field of honor, yes; but the field of honor was so very wet! It makes a difference.

The general engagement that all expected did not occur, none of the small advantages accruing, now to this side and now to that, in isolated and accidental collisions being followed up. Half-hearted attacks provoked a sullen resistance which was satisfied with mere repulse. Orders were obeyed with mechanical fidelity; no one did any more than his duty.

"The army is cowardly today," said General Cameron, the commander of a Federal brigade, to his adjutant general.

"The army is cold," replied the officer addressed, "and—yes, it doesn't wish to be like that."

He pointed to one of the dead bodies, lying in a thin pool of yellow water, its face and clothing bespattered with mud from hoof and wheel.

The army's weapons seemed to share its military delinquency. The rattle of rifles sounded flat and contemptible. It had no meaning and scarcely roused to attention and expectancy the unengaged parts of the line of battle and the waiting reserves. Heard at a little distance, the reports of cannon were feeble in volume and timbre: they lacked sting and resonance. The guns seemed to be fired with light charges, unshotted. And so the futile day wore on to its dreary close, and then to a night of discomfort succeeded a day of apprehension.

An army has a personality. Beneath the individual thoughts and emotions of its component parts it thinks and feels as a unit. And in this large, inclusive sense of things lies a wiser wisdom than the mere sum of all that it knows. On that dismal morning this great brute force, groping at the bottom of a white ocean of fog among trees that seemed as seaweeds, had a dumb consciousness that all was not well; that a day's maneuvering had resulted in a faulty disposition of its parts, a blind diffusion of its strength. The men felt insecure and talked among themselves of such tactical errors as with their meager military vocabulary they were able to name. Field and line officers gathered in groups and spoke more learnedly of what they apprehended with no greater clearness. Commanders of brigades and divisions looked anxiously to their connections on the right and on the left, sent staff officers on errands of inquiry and pushed skirmish lines silently and cautiously forward into the dubious region between the known and the unknown. At some points on the line the troops, apparently of their own volition, constructed such defenses as they could without the silent spade and the noisy ax.

One of these points was held by Captain Ransome's battery of six guns. Provided always with intrenching tools, his men had labored with diligence during the night, and now his guns thrust their black muzzles through the embrasures of a really formidable earthwork. It crowned a slight acclivity devoid of undergrowth and providing an unobstructed fire that would sweep the ground for an unknown distance in front. The position could hardly have been better chosen. It had this peculiarity, which Captain Ransome, who was greatly addicted to the use of the compass, had not failed to observe: it faced northward, whereas he knew that the general line of the army must face eastward. In fact, that part of the line was "refused" —that is to say, bent backward, away from the enemy. This implied that Captain Ransome's battery was somewhere near the left flank of the army; for an army in line of battle retires its flanks if the nature of the ground will permit, they being its vulnerable points. Actually, Captain Ransome appeared to hold the extreme left of the line, no troops being visible in that direction beyond his own. Immediately in rear of his guns occurred that conversation between him and his brigade commander, the concluding and more picturesque part of which is reported above.

III
HOW TO PLAY THE CANNON WITHOUT NOTES

Captain Ransome sat motionless and silent on horseback. A few yards away his men were standing at their guns. Somewhere—everywhere within a few miles—were a hundred thousand men, friends and enemies. Yet he was alone. The mist had isolated him as completely as if he had been in the heart of a desert. His world was a few square yards of wet and trampled earth about the feet of his horse. His comrades in that ghostly domain were invisible and inaudible. These were conditions favorable to thought, and he was thinking. Of the nature of his thoughts his clear-cut handsome features yielded no attesting sign. His face was as inscrutable as that of the Sphinx. Why should it have made a record which there was none to observe? At the sound of a footstep he merely turned his eyes in the direction whence it came; one of his sergeants, looking a giant in stature in the false perspective of the fog, approached, and when clearly defined and reduced to his true dimensions by propinquity, saluted and stood at attention.

"Well, Morris," said the officer, returning his subordinate's salute.

"Lieutenant Price directed me to tell you, sir, that most of the infantry has been withdrawn. We have not sufficient support."

"Yes, I know."

"I am to say that some of our men have been out over the works a hundred yards and report that our front is not picketed."

"Yes."

"They were so far forward that they heard the enemy."

"Yes."

"They heard the rattle of the wheels of artillery and the commands of officers."

"Yes."

"The enemy is moving toward our works."

Captain Ransome, who had been facing to the rear of his line—toward the point where the brigade commander and his cavalcade had been swallowed up by the fog—reined his horse about and faced the other way. Then he sat motionless as before.

"Who are the men who made that statement?" he inquired, without looking at the sergeant. His eyes were directed straight into the fog over the head of his horse.

"Corporal Hassman and Gunner Manning."

Captain Ransome was a moment silent. A slight pallor came into his face, a slight compression affected the lines of his lips, but it would have required a closer observer than Sergeant Morris to note the change. There was none in the voice.

"Sergeant, present my compliments to Lieutenant Price and direct him to open fire with all the guns. Grape."

The sergeant saluted and vanished in the fog.

IV

TO INTRODUCE GENERAL MASTERSON

Searching for his division commander, General Cameron and his escort had followed the line of battle for nearly a mile to the right of Ransome's battery, and there learned that the division commander had gone in search of the corps commander. It seemed that everybody was looking for his immediate superior—an ominous circumstance. It meant that nobody was quite at ease. So General Cameron rode on for another half-mile, where by good luck he met General Masterson, the division commander, returning.

"Ah, Cameron," said the higher officer, reining up, and throwing his right leg across the pommel of his saddle in a most unmilitary way, "anything up? Found a good position for your battery, I hope—if one place is better than another in a fog."

"Yes, general," said the other, with the greater dignity appropriate to his less exalted rank, "my battery is very well placed. I wish I could say that it is as well commanded."

"Eh, what's that? Ransome? I think him a fine fellow. In the army we should be proud of him."

It was customary for officers of the regular army to speak of it as "the army." As the greatest cities are most provincial, so the self-complacency of aristocracies is most frankly plebeian.

"He is too fond of his opinion. By the way, in order to occupy the hill that he holds I had to extend my line dangerously. The hill is on my left—that is to say the left flank of the army."

"Oh, no, Hart's brigade is beyond. It was ordered up from Drytown during the night and directed to hook on to you. Better go and—"

The sentence was unfinished: a lively cannonade had broken out on the left, and both officers, followed by their retinues of aides and orderlies making a great jingle and clank, rode rapidly toward the spot. But they were soon impeded, for they were compelled by the fog to keep within sight of the line of battle, behind which were swarms of men, all in motion across their way. Everywhere the line was assuming a sharper and harder definition, as the men sprang to arms and the officers, with drawn swords, "dressed" the ranks. Colorbearers unfurled the flags, buglers blew the "assembly," hospital attendants appeared with stretchers. Field officers mounted and sent their impedimenta to the rear in care of Negro servants. Back in the ghostly spaces of the forest could be heard the rustle and murmur of the reserves, pulling themselves together.

Nor was all this preparation vain, for scarcely five minutes had passed since Captain Ransome's guns had broken the truce of doubt before the whole region was aroar: the enemy had attacked nearly everywhere.

V

HOW SOUNDS CAN FIGHT SHADOWS

Captain Ransome walked up and down behind his guns, which were firing rapidly but with steadiness. The gunners worked alertly, but without haste or apparent excitement. There was really no reason for excitement; it is not much to point a cannon into a fog and fire it. Anybody can do as much as that.

The men smiled at their noisy work, performing it with a lessening alacrity. They cast curious regards upon their captain, who had now mounted the banquette of the fortification and was looking across the parapet as if observing the effect of his fire. But the only visible effect was the substitution of wide, low-lying sheets of smoke for their bulk of fog. Suddenly out of the obscurity burst a great sound of cheering, which filled the intervals between the reports of the guns with startling distinctness! To the few with leisure and opportunity to observe, the sound was inexpressibly strange—so loud, so near, so menacing, yet nothing seen! The men who had smiled at their work smiled no more, but performed it with a serious and feverish activity.

From his station at the parapet Captain Ransome now saw a great multitude of dim gray figures taking shape in the mist below him and swarming up the slope. But the work of the guns was now fast and furious. They swept the populous declivity with gusts of grape and canister, the whirring of which could be heard through the thunder of the explosions. In this awful tempest of iron the assailants struggled forward foot by foot across their dead, firing into the embrasures, reloading, firing again, and at last falling in their turn, a little in advance of those who had fallen before. Soon the smoke was dense enough to cover all. It settled down upon the attack and, drifting back, involved the defense. The gunners could hardly see to serve their pieces, and when occasional figures of the enemy appeared upon the parapet—having had the good luck to get near enough to it, between two embrasures, to be protected from the guns—they looked so unsubstantial that it seemed hardly worthwhile for the few infantrymen to go to work upon them with the bayonet and tumble them back into the ditch.

As the commander of a battery in action can find something better to do than cracking individual skulls, Captain Ransome had retired from the parapet to his proper post in rear of his guns, where he stood with folded arms, his bugler beside him. Here, during the hottest of the fight, he was approached by Lieutenant Price, who had just sabered a daring assailant inside the work. A spirited colloquy ensued between the two officers—spirited, at least, on the part of the lieutenant, who gesticulated with energy and shouted again and again into his commander's ear in the attempt to make himself heard above the infernal din of the guns. His gestures, if coolly noted by an actor, would have been pronounced to be those of protestation: one would have said that he was opposed to the proceedings. Did he wish to surrender?

Captain Ransome listened without a change of countenance or attitude, and when the other man had finished his harangue, looked him coldly in the eyes and during a seasonable abatement of the uproar said:

"Lieutenant Price, it is not permitted to you to know *anything*. It is sufficient that you obey my orders."

The lieutenant went to his post, and the parapet being now apparently clear Captain Ransome returned to it to have a look over. As he mounted the banquette a man sprang upon the crest, waving a great brilliant flag. The captain drew a pistol from his belt and shot him dead. The body, pitching forward, hung over the inner edge of the embankment, the arms straight downward, both hands still grasping the flag. The man's few followers turned and fled down the slope. Looking over the parapet, the captain saw no living thing. He observed also that no bullets were coming into the work.

He made a sign to the bugler, who sounded the command to cease firing. At all other points the action had already ended with a repulse of the Confederate attack; with the cessation of this cannonade the silence was absolute.

VI

WHY, BEING AFFRONTED BY *A*, IT IS NOT BEST TO AFFRONT *B*

General Masterson rode into the redoubt. The men, gathered in groups, were talking loudly and gesticulating. They pointed at the dead, running from one body to another. They neglected their foul and heated guns and forgot to resume their outer clothing. They ran to the parapet and looked over, some of them leaping down into the ditch. A score were gathered about a flag rigidly held by a dead man.

"Well, my men," said the general cheerily, "you have had a pretty fight of it."

They stared. Nobody replied. The presence of the great man seemed to embarrass and alarm.

Getting no response to his pleasant condescension, the easy-mannered officer whistled a bar or two of a popular air and, riding forward to the parapet, looked over at the dead. In an instant he had whirled his horse about and was spurring along in rear of the guns, his eyes everywhere at once. An officer sat on the trail of one of the guns, smoking a cigar. As the general dashed up he rose and tranquilly saluted.

"Captain Ransome!"—the words fell sharp and harsh, like the clash of steel blades—"you have been fighting our own men —our own men, sir. Do you hear? Hart's brigade!"

"General, I know that."

"You know it—you know that, and you sit here smoking? Oh, damn it, Hamilton, I'm losing my temper"—this to his provost marshal. "Sir—Captain Ransome, be good enough to say—to say why you fought our own men."

"That I am unable to say. In my orders that information was withheld."

Apparently the general did not comprehend.

"Who was the aggressor in this affair, you or General Hart?" he asked.

"I was."

"And could you not have known—could you not see, sir, that you were attacking our own men?"

The reply was astounding!

"I knew that, general. It appeared to be none of my business."

Then, breaking the dead silence that followed his answer, he said:

"I must refer you to General Cameron."

"General Cameron is dead, sir—as dead as he can be—as dead as any man in this army. He lies back yonder under a tree. Do you mean to say that he had anything to do with this horrible business?"

Captain Ransome did not reply. Observing the altercation, his men had gathered about to watch the outcome. They were greatly excited. The fog, which had been partly dissipated by the firing, had again closed in so darkly about them that they drew more closely together till the judge on horseback and the accused standing calmly before him had but a narrow space free from intrusion. It was the most informal of courts-martial, but all felt that the formal one to follow would but affirm its judgment. It had no jurisdiction, but it had the significance of prophecy.

"Captain Ransome," the general cried impetuously, but with something in his voice that was almost entreaty, "if you can say anything to put a better light upon your incomprehensible conduct I beg you will do so."

Having recovered his temper, this generous soldier sought for something to justify his naturally sympathetic attitude toward a brave man in the imminence of a dishonorable death.

"Where is Lieutenant Price?" the captain said.

That officer stood forward, his dark saturnine face looking somewhat forbidding under a bloody handkerchief bound about his brow. He understood the summons and needed no invitation to speak. He did not look at the captain, but addressed the general:

"During the engagement I discovered the state of affairs,

and apprised the commander of the battery. I ventured to urge that the firing cease. I was insulted and ordered to my post."

"Do you know anything of the orders under which I was acting?" asked the captain.

"Of any orders under which the commander of the battery was acting," the lieutenant continued, still addressing the general, "I know nothing."

Captain Ransome felt his world sink away from his feet. In those cruel words he heard the murmur of the centuries breaking upon the short of eternity. He heard the voice of doom; it said, in cold, mechanical, and measured tones: "Ready, aim, fire!" and he felt the bullets tear his heart to shreds. He heard the sound of the earth upon his coffin and (if the good God was so merciful) the song of a bird above his forgotten grave. Quietly detaching his saber from its supports, he handed it up to the provost marshal.

ONE SUMMER
NIGHT

THE fact that Henry Armstrong was buried did not seem to him to prove that he was dead: he had always been a hard man to convince. That he really was buried, the testimony of his senses compelled him to admit. His posture—flat upon his back, with his hands crossed upon his stomach and tied with something that he easily broke without profitably altering the situation—the strict confinement of his entire person, the black darkness and profound silence, made a body of evidence impossible to controvert, and he accepted it without cavil.

But dead—no; he was only very, very ill. He had, withal, the invalid's apathy and did not greatly concern himself about the uncommon fate that had been allotted to him. No philosopher was he—just a plain, commonplace person gifted, for the time being, with a pathological indifference: the organ that he feared consequences with was torpid. So, with no particular apprehension for his immediate future, he fell asleep and all was peace with Henry Armstrong.

But something was going on overhead. It was a dark summer night, shot through with infrequent shimmers of lightning silently firing a cloud lying low in the west and portending a storm. These brief, stammering illuminations brought out with ghastly distinctness the monuments and headstones of the cemetery and seemed to set them dancing. It was not a night in which any credible witness was likely to be straying

about a cemetery, so the three men who were there, digging
into the grave of Henry Armstrong, felt reasonably secure.

Two of them were young students from a medical college
a few miles away; the third was a gigantic Negro known as
Jess. For many years Jess had been employed about the cemetery as a man-of-all-work and it was his favorite pleasantry
that he knew "every soul in the place." From the nature of
what he was now doing it was inferable that the place was
not so populous as its register may have shown it to be.

Outside the wall, at the part of the grounds farthest from
the public road, were a horse and a light wagon, waiting.

The work of excavation was not difficult: the earth with
which the grave had been loosely filled a few hours before
offered little resistance and was soon thrown out. Removal of
the casket from its box was less easy, but it was taken out,
for it was a perquisite of Jess, who carefully unscrewed the
cover and laid it aside, exposing the body in black trousers
and white shirt. At that instant the air sprang to flame, a
cracking shock of thunder shook the stunned world, and Henry

Armstrong tranquilly sat up. With inarticulate cries the men fled in terror, each in a different direction. For nothing on earth could two of them have been persuaded to return. But Jess was of another breed.

In the gray of the morning the two students, pallid and haggard from anxiety and with the terror of their adventure still beating tumultuously in their blood, met at the medical college.

"You saw it?" cried one.

"God! yes—what are we to do?"

They went around to the rear of the building, where they saw a horse, attached to a light wagon, hitched to a gatepost near the door of the dissecting room. Mechanically they entered the room. On a bench in the obscurity sat the Negro Jess. He rose, grinning, all eyes and teeth.

"I'm waiting for my pay," he said.

Stretched naked on a long table lay the body of Henry Armstrong, the head defiled with blood and clay from a blow with a spade.

THREE AND ONE
ARE ONE

I N the year 1861 Barr Lassiter, a young man of twenty-two,
lived with his parents and an elder sister near Carthage,
Tennessee. The family were in somewhat humble circumstances, subsisting by cultivation of a small and not very fertile
plantation. Owning no slaves, they were not rated among "the
best people" of their neighborhood; but they were honest persons of good education, fairly well mannered and as respectable
as any family could be if uncredentialed by personal dominion
over the sons and daughters of Ham. The elder Lassiter had
that severity of manner that so frequently affirms an uncom-
promising devotion to duty, and conceals a warm and affectionate disposition. He was of the iron of which martyrs are
made, but in the heart of the matrix had lurked a nobler metal,
fusible at a milder heat, yet never coloring nor softening the
hard exterior. By both heredity and environment something
of the man's inflexible character had touched the other members of the family; the Lassiter home, though not devoid of
domestic affection, was a veritable citadel of duty, and duty—
ah, duty is as cruel as death!

When the war came on it found in the family, as in so many
others in that state, a divided sentiment; the young man was
loyal to the Union, the others savagely hostile. This unhappy
division begot an insupportable domestic bitterness, and when
the offending son and brother left home with the avowed pur-

pose of joining the Federal army, not a hand was laid in his, not a word of farewell was spoken, not a good wish followed him out into the world whither he went to meet with such spirit as he might whatever fate awaited him.

Making his way to Nashville, already occupied by the army of General Buell, he enlisted in the first organization that he found, a Kentucky regiment of cavalry, and in due time passed through all the stages of military evolution from raw recruit to experienced trooper. A right good trooper he was, too, although in his oral narrative from which this tale is made there was no mention of that; the fact was learned from his surviving comrades. For Barr Lassiter has answered "Here" to the sergeant whose name is Death.

Two years after he had joined it his regiment passed through the region whence he had come. The country thereabout had suffered severely from the ravages of war, having been occupied alternately (and simultaneously) by the belligerent forces, and a sanguinary struggle had occurred in the immediate vicinity of the Lassiter homestead. But of this the young trooper was not aware.

Finding himself in camp near his home, he felt a natural longing to see his parents and sister, hoping that in them, as in him, the unnatural animosities of the period had been softened by time and separation. Obtaining a leave of absence, he set foot in the late summer afternoon, and soon after the rising of the full moon was walking up the gravel path leading to the dwelling in which he had been born.

Soldiers in war age rapidly, and in youth two years are a long time. Barr Lassiter felt himself an old man, and had almost expected to find the place a ruin and a desolation. Nothing, apparently, was changed. At the sight of each dear and familiar object he was profoundly affected. His heart beat audibly, his emotion nearly suffocated him; an ache was in his throat. Unconsciously he quickened his pace until he almost ran, his long shadow making grotesque efforts to keep its place beside him.

The house was unlighted, the door open. As he approached and paused to recover control of himself his father came out and stood bareheaded in the moonlight.

"Father!" cried the young man, springing forward with outstretched hand, "Father!"

The elder man looked him sternly in the face, stood a moment motionless and without a word withdrew into the house. Bitterly disappointed, humiliated, inexpressibly hurt and altogether unnerved, the soldier dropped upon a rustic seat in deep dejection, supporting his head upon his trembling hand. But he would not have it so: he was too good a soldier to accept repulse as defeat. He rose and entered the house, passing directly to the sitting room.

It was dimly lighted by an uncurtained east window. On a low stool by the hearthside, the only article of furniture in the place, sat his mother, staring into a fireplace strewn with blackened embers and cold ashes. He spoke to her—tenderly, interrogatively, and with hesitation, but she neither answered, nor moved, nor seemed in any way surprised. True, there had been time for her husband to apprise her of their guilty son's

return. He moved nearer and was about to lay his hand upon her arm, when his sister entered from an adjoining room, looked him full in the face, passed him without a sign of recognition and left the room by a door that was partly behind him. He had turned his head to watch her, but when she was gone his eyes again sought his mother. She, too, had left the place.

Barr Lassiter strode to the door by which he had entered. The moonlight on the lawn was tremulous, as if the sward were a rippling sea. The trees and their black shadows shook as in a breeze. Blended with its borders, the gravel walk seemed unsteady and insecure to step on. This young soldier knew the optical illusions produced by tears. He felt them on his cheek, and saw them sparkle on the breast of his trooper's jacket. He left the house and made his way back to camp.

The next day, with no very definite intention, with no dominant feeling that he could rightly have named, he again sought the spot. Within a half-mile of it he met Bushrod Albro, a former playfellow and schoolmate, who greeted him warmly.

"I am going to visit my home," said the soldier.

The other looked at him rather sharply, but said nothing.

"I know," continued Lassiter, "that my folks have not changed, but—"

"There have been changes," Albro interrupted. "Everything changes. I'll go with you if you don't mind. We can talk as we go."

But Albro did not talk.

Instead of a house they found only fire-blackened foundations of stone, enclosing an area of compact ashes pitted by rains.

Lassiter's astonishment was extreme.

"I could not find the right way to tell you," said Albro. "In the fight a year ago your house was burned by a Federal shell."

"And my family—where are they?"

"In heaven, I hope. All were killed by the shell."

THE DEATH
OF HALPIN FRAYSER

For by death is wrought greater change than hath been shown. Whereas in general the spirit that removed cometh back upon occasion, and is sometimes seen of those in flesh (appearing in the form of the body it bore), yet it hath happened that the veritable body without the spirit hath walked. And it is attested of those encountering who have lived to speak thereon that a lich so raised up hath no natural affection, nor remembrance thereof, but only hate. Also, it is known that some spirits which in life were benign become by death evil altogether.—Hali

I

ONE dark night in midsummer a man waking from a dreamless sleep in a forest lifted his head from the earth, and staring a few moments into the blackness, said: "Catherine Larue." He said nothing more; no reason was known to him why he should have said so much.

The man was Halpin Frayser. He lived in St. Helena, but where he lives now is uncertain, for he is dead. One who practices sleeping in the woods with nothing under him but the dry leaves and the damp earth, and nothing over him but the branches from which the leaves have fallen and the sky from which the earth has fallen, cannot hope for great longevity, and Frayser had already attained the age of thirty-two. There are persons in this world, millions of persons, and far and away the best persons, who regard that as a very advanced age. They are the children. To those who view the voyage of life from the port of departure the bark that has accomplished any considerable distance appears already in close approach to the farther shore. However, it is not certain that Halpin Frayser came to his death by exposure.

He had been all day in the hills west of the Napa Valley, looking for doves and such small game as was in season. Late in the afternoon it had come on to be cloudy, and he had lost his bearings; and although he had only to go always down-hill—everywhere the way to safety when one is lost—the absence of trails had so impeded him that he was overtaken by night while still in the forest. Unable in the darkness to pene-trate the thickets of manzanita and other undergrowth, utterly bewildered and overcome with fatigue, he had lain down near the root of a large madroño and fallen into a dreamless sleep. It was hours later, in the very middle of the night, that one of God's mysterious messengers, gliding ahead of the incalculable host of his companions sweeping westward with the dawn line, pronounced the awakening word in the ear of the sleeper, who sat upright and spoke, he knew not why, a name, he knew not whose.

Halpin Frayser was not much of a philosopher, nor a scien-tist. The circumstance that, waking from a deep sleep at night in the midst of a forest, he had spoken aloud a name that he had not in memory and hardly had in mind did not arouse an enlightened curiosity to investigate the phenomenon. He thought it odd, and with a little perfunctory shiver, as if in deference to a seasonal presumption that the night was chill, he lay down again and went to sleep. But his sleep was no longer dreamless.

He thought he was walking along a dusty road that showed white in the gathering darkness of a summer night. Whence and whither it led, and why he traveled it, he did not know, though all seemed simple and natural, as is the way in dreams; for in the Land Beyond the Bed surprises cease from troubling and the judgment is at rest. Soon he came to a parting of the ways; leading from the highway was a road less traveled, having the appearance, indeed, of having been long abandoned, because, he thought, it led to something evil; yet he turned into it without hesitation, impelled by some imperious necessity.

As he pressed forward he became conscious that his way was haunted by invisible existences whom he could not definitely figure to his mind. From among the trees on either side he caught broken and incoherent whispers in a strange tongue which yet he partly understood. They seemed to him fragmentary utterances of a monstrous conspiracy against his body and soul.

It was now long after nightfall, yet the interminable forest through which he journeyed was lit with a wan glimmer having no point of diffusion, for in its mysterious lumination nothing cast a shadow. A shallow pool in the guttered depression of an old wheel rut, as from a recent rain, met his eye with a crimson gleam. He stooped and plunged his hand into it. It stained his fingers; it was blood! Blood, he then observed, was about him everywhere. The weeds growing rankly by the roadside showed it in blots and splashes on their big, broad leaves. Patches of dry dust between the wheelways were pitted and spattered as with a red rain. Defiling the trunks of the trees were broad maculations of crimson, and blood dripped like dew from their foliage.

All this he observed with a terror which seemed not incompatible with the fulfillment of a natural expectation. It seemed to him that it was all in expiation of some crime which, though conscious of his guilt, he could not rightly remember. To the menaces and mysteries of his surroundings the consciousness was an added horror. Vainly he sought by tracing life backward in memory, to reproduce the moment of his sin; scenes and incidents came crowding tumultuously into his mind, one picture effacing another, or commingling with it in confusion and obscurity, but nowhere could he catch a glimpse of what he sought. The failure augmented his terror; he felt as one who has murdered in the dark, not knowing whom nor why. So frightful was the situation—the mysterious light burned with so silent and awful a menace; the noxious plants, the trees that by common consent are invested with a melancholy or baleful character, so openly in his sight conspired against his peace; from overhead and all about came so audible and startling whispers and the sighs of creatures so obviously not of earth—that he could endure it no longer, and with a great effort to break some malign spell that bound his faculties to silence and inaction, he shouted with the full strength of his lungs! His voice, broken, it seemed, into an infinite multitude of unfamiliar sounds, went babbling and stammering away into the distant reaches of the forest, died into silence, and all was as before. But he had made a beginning at resistance and was encouraged. He said:

"I will not submit unheard. There may be powers that are not malignant traveling this accursed road. I shall leave them a record and an appeal. I shall relate my wrongs, the persecutions that I endure—I, a helpless mortal, a penitent, an unoffending poet!" Halpin Frayser was a poet only as he was a penitent: in his dream.

Taking from his clothing a small red-leather pocketbook, one-half of which was leaved for memoranda, he discovered that he was without a pencil. He broke a twig from a bush, dipped it into a pool of blood and wrote rapidly. He had hardly touched the paper with the point of his twig when a low, wild peal of laughter broke out at a measureless distance away, and growing ever louder, seemed approaching ever nearer; a soulless, heartless, and unjoyous laugh, like that of the loon, solitary by the lakeside at midnight; a laugh which culminated in an unearthly shout close at hand, then died away by slow gradations, as if the accursed being that uttered it had withdrawn over the verge of the world whence it had come. But the man felt that this was not so—that it was nearby and had not moved.

A strange sensation began slowly to take possession of his body and his mind. He could not have said which, if any, of his senses was affected; he felt it rather as a consciousness—a mysterious mental assurance of some overpowering presence— some supernatural malevolence different in kind from the invisible existences that swarmed about him, and superior to them in power. He knew that it had uttered that hideous laugh. And now it seemed to be approaching him; from what direction he did not know—dared not conjecture. All his former fears were forgotten or merged in the gigantic terror that now held him in thrall. Apart from that, he had but one thought: to complete his written appeal to the benign powers who, traversing the haunted wood, might sometime rescue him if he should be denied the blessing of annihilation. He wrote with terrible rapidity, the twig in his fingers rilling blood without renewal; but in the middle of a sentence his hands denied their service to his will, his arms fell to his sides, the book to the earth; and powerless to move or cry out, he found himself staring into the sharply drawn face and blank, dead eyes of his own mother, standing white and silent in the garments of the grave!

II

In his youth Halpin Frayser had lived with his parents in Nashville, Tennessee. The Fraysers were well-to-do, having a good position in such society as had survived the wreck wrought by civil war. Their children had the social and educational opportunities of their time and place, and had responded to good associations and instruction with agreeable manners and cultivated minds. Halpin being the youngest and not over-robust was perhaps a trifle spoiled. He had the double disadvantage of a mother's assiduity and a father's neglect. Frayser *père* was what no Southern man of means is not—a politician. His country, or rather his section and state, made demands upon his time and attention so exacting that to those of his family he was compelled to turn an ear partly deafened by the thunder of the political captains and the shouting, his own included.

Young Halpin was of a dreamy, indolent and rather romantic turn, somewhat more addicted to literature than law, the profession to which he was bred. Among those of his relations who professed the modern faith of heredity it was well understood that in him the character of the late Myron Bayne, a maternal great-grandfather, had revisited the glimpses of the moon—by which orb Bayne had in his lifetime been sufficiently affected

to be a poet of no small Colonial distinction. If not specially observed, it was observable that while a Frayser who was not the proud possessor of a sumptuous copy of the ancestral "poetical works" (printed at the family expense, and long ago withdrawn from an inhospitable market) was a rare Frayser indeed, there was an illogical indisposition to honor the great deceased in the person of his spiritual successor. Halpin was pretty generally deprecated as an intellectual black sheep who was likely at any moment to disgrace the flock by bleating in meter. The Tennessee Fraysers were a practical folk—not practical in the popular sense of devotion to sordid pursuits, but having a robust contempt for any qualities unfitting a man for the wholesome vocation of politics.

In justice to young Halpin it should be said that while in him were pretty faithfully reproduced most of the mental and moral characteristics ascribed by history and family tradition to the famous Colonial bard, his succession to the gift and faculty divine was purely inferential. Not only had he never been known to court the muse, but in truth he could not have written correctly a line of verse to save himself from the Killer of the Wise. Still, there was no knowing when the dormant faculty might wake and smite the lyre.

In the meantime the young man was rather a loose fish, anyhow. Between him and his mother was the most perfect sympathy, for secretly the lady was herself a devout disciple of the late and great Myron Bayne, though with the tact so generally and justly admired in her sex (despite the hardy calumniators who insist that it is essentially the same thing as cunning) she had always taken care to conceal her weakness from all eyes but those of him who shared it. Their common guilt in respect of that was an added tie between them. If in Halpin's youth his mother had spoiled him, he had assuredly done his part toward being spoiled. As he grew to such manhood as is attainable by a Southerner who does not care which way elections go, the attachment between him and his beautiful mother—whom from early childhood he had called Katy—became yearly stronger and more tender. In these two romantic natures was manifest in a signal way that neglected phenomenon, the dominance of the sexual element in all the relations of life, strengthening, softening, and beautifying even those of consanguinity. The two were nearly inseparable, and by strangers observing their manner were not infrequently mistaken for lovers.

Entering his mother's boudoir one day Halpin Frayser kissed her upon the forehead, toyed for a moment with a lock of her dark hair which had escaped from its confining pins, and said, with an obvious effort at calmness:

"Would you greatly mind, Katy, if I were called away to California for a few weeks?"

It was hardly needful for Katy to answer with her lips a question to which her telltale cheeks had made instant reply. Evidently she would greatly mind; and the tears, too, sprang into her large brown eyes as corroborative testimony.

"Ah, my son," she said, looking up into his face with infinite tenderness, "I should have known that this was coming. Did I not lie awake a half of the night weeping because, during the other half, Grandfather Bayne had come to me in a dream, and standing by his portrait—young, too, and handsome as that—pointed to yours on the same wall? And when I looked it seemed that I could not see the features; you had been painted with a face cloth, such as we put upon the dead. Your father has laughed at me, but you and I, dear, know that such things are not for nothing. And I saw below the edge of the cloth the marks of hands on your throat—forgive me, but we have not been used to keep such things from each other. Perhaps you have another interpretation. Perhaps it does not mean that you will go to California. Or maybe you will take me with you?"

It must be confessed that this ingenious interpretation of the dream in the light of newly discovered evidence did not wholly commend itself to the son's more logical mind; he had, for the moment at least, a conviction that it foreshadowed a more simple and immediate, if less tragic, disaster than a visit to the Pacific Coast. It was Halpin Frayser's impression that he was to be garroted on his native heath.

"Are there not medicinal springs in California?" Mrs. Frayser resumed before he had time to give her the true reading of the dream—"places where one recovers from rheumatism and neuralgia? Look—my fingers feel so stiff; and I am almost sure they have been giving me great pain while I slept."

She held out her hands for his inspection. What diagnosis of her case the young man may have thought it best to conceal with a smile the historian is unable to state, but for himself he feels bound to say that fingers looking less stiff, and showing fewer evidences of even insensible pain, have seldom been submitted for medical inspection by even the fairest patient desiring a prescription of unfamiliar scenes.

The outcome of it was that of these two odd persons having equally odd notions of duty, the one went to California, as the interest of his client required, and the other remained at home in compliance with a wish that her husband was scarcely conscious of entertaining.

While in San Francisco Halpin Frayser was walking one dark night along the waterfront of the city, when, with a suddenness that surprised and disconcerted him, he became a sailor. He was in fact "shanghaied" aboard a gallant, gallant ship, and sailed for a far countree. Nor did his misfortunes end with the voyage; for the ship was cast ashore on an island of the South Pacific, and it was six years afterward when the survivors were taken off by a venturesome trading schooner and brought back to San Francisco.

Though poor in purse, Frayser was no less proud in spirit than he had been in the years that seemed ages and ages ago. He would accept no assistance from strangers, and it was while living with a fellow survivor near the town of St. Helena, awaiting news and remittances from home, that he had gone gunning and dreaming.

III

The apparition confronting the dreamer in the haunted wood— the thing so like, yet so unlike his mother—was horrible! It stirred no love nor longing in his heart; it came unattended with pleasant memories of a golden past—inspired no sentiment of any kind; all the finer emotions were swallowed up in fear. He tried to turn and run from before it, but his legs were as lead; he was unable to lift his feet from the ground. His arms hung helpless at his sides; of his eyes only he retained control, and these he dared not remove from the lusterless orbs of the apparition, which he knew was not a soul without a body, but that most dreadful of all existences infesting that haunted wood—a body without a soul! In its blank stare was neither love, nor pity, nor intelligence—nothing to which to address an appeal for mercy. "An appeal will not lie," he thought, with an absurd reversion to professional slang, making the situation more horrible, as the fire of a cigar might light up a tomb.

For a time, which seemed so long that the world grew gray with age and sin, and the haunted forest, having fulfilled its purpose in this monstrous culmination of its terrors, vanished out of his consciousness with all its sights and sounds, the apparition stood within a pace, regarding him with the mindless malevolence of a wild brute; then thrust its hands forward and sprang upon him with appalling ferocity! The act released his physical energies without unfettering his will; his mind was still spellbound, but his powerful body and agile limbs, endowed with a blind, insensate life of their own, resisted stoutly and well. For an instant he seemed to see this unnatural contest between a dead intelligence and a breathing mechanism only as a spectator—such fancies are in dreams; then he regained his identity almost as if by a leap forward into his body, and the straining automaton had a directing will as alert and fierce as that of its hideous antagonist.

But what mortal can cope with a creature of his dream? The imagination creating the enemy is already vanquished; the combat's result is the combat's cause. Despite his struggles— despite his strength and activity, which seemed wasted in a void, he felt the cold fingers close upon his throat. Borne backward to the earth, he saw above him the dead and drawn face within a hand's breadth of his own, and then all was black. A sound as of the beating of distant drums—a murmur of swarming voices, a sharp, far cry signing all to silence, and Halpin Frayser dreamed that he was dead.

IV

A warm, clear night had been followed by a morning of drench-
ing fog. At about the middle of the afternoon of the preceding
day a little whiff of light vapor—a mere thickening of the atmosphere, the ghost of a cloud—had been observed clinging to
the western side of Mount St. Helena, away up along the barren
altitudes near the summit. It was so thin, so diaphanous, so like
a fancy made visible, that one would have said, "Look quickly!
in a moment it will be gone."

In a moment it was visibly larger and denser. While with
one edge it clung to the mountain, with the other it reached
farther and farther out into the air above the lower slopes. At
the same time it extended itself to north and south, joining
small patches of mist that appeared to come out of the mountainside on exactly the same level, with an intelligent design
to be absorbed. And so it grew and grew until the summit was
shut out of view from the valley, and over the valley itself was
an ever-extending canopy, opaque and gray. At Calistoga,
which lies near the head of the valley and the foot of the mountain, there were a starless night and a sunless morning. The
fog, sinking into the valley, had reached southward, swallowing up ranch after ranch, until it had blotted out the town of
St. Helena, nine miles away. The dust in the road was laid;
trees were adrip with moisture; birds sat silent in their
coverts; the morning light was wan and ghastly, with neither
color nor fire.

Two men left the town of St. Helena at the first glimmer of
dawn, and walked along the road northward up the valley toward Calistoga. They carried guns on their shoulders, yet no
one having knowledge of such matters could have mistaken
them for hunters of bird or beast. They were a deputy sheriff
from Napa and a detective from San Francisco—Holker and
Jaralson, respectively. Their business was man-hunting.

"How far is it?" inquired Holker, as they strode along, their
feet stirring white the dust beneath the damp surface of the
road.

"The White Church? Only a half mile farther," the other answered. "By the way," he added, "it is neither white nor a church; it is an abandoned schoolhouse, gray with age and neglect. Religious services were once held in it—when it was white—and there is a graveyard that would delight a poet. Can you guess why I sent for you, and told you to come heeled?"

"Oh, I never have bothered you about things of that kind. I've always found you communicative when the time came. But if I may hazard a guess, you want me to help you arrest one of the corpses in the graveyard."

"You remember Branscom?" said Jaralson, treating his companion's wit with the inattention that it deserved.

"The chap who cut his wife's throat? I ought. I wasted a week's work on him and had my expenses for my trouble. There is a reward of five hundred dollars, but none of us ever got a sight of him. You don't mean to say—"

"Yes, I do. He has been under the noses of you fellows all the time. He comes by night to the old graveyard at the White Church."

"The devil! That's where they buried his wife."

"Well, you fellows might have had sense enough to suspect that he would return to her grave sometime."

"The very last place that anyone would have expected him to return to."

"But you had exhausted all the other places. Learning your failure at them, I 'laid for him' there."

"And you found him?"

"Damn it, he found *me*! The rascal got the drop on me— regularly held me up and made me travel. It's God's mercy that he didn't go through me. Oh, he's a good one, and I fancy the half of that reward is enough for me if you're needy."

Holker laughed good-humoredly, and explained that his creditors were never more importunate.

"I wanted merely to show you the ground, and arrange a plan with you," the detective explained. "I thought it as well for us to be heeled, even in daylight."

"The man must be insane," said the deputy sheriff. "The reward is for his capture and conviction. If he's mad he won't be convicted."

Mr. Holker was so profoundly affected by that possible

failure of justice that he involuntarily stopped in the middle of the road, then resumed his walk with abated zeal.

"Well, he looks it," assented Jaralson. "I'm bound to admit that a more unshaven, unshorn, unkempt, and uneverything wretch I never saw outside the ancient and honorable order of tramps. But I've gone in for him, and can't make up my mind to let go. There's glory in it for us, anyhow. Not another soul knows that he is this side of the Mountains of the Moon."

"All right," Holker said, "we will go and view the ground," and he added, in the words of a once favorite inscription for tombstones, " 'where you must shortly lie'—I mean, if old Branscom ever gets tired of you and your impertinent intrusion. By the way, I heard the other day that Branscom was not his real name."

"What is?"

"I can't recall it. I had lost all interest in the wretch, and it did not fix itself in my memory—something like Pardee. The woman whose throat he had the bad taste to cut was a widow when he met her. She had come to California to look up some relatives—there are persons who will do that sometimes. But you know all that."

"Naturally."

"But not knowing the right name, by what happy inspiration did you find the right grave? The man who told me what the name was said it had been cut on the headboard."

"I don't know the right grave." Jaralson was apparently a trifle reluctant to admit his ignorance of so important a point of his plan. "I have been watching about the place generally. A part of our work this morning will be to identify that grave. Here is the White Church."

For a long distance the road had been bordered by fields on both sides, but now on the left there was a forest of oaks, madroños, and gigantic spruces whose lower parts only could be seen, dim and ghostly in the fog. The undergrowth was, in places, thick, but nowhere impenetrable. For some moments Holker saw nothing of the building, but as they turned into the woods it revealed itself in faint gray outline through the fog, looking huge and far away. A few steps more, and it was within an arm's length, distinct, dark with moisture, and insignificant in size. It had the usual country-schoolhouse form—belonged to the packing-box order of architecture; had an underpinning of stones, a moss-grown roof, and blank window spaces, whence both glass and sash had long departed. It was ruined, but not a ruin—a typical Californian substitute for what are known to guidebookers abroad as "monuments of the past." With scarcely a glance at this uninteresting structure Jaralson moved on into the dripping undergrowth beyond.

"I will show you where he held me up," he said. "This is the graveyard."

Here and there among the bushes were small enclosures containing graves, sometimes no more than one. They were recognized as graves by the discolored stones or rotting boards at head and foot, leaning at all angles, some prostrate, by the ruined picket fences surrounding them; or, infrequently, by the mound itself showing its gravel through the fallen leaves. In many instances nothing marked the spot where lay the vestiges of some poor mortal—who, leaving "a large circle of sorrowing friends," had been left by them in turn—except a depression in the earth, more lasting than that in the spirits of the mourners. The paths, if any paths had been, were long obliterated; trees of a considerable size had been permitted to grow up from the graves and thrust aside with root or branch the enclosing fences. Over all was that air of abandonment and decay which seems nowhere so fit and significant as in a village of the forgotten dead.

As the two men, Jaralson leading, pushed their way through the growth of young trees, that enterprising man suddenly stopped and brought up his shotgun to the height of his breast, uttered a low note of warning, and stood motionless, his eyes fixed upon something ahead. As well as he could, obstructed by brush, his companion, though seeing nothing, imitated the posture and so stood, prepared for what might ensue. A moment later Jaralson moved cautiously forward, the other following.

Under the branches of an enormous spruce lay the dead body of a man. Standing silent above it they noted such particulars as first strike the attention—the face, the attitude, the clothing; whatever most promptly and plainly answers the unspoken question of a sympathetic curiosity.

The body lay upon its back, the legs wide apart. One arm was thrust upward, the other outward; but the latter was bent acutely, and the hand was near the throat. Both hands were tightly clenched. The whole attitude was that of desperate but ineffectual resistance to—what?

Nearby lay a shotgun and a game bag through the meshes of which was seen the plumage of shot birds. All about were evidences of a furious struggle: small sprouts of poison oak were bent and denuded of leaf and bark; dead and rotting leaves had been pushed into heaps and ridges on both sides of the legs by the action of other feet than theirs; alongside the hips were unmistakable impressions of human knees.

The nature of the struggle was made clear by a glance at the dead man's throat and face. While breast and hands were white, those were purple—almost black. The shoulders lay upon a low mound, and the head was turned back at an angle otherwise impossible, the expanded eyes staring blankly backward in a direction opposite to that of the feet. From the froth filling the open mouth the tongue protruded, black and swollen. The throat showed horrible contusions; not mere finger marks, but bruises and lacerations wrought by two strong hands that must have buried themselves in the yielding flesh, maintaining their terrible grasp until long after death. Breast, throat, face were wet; the clothing was saturated; drops of water, condensed from the fog, studded the hair and mustache.

All this the two men observed without speaking—almost at a glance. Then Holker said:

"Poor devil! He had a rough deal."

Jaralson was making a vigilant circumspection of the forest, his shotgun held in both hands and at full cock, his finger upon the trigger.

"The work of a maniac," he said, without withdrawing his eyes from the enclosing wood. "It was done by Branscom—Pardee."

Something half hidden by the disturbed leaves on the earth caught Holker's attention. It was a red-leather pocketbook. He picked it up and opened it. It contained leaves of white paper for memoranda, and upon the first leaf was the name "Halpin Frayser." Written in red on several succeeding leaves—

scrawled as if in haste and barely legible—were the following lines, which Holker read aloud, while his companion continued scanning the dim gray confines of their narrow world and hearing matter of apprehension in the drip of water from every burdened branch:

Enthralled by some mysterious spell, I stood
In the lit gloom of an enchanted wood.
   The cypress there and myrtle twined their boughs,
Significant, in baleful brotherhood.

The brooding willow whispered to the yew;
Beneath, the deadly nightshade and the rue,
   With immortelles self-woven into strange
Funereal shapes, and horrid nettles grew.

No song of bird nor any drone of bees,
Nor light leaf lifted by the wholesome breeze:
   The air was stagnant all, and Silence was
A living thing that breathed among the trees.

Conspiring spirits whispered in the gloom,
Half-heard, the stilly secrets of the tomb.
   With blood the trees were all adrip; the leaves
Shone in the witch-light with a ruddy bloom.

I cried aloud!—the spell, unbroken still,
Rested upon my spirit and my will.
   Unsouled, unhearted, hopeless and forlorn,
I strove with monstrous presages of ill!

At last the viewless—

Holker ceased reading; there was no more to read. The manuscript broke off in the middle of a line.

"That sounds like Bayne," said Jaralson, who was something of a scholar in his way. He had abated his vigilance and stood looking down at the body.

"Who's Bayne?" Holker asked rather incuriously.

"Myron Bayne, a chap who flourished in the early years of the nation—more than a century ago. Wrote mighty dismal stuff; I have his collected works. That poem is not among them, but it must have been omitted by mistake."

"It is cold," said Holker. "Let us leave here; we must have up the coroner from Napa."

Jaralson said nothing, but made a movement in compliance. Passing the end of the slight elevation of earth upon which the dead man's head and shoulders lay, his foot struck some hard substance under the rotting forest leaves, and he took the trouble to kick it into view. It was a fallen headboard, and painted on it were the hardly decipherable words, "Catherine Larue."

"Larue, Larue!" exclaimed Holker with sudden animation. "Why, that is the real name of Branscom—not Pardee. And— bless my soul! how it all comes to me—the murdered woman's name had been Frayser!"

"There is some rascally mystery here," said Detective Jaralson. "I hate anything of that kind."

There came to them out of the fog—seemingly from a great distance—the sound of a laugh, a low, deliberate, soulless laugh, which had no more of joy than that of a hyena night-prowling in the desert; a laugh that rose by slow gradation, louder and louder, clearer, more distinct and terrible, until it seemed barely outside the narrow circle of their vision; a laugh so unnatural, so unhuman, so devilish, that it filled those hardy man-hunters with a sense of dread unspeakable! They did not move their weapons nor think of them; the menace of that horrible sound was not of the kind to be met with arms. As it had grown out of silence, so now it died away; from a culminating shout which had seemed almost in their ears, it drew itself away into the distance, until its failing notes, joyless and mechanical to the last, sank to silence at a measureless remove.

JOHN BARTINE'S WATCH

A Story by a Physician

T HE exact time? Good God! my friend, why do you insist?
One would think—but what does it matter. It is easily
bedtime— isn't that near enough? But, here, if you must
set your watch, take mine and see for yourself."

With that he detached his watch—a tremendously heavy,
old-fashioned one—from the chain and handed it to me, then
turned away, and walking across the room to a shelf of books,
began an examination of their backs. His agitation and evident
distress surprised me; they appeared reasonless. Having set
my watch by his, I stepped over to where he stood and said,
"Thank you."

As he took his timepiece and reattached it to the guard I
observed that his hands were unsteady. With a tact upon
which I greatly prided myself, I sauntered carelessly to the
sideboard and took some brandy and water, then, begging his
pardon for my thoughtlessness, asked him to have some and
went back to my seat by the fire, leaving him to help himself,
as was our custom. He did so and presently joined me at the
hearth, as tranquil as ever.

This odd little incident occurred in my apartment, where
John Bartine was passing an evening. We had dined together
at the club, had come home in a cab and—in short, everything
had been done in the most prosaic way; and why John Bartine

137

should break in upon the natural and established order of things to make himself spectacular with a display of emotion, apparently for his own entertainment, I could nowise understand. The more I thought of it, while his brilliant conversational gifts were commending themselves to my inattention, the more curious I grew, and of course had no difficulty in persuading myself that my curiosity was friendly solicitude. That is the disguise that curiosity usually assumes to evade resentment. So I ruined one of the finest sentences of his disregarded monologue by cutting it short without ceremony.

"John Bartine," I said, "you must try to forgive me if I am wrong, but with the light that I have at present I cannot concede your right to go all to pieces when asked the time o' night. I cannot admit that it is proper to experience a mysterious reluctance to look your own watch in the face and to cherish in my presence, without explanation, painful emotions which are denied to me, and which are none of my business."

To this ridiculous speech Bartine made no immediate reply, but sat looking gravely into the fire. Fearing that I had offended I was about to apologize and beg him to think no more about the matter, when looking me calmly in the eyes he said:

"My dear fellow, the levity of your manner does not at all disguise the hideous impudence of your demand; but happily I had already decided to tell you what you wish to know, and no manifestation of your unworthiness to hear it shall alter my decision. Be good enough to give me your attention and you shall hear all about the matter.

"This watch," he said, "had been in my family for three generations before it fell to me. Its original owner, for whom it was made, was my great-grandfather, Bramwell Olcott Bartine, a wealthy planter of Colonial Virginia, and as stanch a Tory as ever lay awake nights contriving new kinds of maledictions for the head of Mr. Washington, and new methods of aiding and abetting good King George. One day this worthy gentleman had the deep misfortune to perform for his cause a service of capital importance which was not recognized as legitimate by those who suffered its disadvantages. It does not matter what it was, but among its minor consequences was my excellent ancestor's arrest one night in his own house by a party of Mr. Washington's rebels. He was permitted to say farewell to his weeping family, and was then marched away into the darkness which swallowed him up forever. Not the slenderest clue to his fate was ever found. After the war the most diligent inquiry and the offer of large rewards failed to turn up any of his captors or any fact concerning his disappearance. He had disappeared, and that was all."

Something in Bartine's manner that was not in his words— I hardly knew what it was—prompted me to ask:

"What is your view of the matter—of the justice of it?"

"My view of it," he flamed out, bringing his clenched hand down upon the table as if he had been in a public house dicing with blackguards—"my view of it is that it was a characteristically dastardly assassination by that damned traitor, Washington, and his ragamuffin rebels!"

For some minutes nothing was said. Bartine was recovering his temper, and I waited. Then I said:

"Was that all?"

"No—there was something else. A few weeks after my great-grandfather's arrest his watch was found lying on the porch at the front door of his dwelling. It was wrapped in a sheet of letter paper bearing the name of Rupert Bartine, his only son, my grandfather. I am wearing that watch."

Bartine paused. His usually restless black eyes were staring fixedly into the grate, a point of red light in each, reflected from the glowing coals. He seemed to have forgotten me. A sudden threshing of the branches of a tree outside one of the windows, and almost at the same instant a rattle of rain against the glass, recalled him to a sense of his surroundings. A storm had risen, heralded by a single gust of wind, and in a few moments the steady plash of the water on the pavement was distinctly heard. I hardly know why I relate this incident; it seemed somehow to have a certain significance and relevancy which I am unable now to discern. It at least added an element of seriousness, almost solemnity. Bartine resumed:

"I have a singular feeling toward this watch—a kind of affection for it. I like to have it about me, though partly from its weight, and partly for a reason I shall now explain, I seldom

carry it. The reason is this: Every evening when I have it with
me I feel an unaccountable desire to open and consult it, even
if I can think of no reason for wishing to know the time. But
if I yield to it, the moment my eyes rest upon the dial I am
filled with a mysterious apprehension—a sense of imminent
calamity. And this is the more insupportable the nearer it is
to eleven o'clock—by this watch, no matter what the actual
hour may be. After the hands have registered eleven the desire
to look is gone; I am entirely indifferent. Then I can consult
the thing as often as I like, with no more emotion than you
feel in looking at your own. Naturally I have trained myself
not to look at that watch in the evening before eleven; nothing
could induce me. Your insistence this evening upset me a trifle.
I felt very much as I suppose an opium-eater might feel if his

yearning for his special and particular kind of hell were rein-
forced by opportunity and advice.

"Now that is my story, and I have told it in the interest of
your trumpery science; but if on any evening hereafter you
observe me wearing this damnable watch, and you have the
thoughtfulness to ask me the hour, I shall beg leave to put
you to the inconvenience of being knocked down."

His humor did not amuse me. I could see that in relating his
delusion he was again somewhat disturbed. His concluding
smile was positively ghastly, and his eyes had resumed something more than their old restlessness; they shifted hither and
thither about the room with apparent aimlessness and I fancied had taken on a wild expression, such as is sometimes
observed in cases of dementia. Perhaps this was my own

141

imagination, but at any rate I was now persuaded that my friend was afflicted with a most singular and interesting monomania. Without, I trust, any abatement of my affectionate solicitude for him as a friend, I began to regard him as a patient, rich in possibilities of profitable study. Why not? Had he not described his delusion in the interest of science? Ah, poor fellow, he was doing more for science than he knew: not only his story but himself was in evidence. I should cure him if I could, of course, but first I should make a little experiment in psychology—nay, the experiment itself might be a step in his restoration.

"That is very frank and friendly of you, Bartine," I said cordially, "and I'm rather proud of your confidence. It is all very odd, certainly. Do you mind showing me the watch?"

He detached it from his waistcoat, chain and all, and passed it to me without a word. The case was of gold, very thick and strong, and singularly engraved. After closely examining the dial and observing that it was nearly twelve o'clock, I opened it at the back and was interested to observe an inner case of ivory, upon which was painted a miniature portrait in that exquisite and delicate manner which was in vogue during the eighteenth century.

"Why, bless my soul!" I exclaimed, feeling a sharp artistic delight—"how under the sun did you get that done? I thought miniature painting on ivory was a lost art."

"That," he replied, gravely smiling, "is not I. It is my excellent great-grandfather, the late Bramwell Olcott Bartine, Esquire, of Virginia. He was younger then than later—about my age, in fact. It is said to resemble me. Do you think so?"

"Resemble you? I should say so! Barring the costume, which I supposed you to have assumed out of compliment to the art— or for *vraisemblance*, so to say—and the no mustache, that portrait is you in every feature, line, and expression."

No more was said at that time. Bartine took a book from the table and began reading. I heard outside the incessant plash of the rain in the street. There were occasional hurried footfalls on the sidewalks; and once a slower, heavier tread seemed to cease at my door—a policeman, I thought, seeking shelter in the doorway. The boughs of the trees tapped significantly on the windowpanes, as if asking for admittance. I remember it all through these years and years of a wiser, graver life.

Seeing myself unobserved, I took the old-fashioned key that dangled from the chain and quickly turned back the hands of the watch a full hour; then, closing the case, I handed Bartine his property and saw him replace it on his person.

"I think you said," I began, with assumed carelessness, "that after eleven the sight of the dial no longer affects you. As it is now nearly twelve"—looking at my own timepiece—"perhaps, if you don't resent my pursuit of proof, you will look at it now."

He smiled good-humoredly, pulled out the watch again, opened it, and instantly sprang to his feet with a cry that Heaven has not had the mercy to permit me to forget! His eyes, their blackness strikingly intensified by the pallor of his face, were fixed upon the watch, which he clutched in both hands. For some time he remained in that attitude without uttering another sound; then, in a voice that I should not have recognized as his, he said:

"Damn you! It is two minutes to eleven!"

I was not unprepared for some such outbreak, and without rising replied, calmly enough:

"I beg your pardon. I must have misread your watch in setting my own by it."

He shut the case with a sharp snap and put the watch in his pocket. He looked at me and made an attempt to smile, but his lower lip quivered and he seemed unable to close his mouth. His hands, also, were shaking, and he thrust them, clenched, into the pockets of his sack coat. The courageous spirit was manifestly endeavoring to subdue the coward body. The effort was too great; he began to sway from side to side, as from vertigo, and before I could spring from my chair to support him his knees gave way and he pitched awkwardly forward and fell upon his face. I sprang to assist him to rise; but when John Bartine rises we shall all rise.

The postmortem examination disclosed nothing; every organ was normal and sound. But when the body had been prepared for burial a faint dark circle was seen to have developed around the neck; at least I was so assured by several persons who said they saw it, but of my own knowledge I cannot say if that was true.

Nor can I set limitations to the law of heredity. I do not know that in the spiritual world a sentiment or emotion may not survive the heart that held it, and seek expression in a kindred life, ages removed. Surely, if I were to guess at the fate of Bramwell Olcott Bartine, I should guess that he was hanged at eleven o'clock in the evening, and that he had been allowed several hours in which to prepare for the change.

As to John Bartine, my friend, my patient for five minutes, and—Heaven forgive me!—my victim for eternity, there is no more to say. He is buried, and his watch with him—I saw to that. May God rest his soul in Paradise, and the soul of his Virginian ancestor, if, indeed, they are two souls.

STALEY FLEMING'S HALLUCINATION

O F two men who were talking one was a physician.

"I sent for you, doctor," said the other, "but I don't think you can do me any good. Maybe you can recommend a specialist in psychopathy. I fancy I'm a bit loony."

"You look all right," the physician said.

"You shall judge—I have hallucinations. I wake every night and see in my room, intently watching me, a big black Newfoundland dog with a white forefoot."

"You say you wake. Are you sure about that? 'Hallucinations' are sometimes only dreams."

"Oh, I wake, all right. Sometimes I lie still a long time, looking at the dog as earnestly as the dog looks at me—I always leave the light going. When I can't endure it any longer I sit up in bed—and nothing is there!"

"' 'M, 'm. What is the beast's expression?"

"It seems to me sinister. Of course I know that, except in art, an animal's face in repose has always the same expression. But this is not a real animal. Newfoundland dogs are pretty mild-looking, you know. What's the matter with this one?"

"Really, my diagnosis would have no value. I am not going to treat the dog."

The physician laughed at his own pleasantry, but narrowly watched his patient from the corner of his eye. Presently he said, "Fleming, your description of the beast fits the dog of the late Atwell Barton."

Fleming half-rose from his chair, sat again, and made a visible attempt at indifference. "I remember Barton," he said. "I believe he was—it was reported that—wasn't there something suspicious in his death?"

Looking squarely now into the eyes of his patient, the physician said, "Three years ago the body of your old enemy, Atwell Barton, was found in the woods near his house and yours. He had been stabbed to death. There have been no arrests; there was no clue. Some of us had 'theories.' I had one. Have you?"

"I? Why, bless your soul, what could I know about it? You remember that I left for Europe almost immediately afterward—a considerable time afterward. In the few weeks since my return you could not expect me to construct a 'theory.' In fact, I have not given the matter a thought. What about his dog?"

"It was first to find the body. It died of starvation on his grave."

We do not know the inexorable law underlying coincidences. Staley Fleming did not, or he would perhaps not have sprung to his feet as the night wind brought in through the open window the long wailing howl of a distant dog. He strode several times across the room in the steadfast gaze of the physician; then, abruptly confronting him, almost shouted, "What has all this to do with my trouble, Dr. Halderman? You forget why you were sent for."

Rising, the physician laid his hand upon his patient's arm and said, gently, "Pardon me. I cannot diagnose your disorder offhand—tomorrow, perhaps. Please go to bed, leaving your door unlocked. I will pass the night here with your books. Can you call me without rising?"

"Yes, there is an electric bell."

"Good. If anything disturbs you, push the button without sitting up. Good night."

Comfortably installed in an armchair, the man of medicine stared into the glowing coals and thought deeply and long, but apparently to little purpose, for he frequently rose and, opening a door leading to the staircase, listened intently, then resumed his seat. Presently, however, he fell asleep, and when he woke it was past midnight. He stirred the failing fire, lifted a book from the table at his side and looked at the title. It was Denneker's *Meditations*. He opened it at random and began to read:

"Forasmuch as it is ordained of God that all flesh hath spirit and thereby taketh on spiritual powers, so, also, the spirit hath powers of the flesh, even when it is gone out of the flesh and liveth as a thing apart, as many a violence performed by wraith and lemure sheweth. And there be who say that man is not single in this, but the beasts have the like evil inducement, and—"

The reading was interrupted by a shaking of the house, as by the fall of a heavy object. The reader flung down the book, rushed from the room, and mounted the stairs to Fleming's bedchamber. He tried the door, but contrary to his instructions it was locked. He set his shoulder against it with such force that it gave way. On the floor near the disordered bed, in his night clothes, lay Fleming gasping away his life.

The physician raised the dying man's head from the floor and observed a wound in the throat. "I should have thought of this," he said, believing it suicide.

When the man was dead an examination disclosed the unmistakable marks of an animal's fangs deeply sunken into the jugular vein.

But there was no animal.

OUT
OF
DOG

OIL OF DOG

Y name is Boffer Bings. I was born of honest parents in one of the humbler walks of life, my father being a manufacturer of dog oil and my mother having a small studio in the shadow of the village church, where she disposed of unwelcome babes. In my boyhood I was trained to habits of industry; I not only assisted my father in procuring dogs for his vats, but was frequently employed by my mother to carry away the debris of her work in the studio. In performance of this duty I sometimes had need of all my natural intelligence, for all the law officers of the vicinity were opposed to my mother's business. They were not elected on an opposition ticket, and the matter had never been made a political issue; it just happened so. My father's business of making dog oil was, naturally, less unpopular, though the owners of missing dogs sometimes regarded him with suspicion, which was reflected, to some extent, upon me. My father had, as silent partners, all the physicians of the town, who seldom wrote a prescription which did not contain what they were pleased to designate as *Ol. can.* It is really the most valuable medicine ever discovered. But most persons are unwilling to make personal sacrifices for the afflicted, and it was evident that many of the fattest dogs in town had been forbidden to play with me—a fact which pained my young sensibilities, and at one time came near driving me to become a pirate.

Looking back upon those days, I cannot but regret, at times, that by indirectly bringing my beloved parents to their death I was the author of misfortunes profoundly affecting my future.

One evening while passing my father's oil factory with the body of a foundling from my mother's studio I saw a constable who seemed to be closely watching my movements. Young as I was, I had learned that a constable's acts, of whatever apparent character, are prompted by the most reprehensible motives, and I avoided him by dodging into the oilery by a side door which happened to stand ajar. I locked it at once and was alone with my dead. My father had retired for the night. The only light in the place came from the furnace, which glowed a deep, rich crimson under one of the vats, casting ruddy reflections on the walls. Within the cauldron the oil still rolled in indolent ebullition, occasionally pushing to the surface a piece of dog. Seating myself to wait for the constable to go away, I held the naked body of the foundling in my lap and tenderly stroked its short, silken hair. Ah, how beautiful it was! Even at that early age I was passionately fond of children, and as I looked upon this cherub I could almost find it in my heart to wish that the small, red wound upon its breast—the work of my dear mother—had not been mortal.

It had been my custom to throw the babes into the river which nature had thoughtfully provided for the purpose, but that night I did not dare to leave the oilery for fear of the constable. "After all," I said to myself, "it cannot greatly matter if I put it into this cauldron. My father will never know the bones from those of a puppy, and the few deaths which may result from administering another kind of oil for the incomparable *Ol. can.* are not important in a population which increases so rapidly." In short, I took the first step in crime and brought myself untold sorrow by casting the babe into the cauldron.

The next day, somewhat to my surprise, my father, rubbing his hands with satisfaction, informed me and my mother that he had obtained the finest quality of oil that was ever seen; that the physicians to whom he had shown samples had so pronounced it. He added that he had no knowledge as to how the result was obtained; the dogs had been treated in all respects as usual, and were of an ordinary breed. I deemed it my duty to explain—which I did, though palsied would have been my tongue if I could have foreseen the consequences. Bewailing their previous ignorance of the advantages of combining their industries, my parents at once took measures to repair the error. My mother removed her studio to a wing of the factory building and my duties in connection with the business ceased; I was no longer required to dispose of the bodies of the small superfluous, and there was no need of alluring dogs to their doom, for my father discarded them altogether, though they still had an honorable place in the name of the oil. So suddenly thrown into idleness, I might naturally have been expected to become vicious and dissolute, but I did not. The holy influence of my dear mother was ever about me to protect me from the temptations which beset youth, and my father was a deacon in a church. Alas, that

through my fault these estimable persons should have come to so bad an end!

Finding a double profit in her business, my mother now devoted herself to it with a new assiduity. She removed not only superfluous and unwelcome babes to order, but went out into the highways and byways, gathering in children of a larger growth, and even such adults as she could entice to the oilery. My father, too, enamored of the superior quality of oil produced, purveyed for his vats with diligence and zeal. The conversion of their neighbors into dog oil became, in short, the one passion of their lives—an absorbing and overwhelming greed took possession of their souls and served them in place of a hope in heaven—by which, also, they were inspired.

So enterprising had they now become that a public meeting was held and resolutions passed severely censuring them. It was intimated by the chairman that any further raids upon

the population would be met in a spirit of hostility. My poor parents left the meeting brokenhearted, desperate and, I believe, not altogether sane. Anyhow, I deemed it prudent not to enter the oilery with them that night, but slept outside in a stable.

At about midnight some mysterious impulse caused me to rise and peer through a window into the furnace room, where I knew my father now slept. The fires were burning as brightly as if the following day's harvest had been expected to be abundant. One of the large cauldrons was slowly "walloping" with a mysterious appearance of self-restraint, as if it bided its time to put forth its full energy. My father was not in bed; he had risen in his night clothes and was preparing a noose in a strong cord. From the looks which he cast at the door of my mother's bedroom I knew too well the purpose that he had in mind. Speechless and motionless with terror, I could do nothing in prevention or warning. Suddenly the door of my mother's apartment was opened, noiselessly, and the two confronted each other, both apparently surprised. The lady, also, was in her night clothes, and she held in her right hand the tool of her trade, a long, narrow-bladed dagger.

She, too, had been unable to deny herself the last profit which the unfriendly action of the citizens and my absence had left her. For one instant they looked into each other's blazing eyes and then sprang together with indescribable fury. Round and round the room they struggled, the man cursing, the woman shrieking, both fighting like demons—she to strike him with the dagger, he to strangle her with his great bare hands. I know not how long I had the unhappiness to observe this disagreeable instance of domestic infelicity, but at last, after a more than usually vigorous struggle, the combatants suddenly moved apart.

My father's breast and my mother's weapon showed evidences of contact. For another instant they glared at each other in the most unamiable way; then my poor, wounded father, feeling the hand of death upon him, leaped forward, unmindful of resistance, grasped my dear mother in his arms, dragged her to the side of the boiling cauldron, collected all his failing energies, and sprang in with her! In a moment, both had disappeared and were adding their oil to that of the committee of citizens who had called the day before with an invitation to the public meeting.

Convinced that these unhappy events closed to me every avenue to an honorable career in that town, I removed to the famous city of Otumwee, where these memoirs are written with a heart full of remorse for a heedless act entailing so dismal a commercial disaster.

THE HYPNOTIST

B Y those of my friends who happen to know that I sometimes amuse myself with hypnotism, mind reading and
kindred phenomena, I am frequently asked if I have a
clear conception of the nature of whatever principle underlies
them. To this question I always reply that I neither have nor
desire to have. I am no investigator with an ear at the keyhole
of Nature's workshop, trying with vulgar curiosity to steal
the secrets of her trade. The interests of science are as little
to me as mine seem to have been to science.

Doubtless the phenomena in question are simple enough,
and in no way transcend our powers of comprehension if only
we could find the clue; but for my part I prefer not to find it,
for I am of a singularly romantic disposition, deriving more
gratification from mystery than from knowledge. It was commonly remarked of me when I was a child that my big blue
eyes appeared to have been made rather to look into than look
out of—such was their dreamful beauty, and in my frequent
periods of abstraction, their indifference to what was going on.
In those peculiarities they resembled, I venture to think, the
soul which lies behind them, always more intent upon some
lovely conception which it has created in its own image than
concerned about the laws of nature and the material frame of
things. All this, irrelevant and egotistic as it may seem, is
related by way of accounting for the meagerness of the light
that I am able to throw upon a subject that has engaged so

156

much of my attention, and concerning which there is so keen and general a curiosity. With my powers and opportunities, another person might doubtless have an explanation for much of what I present simply as narrative.

My first knowledge that I possessed unusual powers came to me in my fourteenth year, when at school. Happening one day to have forgotten to bring my noonday luncheon, I gazed longingly at that of a small girl who was preparing to eat hers. Looking up, her eyes met mine and she seemed unable to withdraw them. After a moment of hesitancy she came forward in an absent kind of way and without a word surrendered her little basket with its tempting contents and walked away. Inexpressibly pleased, I relieved my hunger and destroyed the basket. After that I had not the trouble to bring a luncheon for myself: that little girl was my daily purveyor; and not infrequently in satisfying my simple need from her frugal store I combined pleasure and profit by constraining her attendance at the feast and making misleading proffer of the viands, which eventually I consumed to the last fragment. The girl was always persuaded that she had eaten all herself; and later in the day her tearful complaints of hunger surprised the teacher, entertained the pupils, earned for her the sobriquet of Greedy-Gut, and filled me with a peace past understanding.

A disagreeable feature of this otherwise satisfactory condition of things was the necessary secrecy: the transfer of the luncheon, for example, had to be made at some distance from the madding crowd, in a wood; and I blush to think of the many other unworthy subterfuges entailed by the situation. As I was (and am) naturally of a frank and open disposition, these became more and more irksome, and but for the reluctance of my parents to renounce the obvious advantages of the new regime I would gladly have reverted to the old. The plan that I finally adopted to free myself from the consequences of my own powers excited a wide and keen interest at the time, and that part of it which consisted in the death of the girl was severely condemned, but it is hardly pertinent to the scope of this narrative.

For some years afterward I had little opportunity to practice hypnotism; such small essays as I made at it were com-

monly barren of other recognition than solitary confinement
on a bread-and-water diet; sometimes, indeed, they elicited
nothing better than the cat-o'-nine-tails. It was when I was
about to leave the scene of these small disappointments that
my one really important feat was performed.

I had been called into the warden's office and given a suit of
civilian's clothing, a trifling sum of money, and a great deal
of advice, which I am bound to confess was of a much better
quality than the clothing. As I was passing out of the gate
into the light of freedom I suddenly turned and looking the
warden gravely in the eye, soon had him in control.

"You are an ostrich," I said.

At the postmortem examination the stomach was found to
contain a great quantity of indigestible articles mostly of
wood or metal. Stuck fast in the esophagus and constituting,
according to the coroner's jury, the immediate cause of death,
one doorknob.

I was by nature a good and affectionate son, but as I took
my way into the great world from which I had been so long
secluded I could not help remembering that all my misfortunes
had flowed like a stream from the niggard economy of my
parents in the matter of school luncheons; and I knew of no
reason to think they had reformed.

On the road between Succotash Hill and South Asphyxia is
a little open field which once contained a shanty known as Pete
Gilstrap's Place, where that gentleman used to murder travelers for a living. The death of Mr. Gilstrap and the diversion
of nearly all the travel to another road occurred so nearly at
the same time that no one has ever been able to say which
was cause and which effect. Anyhow, the field was now a
desolation and the Place had long been burned. It was while
going afoot to South Asphyxia, the home of my childhood,
that I found both my parents on their way to the Hill. They
had hitched their team and were eating luncheon under an oak
tree in the center of the field. The sight of the luncheon called
up painful memories of my schooldays and roused the sleeping
lion in my breast. Approaching the guilty couple, who at once
recognized me, I ventured to suggest that I share their
hospitality.

As I was passing
out of the gate and
into the light of free
dom I suddenly turn
ed and looking the
warden gravely in the
eye, soon had him in
control.
"You are an ostrich,"
        I said.

"Of this cheer, my son," said the author of my being, with characteristic pomposity, which age had not withered, "there is sufficient for but two. I am not, I hope, insensible to the hunger-light in your eyes, but—"

My father has never completed that sentence; what he mistook for hunger-light was simply the earnest gaze of the hypnotist. In a few seconds he was at my service. A few more sufficed for the lady, and the dictates of a just resentment could be carried into effect. "My former father," I said, "I presume that it is known to you that you and this lady are no longer what you were?"

"I have observed a certain subtle change" was the rather dubious reply of the old gentleman. "It is perhaps attributable to age."

"It is more than that," I explained. "It goes to character—to species. You and the lady here are, in truth, two broncos—wild stallions both, and unfriendly."

"Why, John," exclaimed my dear mother, "you don't mean to say that I am—"

"Madam," I replied, solemnly, fixing my eyes again upon hers, "you are."

Scarcely had the words fallen from my lips when she dropped upon her hands and knees, and backing up to the old man squealed like a demon and delivered a vicious kick upon his shin! An instant later he was himself down on all fours, headed away from her and flinging his feet at her simultaneously and successively. With equal earnestness but inferior agility, because of her hampering body gear, she plied her own. Their flying legs crossed and mingled in the most bewildering way; their feet sometimes meeting squarely in midair, their bodies thrust forward, falling flat upon the ground and for a moment helpless. On recovering themselves they would resume the combat, uttering their frenzy in the nameless sounds of the furious brutes which they believed themselves to be—the whole region rang with their clamor! Round and round they wheeled, the blows of their feet falling "like lightnings from the mountain cloud." They plunged and reared backward upon their knees, struck savagely at each other with awkward descending blows of both fists at once, and dropped again upon their hands as if unable to maintain the upright position of the body. Grass and pebbles were torn from the soil by hands and feet; clothing, hair, faces inexpressibly defiled with dust and blood. Wild, inarticulate screams of rage attested the delivery of the blows; groans, grunts and gasps their receipt. Nothing more truly military was ever seen at Gettysburg or Waterloo: the valor of my dear parents in the hour of danger can never cease to be to me a source of pride and gratification. At the end of it all two battered, tattered, bloody and fragmentary vestiges of mortality attested the solemn fact that the author of the strife was an orphan.

Arrested for provoking a breach of the peace, I was, and have ever since been, tried in the Court of Technicalities and Continuances whence, after fifteen years of proceedings, my attorney is moving heaven and earth to get the case taken to the Court of Remandment for New Trials.

Such are a few of my principal experiments in the mysterious force or agency known as hypnotic suggestion. Whether or not it could be employed by a bad man for an unworthy purpose I am unable to say.

THE DIFFICULTY OF CROSSING A FIELD

ONE morning in July 1854, a planter named Williamson, living six miles from Selma, Alabama, was sitting with his wife and a child on the veranda of his dwelling. Immediately in front of the house was a lawn, perhaps fifty yards in extent between the house and public road, or, as it was called, the "pike." Beyond this road lay a close-cropped pasture of some ten acres, level and without a tree, rock, or any natural or artificial object on its surface. At the time there was not even a domestic animal in the field. In another field, beyond the pasture, a dozen slaves were at work under an overseer.

Throwing away the stump of a cigar, the planter rose, saying, "I forgot to tell Andrew about those horses." Andrew was the overseer.

Williamson strolled leisurely down the gravel walk, plucking a flower as he went, passed across the road and into the pasture, pausing a moment as he closed the gate leading into it, to greet a passing neighbor, Armour Wren, who lived on an adjoining plantation. Mr. Wren was in an open carriage with his son James, a lad of thirteen. When he had driven some two hundred yards from the point of meeting, Mr. Wren said to his son, "I forgot to tell Mr. Williamson about those horses."

Mr. Wren had sold to Mr. Williamson some horses, which were to have been sent for that day, but for some reason not now remembered it would be inconvenient to deliver them until

162

the morrow. The coachman was directed to drive back, and as the vehicle turned Williamson was seen by all three, walking leisurely across the pasture. At that moment one of the coach horses stumbled and came near falling. It had no more than fairly recovered itself when James Wren cried, "Why, father, what has become of Mr. Williamson?"

It is not the purpose of this narrative to answer that question.

Mr. Wren's strange account of the matter, given under oath in the course of legal proceedings relating to the Williamson estate, here follows:

"My son's exclamation caused me to look toward the spot where I had seen the deceased [sic] an instant before, but he was not there, nor was he anywhere visible. I cannot say that at the moment I was greatly startled, or realized the gravity of the occurrence, though I thought it singular. My son, however, was greatly astonished and kept repeating his question in different forms until we arrived at the gate. My black boy Sam was similarly affected, even in a greater degree, but I reckon more by my son's manner than by anything he had himself observed. [This sentence in the testimony was stricken out.] As we got out of the carriage at the gate of the field, and while Sam was hanging [sic] the team to the fence, Mrs. Williamson, with her child in her arms and followed by several servants, came running down the walk in great excitement, crying, 'He is gone, he is gone! O God! what an awful thing!' and many other such exclamations, which I do not distinctly recollect. I got from them the impression that they related to something more than the mere disappearance of her husband, even if that had occurred before her eyes. Her manner was wild, but not more so, I think, than was natural under the circumstances. I have no reason to think she had at that time lost her mind. I have never since seen nor heard of Mr. Williamson."

This testimony, as might have been expected, was corroborated in almost every particular by the only other eyewitness (if that is a proper term)—the lad James. Mrs. Williamson had lost her reason and the servants were, of course, not competent to testify. The boy James Wren had declared at first that he *saw* the disappearance, but there is nothing of this in his testimony given in court. None of the field hands working in the field to which Williamson was going had seen him at all, and the most rigorous search of the entire plantation and adjoining country failed to supply a clue. The most monstrous and grotesque fictions, originating with the blacks, were current in that part of the state for many years, and probably are to this day; but what has been here related is all that is certainly known of the matter. The courts decided that Williamson was dead, and his estate was distributed according to law.

AN ARREST

HAVING murdered his brother-in-law, Orrin Brower of Kentucky was a fugitive from justice. From the county jail where he had been confined to await his trial he had escaped by knocking down his jailer with an iron bar, robbing him of his keys and, opening the outer door, walking out into the night. The jailer being unarmed, Brower got no weapon with which to defend his recovered liberty. As soon as he was out of the town he had the folly to enter a forest; this was many years ago, when that region was wilder than it is now.

The night was pretty dark, with neither moon nor stars visible, and as Brower had never dwelt thereabout, and knew nothing of the lay of the land, he was, naturally, not long in losing himself. He could not have said if he were getting farther away from the town or going back to it—a most important matter to Orrin Brower. He knew that in either case a posse of citizens with a pack of bloodhounds would soon be on his track and his chance of escape was very slender; but he did not wish to assist in his own pursuit. Even an added hour of freedom was worth having.

Suddenly he emerged from the forest into an old road, and there before him saw, indistinctly, the figure of a man, motionless in the gloom. It was too late to retreat: the fugitive felt that at the first movement back toward the wood he would be, as he afterward explained, "filled with buckshot." So the two

165

stood there like trees, Brower nearly suffocated by the activity
of his own heart; the other—the emotions of the other are not
recorded.

A moment later—it may have been an hour—the moon sailed
into a patch of unclouded sky and the hunted man saw that
visible embodiment of Law lift an arm and point significantly
toward and beyond him. He understood. Turning his back to his
captor, he walked submissively away in the direction indicated,
looking to neither the right nor the left, hardly daring to
breathe, his head and back actually aching with a prophecy of
buckshot.

Brower was as courageous a criminal as ever lived to be
hanged; that was shown by the conditions of awful personal
peril in which he had coolly killed his brother-in-law. It is
needless to relate them here; they came out at his trial, and
the revelation of his calmness in confronting them came near
to saving his neck. But what would you have?—when a brave
man is beaten, he submits.

So they pursued their journey jailward along the old road
through the woods. Only once did Brower venture a turn of
the head: just once, when he was in deep shadow and he knew

that the other was in moonlight, he looked backward. His captor was Burton Duff, the jailer, as white as death and bearing upon his brow the livid mark of the iron bar. Orrin Brower had no further curiosity.

Eventually they entered the town, which was all alight, but deserted; only the women and children remained, and they were off the streets. Straight toward the jail the criminal held his way. Straight up to the main entrance he walked, laid his hand upon the knob of the heavy iron door, pushed it open without command, entered and found himself in the presence of a half-dozen armed men. Then he turned. Nobody else entered.

On a table in the corridor lay the dead body of Burton Duff.

MOXON'S MASTER

RE YOU serious?—Do you really believe that a machine thinks?"

I got no immediate reply. Moxon was apparently intent upon the coals in the grate, touching them deftly here and there with the fire-poker till they signified a sense of his attention by a brighter glow. For several weeks I had been observing in him a growing habit of delay in answering even the most trivial of commonplace questions. His air, however, was that of preoccupation rather than deliberation. One might have said that he had something on his mind.

Presently he said:

"What is a 'machine'? The word has been variously defined. Here is one definition from a popular dictionary: 'Any instrument or organization by which power is applied and made effective, or a desired effect produced.' Well, then, is not a man a machine? And you will admit that he thinks—or thinks he thinks."

"If you do not wish to answer my question," I said, rather testily, "why not say so? All that you say is mere evasion. You know well enough that when I say 'machine' I do not mean a man, but something that man has made and controls."

"When it does not control him," he said, rising abruptly and looking out of a window, whence nothing was visible in the blackness of a stormy night. A moment later he turned about and with a smile said, "I beg your pardon; I had no thought of evasion. I considered the dictionary man's unconscious testi-

168

mony suggestive and worth something in the discussion. I can give your question a direct answer easily enough: I do believe that a machine thinks about the work that it is doing."

That was direct enough, certainly. It was not altogether pleasing, for it tended to confirm a sad suspicion that Moxon's devotion to study and work in his machine shop had not been good for him. I knew, for one thing, that he suffered from insomnia, and that is no light affliction. Had it affected his mind? His reply to my question seemed to me then evidence that it had; perhaps I should think differently about it now. I was younger then, and among the blessings that are not denied to youth is ignorance. Incited by that great stimulant to controversy, I said:

"And what, pray, does it think with—in the absence of a brain?"

The reply, coming with less than his customary delay, took his favorite form of counterinterrogation:

"With what does a plant think—in the absence of a brain?"

"Ah, plants also belong to the philosopher class! I should be pleased to know some of their conclusions; you may omit the premises."

"Perhaps," he replied, apparently unaffected by my foolish irony, "you may be able to infer their convictions from their acts. I will spare you the familiar examples of the sensitive mimosa, the several insectivorous flowers and those whose stamens bend down and shake their pollen upon the entering bee in order that he may fertilize their distant mates. But observe this. In an open spot in my garden I planted a climbing vine. When it was barely above the surface I set a stake into the soil a yard away. The vine at once made for it, but as it was about to reach it after several days I removed it a few feet. The vine at once altered its course, making an acute angle, and again made for the stake. This maneuver was repeated several times, but finally, as if discouraged, the vine abandoned the pursuit and ignoring further attempts to divert it traveled to a small tree, farther away, which it climbed.

"Roots of the eucalyptus will prolong themselves incredibly in search of moisture. A well-known horticulturist relates that one entered an old drain pipe and followed it until it came to a break, where a section of the pipe had been removed to make way for a stone wall that had been built across its course. The root left the drain and followed the wall until it found an opening where a stone had fallen out. It crept through and, following the other side of the wall back to the drain, entered the unexplored part and resumed its journey."

"And all this?"

"Can you miss the significance of it? It shows the consciousness of plants. It proves that they think."

"Even if it did—what then? We were speaking, not of plants, but of machines. They may be composed partly of wood —wood that no longer has vitality—or wholly of metal. Is thought an attribute also of the mineral kingdom?"

"How else do you explain the phenomena, for example, of crystallization?"

"I do not explain them."

"Because you cannot without affirming what you wish to deny, namely, intelligent cooperation among the constituent elements of the crystals. When soldiers form lines, or hollow squares, you call it reason. When wild geese in flight take the form of a letter V you say instinct. When the homogeneous atoms of a mineral, moving freely in solution, arrange themselves into shapes mathematically perfect, or particles of frozen moisture into the symmetrical and beautiful forms of snowflakes, you have nothing to say. You have not even invented a name to conceal your heroic unreason."

Moxon was speaking with unusual animation and earnestness. As he paused I heard in an adjoining room known to me as his machine shop, which no one but himself was permitted to enter, a singular thumping sound, as of someone pounding upon a table with an open hand. Moxon heard it at the same moment and, visibly agitated, rose and hurriedly passed into the room whence it came. I thought it odd that anyone else should be in there, and my interest in my friend—with doubtless a touch of unwarrantable curiosity—led me to listen intently, though, I am happy to say, not at the keyhole. There were confused sounds, as of a struggle or scuffle; the floor shook. I distinctly heard hard breathing and a hoarse whisper which said, "Damn you!" Then all was silent, and presently Moxon reappeared and said, with a rather sorry smile:

"Pardon me for leaving you so abruptly. I have a machine in there that lost its temper and cut up rough."

Fixing my eyes steadily upon his left cheek, which was traversed by four parallel excoriations showing blood, I said: "How would it do to trim its nails?"

I could have spared myself the jest; he gave it no attention, but seated himself in the chair that he had left and resumed the interrupted monologue as if nothing had occurred.

"Doubtless you do not hold with those (I need not name them to a man of your reading) who have taught that all matter is sentient, that every atom is a living, feeling, conscious being. *I* do. There is no such thing as dead, inert matter. It is all alive; all instinct with force, actual and potential; all sensitive to the same forces in its environment and susceptible to the contagion of higher and subtler ones residing in such superior organisms as it may be brought into relation with, as those of man when he is fashioning it into an instrument of his will. It absorbs something of his intelligence and purpose— more of them in proportion to the complexity of the resulting machine and that of its work.

"Do you happen to recall Herbert Spencer's definition of life? I read it thirty years ago. He may have altered it afterward, for anything I know, but in all that time I have been unable to think of a single word that could profitably be changed or added or removed. It seems to me not only the best definition, but the only possible one.

" 'Life,' he says, 'is a definite combination of heterogeneous changes, both simultaneous and successive, in correspondence with external coexistences and sequences.' "

"That defines the phenomenon," I said, "but gives no hint of its cause."

"That," he replied, "is all that any definition can do. As Mill points out, we know nothing of cause except as an antecedent— nothing of effect except as a consequent. Of certain phenomena, one never occurs without another, which is dissimilar: the first in point of time we call cause, the second, effect. One who had many times seen a rabbit pursued by a dog, and had never seen rabbits and dogs otherwise, would think the rabbit the cause of the dog.

"But I fear," he added, laughing naturally enough, "that my rabbit is leading me a long way from the track of my legitimate quarry. I'm indulging in the pleasure of the chase for its own sake. What I want you to observe is that in Herbert Spencer's definition of life the activity of a machine is included—there is nothing in the definition that is not applicable to it. According to this sharpest of observers and deepest of thinkers, if a man during his period of activity is alive, so is a machine when in operation. As an inventor and constructor of machines I know that to be true."

Moxon was silent for a long time, gazing absently into the fire. It was growing late and I thought it time to be going, but somehow I did not like the notion of leaving him in that isolated house, all alone except for the presence of some person of whose nature my conjectures could go no further than that it was unfriendly, perhaps malign. Leaning toward him and looking earnestly into his eyes while making a motion with my hand through the door of his workshop, I said:

"Moxon, whom have you in there?"

Somewhat to my surprise he laughed lightly and answered without hesitation:

"Nobody. The incident that you have in mind was caused by my folly in leaving a machine in action with nothing to act upon, while I undertook the interminable task of enlightening your understanding. Do you happen to know that Consciousness is the creature of Rhythm?"

"O bother them both!" I replied, rising and laying hold of my overcoat. "I'm going to wish you good night. And I'll add the hope that the machine which you inadvertently left in action will have her gloves on the next time you think it needful to stop her."

Without waiting to observe the effect of my shot I left the house.

Rain was falling, and the darkness was intense. In the sky beyond the crest of a hill toward which I groped my way along precarious plank sidewalks and across miry, unpaved streets I could see the faint glow of the city's lights, but behind me nothing was visible but a single window of Moxon's house. It glowed with what seemed to me a mysterious and fateful meaning. I knew it was an uncurtained aperture in my friend's machine shop, and I had little doubt that he had resumed the studies interrupted by his duties as my instructor in mechanical consciousness and the fatherhood of Rhythm. Odd, and in some degree humorous, as his convictions seemed to me at that time, I could not wholly divest myself of the feeling that they had some tragic relation to his life and character—perhaps to his destiny—although I no longer entertained the notion that they were the vagaries of a disordered mind. Whatever might be thought of his views, his exposition of them was too logical for that. Over and over, his last words came back to me: "Consciousness is the creature of Rhythm." Bald and terse as the statement was, I now found it infinitely alluring. At each recurrence it broadened in meaning and deepened in suggestion. Why, here (I thought) is something upon which to found a philosophy. If consciousness is the product of rhythm, all things *are* conscious, for all have motion, and all motion is rhythmic. I wondered if Moxon knew the significance and breadth of his thought—the scope of this momentous generalization; or had he arrived at his philosophic faith by the tortuous and uncertain road of observation?

That faith was then new to me, and all Moxon's expounding had failed to make me a convert; but now it seemed as if a great light shone about me, like that which fell upon Saul of Tarsus; and out there in the storm and darkness and solitude I experienced what Lewes calls "the endless variety and excitement of philosophic thought." I exulted in a new sense of knowledge, a new pride of reason. My feet seemed hardly to touch the earth; it was as if I were uplifted and borne through the air by invisible wings.

Yielding to an impulse to seek further light from him whom I now recognized as my master and guide, I had unconsciously turned about, and almost before I was aware of having done so found myself again at Moxon's door. I was drenched with rain, but felt no discomfort. Unable in my excitement to find the doorbell I instinctively tried the knob. It turned and, entering, I mounted the stairs to the room that I had so recently left. All was dark and silent; Moxon, as I had supposed, was in the adjoining room—the machine shop. Groping along the wall until I found the communicating door I knocked loudly several times but got no response, which I attributed to the uproar outside, for the wind was blowing a gale and dashing the rain against the thin-walls in sheets. The drumming upon the shingle roof spanning the unceiled room was loud and incessant.

I had never been invited into the machine shop—had, indeed, been denied admittance, as had all others, with one exception, a skilled metalworker, of whom no one knew anything except that his name was Haley and his habit silence. But in my spiritual exaltation, discretion and civility were alike forgotten and I opened the door. What I saw took all philosophical speculation out of me in short order.

Moxon sat facing me at the farther side of a small table upon which a single candle made all the light that was in the room. Opposite him, his back toward me, sat another person. On the table between the two was a chessboard; the men were playing. I knew little of chess, but as only a few pieces were on the board it was obvious that the game was near its close. Moxon was intensely interested—not so much, it seemed to me, in the game as in his antagonist, upon whom he had fixed so intent a look that, standing though I did directly in the line of his vision, I was altogether unobserved. His face was ghastly white, and his eyes glittered like diamonds. Of his antagonist I had only a back view, but that was sufficient; I should not have cared to see his face.

He was apparently not more than five feet in height, with proportions suggesting those of a gorilla—a tremendous breadth of shoulders, thick, short neck and broad, squat head, which had a tangled growth of black hair and was topped with a crimson fez. A tunic of the same color, belted tightly to the waist, reached the seat—apparently a box—upon which he sat; his legs and feet were not seen. His left forearm appeared to rest in his lap; he moved his pieces with his right hand, which seemed disproportionately long.

I had shrunk back and now stood a little to one side of the doorway and in shadow. If Moxon had looked farther than the face of his opponent he could have observed nothing now, except that the door was open. Something forbade me either to enter or to retire, a feeling—I know not how it came—that I was in the presence of an imminent tragedy and might serve my friend by remaining. With a scarcely conscious rebellion against the indelicacy of the act, I remained.

The play was rapid. Moxon hardly glanced at the board before making his moves, and to my unskilled eye seemed to move the piece most convenient to his hand, his motions in doing so being quick, nervous and lacking in precision. The response of his antagonist, while equally prompt in the inception, was made with a slow, uniform, mechanical and, I thought, somewhat theatrical movement of the arm that was a sore trial to my patience. There was something unearthly about it all, and I caught myself shuddering. But I was wet and cold.

Two or three times after moving a piece the stranger slightly inclined his head, and each time I observed that Moxon shifted his king. All at once the thought came to me that the man was dumb. And then that he was a machine—an automaton chess-player! Then I remembered that Moxon had once spoken to me of having invented such a piece of mechanism, though I did not understand that it had actually been constructed. Was all his talk about the consciousness and intelligence of machines merely a prelude to eventual exhibition of this device—only a trick to intensify the effect of its mechanical action upon me in my ignorance of its secret?

A fine end, this, of all my intellectual transports—my "endless variety and excitement of philosophic thought"! I was about to retire in disgust when something occurred to hold my curiosity. I observed a shrug of the thing's great shoulders, as if it were irritated, and so natural was this—so entirely human—that in my new view of the matter it startled me. Nor was that all, for a moment later it struck the table sharply with its clenched hand. At that gesture Moxon seemed even more startled than I. He pushed his chair a little backward, as in alarm.

Presently Moxon, whose play it was, raised his hand high above the board, pounced upon one of his pieces like a sparrow hawk and with the exclamation "Checkmate!" rose quickly to his feet and stepped behind his chair. The automaton sat motionless.

The wind had now gone down, but I heard, at lessening in-

tervals and progressively louder, the rumble and roll of thunder. In the pauses between I now became conscious of a low humming or buzzing which, like the thunder, grew momentarily louder and more distinct. It seemed to come from the body of the automaton, and was unmistakably a whirring of wheels. It gave me the impression of a disordered mechanism which had escaped the repressive and regulating action of some controlling part—an effect such as might be expected if a pawl should be jostled from the teeth of a ratchet wheel. But before I had time for much conjecture as to its nature my attention was taken by the strange motions of the automaton itself. A slight but continuous convulsion appeared to have

possession of it. In body and head it shook like a man with palsy or an ague chill, and the motion augmented every moment until the entire figure was in violent agitation. Suddenly it sprang to its feet and with a movement almost too quick for the eye to follow shot forward across table and chair, with both arms thrust forth to their full length—the posture and lunge of a diver. Moxon tried to throw himself backward out of reach, but he was too late: I saw the horrible thing's hands close upon his throat, his own clutch its wrists. Then the table was overturned, the candle thrown to the floor and extinguished, and all was black dark. But the noise of the struggle was dreadfully distinct, and most terrible of all were the raucous, squawking sounds made by the strangled man's efforts to breathe. Guided by the infernal hubbub, I sprang to the rescue of my friend, but had hardly taken a stride in the darkness when the whole room blazed with a blinding white light that burned into my brain and heart and memory a vivid picture of the combatants on the floor, Moxon underneath, his throat still in the clutch of those iron hands, his head forced backward, his eyes protruding, his mouth wide open and his tongue thrust out; and—horrible contrast!—upon the painted face of his assassin an expression of tranquil and profound thought, as in the solution of a problem in chess! This I observed, then all was blackness and silence.

Three days later I recovered consciousness in a hospital. As the memory of that tragic night slowly evolved in my ailing brain I recognized in my attendant Moxon's confidential workman, Haley. Responding to a look he approached, smiling.

"Tell me about it," I managed to say, faintly—"all about it."

"Certainly," he said. "You were carried unconscious from a burning house—Moxon's. Nobody knows how you came to be there. You may have to do a little explaining. The origin of the fire is a bit mysterious, too. My own notion is that the house was struck by lightning."

"And Moxon?"

"Buried yesterday—what was left of him."

Apparently this reticent person could unfold himself on occasion. When imparting shocking intelligence to the sick he was affable enough. After some moments of the keenest mental suffering I ventured to ask another question:

"Who rescued me?"

"Well, if that interests you—I did."

"Thank you, Mr. Haley, and may God bless you for it. Did you rescue, also, that charming product of your skill, the automaton chess-player that murdered its inventor?"

The man was silent a long time, looking away from me. Presently he turned and gravely said:

"Do you know that?"

"I do," I replied. "I saw it done."

That was many years ago. If asked today I should answer less confidently.

KILLED AT
RESACA

HE best soldier of our staff was Lieutenant Herman Brayle, one of the two aides-de-camp. I don't remember where the general picked him up; from some Ohio regiment, I think. None of us had previously known him, and it would have been strange if we had, for no two of us came from the same state, nor even from adjoining states. The general seemed to think that a position on his staff was a distinction that should be so judiciously conferred as not to beget any sectional jealousies and imperil the integrity of that part of the country which was still an integer. He would not even choose officers from his own command, but by some jugglery at department headquarters obtained them from other brigades. Under such circumstances, a man's service had to be very distinguished indeed to be heard of by his family and the friends of his youth; and "the speaking trump of fame" was a trifle hoarse from loquacity, anyhow.

Lieutenant Brayle was more than six feet in height and of splendid proportions, with the light hair and gray-blue eyes which men so gifted usually find associated with a high order of courage. As he was commonly in full uniform, especially in action, when most officers are content to be less flamboyantly attired, he was a very striking and conspicuous figure. As to the rest, he had a gentleman's manners, a scholar's head, and a lion's heart. His age was about thirty.

We all soon came to like Brayle as much as we admired him,

and it was with sincere concern that in the engagement at Stone's River—our first action after he joined us—we observed that he had one most objectionable and unsoldierly quality: he was vain of his courage. During all the vicissitudes and mutations of that hideous encounter, whether our troops were fighting on the open cotton fields, in the cedar thickets, or behind the railway embankment, he did not once take cover, except when sternly commanded to do so by the general, who usually had other things to think of than the lives of his staff officers—or those of his men, for that matter.

In every later engagement while Brayle was with us it was the same way. He would sit his horse like an equestrian statue, in a storm of bullets and grape, in the most exposed places— wherever, in fact, duty, requiring him to go, permitted him to remain—when, without trouble and with distinct advantage to his reputation for common sense, he might have been in such security as is possible on a battlefield in the brief intervals of personal inaction.

On foot, from necessity or in deference to his dismounted commander or associates, his conduct was the same. He would stand like a rock in the open when officers and men alike had taken to cover; while men older in service and years, higher in rank and of unquestionable intrepidity, were loyally preserving behind the crest of a hill lives infinitely precious to their country, this fellow would stand, equally idle, on the ridge, facing in the direction of the sharpest fire.

When battles are going on in open ground it frequently occurs that the opposing lines, confronting each other within a stone's throw for hours, hug the earth as closely as if they loved it. The line officers in their proper places flatten themselves no less, and the field officers, their horses all killed or sent to the rear, crouch beneath the infernal canopy of hissing lead and screaming iron without a thought of personal dignity.

In such circumstances the life of a staff officer of a brigade is distinctly not a happy one, mainly because of its precarious tenure and the unnerving alternations of emotion to which he is exposed. From a position of that comparative security from which a civilian would ascribe his escape to a "miracle," he may be dispatched with an order to some commander of a prone regiment in the front line—a person for the moment inconspicuous and not always easy to find without a deal of search among men somewhat preoccupied, and in a din in which question and answer alike must be imparted in the sign language. It is customary in such cases to duck the head and scuttle away on a keen run, an object of lively interest to some thousands of admiring marksmen. In returning—well, it is not customary to return.

Brayle's practice was different. He would consign his horse to the care of an orderly—he loved his horse—and walk quietly away on his perilous errand with never a stoop of the back, his splendid figure, accentuated by his uniform, holding the eye with a strange fascination. We watched him with suspended breath, our hearts in our mouths. On one occasion of this kind, indeed, one of our number, an impetuous stammerer, was so possessed by his emotion that he shouted at me:

"I'll b-b-bet you t-two d-d-dollars they d-drop him b-b-before he g-gets to that d-d-ditch!"

I did not accept the brutal wager. I thought they would.

Let me do justice to a brave man's memory; in all these needless exposures of life there was no visible bravado nor subsequent narration. In the few instances when some of us had ventured to remonstrate, Brayle had smiled pleasantly and made some light reply, which, however, had not encouraged a further pursuit of the subject. Once he said:

"Captain, if ever I come to grief by forgetting your advice, I hope my last moments will be cheered by the sound of your beloved voice breathing into my ear the blessed words, 'I told you so.'"

We laughed at the captain—just why we could probably not have explained—and that afternoon when he was shot to rags from an ambuscade Brayle remained by the body for some time, adjusting the limbs with needless care—there in the middle of a road swept by gusts of grape and canister! It is easy to condemn this kind of thing, and not very difficult to refrain from imitation, but it is impossible not to respect, and Brayle was liked none the less for the weakness which had so heroic an expression. We wished he were not a fool, but he went on that way to the end, sometimes hard hit, but always returning to duty about as good as new.

Of course, it came at last; he who ignores the law of probabilities challenges an adversary that is seldom beaten. It was at Resaca, in Georgia, during the movement that resulted in the taking of Atlanta. In front of our brigade the enemy's line of earthworks ran through open fields along a slight crest. At each end of this open ground we were close up to him in the woods, but the clear ground we could not hope to occupy until night, when darkness would enable us to burrow like moles and throw up earth. At this point our line was a quarter-mile away in the edge of a wood. Roughly, we formed a semicircle, the enemy's fortified line being the chord of the arc.

"Lieutenant, go tell Colonel Ward to work up as close as he can get cover, and not to waste much ammunition in unnecessary firing. You may leave your horse."

When the general gave this direction we were in the fringe of the forest, near the right extremity of the arc. Colonel Ward was at the left. The suggestion to leave the horse obviously enough meant that Brayle was to take the longer line, through the woods and among the men. Indeed, the suggestion was needless; to go by the short route meant absolutely certain failure to deliver the message. Before anybody could interpose, Brayle had cantered lightly into the field and the enemy's works were crackling in conflagration.

"Stop that damned fool!" shouted the general.

A private of the escort, with more ambition than brains, spurred forward to obey, and within ten yards left himself and his horse dead on the field of honor.

Brayle was beyond recall, galloping easily along, parallel to the enemy and less than two hundred yards distant. He was a picture to see! His hat had been blown or shot from his head, and his long, blond hair rose and fell with the motion of his horse. He sat erect in the saddle, holding the reins lightly in his left hand, his right hanging carelessly at his side. An occasional glimpse of his handsome profile as he turned his head one way or the other proved that the interest which he took in what was going on was natural and without affectation.

The picture was intensely dramatic, but in no degree theatrical. Successive scores of rifles spat at him viciously as he came within range, and our own line in the edge of the timber broke out in visible and audible defense. No longer regardful of themselves or their orders, our fellows sprang to their feet, and swarming into the open sent broad sheets of bullets against the blazing crest of the offending works, which poured an answering fire into their unprotected groups with deadly effect. The artillery on both sides joined the battle, punctuating the rattle and roar with deep, earth-shaking explosions and tearing the air with storms of screaming grape, which from the enemy's side splintered the trees and spattered them with blood, and from ours defiled the smoke of his arms with banks and clouds of dust from his parapet.

My attention had been for a moment drawn to the general combat, but now, glancing down the unobscured avenue between these two thunderclouds, I saw Brayle, the cause of the carnage. Invisible now from either side, and equally doomed by friend and foe, he stood in the shot-swept space, motionless, his face toward the enemy. At some little distance lay his horse. I instantly saw what had stopped him.

As topographical engineer I had, early in the day, made a hasty examination of the ground, and now remembered that at that point was a deep and sinuous gully, crossing half the field from the enemy's line, its general course at right angles to it. From where we now were it was invisible, and Brayle had evidently not known about it. Clearly, it was impassable. Its salient angles would have afforded him absolute security if he had chosen to be satisfied with the miracle already wrought in his favor and leapt into it. He could not go forward, he would not turn back; he stood awaiting death. It did not keep him long waiting.

By some mysterious coincidence, almost instantaneously as he fell, the firing ceased, a few desultory shots at long intervals serving rather to accentuate than break the silence. It was as if both sides had suddenly repented of their profitless crime. Four stretcher-bearers of ours, following a sergeant with a white flag, soon afterward moved unmolested into the field, and made straight for Brayle's body. Several Confederate officers and men came out to meet them, and with uncovered heads assisted them to take up their sacred burden. As it was borne toward us we heard beyond the hostile works fifes and a muffled drum—a dirge. A generous enemy honored the fallen brave.

Among the dead man's effects was a soiled Russia-leather pocketbook. In the distribution of mementos of our friend, which the general, as administrator, decreed, this fell to me.

A year after the close of the war, on my way to California, I opened and idly inspected it. Out of an overlooked compartment fell a letter without envelope or address. It was in a woman's handwriting, and began with words of endearment, but no name.

It had the following dateline: "San Francisco, Cal., July 9, 1862." The signature was "Darling," in marks of quotation. Incidentally, in the body of the text, the writer's full name was given—Marian Mendenhall.

The letter showed evidence of cultivation and good breeding, but it was an ordinary love letter, if a love letter can be ordinary. There was not much in it, but there was something. It was this:

"Mr. Winters, whom I shall always hate for it, has been telling that at some battle in Virginia, where he got his hurt, you were seen crouching behind a tree. I think he wants to injure you in my regard, which he knows the story would do if I believed it. I could bear to hear of my soldier lover's death, but not of his cowardice."

These were the words which on that sunny afternoon, in a distant region, had slain a hundred men. Is woman weak?

One evening I called on Miss Mendenhall to return the letter to her. I intended, also, to tell her what she had done—but not that she did it. I found her in a handsome dwelling on Rincon Hill. She was beautiful, well-bred—in a word, charming.

"You knew Lieutenant Herman Brayle," I said, rather abruptly. "You know, doubtless, that he fell in battle. Among his effects was found this letter from you. My errand here is to place it in your hands."

She mechanically took the letter, glanced through it with

deepening color, and then, looking at me with a smile, said:
"It is very good of you, though I am sure it was hardly
worthwhile." She started suddenly and changed color. "This
stain," she said, "is it—surely it is not—"

"Madam," I said, "pardon me, but that is the blood of the
truest and bravest heart that ever beat."

She hastily flung the letter on the blazing coals. "Uh! I
cannot bear the sight of blood!" she said. "How did he die?"

I had involuntarily risen to rescue that scrap of paper,
sacred even to me, and now stood partly behind her. As she
asked the question she turned her face about and slightly
upward. The light of the burning letter was reflected in her
eyes and touched her cheek with a tingle of crimson like the
stain upon its page. I had never seen anything so beautiful as
this detestable creature.

"He was bitten by a snake," I replied.

HAÏTA
THE SHEPHERD

IN the heart of Haïta the illusions of youth had not been supplanted by those of age and experience. His thoughts were pure and pleasant, for his life was simple and his soul devoid of ambition. He rose with the sun and went forth to pray at the shrine of Hastur, the god of shepherds, who heard and was pleased. After performance of this pious rite Haïta unbarred the gate of the fold and with a cheerful mind drove his flock afield, eating his morning meal of curds and oat cake as he went, occasionally pausing to add a few berries, cold with dew, or to drink of the waters that came away from the hills to join the stream in the middle of the valley and be borne along with it, he knew not whither.

During the long summer day, as his sheep cropped the good grass which the gods had made to grow for them, or lay with their forelegs doubled under their breasts and chewed the cud, Haïta, reclining in the shadow of a tree, or sitting upon a rock, played so sweet music upon his reed pipe that sometimes from the corner of his eye he got accidental glimpses of the minor sylvan deities, leaning forward out of the copse to hear; but if he looked at them directly they vanished. From this— for he must be thinking if he would not turn into one of his own sheep—he drew the solemn inference that happiness may come if not sought, but if looked for will never be seen; for next to the favor of Hastur, who never disclosed himself, Haïta most valued the friendly interest of his neighbors, the shy immortals of the wood and stream. At nightfall he drove his flock back to the fold, saw that the gate was secure, and retired to his cave for refreshment and for dreams.

So passed his life, one day like another, save when the storms uttered the wrath of an offended god. Then Haïta cowered in his cave, his face hidden in his hands, and prayed that he alone might be punished for his sins and the world saved from destruction. Sometimes when there was a great rain, and the stream came out of its banks, compelling him to urge his terrified flock to the uplands, he interceded for the people in the cities which he had been told lay in the plain beyond the two blue hills forming the gateway of his valley.

"It is kind of thee, O Hastur," so he prayed, "to give me mountains so near my dwelling and my fold that I and my sheep can escape the angry torrents; but the rest of the world thou must thyself deliver in some way that I know not of, or I will no longer worship thee."

And Hastur, knowing that Haïta was a youth who kept his word, spared the cities and turned the waters into the sea.

So he had lived since he could remember. He could not rightly conceive any other mode of existence. The holy hermit who dwelt at the head of the valley, a full hour's journey away, from whom he had heard the tale of the great cities where dwelt people—poor souls!—who had no sheep, gave him no knowledge of that early time, when, so he reasoned, he must have been small and helpless like a lamb.

It was through thinking on these mysteries and marvels, and on that horrible change to silence and decay which he felt sure must sometime come to him, as he had seen it come to so many of his flock—as it came to all living things except the birds—that Haïta first became conscious how miserable and hopeless was his lot.

"It is necessary," he said, "that I know whence and how I came; for how can one perform his duties unless able to judge what they are by the way in which he was entrusted with them? And what contentment can I have when I know not how long it is going to last? Perhaps before another sun I may be changed, and then what will become of the sheep? What, indeed, will have become of me?"

Pondering these things Haïta became melancholy and morose. He no longer spoke cheerfully to his flock, nor ran with alacrity to the shrine of Hastur. In every breeze he heard whispers of malign deities whose existence he now first observed. Every cloud was a portent signifying disaster, and the darkness was full of terrors. His reed pipe when applied to his lips gave out no melody, but a dismal wail; the sylvan and riparian intelligences no longer thronged the thicketside to listen, but fled from the sound, as he knew by the stirred leaves and bent flowers. He relaxed his vigilance, and many of his sheep strayed away into the hills and were lost. Those that remained became lean and ill for lack of good pasturage, for he would not seek it for them, but conducted them day after day to the same spot, through mere abstraction, while puzzling about life and death—of immortality he knew not.

One day while indulging in the gloomiest reflections he suddenly sprang from the rock upon which he sat, and with a determined gesture of the right hand exclaimed, "I will no longer be a suppliant for knowledge which the gods withhold. Let them look to it that they do me no wrong. I will do my duty as best I can and if I err upon their own heads be it!"

Suddenly, as he spoke, a great brightness fell about him, causing him to look upward, thinking the sun had burst through a rift in the clouds; but there were no clouds. No more than an arm's length away stood a beautiful maiden. So beautiful she was that the flowers about her feet folded their petals in despair and bent their heads in token of submission; so sweet her look that the hummingbirds thronged her eyes, thrusting their thirsty bills almost into them, and the wild bees were about her lips. And such was her brightness that the shadows of all objects lay divergent from her feet, turning as she moved.

Haïta was entranced. Rising, he knelt before her in adoration, and she laid her hand upon his head.

"Come," she said in a voice that had the music of all the bells of his flock, "come, thou art not to worship me, who am no goddess, but if thou art truthful and dutiful I will abide with thee."

Haïta seized her hand, and stammering his joy and gratitude arose, and hand in hand they stood and smiled into each other's eyes. He gazed on her with reverence and rapture. He said, "I pray thee, lovely maid, tell me thy name and whence and why thou comest."

At this she laid a warning finger on her lip and began to withdraw. Her beauty underwent a visible alteration that made him shudder, he knew not why, for still she was beautiful. The landscape was darkened by a giant shadow sweeping across the valley with the speed of a vulture. In the obscurity the maiden's figure grew dim and indistinct and her voice seemed to come from a distance, as she said, in a tone of sorrowful reproach, "Presumptuous and ungrateful youth! Must I then so soon leave thee? Would nothing do but thou must at once break the eternal compact?"

Inexpressibly grieved, Haïta fell upon his knees and implored her to remain—rose and sought her in the deepening darkness—ran in circles, calling to her aloud, but all in vain. She was no longer visible, but out of the gloom he heard her voice saying, "Nay, thou shalt not have me by seeking. Go to thy duty, faithless shepherd, or we shall never meet again."

Night had fallen; the wolves were howling in the hills and the terrified sheep crowding about Haïta's feet. In the demands of the hour he forgot his disappointment, drove his sheep to the fold, and repairing to the place of worship poured out his heart in gratitude to Hastur for permitting him to save his flock, then retired to his cave and slept.

When Haïta awoke the sun was high and shone in at the cave, illuminating it with a great glory. And there, beside him, sat the maiden. She smiled upon him with a smile that seemed the visible music of his pipe of reeds. He dared not speak, fearing to offend her as before, for he knew not what he could venture to say.

"Because," she said, "thou didst thy duty by the flock, and didst not forget to thank Hastur for staying the wolves of the night, I am come to thee again. Wilt thou have me for a companion?"

"Who would not have thee forever?" replied Haïta. "Oh! never again leave me until—until I—change and become silent and motionless."

Haïta had no word for death.

"I wish, indeed," he continued, "that thou wert of my own sex, that we might wrestle and run races and so never tire of being together."

At these words the maiden arose and passed out of the cave, and Haïta, springing from his couch of fragrant boughs to overtake and detain her, observed to his astonishment that the rain was falling and the stream in the middle of the valley had come out of its banks. The sheep were bleating in terror, for the rising waters had invaded their fold. And there was danger for the unknown cities of the distant plain.

It was many days before Haïta saw the maiden again. One day he was returning from the head of the valley, where he had gone with ewe's milk and oat cake and berries for the holy hermit, who was too old and feeble to provide himself with food.

"Poor old man!" he said aloud, as he trudged along homeward. "I will return tomorrow and bear him on my back to my own dwelling, where I can care for him. Doubtless it is for this that Hastur has reared me all these many years, and gives me health and strength."

As he spoke, the maiden, clad in glittering garments, met him in the path with a smile that took away his breath.

"I am come again," she said, "to dwell with thee if thou wilt now have me, for none else will. Thou mayest have learned wisdom, and art willing to take me as I am, nor care to know."

Haïta threw himself at her feet. "Beautiful being," he cried, "if thou wilt but deign to accept all the devotion of my heart and soul—after Hastur be served—it is thine forever. But, alas! thou art capricious and wayward. Before tomorrow's sun I may lose thee again. Promise, I beseech thee, that however in my ignorance I may offend, thou wilt forgive and remain always with me."

Scarcely had he finished speaking when a troop of bears came out of the hills, racing toward him with crimson mouths and fiery eyes. The maiden again vanished, and he turned and fled for his life. Nor did he stop until he was in the cot of the holy hermit, whence he had set out. Hastily barring the door against the bears he cast himself upon the ground and wept.

"My son," said the hermit from his couch of straw, freshly gathered that morning by Haïta's hands, "it is not like thee to weep for bears—tell me what sorrow hath befallen thee, that age may minister to the hurts of youth which such balms as it hath of its wisdom."

Haïta told him all: how thrice he had met the radiant maid, and thrice she had left him forlorn. He related minutely all that had passed between them, omitting no word of what had been said.

When he had ended, the holy hermit was a moment silent, then said, "My son, I have attended to thy story, and I know the maiden. I have myself seen her, as have many. Know, then, that her name, which she would not even permit thee to inquire, is Happiness. Thou saidst the truth to her, that she is capricious, for she imposeth conditions that man cannot fulfill, and delinquency is punished by desertion. She cometh only when unsought, and will not be questioned. One manifestation of curiosity, one sign of doubt, one expression of misgiving, and she is away! How long didst thou have her at any time before she fled?"

"Only a single instant," answered Haïta, blushing with shame at the confession. "Each time I drove her away in one moment."

"Unfortunate youth!" said the holy hermit, "but for thine indiscretion thou mightst have had her for two."

PRESENT AT A HANGING

A N OLD man named Daniel Baker, living near Lebanon,
Iowa, was suspected by his neighbors of having murdered a peddler who had obtained permission to pass
the night at his house. This was in 1853, when peddling was
more common in the Western country than it is now, and was
attended with considerable danger. The peddler with his pack
traversed the country by all manner of lonely roads, and was
compelled to rely upon the country people for hospitality. This
brought him into relation with queer characters, some of
whom were not altogether scrupulous in their methods of
making a living, murder being an acceptable means to that
end. It occasionally occurred that a peddler with diminished
pack and swollen purse would be traced to the lonely dwelling
of some rough character and never could be traced beyond.
This was so in the case of "old man Baker," as he was always
called. (Such names are given in the Western settlements only
to elderly persons who are not esteemed; to the general dis-
repute of social unworth is affixed the special reproach of age.)
A peddler came to his house and none went away—that is all
that anybody knew.

Seven years later the Rev. Mr. Cummings, a Baptist minister well known in that part of the country, was driving by
Baker's farm one night. It was not very dark: there was a
bit of moon somewhere above the light veil of mist that lay

194

along the earth. Mr. Cummings, who was at all times a cheerful person, was whistling a tune, which he would occasionally interrupt to speak a word of friendly encouragement to his horse. As he came to a little bridge across a dry ravine he saw the figure of a man standing upon it, clearly outlined against the gray background of a misty forest. The man had something strapped on his back and carried a heavy stick—obviously an itinerant peddler. His attitude had in it a suggestion of abstraction, like that of a sleepwalker. Mr. Cummings reined in his horse when he arrived in front of him, gave him a pleasant salutation and invited him to a seat in the vehicle— "if you are going my way," he added. The man raised his head, looked him full in the face, but neither answered nor made any further movement. The minister, with good-natured persistence, repeated his invitation. At this the man threw his right hand forward from his side and pointed downward as he stood on the extreme edge of the bridge. Mr. Cummings looked past him, over into the ravine, saw nothing unusual and withdrew his eyes to address the man again. He had disappeared. The horse, which all this time had been uncommonly restless, gave at the same moment a snort of terror and started to run away. Before he had regained control of the animal the minister was at the crest of the hill a hundred yards along. He looked back and saw the figure again, at the same place and in the same attitude as when he had first observed it. Then for the first time he was conscious of a sense of the supernatural and drove home as rapidly as his willing horse would go.

On arriving at home he related his adventure to his family, and early the next morning, accompanied by two neighbors, John White Corwell and Abner Raiser, returned to the spot. They found the body of old man Baker hanging by the neck from one of the beams of the bridge, immediately beneath the spot where the apparition had stood. A thick coating of dust, slightly dampened by the mist, covered the floor of the bridge, but the only footprints were those of Mr. Cummings' horse.

In taking down the body the men disturbed the loose, friable earth of the slope below it, disclosing human bones already nearly uncovered by the action of water and frost. They were identified as those of the lost peddler. At the double inquest the coroner's jury found that Daniel Baker died by his own hand while suffering from temporary insanity, and that Samuel Morritz was murdered by some person or persons to the jury unknown.

AN INHABITANT
OF CARCOSA

For there be divers sorts of death—some wherein the body remaineth; and in some it vanisheth quite away with the spirit. This commonly occurreth only in solitude (such is God's will) and, none seeing the end, we say the man is lost, or gone on a long journey—which indeed he hath; but sometimes it hath happened in sight of many, as abundant testimony showeth. In one kind of death the spirit also dieth, and this it hath been known to do while yet the body was in vigor for many years. Sometimes, as is veritably attested, it dieth with the body, but after a season is raised up again in that place where the body did decay.

PONDERING these words of Hali (whom God rest) and questioning their full meaning, as one who, having an intimation, yet doubts if there be not something behind, other than that which he has discerned, I noted not whither I had strayed until a sudden chill wind striking my face revived in me a sense of my surroundings. I observed with astonishment that everything seemed unfamiliar. On every side of me stretched a bleak and desolate expanse of plain, covered with a tall overgrowth of sere grass, which rustled and whistled in the autumn wind with heaven knows what mysterious and disquieting suggestion. Protruded at long intervals above it stood strangely shaped and somber-colored

197

rocks, which seemed to have an understanding with one another and to exchange looks of uncomfortable significance, as if they had reared their heads to watch the issue of some foreseen event. A few blasted trees here and there appeared as leaders in this malevolent conspiracy of silent expectation.

The day, I thought, must be far advanced, though the sun was invisible; and although sensible that the air was raw and chill my consciousness of that fact was rather mental than physical—I had no feeling of discomfort. Over all the dismal landscape a canopy of low, lead-colored clouds hung like a visible curse. In all this there were a menace and a portent—a hint of evil, an intimation of doom. Bird, beast, or insect there was none. The wind sighed in the bare branches of the dead trees and the gray grass bent to whisper its dread secret to the earth; but no other sound nor motion broke the awful repose of that dismal place.

I observed in the herbage a number of weatherworn stones, evidently shaped with tools. They were broken, covered with moss, and half sunken in the earth. Some lay prostrate, some leaned at various angles, none was vertical. They were obviously headstones of graves, though the graves themselves no longer existed as either mounds or depressions; the years had leveled all. Scattered here and there, more massive blocks showed where some pompous tomb or ambitious monument had once flung its feeble defiance at oblivion. So old seemed these relics, these vestiges of vanity and memorials of affection and piety, so battered and worn and stained—so neglected, deserted, forgotten the place—that I could not help thinking myself the discoverer of the burial ground of a prehistoric race of men whose very name was long extinct.

Filled with these reflections, I was for some time heedless of the sequence of my own experiences, but soon I thought, How came I hither? A moment's reflection seemed to make this all clear and explain at the same time, though in a disquieting way, the singular character with which my fancy had invested all that I saw or heard. I was ill. I remembered now that I had been prostrated by a sudden fever, and that my family had told me that in my periods of delirium I had constantly cried out for liberty and air, and had been held in bed to prevent my escape out-of-doors. Now I had eluded the vigilance of my attendants and had wandered hither to—to where? I could not conjecture. Clearly I was at a considerable distance from the city where I dwelt—the ancient and famous city of Carcosa.

No signs of human life were anywhere visible nor audible; no rising smoke, no watchdog's bark, no lowing of cattle, no shouts of children at play—nothing but that dismal burial place with its air of mystery and dread, due to my own disordered brain. Was I not becoming again delirious, there beyond human aid? Was it not indeed *all* an illusion of my madness? I called aloud the names of my wives and sons, reached out my hands in search of theirs, even as I walked among the crumbling stones and in the withered grass.

A noise behind me caused me to turn about. A wild animal— a lynx—was approaching. The thought came to me: If I break down here in the desert—if the fever return and I fail, this beast will be at my throat. I sprang toward it, shouting. It trotted tranquilly by within a hand's-breadth of me and disappeared behind a rock.

A moment later a man's head appeared to rise out of the ground a short distance away. He was ascending the farther slope of a low hill whose crest was hardly to be distinguished from the general level. His whole figure soon came into view against the background of gray cloud. He was half naked, half clad in skins. His hair was unkempt, his beard long and ragged. In one hand he carried a bow and arrow; the other held a blazing torch with a long trail of black smoke. He walked slowly and with caution, as if he feared falling into some open grave concealed by the tall grass. This strange apparition surprised but did not alarm, and taking such a course as to intercept him I met him almost face to face, accosting him with the familiar salutation, "God keep you."

He gave no heed, nor did he arrest his pace.

"Good stranger," I continued, "I am ill and lost. Direct me, I beseech you, to Carcosa."

The man broke into a barbarous chant in an unknown tongue, passing on and away.

An owl on the branch of a decayed tree hooted dismally and

was answered by another in the distance. Looking upward, I
saw through a sudden rift in the clouds Aldebaran and the
Hyades! In all this there was a hint of night—the lynx, the
man with the torch, the owl. Yet I saw—I saw even the stars
in absence of the darkness. I saw, but was apparently not seen
nor heard. Under what awful spell did I exist?

I seated myself at the root of a great tree, seriously to consider what it were best to do. That I was mad I could no longer
doubt, yet recognized a ground of doubt in the conviction. Of
fever I had no trace. I had, withal, a sense of exhilaration and
vigor altogether unknown to me—a feeling of mental and
physical exaltation. My senses seemed all alert; I could feel
the air as a ponderous substance; I could hear the silence.

A great root of the giant tree against whose trunk I leaned as I sat held enclosed in its grasp a slab of stone, a part of which protruded into a recess formed by another root. The stone was thus partly protected from the weather, though greatly decomposed. Its edges were worn round, its corners eaten away, its surface deeply furrowed and scaled. Glittering particles of mica were visible in the earth about it—vestiges of its decomposition. This stone had apparently marked the grave out of which the tree had sprung ages ago. The tree's exacting roots had robbed the grave and made the stone a prisoner.

A sudden wind pushed some dry leaves and twigs from the uppermost face of the stone; I saw the low-relief letters of an inscription and bent to read it. God in Heaven! *My* name in full!—the date of *my* birth—the date of *my* death!

A level shaft of light illuminated the whole side of the tree as I sprang to my feet in terror. The sun was rising in the rosy east. I stood between the tree and his broad red disk— no shadow darkened the trunk!

A chorus of howling wolves saluted the dawn. I saw them sitting on their haunches, singly and in groups, on the summits of irregular mounds and tumuli filling a half of my desert prospect and extending to the horizon. And then I knew that these were ruins of the ancient and famous city of Carcosa.

———

Such are the facts imparted to the medium Bayrolles by the spirit Hoseib Alar Robardin.

ONE OFFICER,
ONE MAN

C APTAIN Graffenreid stood at the head of his company. The regiment was not engaged. It formed a part of the front line of battle, which stretched away to the right with a visible length of nearly two miles through the open ground. The left flank was veiled by woods; to the right also the line was lost to sight, but it extended many miles. A hundred yards in rear was a second line, behind this, the reserve brigades and divisions in column. Batteries of artillery occupied the spaces between and crowned the low hills. Groups of horsemen—generals with their staffs and escorts, and field officers of regiments behind the colors—broke the regularity of the lines and columns. Numbers of these figures of interest had field glasses at their eyes and sat motionless, stolidly scanning the country in front; others came and went at a slow canter, bearing orders. There were squads of stretcher-bearers, ambulances, wagon trains with ammunition, and officers' servants in rear of all—of all that was visible—for still in rear of these, along the roads, extended for many miles all that vast multitude of noncombatants who with their various impedimenta are assigned to the inglorious but important duty of supplying the fighters' many needs.

An army in line of battle awaiting attack, or prepared to deliver it, presents strange contrasts. At the front are precision, formality, fixity, and silence. Toward the rear these characteristics are less and less conspicuous, and finally, in point of space, are lost altogether in confusion, motion, and noise. The homogeneous becomes heterogeneous. Definition is lacking; repose is replaced by an apparently purposeless activity; harmony vanishes in hubbub, form in disorder. Commotion everywhere and ceaseless unrest. The men who do not fight are never ready.

From his position at the right of his company in the front rank, Captain Graffenreid had an unobstructed outlook toward the enemy. A half-mile of open and nearly level ground lay before him, and beyond it an irregular wood, covering a slight acclivity; not a human being anywhere visible. He could imagine nothing more peaceful than the appearance of that pleasant landscape with its long stretches of brown fields over which the atmosphere was beginning to quiver in the heat of the morning sun. Not a sound came from forest or field—not even the barking of a dog or the crowing of a cock at the half-seen plantation house on the crest among the trees. Yet every man in those miles of men knew that he and death were face to face.

Captain Graffenreid had never in his life seen an armed enemy, and the war in which his regiment was one of the first to take the field was two years old. He had had the rare advantage of a military education, and when his comrades had marched to the front he had been detached for administrative service at the capital of his state, where it was thought that he could be most useful. Like a bad soldier he protested, and like a good one obeyed. In close official and personal relations with the governor of his state, and enjoying his confidence and favor, he had firmly refused promotion and seen his juniors elevated above him. Death had been busy in his distant regiment; vacancies among the field officers had occurred again and again; but from a chivalrous feeling that war's rewards belonged of right to those who bore the storm and stress of battle, he had held his humble rank and generously advanced the fortunes of others. His silent devotion to principle had conquered at last: he had been relieved of his hateful duties and ordered to the front, and now, untried by fire, stood in the van of battle in command of a company of hardy veterans, to whom he had been only a name, and that name a byword. By none—not even by those of his brother officers in whose favor he had waived his rights—was his devotion to duty understood. They were too busy to be just; he was looked upon as one who had shirked his duty, until forced unwillingly into the field. Too proud to explain, yet not too insensible to feel, he could only endure and hope.

Of all the Federal army on that summer morning none had accepted battle more joyously than Anderton Graffenreid. His spirit was buoyant, his faculties were riotous. He was in a state of mental exaltation and scarcely could endure the enemy's tardiness in advancing to the attack. To him this was opportunity—for the result he cared nothing. Victory or defeat, as God might will. In one or in the other he should prove himself a soldier and a hero; he should vindicate his right to the respect of his men and the companionship of his brother officers—to the consideration of his superiors. How his heart leaped in his breast as the bugle sounded the stirring notes of the "assembly"! With what a light tread, scarcely conscious of the earth beneath his feet, he strode forward at the head of his company, and how exultingly he noted the tactical dispositions which placed his regiment in the front line! And if perchance some memory came to him of a pair of dark eyes that might take on a tenderer light in reading the account of that day's doings, who shall blame him for the unmartial thought or count it a debasement of soldierly ardor?

Suddenly, from the forest a half-mile in front—apparently from among the upper branches of the trees, but really from the ridge beyond—rose a tall column of white smoke. A moment later came a deep, jarring explosion, followed—almost attended—by a hideous rushing sound that seemed to leap forward across the intervening space with inconceivable rapidity, rising from whisper to roar with too quick a gradation for attention to note the successive stages of its horrible progression! A visible tremor ran along the lines of men; all were startled into motion. Captain Graffenreid dodged and threw up his hands to one side of his head, palms outward. As he did so he heard a keen, ringing report, and saw on a hillside behind the line a fierce roll of smoke and dust—the shell's explosion. It had passed a hundred feet to his left! He heard, or fancied he heard, a low, mocking laugh, and turning in the direction whence it came saw the eyes of his first lieutenant fixed upon him with an unmistakable look of amusement. He looked along the line of faces in the front ranks. The men were laughing. At him? The thought restored the color to his bloodless face—restored too much of it. His cheeks burned with a fever of shame.

The enemy's shot was not answered: the officer in command at that exposed part of the line had evidently no desire to provoke a cannonade. For the forbearance Captain Graffenreid was conscious of a sense of gratitude. He had not known that the flight of a projectile was a phenomenon of so appalling character. His conception of war had already undergone a profound change, and he was conscious that his new feeling was manifesting itself in visible perturbation. His blood was boiling in his veins; he had a choking sensation and felt that if he had a command to give it would be inaudible, or at least unintelligible. The hand in which he held his sword trembled; the other moved automatically, clutching at various parts of his clothing. He found a difficulty in standing still and fancied that his men observed it. Was it fear? He feared it was.

From somewhere away to the right came, as the wind served, a low, intermittent murmur like that of ocean in a storm— like that of a distant railway train—like that of wind among the pines—three sounds so nearly alike that the ear, unaided by the judgment, cannot distinguish them one from another. The eyes of the troops were drawn in that direction; the mounted officers turned their field glasses that way. Mingled with the sound was an irregular throbbing. He thought it, at first, the beating of his fevered blood in his ears; next, the distant tapping of a bass drum.

"The ball is opened on the right flank," said an officer.

Captain Graffenreid understood: the sounds were musketry and artillery. He nodded and tried to smile. There was apparently nothing infectious in the smile.

Presently a light line of blue smoke puffs broke out along the edge of the wood in front, succeeded by a crackle of rifles. There were keen, sharp hissings in the air, terminating abruptly with a thump nearby. The man at Captain Graffen-reid's side dropped his rifle; his knees gave way and he pitched awkwardly forward, falling upon his face. Somebody shouted "Lie down!" and the dead man was hardly distinguishable from the living. It looked as if those few rifle shots had slain ten thousand men. Only the field officers remained erect; their concession to the emergency consisted in dismounting and sending their horses to the shelter of the low hills immediately in rear.

Captain Graffenreid lay alongside the dead man, from be-neath whose breast flowed a little rill of blood. It had a faint, sweetish odor that sickened him. The face was crushed into the earth and flattened. It looked yellow already, and was re-pulsive. Nothing suggested the glory of a soldier's death nor mitigated the loathsomeness of the incident. He could not turn his back upon the body without facing away from his company.

He fixed his eyes upon the forest, where all again was silent. He tried to imagine what was going on there—the lines of troops forming to attack, the guns being pushed forward by hand to the edge of the open. He fancied he could see their black muzzles protruding from the undergrowth, ready to de-liver their storm of missiles—such missiles as the one whose shriek had so unsettled his nerves. The distention of his eyes became painful. A mist seemed to gather before them; he could no longer see across the field, yet would not withdraw his gaze lest he see the dead man at his side.

The fire of battle was not now burning very brightly in this warrior's soul. From inaction had come introspection. He sought rather to analyze his feelings than distinguish himself by courage and devotion. The result was profoundly disap-pointing. He covered his face with his hands and groaned aloud.

The hoarse murmur of battle grew more and more distinct upon the right; the murmur had, indeed, become a roar, the throbbing, a thunder. The sounds had worked round obliquely to the front; evidently the enemy's left was being driven back, and the propitious moment to move against the salient angle of his line would soon arrive. The silence and mystery in front were ominous; all felt that they boded evil to the assailants.

Behind the prostrate lines sounded the hoofbeats of galloping horses; the men turned to look. A dozen staff officers were riding to the various brigade and regimental commanders, who had remounted. A moment more and there was a chorus of voices, all uttering out of time the same words—"Attention, battalion!" The men sprang to their feet and were aligned by the company commanders. They awaited the word "forward"— awaited, too, with beating hearts and set teeth the gusts of lead and iron that were to smite them at their first movement in obedience to that word. The word was not given; the tempest did not break out. The delay was hideous, maddening! It unnerved like a respite at the guillotine.

Captain Graffenreid stood at the head of his company, the dead man at his feet. He heard the battle on the right—rattle and crash of musketry, ceaseless thunder of cannon, desultory cheers of invisible combatants. He marked ascending clouds of smoke from distant forests. He noted the sinister silence of the forest in front. These contrasting extremes affected the whole range of his sensibilities. The strain upon his nervous organization was insupportable. He grew hot and cold by turns. He panted like a dog, and then forgot to breathe until reminded by vertigo.

Suddenly he grew calm. Glancing downward, his eyes had fallen upon his naked sword, as he held it, point to earth. Foreshortened to his view, it resembled somewhat, he thought, the short, heavy blade of the ancient Roman. The fancy was full of suggestion, malign, fateful, heroic!

The sergeant in the rear rank, immediately behind Captain Graffenreid, now observed a strange sight. His attention drawn by an uncommon movement made by the captain—a sudden reaching forward of the hands and their energetic withdrawal, throwing the elbows out, as in pulling an oar—he saw spring from between the officer's shoulders a bright point of metal which prolonged itself outward, nearly a half-arm's length— a blade! It was faintly streaked with crimson, and its point approached so near to the sergeant's breast, and with so quick a movement, that he shrank backward in alarm. That moment Captain Graffenreid pitched heavily forward upon the dead man and died.

A week later the major general commanding the left corps of the Federal army submitted the following official report:

"Sir: I have the honor to report, with regard to the action of the 19th inst., that owing to the enemy's withdrawal from my front to reinforce his beaten left, my command was not seriously engaged. My loss was as follows: Killed, one officer, one man."

THE DAMNED
THING

I
ONE DOES NOT ALWAYS EAT
WHAT IS ON THE TABLE

BY the light of a tallow candle which had been placed on one end of a rough table a man was reading something written in a book. It was an old account book, greatly worn; and the writing was not, apparently, very legible, for the man sometimes held the page close to the flame of the candle to get a stronger light on it. The shadow of the book would then throw into obscurity a half of the room, darkening a number of faces and figures; for besides the reader, eight other men were present. Seven of them sat against the rough log walls, silent, motionless, and the room being small, not very far from the table. By extending an arm any one of them could have touched the eighth man, who lay on the table, face upward, partly covered by a sheet, his arms at his sides. He was dead.

The man with the book was not reading aloud, and no one spoke. All seemed to be waiting for something to occur; the dead man only was without expectation. From the blank darkness outside came in, through the aperture that served for a window, all the ever unfamiliar noises of night in the wilderness—the long nameless note of a distant coyote; the stilly pulsing trill of tireless insects in trees; strange cries of night birds, so different from those of the birds of day; the drone of great blundering beetles, and all that mysterious chorus of small sounds that seem always to have been but half heard when they have suddenly ceased, as if conscious of an indiscretion. But nothing of all this was noted in that company; its members were not overmuch addicted to idle interest in matters of no practical importance; that was obvious in every line of their rugged faces—obvious even in the dim light of the single candle. They were evidently men of the vicinity—farmers and woodsmen.

The person reading was a trifle different; one would have said of him that he was of the world, worldly, albeit there was that in his attire which attested a certain fellowship with the organisms of his environment. His coat would hardly have passed muster in San Francisco; his footgear was not of urban origin, and the hat that lay by him on the floor (he was the only one uncovered) was such that if one had considered it as an article of mere personal adornment he would have missed its meaning. In countenance the man was rather prepossessing, with just a hint of sternness; though that he may have assumed or cultivated, as appropriate to one in authority. For he was a coroner. It was by virtue of his office that he had possession of the book in which he was reading. It had been found among the dead man's effects—in his cabin, where the inquest was now taking place.

When the coroner had finished reading he put the book into his breast pocket. At that moment the door was pushed open and a young man entered. He, clearly, was not of mountain birth and breeding: he was clad as those who dwell in cities. His clothing was dusty, however, as from travel. He had, in fact, been riding hard to attend the inquest.

The coroner nodded. No one else greeted him.

"We have waited for you," said the coroner. "It is necessary to have done with this business tonight."

The young man smiled. "I am sorry to have kept you," he said. "I went away, not to evade your summons, but to post to my newspaper an account of what I suppose I am called back to relate."

The coroner smiled.

"The account that you posted to your newspaper," he said, "differs, probably, from that which you will give here under oath."

"That," replied the other, rather hotly and with a visible flush, "is as you please. I used manifold paper and have a copy of what I sent. It was not written as news, for it is incredible, but as fiction. It may go as a part of my testimony under oath."

"But you say it is incredible."

"That is nothing to you, sir, if I also swear that it is true."

The coroner was silent for a time, his eyes upon the floor. The men about the sides of the cabin talked in whispers, but seldom withdrew their gaze from the face of the corpse. Presently the coroner lifted his eyes and said, "We will resume the inquest."

The men removed their hats. The witness was sworn.

"What is your name?" the coroner asked.

"William Harker."

"Age?"

"Twenty-seven."

"You knew the deceased, Hugh Morgan?"

"Yes."

"You were with him when he died?"

"Near him."

"How did that happen—your presence, I mean?"

"I was visiting him at this place to shoot and fish. A part of my purpose, however, was to study him and his odd, solitary way of life. He seemed a good model for a character in fiction. I sometimes write stories."

"I sometimes read them."

"Thank you."

"Stories in general—not yours."

Some of the jurors laughed. Against a somber background humor shows high lights. Soldiers in the intervals of battle laugh easily, and a jest in the death chamber conquers by surprise.

"Relate the circumstances of this man's death," said the coroner. "You may use any notes or memoranda that you please."

The witness understood. Pulling a manuscript from his breast pocket he held it near the candle and turning the leaves until he found the passage that he wanted began to read.

II
WHAT MAY HAPPEN IN A FIELD
OF WILD OATS

"... The sun had hardly risen when we left the house. We were looking for quail, each with a shotgun, but we had only one dog. Morgan said that our best ground was beyond a certain ridge that he pointed out, and we crossed it by a trail through the chaparral. On the other side was comparatively level ground, thickly covered with wild oats. As we emerged from the chaparral Morgan was but a few yards in advance. Suddenly we heard, at a little distance to our right and partly in front, a noise as of some animal thrashing about in the bushes, which we could see were violently agitated.

" 'We've started a deer,' I said. 'I wish we had brought a rifle.'

"Morgan, who had stopped and was intently watching the agitated chaparral, said nothing, but had cocked both barrels of his gun and was holding it in readiness to aim. I thought him a trifle excited, which surprised me, for he had a reputation for exceptional coolness, even in moments of sudden and imminent peril.

" 'O, come,' I said. 'You are not going to fill up a deer with quail-shot, are you?'

"Still he did not reply, but catching a sight of his face as he turned it slightly toward me I was struck by the intensity of his look. Then I understood that we had serious business in hand, and my first conjecture was that we had jumped a grizzly. I advanced to Morgan's side, cocking my piece as I moved.

"The bushes were now quiet and the sounds had ceased, but Morgan was as attentive to the place as before.

" 'What is it? What the devil is it?' I asked.

" 'That Damned Thing!' he replied, without turning his head. His voice was husky and unnatural. He trembled visibly.

"I was about to speak further, when I observed the wild oats near the place of the disturbance moving in the most inexplicable way. I can hardly describe it. It seemed as if stirred by a streak of wind, which not only bent it, but pressed it down—crushed it so that it did not rise—and this movement was slowly prolonging itself directly toward us.

"Nothing that I had ever seen had affected me so strangely as this unfamiliar and unaccountable phenomenon, yet I am unable to recall any sense of fear. I remember—and tell it here because, singularly enough, I recollected it then—that once in looking carelessly out of an open window I momentarily mistook a small tree close at hand for one of a group of larger trees at a little distance away. It looked the same size as the others, but being more distinctly and sharply defined in mass and detail seemed out of harmony with them. It was a mere falsification of the law of aerial perspective, but it startled, almost terrified me. We so rely upon the orderly operation of familiar natural laws that any seeming suspension of them is noted as a menace to our safety, a warning of unthinkable calamity. So now the apparently causeless movement of the herbage and the slow, undeviating approach of the line of disturbance were distinctly disquieting. My companion appeared actually frightened, and I could hardly credit my senses when I saw him suddenly throw his gun to his shoulder and fire both barrels at the agitated grain! Before the smoke of the discharge had cleared away I heard a loud savage cry—a scream like that of a wild animal—and flinging his gun upon the ground Morgan sprang away and ran swiftly from the spot. At the same instant I was thrown violently to the ground by the impact of something unseen in the smoke—some soft, heavy substance that seemed thrown against me with great force.

"Before I could get upon my feet and recover my gun, which seemed to have been struck from my hands, I heard Morgan crying out as if in mortal agony, and mingling with his cries were such hoarse, savage sounds as one hears from fighting dogs. Inexpressibly terrified, I struggled to my feet and looked

in the direction of Morgan's retreat—and may Heaven in
mercy spare me from another sight like that! At a distance of
less than thirty yards was my friend, down upon one knee, his
head thrown back at a frightful angle, hatless, his long hair
in disorder and his whole body in violent movement from side
to side, backward and forward. His right arm was lifted and
seemed to lack the hand—at least, I could see none. The other
arm was invisible. At times, as my memory now reports this
extraordinary scene, I could discern but a part of his body. It
was as if he had been partly blotted out—I cannot otherwise
express it—then a shifting of his position would bring it all
into view again.

"All this must have occurred within a few seconds, yet in
that time Morgan assumed all the postures of a determined
wrestler vanquished by superior weight and strength. I saw
nothing but him, and him not always distinctly. During the
entire incident his shouts and curses were heard, as if through
an enveloping uproar of such sounds of rage and fury as I had
never heard from the throat of man or brute!

"For a moment only I stood irresolute, then throwing down
my gun I ran forward to my friend's assistance. I had a vague
belief that he was suffering from a fit, or some form of convulsion. Before I could reach his side he was down and quiet. All
sounds had ceased, but with a feeling of such terror as even
these awful events had not inspired I now saw again the
mysterious movement of the wild oats, prolonging itself from
the trampled area about the prostrate man toward the edge of
a wood. It was only when it had reached the wood that I was
able to withdraw my eyes and look at my companion. He was
dead."

III

A MAN THOUGH NAKED MAY BE
IN RAGS

The coroner rose from his seat and stood beside the dead man.
Lifting an edge of the sheet he pulled it away, exposing the
entire body, altogether naked and showing in the candlelight a
claylike yellow. It had, however, broad maculations of bluish

black, obviously caused by extravasated blood from contusions. The chest and sides looked as if they had been beaten with a bludgeon. There were dreadful lacerations; the skin was torn in strips and shreds.

The coroner moved round to the end of the table and undid a silk handkerchief which had been passed under the chin and knotted on the top of the head. When the handkerchief was drawn away it exposed what had been the throat. Some of the jurors who had risen to get a better view repented their curiosity and turned away their faces. Witness Harker went to the open window and leaned out across the sill, faint and sick. Dropping the handkerchief upon the dead man's neck the coroner stepped to an angle of the room and from a pile of clothing produced one garment after another, each of which he held up a moment for inspection. All were torn, and stiff with blood. The jurors did not make a closer inspection. They seemed rather uninterested. They had, in truth, seen all this before, the only thing that was new to them being Harker's testimony.

"Gentlemen," the coroner said, "we have no more evidence, I think. Your duty has been already explained to you. If there is nothing you wish to ask you may go outside and consider your verdict."

The foreman rose—a tall, bearded man of sixty, coarsely clad.

"I should like to ask one question, Mr. Coroner," he said. "What asylum did this yer last witness escape from?"

"Mr. Harker," said the coroner, gravely and tranquilly, "from what asylum did you last escape?"

Harker flushed crimson again, but said nothing, and the seven jurors rose and solemnly filed out of the cabin.

"If you have done insulting me, sir," said Harker, as soon as he and the officer were left alone with the dead man, "I suppose I am at liberty to go?"

"Yes."

Harker started to leave, but paused, with his hand on the door latch. The habit of his profession was strong in him—stronger than his sense of personal dignity. He turned about and said:

"The book that you have there—I recognize it as Morgan's diary. You seemed greatly interested in it; you read in it while I was testifying. May I see it? The public would like—"

"The book will cut no figure in this matter," replied the official, slipping it into his coat pocket. "All the entries in it were made before the writer's death."

As Harker passed out of the house the jury reentered and stood about the table, on which the now covered corpse showed under the sheet with sharp definition. The foreman seated himself near the candle, produced from his breast pocket a pencil and scrap of paper and wrote rather laboriously the following verdict, which with various degrees of effort all signed:

"We, the jury, do find that the remains come to their death at the hands of a mountain lion, but some of us thinks, all the same, they had fits."

IV
AN EXPLANATION FROM THE TOMB

In the diary of the late Hugh Morgan are certain interesting entries having, possibly, a scientific value as suggestions. At the inquest upon his body the book was not put in evidence; possibly the coroner thought it not worthwhile to confuse the jury. The date of the first of the entries mentioned cannot be ascertained; the upper part of the leaf is torn away. The part of the entry remaining follows:

". . . would run in a half-circle, keeping his head turned always toward the center, and again he would stand still, barking furiously. At last he ran away into the brush as fast as he could go. I thought at first that he had gone mad, but on returning to the house found no other alteration in his manner than what was obviously due to fear of punishment.

"Can a dog see with his nose? Do odors impress some cerebral center with images of the thing that emitted them? . . .

"Sept. 2—Looking at the stars last night as they rose above the crest of the ridge east of the house, I observed them successively disappear—from left to right. Each was eclipsed but an instant, and only a few at the same time, but along the entire length of the ridge all that were within a degree or two of the crest were blotted out. It was as if something had passed along between me and them; but I could not see it, and the stars were not thick enough to define its outline. Ugh! I don't like this."

Several weeks' entries are missing, three leaves being torn from the book.

"Sept. 27—It has been about here again—I find evidences of its presence every day. I watched again all last night in the same cover, gun in hand, double-charged with buckshot. In the morning the fresh footprints were there, as before. Yet I would have sworn that I did not sleep—indeed, I hardly sleep at all. It is terrible, insupportable! If these amazing experiences are real I shall go mad; if they are fanciful I am mad already.

"Oct. 3—I shall not go—it shall not drive me away. No, this is *my* house, *my* land. God hates a coward. . . .

"Oct. 5—I can stand it no longer; I have invited Harker to pass a few weeks with me—he has a level head. I can judge from his manner if he thinks me mad.

"Oct. 7—I have the solution of the mystery; it came to me last night—suddenly, as by revelation. How simple—how terribly simple!

"There are sounds that we cannot hear. At either end of the scale are notes that stir no chord of that imperfect instrument, the human ear. They are too high or too grave. I have observed a flock of blackbirds occupying an entire treetop—the tops of several trees—and all in full song. Suddenly—in a moment—at absolutely the same instant—all spring into the air and fly away. How? They could not all see one another—whole treetops intervened. At no point could a leader have been visible to all. There must have been a signal of warning or command, high and shrill above the din, but by me unheard. I have observed, too, the same simultaneous flight when all were silent, among not only blackbirds, but other birds—quail, for example, widely separated by bushes—even on opposite sides of a hill.

"It is known to seamen that a school of whales basking or sporting on the surface of the ocean, miles apart, with the convexity of the earth between, will sometimes dive at the same instant—all gone out of sight in a moment. The signal has been sounded—too grave for the ear of the sailor at the masthead and his comrades on the deck—who nevertheless feel its vibrations in the ship as the stones of a cathedral are stirred by the bass of the organ.

"As with sounds, so with colors. At each end of the solar spectrum the chemist can detect the presence of what are known as actinic rays. They represent colors—integral colors in the composition of light—which we are unable to discern. The human eye is an imperfect instrument; its range is but a few octaves of the real chromatic scale. I am not mad; there are colors that we cannot see.

"And, God help me! the Damned Thing is of such a color!"

FABLES

THE MAN WITH NO ENEMIES

An Inoffensive Person walking in a public place was assaulted by a Stranger with a Club, and severely beaten.

When the Stranger with a Club was brought to trial, the complainant said to the Judge:

"I do not know why I was assaulted. I have not an enemy in the world."

"That," said the defendant, "is why I struck him."

"Let the prisoner be discharged," said the Judge. "A man who has no enemies has no friends. The courts are not for such."

THE LIFESAVER

Seventy-five Men presented themselves before the President of the Humane Society and demanded the great gold medal for lifesaving.

"Why, yes," said the President. "By diligent effort so many men must have saved a considerable number of lives. How many did you save?"

"Seventy-five, sir," replied their Spokesman.

"Ah, yes, that is one each—very good work—very good work, indeed," the President said. "You shall not only have the Society's great gold medal, but its recommendation for employment at the several lifeboat stations along the coast. But how did you save so many lives?"

The Spokesman of the Men replied:

"We are officers of the law, and have just abandoned the pursuit of two murderous outlaws."

221

SAINT AND SINNER

"My friend," said a distinguished officer of the Salvation Army to a Most Wicked Sinner, "I was once a drunkard, a thief, an assassin. The Divine Grace has made me what I am."

The Most Wicked Sinner looked at him from head to foot. "Henceforth," he said, "the Divine Grace, I fancy, will let well enough alone."

SAINT AND SOUL

St. Peter was sitting at the gate of Heaven when a Soul approached, and, bowing civilly, handed him its card.

"I am very sorry, sir," said St. Peter, after reading the card, "but I really cannot admit you. You will have to go to the Other Place. Sorry, sir, very sorry."

"Don't mention it," said the Soul. "I have been all the month at a watering place, and it will be an agreeable change. I called only to ask if my friend Elihu Root is here."

"No, sir," the Saint replied, "Mr. Root is not dead."

"Oh, I know that," said the Soul. "I thought he might be visiting God."

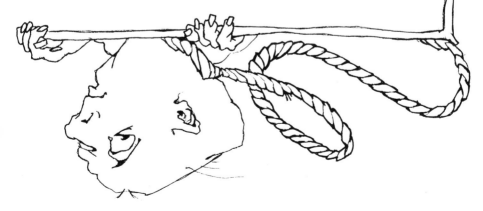

THE LASSOED BEAR

A Hunter who had lassoed a Bear was trying to disengage himself from the rope, but the slip-knot about his wrist would not yield, for the Bear was all the time pulling in the slack with his paws. In the midst of his trouble the Hunter saw a Showman passing by and managed to attract his attention.

"What will you give me," he said, "for my Bear?"

"It will be some five or ten minutes," said the Showman, "before I shall want a bear, and it looks to me as if prices would fall during that time. I think I'll wait and watch the market."

"The price of this animal," the Hunter replied, "is down to bedrock. You can have him for a cent a pound, spot cash, and I'll throw in the next one that I lasso. But the purchaser must remove the goods from the premises forthwith, to make room for the three man-eating tigers, a cat-headed gorilla and an armful of rattlesnakes."

But the Showman passed on in maiden meditation, fancy free, and being joined soon afterward by the Bear, who was absently picking his teeth, it was inferred that they were not unacquainted.

THE AUSTRALIAN GRASSHOPPER

A Distinguished Naturalist was traveling in Australia, when he saw a Kangaroo in session and flung a stone at it. The Kangaroo immediately adjourned, tracing against the sunset sky a parabolic curve spanning seven provinces, and vanished below the horizon. The Distinguished Naturalist looked interested, but said nothing for an hour; then he said to his native Guide:

"You have pretty wide meadows here, I suppose?"

"No, not very wide," the Guide answered. "About the same as in England and America."

After another long silence the Distinguished Naturalist said:

"The hay which we shall purchase for our horses this evening—I shall expect to find the stalks about fifty feet long. Am I right?"

"Why, no," said the Guide, "a foot or two is about the usual length of our hay. What can you be thinking of?"

The Distinguished Naturalist made no immediate reply, but later, as in the shades of night they journeyed through the desolate vastness of the Great Lone Land, he broke the silence:

"I was thinking," he said, "of the uncommon magnitude of that grasshopper."

THE DISCONTENTED MALEFACTOR

A Judge having sentenced a Malefactor to the penitentiary was proceeding to point out to him the disadvantages of crime and the profit of reformation.

"Your Honor," said the Malefactor, interrupting, "would you be kind enough to alter my punishment to ten years in the penitentiary and nothing else?"

"Why," said the Judge, surprised, "I have given you only three years!"

"Yes, I know," assented the Malefactor—"three years' imprisonment and the preaching. If you please, I should like to commute the preaching."

TWO POETS

Two Poets were quarreling for the Apple of Discord and the Bone of Contention, for they were very hungry.

"My sons," said Apollo, "I will part the prizes between you. You," he said to the First Poet, "excel in Art—take the Apple. And you," he said to the Second Poet, "in Imagination—take the Bone."

"To Art the best prize!" said the First Poet, triumphantly, and endeavoring to devour his award broke all his teeth. The Apple was a work of Art.

"That shows our master's contempt for mere Art," said the Second Poet, grinning.

Thereupon he attempted to gnaw his Bone, but his teeth passed through it without encountering resistance. It was an imaginary Bone.

THE AUSTERE GOVERNOR

A Governor visiting a state prison was implored by a Convict to pardon him.

"What are you in for?" asked the Governor.

"I held a high office," the Convict humbly replied, "and sold subordinate appointments."

"Then I decline to interfere," said the Governor, with asperity. "A man who abuses his office by making it serve a private end and purvey a personal advantage is unfit to be free. By the way, Mr. Warden," he added to that official, as the Convict slunk away, "in appointing you to this position, I was given to understand that your friends could make the Shikane County delegation to the next state convention solid for—for the present administration. Was I rightly informed?"

"You were, sir."

"Very well, then, I will bid you good day. Please be so good as to appoint my nephew Night Chaplain and Reminder of Mothers and Sisters."

THE REFORM SCHOOL BOARD

The members of the School Board in Doosnoswair being suspected of appointing female teachers for an improper consideration, the people elected a Board composed wholly of women. In a few years the scandal was at an end; there were no female teachers in the Department.

THE WITCH'S STEED

A Broomstick that had long served a witch as a steed complained of the nature of its employment, which it thought degrading.

"Very well," said the Witch, "I will give you work in which you will be associated with intellect—you will come in contact with brains. I shall present you to a housewife."

"What!" said the Broomstick, "do you consider the hands of a housewife intellectual?"

"I referred," said the Witch, "to the head of her good man."

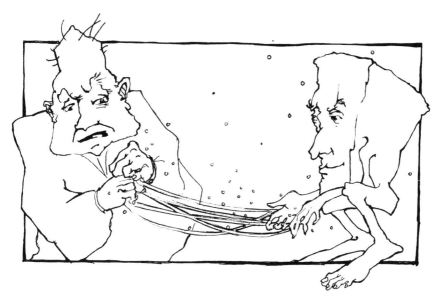

LEGISLATOR AND SOAP

A member of the Kansas Legislature meeting a Cake of Soap
was passing it by without recognition, but the Cake of Soap
insisted on stopping and shaking hands. Thinking it might
possibly be in the enjoyment of the elective franchise, he gave
it a cordial and earnest grasp. On letting it go he observed that
a part of it adhered to his fingers, and running to a brook in
great alarm, proceeded to wash it off. In doing so he neces-
sarily got some on the other hand, and when he had finished
washing both were so white that he went to bed and sent for
a physician.

THE TRIED ASSASSIN

An Assassin being put upon trial in a New England court, his
Counsel rose and said, "Your Honor, I move for a discharge
on the ground of 'once in jeopardy': my client has been already
tried for that murder and acquitted."

"In what court?" asked the Judge.

"In the Superior Court of San Francisco," the Counsel replied.

"Let the trial proceed—your motion is denied," said the
Judge. "An Assassin is not in jeopardy when tried in California."

THE BUMBO OF JIAM

The Pahdour of Patagascar and the Gookul of Madagonia were disputing about an island that both claimed. Finally, at the suggestion of the International League of Cannon Founders, which had important branches in both countries, they decided to refer their claims to the Bumbo of Jiam, and abide by his judgment. In settling the preliminaries of the arbitration they had, however, the misfortune to disagree, and appealed to arms. At the end of a long and disastrous war, when both sides were exhausted and bankrupt, the Bumbo of Jiam intervened in the interest of peace.

"My great and good friends," he said to his brother sovereigns, "it will be advantageous to you to learn that some questions are more complex and perilous than others, presenting a greater number of points upon which it is possible to differ. For four generations your royal predecessors disputed about possession of that island without falling out. Beware, oh, beware the perils of international arbitration!—against which I feel it my duty to protect you henceforth."

So saying, he annexed both countries, and after a long, peaceful and happy reign was poisoned by his Prime Minister.

THE CITY OF POLITICAL DISTINCTION

Jamrach the Rich, being anxious to reach the City of Political Distinction before nightfall, arrived at a fork of the road and was undecided which branch to follow; so he consulted a Wise-Looking Person who sat by the wayside.

"Take *that* road," said the Wise-Looking Person, pointing it out. "It is known as the Political Highway."

"Thank you," said Jamrach, and was about to proceed.

"About how much do you thank me?" was the reply. "Do you suppose I am here for my health?"

As Jamrach had not become rich by stupidity he handed something to his guide and hastening on soon came to a toll gate kept by a Benevolent Gentleman, to whom he gave something and was suffered to pass. A little farther along he came to a bridge across an imaginary stream, where a Civil Engineer (who had built the bridge) demanded something for interest on his investment, and it was forthcoming. It was growing late when Jamrach came to the margin of what appeared to be a lake of black ink, and there the road terminated. Seeing a Ferryman in his boat he paid something for his passage and was about to embark.

"No," said the Ferryman. "Put your neck in this noose, and I will tow you over. It is the only way," he added, seeing that the passenger was about to complain of the accommodations.

In due time he was dragged across, half strangled and dreadfully beslubbered by the feculent waters. "There," said the Ferryman, hauling him ashore and disengaging him, "you are now in the City of Political Distinction. It has fifty millions of inhabitants, and as the color of the Filthy Pool does not wash off, they all look exactly alike."

"Alas!" exclaimed Jamrach, weeping and bewailing the loss of all his possessions, paid out in tips and tolls. "I will go back with you."

"I don't think you will," said the Ferryman, pushing off. "This city is situated on the Island of the Unreturning."

THE TOLERANT SOVEREIGN

The Gamdoodle of Moop summoned his Secretary of War to an audience and said:

"Sir, you cannot be unaware of the great outcry that my loyal subjects are making against you. They say that you are a rascal."

"Your Majesty," replied the Secretary of War, "it is untrue."

"I'm right glad to hear it," the Gamdoodle replied, rising to intimate that the interview was at an end. But observing that the official did not depart, he added, "Is there anything to say?"

"Yes, your Majesty," the Secretary of War answered. "I wish to surrender my portfolio, for while the public outcry is untrue it is not unjust. I am a fool."

At this the Gamdoodle was graciously pleased to smile. "My good man," he said, "return to your duties. I am that way myself."

A LITTLE LEARNING

Having been taught Greek, a Parrot was puffed up with conceit.

"Observe," said he, "the advantages of a classical education! I can chatter nonsense in the tongue of Plato."

"I should advise you," said his Master, quietly, "to let it be nonsense of a character somewhat different from that of some of Plato's most admired compatriots if you value the privilege of hanging at that open window. Commit no mythology, please."

THE FLYING MACHINE

An Ingenious Man who had built a flying machine invited a great concourse of people to see it go up. At the appointed moment, everything being ready, he boarded the car and turned on the power. The machine immediately broke through the massive substructure upon which it was builded, and sank out of sight into the earth, the aeronaut springing out barely in time to save himself.

"Well," said he, "I have done enough to demonstrate the correctness of my details. The defects," he added, with a look at the ruined brickwork, "are merely basic and fundamental."

On this assurance the people came forward with subscriptions to build a second machine.

THE INCREDULOUS SUBORDINATE

A Commanding General retreating after defeat came upon the camp of a Subordinate, who was playing cards with his men.

"Why did you not march to my assistance, sir?" thundered the Commanding General. "Did you not hear the reports of my guns?"

"Reports? Oh, yes," the Subordinate replied. "I heard them all right, but I did not believe them. I used to be a reporter."

THE STATUE AT BUMBOOGLE

On a high hill overlooking the ancient city of Bumboogle is a colossal statue, erected by the nation, to the memory of the illustrious Gaaka-Wolwol, "the best and wisest of mankind." A Traveler from a distant country said to the Custodian of the Statue, who is the highest officer of the realm, "The winds of the sea, O Most Exalted, have not blown the fame of your great countryman to my native shores. What did he do?"

"Nothing. That is how we know him to have been good."

"But his wisdom—what did he say?"

"Nothing. That is how we know him to have been wise."

TWO POLITICIANS

Two Politicians were exchanging ideas regarding the rewards for public service.

"The reward that I most desire," said the First Politician, "is the gratitude of my fellow citizens."

"That would be very gratifying, no doubt," said the Second Politician, "but, alas! in order to obtain it one has to retire from politics."

For an instant they gazed upon each other with inexpressible tenderness; then the First Politician murmured, "God's will be done! Since we cannot hope for reward, let us be content with what we have."

And lifting their right hands for a moment from the public treasury they swore to be content.

A FAULTY PERFORMANCE

A pet Opossum belonging to a Great Critic stole his favorite kitten and was about to kill and eat it when she saw him approaching, and fearing detection she concealed it in her pouch.

"Well, my pretty one," said the Great Critic, with condescension, "what new charms and graces have you today?"

Before she could reply the kitten set up a diligent and persistent mewing. When at last the music had ceased the Opossum said:

"I've been dabbling a little in mimicry and ventriloquism. I thought it would please you, sir."

"The desire to please is ever pleasing," the Great Critic answered, not without a touch of professional dignity, "but you have much to learn about the mewing of kittens."

A DEFECTIVE PETITION

An Associate Justice of the Supreme Court was sitting by a river when a Traveler approached and said:

"I wish to cross. Will it be lawful to use this boat?"

"It will" was the reply. "It is my boat."

The Traveler thanked him, and pushing the boat into the water embarked and rowed away. But the boat sank and he was drowned.

"Heartless man!" said an Indignant Spectator. "Why did you not tell him that your boat had a hole in it?"

"The matter of the boat's condition," said the great jurist, "was not brought before me."

THE REFORMED ANARCHIST

A famous Anarchist wrecked at sea was cast ashore upon the island of Gowqueechy, inhabited by the ancient and powerful tribe of Tumtums. He was found and taken before the Jamgrogrum, who asked him his political faith.

"We ask all strangers that," the Jamgrogrum explained, "in the hope that someday we shall hear of political principles that are superior to ours."

"I am an Anarchist," answered the stranger. "I hold that all government is wicked, all laws are oppressive. I teach that all Jamgrogra should be assassinated."

The monarch called his Prime Minister to his side and giving him some whispered instructions retired.

The next day, when the Prime Minister had presented himself at the palace and had eaten a handful of clay, as court etiquette required, he was asked by the Jamgrogrum for news of the Anarchist.

"May your Majesty's tomb stand forever," said the Prime Minister. "I had him taken to the baths and carefully washed all over."

"Well?"

"When asked, according to your Majesty's instructions, if he were still an Anarchist, he replied that no treatment, however harsh and cruel, could alter his convictions."

"Indeed," exclaimed the Jamgrogrum, with the dejected air of one deprived of a cherished illusion, "then my theory of the unity of dirt and anarchism is overthrown."

"No, your Majesty," said the Prime Minister. "He died ten minutes after the bath."

PATRIOT AND BANKER

A Patriot who had taken office poor and retired rich was introduced at a bank where he desired to open an account.

"With pleasure," said the Honest Banker. "We shall be glad to do business with you, but first you must make yourself an honest man by restoring what you stole from the Government."

"Good heavens!" cried the Patriot. "If I do that, I shall have nothing to deposit with you."

"I don't see that," the Honest Banker replied. "We are not the whole American people."

"Ah, I understand," said the Patriot, musing. "At what sum do you estimate this bank's proportion of the country's loss by me?"

"About a dollar," answered the Honest Banker.

And with a proud consciousness of serving his country wisely and well he charged that sum to the account.

A HASTY SETTLEMENT

"Your Honor," said an Attorney, rising, "what is the present status of this case—as far as it has gone?"

"I have given a judgment for the residuary legatee under the will," said the Court, "put the costs upon the contestants, decided all questions relating to fees and other charges; and, in short, the estate in litigation has been settled, with all controversies, disputes, misunderstandings and differences of opinion thereunto appertaining."

"Ah, yes, I see," said the Attorney, thoughtfully, "we are making progress—we are getting on famously."

"Progress?" echoed the Judge. "Progress? Why, sir, the matter is concluded!"

"Exactly, exactly. It had to be concluded in order to give relevancy to the motion that I am about to make. Your Honor, I move that the judgment of the Court be set aside and the case reopened."

"Upon what ground, sir?" the Judge asked in surprise.

"Upon the ground," said the Attorney, "that after paying all fees and expenses of litigation and all charges against the estate there will still be something left."

"There may have been an error," said his Honor, thoughtfully. "The Court may have underestimated the value of the estate. The motion is taken under advisement."

THE CRIMSON CANDLE

A Man lying at the point of death called his wife to his bedside and said:

"I am about to leave you forever; give me, therefore, one last proof of your affection and fidelity. In my desk you will find a crimson candle, which has been blessed by the High Priest and has a peculiar mystical significance. Swear to me that while it is in existence you will not remarry."

The Woman swore and the Man died. At the funeral the Woman stood at the head of the bier, holding a lighted crimson candle till it was wasted entirely away.

THE FOOLISH WOMAN

A Married Woman, whose lover was about to reform by running away, procured a pistol and shot him dead.

"Why did you do that, madam?" inquired a Policeman, sauntering by.

"Because," replied the Married Woman, "he was a wicked man, and had purchased a ticket to Chicago."

"My sister," said an adjacent Man of God, solemnly, "you cannot stop the wicked from going to Chicago by killing them."

THE FUGITIVE OFFICE

A Traveler arriving at the capital of a nation saw a vast plain outside the wall, filled with struggling and shouting men. While he looked upon the alarming spectacle an Office broke away from the throng and took shelter in a tomb near to where he stood, the crowd being too intent upon hammering one another to observe that the cause of their contention had departed.

"Poor bruised and bleeding creature," said the compassionate Traveler, "what was your offense?"

"I sought the man," said the Office.

THE ELIGIBLE SON-IN-LAW

A Truly Clever Person who conducted a savings bank and lent money to his sisters and his cousins and his aunts was approached by a Tatterdemalion who applied for a loan of one hundred thousand dollars.

"What security have you to offer?" asked the Truly Clever Person.

"The best in the world," the applicant replied, confidentially. "I am about to become your son-in-law."

"That would indeed be gilt-edged," said the Banker, gravely, "but what claim have you to the hand of my daughter?"

"One that cannot be lightly denied," said the Tatterdemalion. "I am about to become worth one hundred thousand dollars."

Unable to detect a weak point in this scheme of mutual advantage, the Financier gave the Promoter in Disguise an order for the money and wrote a note to his wife directing her to count out the girl.

HIGHWAYMAN AND TRAVELER

A Highwayman confronted a Traveler, and covering him with a firearm, shouted, "Your money or your life!"

"My good friend," said the Traveler, "according to the terms of your demand my money will save my life, my life my money. You imply that you will take one or the other, but not both. If that is what you mean, please be good enough to take my life."

"That is not what I mean," said the Highwayman. "You cannot save your money by giving up your life."

"Then take it anyhow," the Traveler said. "If it will not save my money, it is good for nothing."

The Highwayman was so pleased with the Traveler's philosophy and wit that he took him into partnership and this splendid combination of talent started a newspaper.

POLICEMAN AND CITIZEN

A Policeman, finding a man who had fallen in a fit, said, "This man is drunk," and began beating him on the head with his club. A passing Citizen said:

"Why do you murder a man that is already harmless?"

Thereupon the Policeman left the man in a fit and attacked the Citizen, who after receiving several severe contusions ran away.

"Alas," said the Policeman, "why did I not attack the sober one before exhausting myself upon the other?"

Thenceforward he pursued that plan, and by zeal and diligence rose to be Chief, and sobriety is unknown in the region subject to his sway.

MORAL PRINCIPLE AND MATERIAL INTEREST

A Moral Principle met a Material Interest on a bridge wide enough for but one.

"Down, you base thing!" thundered the Moral Principle, "and let me pass over you!"

The Material Interest merely looked in the other's eyes without saying anything.

"Ah," said the Moral Principle, hesitatingly, "let us draw lots to see which one of us shall retire till the other has crossed."

The Material Interest maintained an unbroken silence and an unwavering stare.

"In order to avoid a conflict," the Moral Principle resumed, somewhat uneasily, "I shall myself lie down and let you walk over me."

Then the Material Interest found his tongue. "I don't think you are very good walking," he said. "I am a little particular about what I have underfoot. Suppose you get off into the water."

It occurred that way.

THE DUTIFUL SON

A Millionaire who had gone to an almshouse to visit his father met a Neighbor there, who was greatly surprised.

"What!" said the Neighbor, "you do sometimes visit your father?"

"If our situations were reversed," said the Millionaire, "I am sure he would visit me. The old man has always been rather proud of me. Besides," he added softly, "I had to have his signature. I am insuring his life."

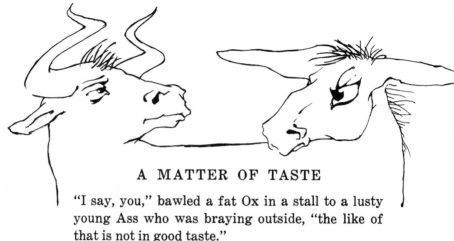

A MATTER OF TASTE

"I say, you," bawled a fat Ox in a stall to a lusty young Ass who was braying outside, "the like of that is not in good taste."

"In whose good taste, my adipose censor?" inquired the Ass, not too respectfully.

"Why—ah—h'm. I mean that it does not suit me. You should bellow."

"May I ask how it concerns you whether I bellow or bray, or do both, or neither?"

"I cannot tell you," said the Ox, shaking his head despondingly. "I do not at all understand the matter. I can only say that I have been used to censure all discourse that differs from my own."

"Exactly," said the Ass. "You have tried to make an art of impudence by calling preferences principles. In 'taste' you have invented a word incapable of definition to denote an idea impossible of expression, and by employing the word 'good' or 'bad' in connection with it you indicate a merely subjective process, in terms of an objective quality. Such presumption transcends the limits of mere effrontery and passes into the boundless empyrean of pure gall!"

The bovine critic, having no words to express his disapproval of this remarkable harangue, said it was in bad taste.

THE FABULIST

An Illustrious Satirist was visiting a traveling menagerie with a view to collecting literary materials. As he was passing near the Elephant that animal said:

"How sad that so justly famous a censor should mar his work by ridicule of persons with pendulous noses—who are the salt of the earth!"

240

The Kangaroo said:

"I do so enjoy that great man's censure of the ridiculous—particularly his attacks on the proboscidae, but, alas! he has no reverence for the marsupials, and laughs at our way of carrying our young in a pouch."

The Camel said:

"If he would only respect the Sacred Hump, he would be faultless. As it is, I cannot permit his work to be read in the presence of my family."

The Ostrich, seeing his approach, thrust her head into the straw, saying:

"If I do not conceal myself, he may be reminded to write something disagreeable about my lack of a crest, or my appetite for scrap iron; and although he is inexpressibly brilliant when he devotes himself to ridicule of folly and greed, his dullness is matchless when he transcends the limits of legitimate comment."

"That," said the Buzzard to his mate, "is the distinguished author of that glorious fable, 'The Ostrich and the Keg of Raw Nails.' I regret to add, that he wrote also, 'The Buzzard's Feast,' in which a carrion diet is contumeliously disparaged. A carrion diet is the foundation of sound health. If nothing but corpses were eaten, death would be unknown."

Seeing an attendant approaching, the Illustrious Satirist passed out of the tent and mingled with the crowd. It was afterward discovered that he had crept in under the canvas without paying.

TWO OF THE PIOUS

A Christian and a Heathen in His Blindness were disputing, when the Christian, with that charming consideration which serves to distinguish the truly pious from wolves that perish, exclaimed:

"If I could have my way, I'd blow up all your gods with dynamite."

"And if I could have mine," retorted the Heathen in His Blindness, bitterly malevolent but oleaginously suave, "I'd fan all yours out of the universe."

THE SECRET OF HAPPINESS

Having been told by an angel that Noureddin Becar was the happiest man in the world, the Sultan caused him to be brought to the palace and said:

"Impart to me, I command thee, the secret of thy happiness."

"O father of the sun and the moon," answered Noureddin Becar, "I did not know that I was happy."

"That," said the Sultan, "is the secret that I sought."

Noureddin Becar retired in deep dejection, fearing that his new-found happiness might forsake him.

ATONEMENT

Two Women in heaven claimed one Man newly arrived.

"I was his wife," said one.

"I his sweetheart," said the other.

St. Peter said to the Man, "Go down to the Other Place—you have suffered enough."

A PART OF THE WAGES

"Ours is a life of self-sacrifice," said a Clergyman. "While others pursue gain or pleasure, we burn the midnight oil in studying how to crack the hardest theological nuts. And all for what earthly reward?"

"Well," said his Parishioner, thoughtfully, "there are, for example, the kernels."

SHEEP AND LION

"You are a beast of war," said the Sheep to the Lion, "yet men go gunning for you. Me, a believer in nonresistance, they do not hunt."

"They do not need to," replied the son of the desert. "They can breed you."

OFFICER AND THUG

A Chief of Police who had seen an Officer beating a Thug was very indignant, and said he must not do so any more on pain of dismissal.

"Don't be too hard on me," said the Officer, smiling. "I was beating him with a stuffed club."

"Nevertheless," persisted the Chief of Police, "it was a liberty that must have been very disagreeable, though it may not have hurt. Please do not repeat it."

"But," said the Officer, still smiling, "it was a stuffed Thug."

In attempting to express his gratification the Chief of Police thrust out his right hand with such violence that his skin was ruptured at the armpit and a stream of sawdust poured from the wound. He was a stuffed Chief of Police.

FAMINE VERSUS PESTILENCE

"It is hard on you, my gallant friend," said the Victorious Besieger, "but I must say it. Pestilence was among my troops, and if you had not surrendered to me I should have surrendered to you."

"That is what I feared you would do," replied the Vanquished Commander. "My men were eating their belts and cartridge boxes. We could not properly provide for you."

THE INCONSOLABLE WIDOW

A Woman in widow's weeds was weeping upon a grave.

"Console yourself, madam," said a Sympathetic Stranger. "Heaven's mercies are infinite. There is another man somewhere, besides your husband, with whom you can still be happy."

"There was"—she sobbed—"there was, but this is his grave."

THE MYSTERIOUS WORD

The Chief of a battalion of war correspondents read a manuscript account of a battle.

"My son," he said to its Author, "your story is distinctly unavailable. You say we lost only two men instead of a hundred, that the enemy's loss is unknown, instead of ten thousand, and that we were defeated and ran away. That is no way to write."

"But consider," expostulated the conscientious scribe, "my story may be tame with regard to the number of our casualties, disappointing as to the damage done to the enemy, and shocking in its denouement, but it has the advantage of being the truth."

"I don't quite understand," said the Chief, scratching his head.

"Why, the advantage," the other exclaimed, "the merit—the distinction—the profitable excellence—the—"

"Oh," said the Chief, "I know very well the signification of 'advantage,' but what the devil do you mean by 'truth'?"

A PLUCKED GOOSE

A Man was plucking a live Goose, when the bird addressed him thus:

"Suppose that you were a goose. Do you think that you would relish this sort of thing?"

"Suppose that I were," said the Man. "Do you think that you would like to pluck me?"

"Indeed I should!" was the natural, emphatic, but injudicious reply.

"Just so," concluded her tormentor, pulling out another handful of feathers, "that is the way that *I* feel about it."

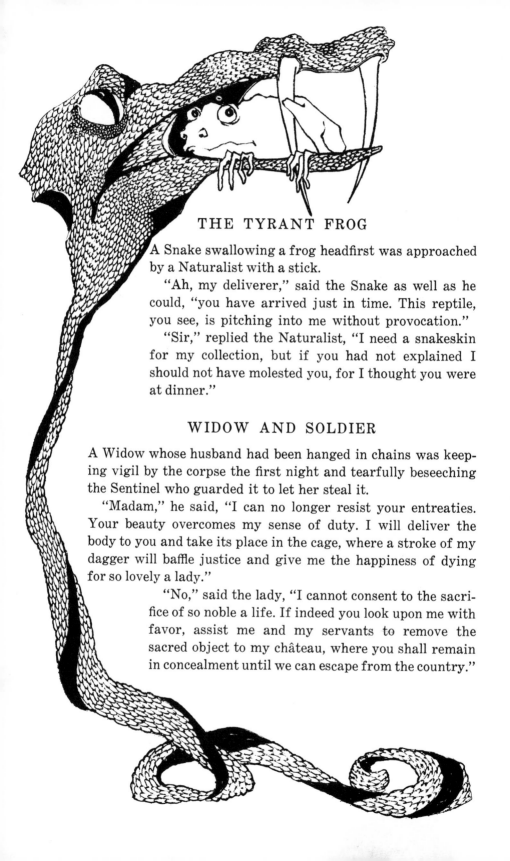

THE TYRANT FROG

A Snake swallowing a frog headfirst was approached by a Naturalist with a stick.

"Ah, my deliverer," said the Snake as well as he could, "you have arrived just in time. This reptile, you see, is pitching into me without provocation."

"Sir," replied the Naturalist, "I need a snakeskin for my collection, but if you had not explained I should not have molested you, for I thought you were at dinner."

WIDOW AND SOLDIER

A Widow whose husband had been hanged in chains was keeping vigil by the corpse the first night and tearfully beseeching the Sentinel who guarded it to let her steal it.

"Madam," he said, "I can no longer resist your entreaties. Your beauty overcomes my sense of duty. I will deliver the body to you and take its place in the cage, where a stroke of my dagger will baffle justice and give me the happiness of dying for so lovely a lady."

"No," said the lady, "I cannot consent to the sacrifice of so noble a life. If indeed you look upon me with favor, assist me and my servants to remove the sacred object to my château, where you shall remain in concealment until we can escape from the country."

"Nay," said the Sentinel, "I should surely be discovered and torn from your arms. In three days you can claim the body of your beloved husband; then you can confer upon an honorable soldier such happiness and distinction as you may think his devotion merits."

"Three days!" the lady exclaimed. "That is long for waiting and short for flight. If unencumbered we may reach the frontier. Already the day begins to break—let us leave the body and set out."

TWO SONS

A Man had Two Sons. The elder was virtuous and dutiful, the younger wicked and crafty. When the father was about to die, he called them before him and said, "I have only two things of value—my herd of camels and my blessing. How shall I allot them?"

"Give to me," said the Younger Son, "thy blessing, for it may reform me. The camels I should be sure to sell and squander the money."

The Elder Son, disguising his joy, said that he would try to be content with the camels and a pious mind.

It was so arranged, and the Man died. Then the wicked Younger Son went before the Cadi and said, "Behold, my brother has defrauded me of my lawful heritage. He is so bad that our father, as is well known, denied him his blessing. Is it likely that he gave him the camels?"

So the Elder Son was compelled to give up the herd and was soundly bastinadoed for his rapacity.

CONSOLATION

A great country having vindicated its courage and prowess by fifteen defeats in which none of its enemy's troops suffered any damage, its Prime Minister sued for peace.

"I'll not be hard on you," said the Victor. "You shall keep everything except your colonies, your liberty, your credit and your self-respect."

"Ah," said the Prime Minister, "you are indeed magnanimous. You leave us our honor."

THE SEEKER FOR SIMPLICITY

Laden with a grain of wheat which he had acquired with infinite toil, an Ant was breasting a current of his fellows, each of whom, as is their etiquette, insisted on stopping him, feeling him all over and shaking hands. It occurred to him that excess of ceremony is abuse of courtesy; so he laid down his burden, sat upon it, folded all his legs and smiled a smile of great grimness.

"Hello!" said his Fellow Ants, "what is the matter with you?"

"Sick of the hollow conventionalities of an effete civilization," was the rasping reply—"returned to the simplicity of primitive life."

"Ah! then we must trouble you for that grain. In the primitive life there are no rights of property."

A great white light fell upon the understanding of that rebellious insect. He rose and, grappling the grain of wheat, trotted away with alacrity. It was observed that he submitted with a wealth of patience to manipulation of his friends and neighbors and went long distances out of his way to shake hands with strangers on competing lines of traffic.

REVELATION

A Lion was attacked by a pack of famishing Wolves, who circled about him, howling as loud as they could, though none dared approach him.

"These are very useful creatures," said the Lion, as he lay down for his afternoon nap. "They apprise me of my virtues. I never before knew that I was good to eat."

DISAPPOINTMENT

A Dog that had been engaged in pursuit of his own tail abandoned the chase and, lying down, curled up for repose. In his new posture he found his tail within easy reach of his teeth and seized it with avidity, but immediately released it, wincing with pain.

"After all," he said, "there is more joy in pursuit than in possession."

THE JUSTICE AND HIS ACCUSER

An eminent Justice of the Supreme Court of Gowk was accused of having obtained his appointment by fraud.

"You wander," he said to the Accuser. "It is of little importance how I obtained my power. It is only important how I have used it."

"I confess," said the Accuser, "that in comparison with the rascally way in which you have conducted yourself on the Bench the rascally way in which you got there does seem rather a trifle."

WOLF AND TORTOISE

A Wolf, meeting a Tortoise, said, "My friend, you are the slowest thing out of doors. I do not see how you manage to escape from your enemies."

"As I lack the power to run away," replied the Tortoise, "Providence has thoughtfully supplied me with an impenetrable shell."

The Wolf reflected a long time; then he said:

"It seems to me that it would have been just as easy to give you long legs."

ALARM AND PRIDE

"Good morning, my friend," said Alarm to Pride. "How are you this morning?"

"Very tired," answered Pride, seating himself on a stone by the wayside and mopping his steaming brow. "The politicians are wearing me out by pointing to their dirty records with *me*, when they could as well use a stick."

Alarm sighed sympathetically and said:

"It is pretty much the same way here. Instead of using an opera glass they view the acts of their opponents with *me!*"

As these patient drudges were mingling their tears, they were notified that they must go on duty again, for one of the political parties had nominated a thief and was about to hold a gratification meeting.

ENVIRONMENT

"Prisoner," said the Judge, austerely, "you are justly convicted of murder. Are you guilty, or were you brought up in Kentucky?"

A CAUSEWAY

A Rich Woman having returned from abroad disembarked at the foot of Kneedeep Street, and was about to walk to her hotel through the mud.

"Madam," said a Policeman, "I cannot permit you to do that. You would soil your shoes and stockings."

"Oh, that is of no importance, really," replied the Rich Woman, with a cheerful smile.

"But, madam, it is needless. From the wharf to the hotel, as you observe, extends an unbroken line of prostrate newspapermen who crave the honor of having you walk upon them."

"In that case," she said, seating herself in a doorway and unlocking her satchel, "I shall have to put on my rubber boots."

A TALISMAN

Having been summoned to serve as a juror, a Prominent
Citizen sent a physican's certificate stating that he was afflicted
with softening of the brain.

"The gentleman is excused," said the Judge, handing back
the certificate to the person who had brought it. "He has a
brain."

THE SHADOW OF THE LEADER

A Political Leader was walking out one sunny day, when he
observed his Shadow leaving him and walking rapidly away.

"Come back here, you scoundrel," he cried.

"If I had been a scoundrel," answered the Shadow, increas-
ing its speed, "I should not have left you."

A RADICAL PARALLEL

Some White Christians engaged in driving Chinese Heathens
out of an American town found a newspaper published in
Peking in the Chinese tongue and compelled one of their vic-
tims to translate an editorial. It turned out to be an appeal to
the people of the province of Pang Ki to drive the foreign
devils out of the country and burn their dwellings and churches.
At this evidence of Mongolian barbarity the White Christians
were so greatly incensed that they carried out their original
design.

PHYSICIANS TWO

A Wicked Old Man finding himself ill sent for a Physician, who
prescribed for him and went away. Then the Wicked Old Man
sent for Another Physician, saying nothing of the first, and
an entirely different treatment was ordered. This continued
for some weeks, the physicians visiting him on alternate days

and treating him for two different disorders, with constantly enlarging doses of medicine and more and more rigorous nursing. But one day they accidentally met at his bedside while he slept and, the truth coming out, a violent quarrel ensued.

"My good friends," said the patient, awakened by the noise of the dispute, and apprehending the cause of it, "pray be more reasonable. If I could for weeks endure you both, can you not for a little while endure each other? I have been well for ten days, but have remained in bed in the hope of gaining by repose the strength that would justify me in taking your medicines. So far I have touched none of them."

THE THISTLES UPON THE GRAVE

A Mind Reader made a wager that he would be buried alive and remain so for six months, then be dug up alive. In order to secure the grave against secret disturbance, it was sown with thistles. At the end of three months the Mind Reader lost his bet. He had come up to eat the thistles.

KANGAROO AND ZEBRA

A Kangaroo, hopping awkwardly along with some bulky object concealed in her pouch, met a Zebra, and desirous of keeping his attention upon himself, said:

"Your costume looks as if you might have come out of the penitentiary."

"Appearances are deceitful," replied the Zebra, smiling in the consciousness of a more insupportable wit, "or I should have to think that you had come out of the Legislature."

THE HONEST CADI

A Robber who had plundered a merchant of one thousand pieces of gold was taken before the Cadi, who asked him if he had anything to say why he should not be decapitated.

254

"Your Honor," said the Robber, "I could do no otherwise than take the money, for Allah made me that way."

"Your defense is ingenious and sound," said the Cadi, "and I must acquit you of criminality. Unfortunately, Allah has also made me so that I must take off your head—unless," he added, thoughtfully, "you offer me a half of the gold; for He made me weak under temptation."

Thereupon the Robber put five hundred pieces of gold into the Cadi's hand.

"Good," said the Cadi. "I shall now remove only one-half your head. To show my trust in your discretion I shall leave intact the half that you talk with."

THE OVERLOOKED FACTOR

A Man that owned a fine Dog, and by a careful selection of its mate had bred a number of animals but a little lower than the angels, fell in love with his washerwoman, married her, and reared a family of dolts.

"Alas!" he exclaimed, contemplating the melancholy result, "had I but chosen a mate for myself with half the care that I did for my Dog I should now be a proud and happy father."

"I'm not so sure of that," said the Dog, overhearing the lament. "There's a difference, certainly, between your whelps and mine, but I flatter myself that it is not due altogether to the mothers. You and I are not entirely alike ourselves."

THE RETURNED CALIFORNIAN

A Man was hanged by the neck until he was dead. This was in 1893.

"Whence do you come?" Saint Peter asked when the Man presented himself at the gate of Heaven.

"From California," replied the applicant.

"Enter, my son, enter. You bring joyous tidings."

When the Man had vanished inside, Saint Peter took his memorandum tablet and made the following entry:

"February 16, 1893. California settled by the Christians."

THE NO CASE

A Statesman who had been indicted by an unfeeling Grand Jury was arrested by a Sheriff and thrown into jail. As this was abhorrent to his fine spiritual nature, he sent for the District Attorney and asked that the case against him be dismissed.

"Upon what grounds?" asked the District Attorney.

"Lack of evidence to convict," replied the accused.

"Do you happen to have the lack with you?" the official asked. "I should like to see it."

"With pleasure," said the other. "Here it is."

So saying he handed the other a check, which the District Attorney carefully examined, and then pronounced it the most complete absence of both proof and presumption that he had ever seen. He said it would acquit the poorest man in the world.

TWO OF THE DAMNED

Two Blighted Beings, haggard, lacrymose and detested, met on a blasted heath in the light of a struggling moon.

"I wish you a merry Christmas," said the First Blighted Being, in a voice like that of a singing tomb.

"And I you a happy New Year," responded the Second Blighted Being, with the accent of a penitent accordion.

They then fell upon each other's neck and wept scalding rills down each other's spine in token of their banishment to the Realm of Ineffable Bosh. For one of these accursed creatures was the First of January, and the other the Twenty-fifth of December.

RELIGIONS OF ERROR

Hearing a sound of strife, a Christian in the Orient asked his Dragoman the cause of it.

"The Buddhists are cutting Mohammedan throats," the Dragoman replied, with Oriental composure.

"I did not know," remarked the Christian, with scientific interest, "that that would make so much noise."

"The Mohammedans are cutting Buddhist throats," added the Dragoman.

"It is astonishing," mused the Christian, "how violent and how general are religious animosities."

So saying he visibly smugged and went off to telegraph for a brigade of cutthroats to protect Christian interests.

THE HUMBLE PEASANT

An Office Seeker whom the President had ordered out of Washington was watering the homeward highway with his tears.

"Ah," he said, "how disastrous is ambition! How unsatisfying its rewards! How terrible its disappointments! Behold yonder peasant tilling his field in peace and contentment! He rises with the lark, passes the day in wholesome toil, and lies down at night to pleasant dreams. In the mad struggle for place and power he has no part; the roar of the strife reaches his ear like the distant murmur of the ocean. Happy, thrice happy man! I will approach him and bask in the sunshine of his humble felicity. Peasant, hail!"

Leaning upon his rake, the Peasant returned the salutation with a nod, but said nothing.

"My friend," said the Office Seeker, "you see before you the wreck of an ambitious man—ruined by the pursuit of place and power. This morning when I set out from the national capital—"

"Stranger," the Peasant interrupted, "if you're going back there soon maybe you wouldn't mind using your influence to make me Postmaster at Smith's Corners."

The traveler passed on.

JUDGE AND RASH ACT

A Judge who had for years looked in vain for an opportunity for infamous distinction, but whom no litigant thought worth bribing, sat one day upon the Bench, lamenting his hard lot and threatening to put an end to his life if business did not improve. Suddenly he found himself confronted by a dreadful figure clad in a shroud, whose pallor and stony eyes smote him with a horrible apprehension.

"Who are you," he faltered, "and why do you come here?"

"I am the Rash Act," was the sepulchral reply. "You may commit me."

"No," the Judge said thoughtfully, "no, that would be quite irregular. I do not sit today as a committing magistrate."

DECEASED AND HEIRS

A Man died leaving a large estate and many sorrowful relations who claimed it. After some years, when all but one had had judgment given against them, that one was awarded the estate, which he asked his Attorney to have appraised.

"There is nothing to appraise," said the Attorney, pocketing his last fee.

"Then," said the Successful Claimant, "what good has all this litigation done me?"

"You have been a good client to me," the Attorney replied, gathering up his books and papers, "but I must say you betray a surprising ignorance of the purpose of litigation."

AN OPTIMIST

Two Frogs in the belly of a snake were considering their altered circumstances.

"This is pretty hard luck," said one.

"Don't jump to conclusions," the other said. "We are out of the wet and provided with board and lodging."

"With lodging, certainly," said the First Frog, "but I don't see the board."

"You are a croaker," the other explained. "We are the board."

THE COMPASSIONATE PHYSICIAN

A Kindhearted Physician sitting at the bedside of a patient afflicted with an incurable and painful disease heard a noise behind him and turning saw a Cat laughing at the feeble efforts of a wounded Mouse to drag itself out of the room.

"You cruel beast!" he cried. "Why don't you kill it at once, like a lady?"

Rising, he kicked the Cat out of the door and picking up the Mouse compassionately put it out of its misery by pulling off its head. Recalled to the bedside by the moans of his patient, the Kindhearted Physician administered a stimulant, a tonic and a nutrient, and went away.

A FORFEITED RIGHT

The Chief of the Weather Bureau having predicted a fair day, a Thrifty Person hastened to lay in a large stock of umbrellas, which he exposed for sale on the sidewalk; but the weather remained clear and nobody would buy. Thereupon the Thrifty Person brought an action against the Chief of the Weather Bureau for the cost of the umbrellas.

"Your Honor," said the Defendant's Attorney, when the case was called, "I move that this astonishing action be dismissed. Not only is my client in no way responsible for the loss, but he distinctly forecast the fair weather that caused it."

"That is just it, your Honor," replied the Counsel for the Plaintiff. "By making a correct forecast the defendant fooled my client in the only way that he could do so. He has lied so much and so notoriously that he has no right to tell the truth."

Judgment for the plaintiff.

REVENGE

An Insurance Agent was trying to induce a Hard Man to Deal With to take out a policy on his house. After listening to him for an hour, while he painted in vivid colors the extreme danger of fire consuming the house, the Hard Man to Deal With said:

"Do you really think it likely that my house will burn down inside the time that my policy will run?"

"Certainly," replied the Insurance Agent. "Have I not been trying all this time to convince you that I do?"

"Then," said the Hard Man to Deal With, "why are you so eager to have your Company bet me money that it will not?"

The Agent was silent and thoughtful for a moment; then he drew the other apart into an unfrequented place and whispered in his ear:

"My friend, I will impart to you a dark secret. Years ago the Company betrayed my sweetheart by promise of marriage. Under an assumed name I have wormed myself into its service for revenge; and as there is a heaven above us, I will have its heart's blood!"

MAN AND WART

A Person with a Wart on His Nose met a Person Similarly
Afflicted, and said:

"Let me propose your name for membership in the Im-
perial Order of Abnormal Proboscidians, of which I am
the High Noble Toby and Surreptitious Treasurer. Two
months ago I was the only member. One month ago there
were two. Today we number four Emperors of the Abnormal Proboscis in good standing—doubles every four
weeks, see? That's geometrical progression—you know
how that piles up. In a year and a half every man in the
country will have a wart on his nose. Powerful Order!
Initiation, five dollars."

"My friend," said the Person Similarly Afflicted, "here
are five dollars. Keep my name off your books."

"Thank you kindly," the Man with a Wart on His Nose
replied, pocketing the money. "It is just the same to us as
if you joined. Good-by."

He went away, but in a little while he was back.

"I quite forgot to mention the monthly dues," he said.

AN UNSPEAKABLE IMBECILE

A Judge said to a Convicted Assassin:

"Prisoner at the bar, have you anything to say why the death sentence should not be passed upon you?"

"Will what I say make any difference?" asked the Convicted Assassin.

"I do not see how it can," the Judge answered, reflectively. "No, it will not."

"Then," said the doomed one, "I should like to remark that you are the most unspeakable old imbecile in seven states and the District of Columbia."

AT HEAVEN'S GATE

Having risen from the tomb, a Woman presented herself at the gate of Heaven, and knocked with a trembling hand.

"Madam," said Saint Peter, rising and approaching the wicket, "whence do you come?"

"From San Francisco," replied the Woman, with embarrassment, as great beads of perspiration spangled her spiritual brow.

"Never mind, my good girl," the Saint said, compassionately. "Eternity is a long time. You can live that down."

"But that, if you please, is not all." The Woman was growing more and more confused. "I poisoned my husband. I chopped up my babies. I—"

"Ah," said the Saint, with sudden austerity, "your confession suggests a grave possibility. Were you a member of the Women's Press Association?"

The lady drew herself up and replied with warmth:

"I was not."

The gates of pearl and jasper swung back upon their golden hinges, making the most ravishing music, and the Saint, stepping aside, bowed low, saying:

"Enter, then, into thine eternal rest."

But the Woman hesitated.

"The poisoning—the chopping—the—the—"she stammered.

"Of no consequence, I assure you. We are not going to be

hard on a lady who did not belong to the Women's Press Association. Take a harp."

"But I applied for membership—I was blackballed."

"Take two harps."

FOGY AND SHEIK

A Fogy who lived in a cave near a great caravan route returned to his home one day and saw, nearby, a great concourse of men and animals, and in their midst a tower, at the foot of which something with wheels smoked and panted like an exhausted horse. He sought the Sheik of the Outfit.

"What sin art thou committing now, O son of a Christian dog?" said the Fogy, with a truly Oriental politeness.

"Boring for water, you black-and-tan galoot!" replied the Sheik of the Outfit, with that ready repartee which distinguishes the Unbeliever.

"Knowest thou not, thou whelp of darkness and father of disordered livers," cried the Fogy, "that water will cause grass to spring up here, and trees and possibly even flowers? Knowest thou not that thou art, in truth, producing an oasis?"

"And don't you know," said the Sheik of the Outfit, "that caravans will then stop here for rest and refreshment, giving you a chance to steal the camels, the horses and the goods?"

"May the wild hog defile my grave, but thou speakest wisdom!" the Fogy replied, with the dignity of his race, extending his hand. "Sheik."

They shook.

SPORTSMAN AND SQUIRREL

A Sportsman who had wounded a Squirrel, which was making desperate efforts to drag itself away, ran after it with a stick, exclaiming:

"Poor thing! I will put it out of its misery."

At that moment the Squirrel stopped from exhaustion, and looking up at its enemy, said:

"I don't venture to doubt the sincerity of your compassion, though it comes rather late, but you seem to lack the faculty of observation. Do you not perceive by my actions that the dearest wish of my heart is to continue in my misery?"

At this exposure of his hypocrisy the Sportsman was so overcome with shame and remorse that he would not strike the Squirrel, but pointing it out to his dog, walked thoughtfully away.

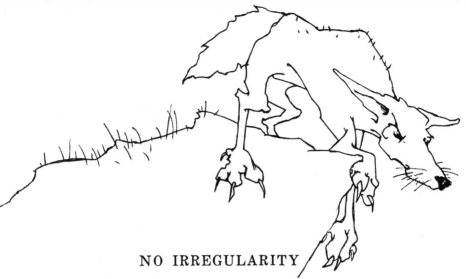

NO IRREGULARITY

A Jackal in pursuit of a Deer was about to seize it, when an earthquake opened a broad and deep chasm between him and his prey.

"This," he said, "is a pernicious interference with the laws of Nature. I refuse to recognize any such irregularity."

So he resumed the chase, endeavoring to cross the abyss by two leaps.

A TRANSPOSITION

Traveling through the sagebrush country a Jackass met a Rabbit, who exclaimed in great astonishment:

"Good heavens! How did you grow so big? You are doubtless the largest rabbit living."

"No," said the Jackass, "you are the smallest donkey."

After a good deal of fruitless argument the question was referred for decision to a passing Coyote, who was a bit of a demagogue and desirous to stand well with both.

"Gentlemen," said he, "you are both right, as was to have been expected of persons so gifted with appliances for receiving instruction from the wise. You, sir"—turning to the superior animal—"are, as he has accurately observed, a rabbit. And you"—to the other—"are correctly described as a jackass. In transposing your names man has acted with incredible folly."

They were so pleased with the decision that they declared the Coyote their candidate for the Grizzly Bearship; but whether he ever obtained the office history does not relate.

OLD MAN AND PUPIL

A Beautiful Old Man, meeting a Sunday school Pupil, laid his hand tenderly upon the lad's head, saying, "Listen, my son, to the words of the wise and heed the advice of the righteous."

"All right," said the Sunday school Pupil, "go ahead."

"Oh, I haven't anything to tell you, really," said the Beautiful Old Man. "I am only observing one of the customs of age. I am a pirate."

And when he had taken his hand from the lad's head the latter observed that his hair was full of clotted blood. Then the Beautiful Old Man went his way, instructing other youth.

TWO FOOTPADS

Two Footpads sat at their grog in a roadside resort, comparing the evening's adventures.

"I held up the Chief of Police," said the First Footpad, "and got away with what he had."

"And I," said the Second Footpad, "held up the United States District Attorney, and got away with—"

"Good Lord!" interrupted the other in astonishment and admiration, "you got away with what that fellow had?"

"No," the unfortunate narrator explained, "with a small part of what *I* had."

DOG AND DOCTOR

A Dog that had seen a Doctor attending the burial of a wealthy patient, said, "When do you expect to dig it up?"

"Why should I dig it up?" the Doctor asked.

"When I bury a bone," said the Dog, "it is with an intention to uncover it later and pick it."

"The bones that I bury," said the Doctor, "are those that I can no longer pick."

THE MONK
AND THE HANGMAN'S
DAUGHTER

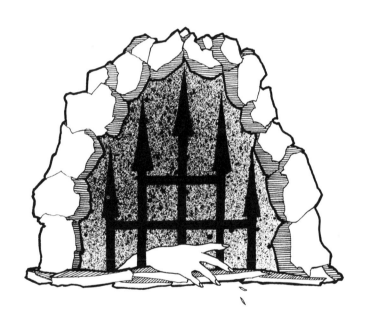

Written in Collaboration with
G. A. DANZIGER

PREFACE

Many years ago—probably in 1890—Dr. Gustav Adolf Danziger brought to me in San Francisco what he said was a translation by himself of a German story by that brilliant writer Herr Richard Voss, of Heidelberg. As Dr. Danziger had at that time a most imperfect acquaintance with the English language, he asked me to rewrite his version of Herr Voss's work for publication in this country. In reading it I was struck by what seemed to me certain possibilities of amplification, and I agreed to do the work if given a free hand by both author and translator. To this somewhat ill-considered proposal, which I supposed would make an end of the matter, I was afterward assured that the author, personally known to the translator, had assented. The result was this book, published by F. J. Schulte & Company of Chicago. Almost coincidentally in point of time the publishers failed, and it was, so far as I know, never put upon the market.

Never having seen the original story, and having no skill in German anyhow, I am unable to say what liberties Dr. Danziger may have taken with his author's text. To me he professed to have taken none; yet, in recent books of his, he is described on the title pages as "Author of The Monk and the Hangman's Daughter"—a statement that seems to justify, if not compel, this brief account of a matter which, though not particularly important, has given rise to more discussion than I have cared to engage in.

By a merely literary artifice the author of the German tale professed to have derived it from another writing, and in the Schulte version appeared the note following:

"The foundation of this narrative is an old manuscript originally belonging to the Franciscan monastery at Berchtesgaden, Bavaria. The manuscript was obtained from a peasant by Herr Richard Voss, of Heidelberg, from whose German version this is an adaptation."

I have always felt that this was inadequate acknowledgment of the work of Herr Voss, for whom I have the profoundest admiration. Not the least part of my motive and satisfaction in republishing lies in the opportunity that it supplies for doing justice to one to whose splendid imagination the chief credit of the tale is due. My light opinion of the credit due to anyone else is attested by my retention of Dr. Danziger's name on the title page. In this version the work that came into my hands from his has been greatly altered and extended.

Washington, D.C.   AMBROSE BIERCE
November 29, 1906

The Monk

and the

Hangman's
Daughter

I

ON the first day of May in the year of our Blessed Lord
1680, the Franciscan monks Aegidius, Romanus and
Ambrosius were sent by their superior from the
Christian city of Passau to the monastery of Berchtesgaden,
near Salzburg. I, Ambrosius, was the strongest and youngest
of the three, being but twenty-one years of age.

The monastery of Berchtesgaden was, we knew, in a wild
and mountainous country, covered with dismal forests, which
were infested with bears and evil spirits; and our hearts were
filled with sadness to think what might become of us in so
dreadful a place. But since it is Christian duty to obey the
mandates of the Church, we did not complain, and were even
glad to serve the wish of our beloved and revered superior.

Having received the benediction, and prayed for the last
time in the church of our saint, we tied up our cowls, put new
sandals on our feet, and set out, attended by the blessings
of all. Although the way was long and perilous, we did not
lose our hope, for hope is not only the beginning and the end
of religion, but also the strength of youth and the support of
age. Therefore our hearts soon forgot the sadness of parting,
and rejoiced in the new and varying scenes that gave us our
first real knowledge of the beauty of the earth as God has made
it. The color and brilliance of the air were like the garment of
the Blessed Virgin; the sun shone like the Golden Heart of
the Savior, from which streameth light and life for all man-

273

kind; the dark-blue canopy that hung above formed a grand and beautiful house of prayer, in which every blade of grass, every flower and living creature praised the glory of God.

As we passed through the many hamlets, villages and cities that lay along our way, the thousands of people, busy in all the vocations of life, presented to us poor monks a new and strange spectacle, which filled us with wonder and admiration. When so many churches came into view as we journeyed on, and the piety and ardor of the people were made manifest by the acclamations with which they hailed us and their alacrity in ministering to our needs, our hearts were full of gratitude and happiness. All the institutions of the Church were prosperous and wealthy, which showed that they had found favor in the sight of the good God whom we serve. The gardens and orchards of the monasteries and convents were well-kept, proving the care and industry of the pious peasantry and the holy inmates of the cloisters. It was glorious to hear the peals of bells announcing the hours of the day: we actually breathed music in the air—the sweet tones were like the notes of angels singing praise to the Lord.

Wherever we went we greeted the people in the name of our Patron saint. On all sides were manifest humility and joy: women and children hastened to the wayside, crowding about us to kiss our hands and beseech a blessing. It almost seemed as if we were no longer poor servitors of God and man, but lords and masters of this whole beautiful earth. Let us, however, not grow proud in spirit, but remain humble, looking carefully into our hearts lest we deviate from the rules of our holy order and sin against our blessed saint.

I, Brother Ambrosius, confess with penitence and shame that my soul caught itself upon exceedingly worldly and sinful thoughts. It seemed to me that the women sought more eagerly to kiss my hands than those of my companions—which surely was not right, since I am not more holy than they; besides, I am younger and less experienced and tried in the fear and commandments of the Lord. When I observed this error of the women, and saw how the maidens kept their eyes upon me, I became frightened, and wondered if I could resist should temptation accost me; and often I thought, with fear and trembling, that vows and prayer and penance alone do not make one a saint; one must be so pure in heart that temptation is unknown. Ah me!

At night we always lodged in some monastery, invariably receiving a pleasant welcome. Plenty of food and drink was set before us, and as we sat at table the monks would crowd about, asking for news of the great world of which it was our blessed privilege to see and learn so much. When our destination was learned we were usually pitied for being doomed to live in the mountain wilderness. We were told of ice fields, snow-crowned mountains and tremendous rocks, roaring torrents, caves and gloomy forests; also of a lake so mysterious and terrible that there was none like it in the world. God be with us!

On the fifth day of our journey, while but a short distance beyond the city of Salzburg, we saw a strange and ominous sight. On the horizon, directly in our front, lay a bank of mighty clouds, with many gray points and patches of darker hue, and above, between them and the blue sky, a second firmament of perfect white. This spectacle greatly puzzled and alarmed us. The clouds had no movement; we watched them for hours and could see no change. Later in the afternoon, when the sun was sinking into the west, they became ablaze with light. They glowed and gleamed in a wonderful manner, and looked at times as if they were on fire!

No one can imagine our surprise when we discovered that what we had mistaken for clouds was simply earth and rocks. These, then, were the mountains of which we had heard so much, and the white firmament was nothing else than the snowy summit of the range—which the Lutherans say their faith can remove. I greatly doubt it.

II

When we stood at the opening of the pass leading into the mountains we were overcome with dejection; it looked like the mouth of hell. Behind us lay the beautiful country through which we had come, and which now we were compelled to leave forever; before us frowned the mountains with their inhospitable gorges and haunted forests, forbidding to the sight and full of peril to the body and the soul. Strengthening our hearts with prayer and whispering anathemas against evil spirits, we entered the narrow pass in the name of God, and pressed forward, prepared to suffer whatever might befall.

As we proceeded cautiously on our way, giant trees barred our progress and dense foliage almost shut out the light of day, the darkness being deep and chill. The sound of our footfalls and of our voices, when we dared to speak, was returned to us from the great rocks bordering the pass, with such distinctness and so many repetitions, yet withal so changed, that we could hardly believe we were not accompanied by troops of invisible beings who mocked us and made a sport of our fears. Great birds of prey, startled from their nests in the treetops and the sides of the cliffs, perched upon high pinnacles of rock and eyed us malignly as we passed; vultures and ravens croaked above us in hoarse and savage tones that made our blood run cold. Nor could our prayers and hymns give us peace; they only called forth other fowl and by their own echoes multiplied the dreadful noises that beset us. It surprised us to observe that huge trees had been plucked out of the earth by the roots and hurled down the sides of the hills, and we shuddered to think by what powerful hands this had been done. At times we passed along the edges of high precipices, and the dark chasms that yawned below were a terrible sight. A storm arose, and we were half-blinded by the fires of heaven and stunned by thunder a thousand times louder than we had ever heard. Our fears were at last worked up to so great a degree that we expected every minute to see some devil from hell leap from behind a rock in our front, or a ferocious bear appear from the undergrowth to dispute our progress. But only deer and foxes crossed our path, and our fears were somewhat quieted to perceive that our blessed saint was no less powerful in the mountains than on the plains below.

At length we reached the bank of a stream whose silvery waters presented a most refreshing sight. In its crystal depths between the rocks we could see beautiful golden trout as large as the carp in the pond of our monastery at Passau. Even in these wild places heaven had provided bountifully for the fasting of the faithful.

Beneath the black pines and close to the large lichen-covered rocks bloomed rare flowers of dark blue and golden yellow. Brother Aegidius, who was as learned as pious, knew them from his herbarium and told us their names. We were delighted by the sight of various brilliant beetles and butterflies which had come out of their hiding places after the rain. We gathered handfuls of flowers and chased the pretty winged insects, forgetting our fears and prayers, the bears and evil spirits, in the exuberance of our joy.

For many hours we had not seen a dwelling nor a human being. Deeper and deeper we penetrated the mountain region; greater and greater became the difficulties we experienced in forest and ravine, and all the horrors of the wilderness that we had already passed were repeated, but without so great an effect upon our souls, for we all perceived that the good God was preserving us for longer service to his holy will. A branch of the friendly river lay in our course, and, approaching it, we were delighted to find it spanned by a rough but substantial bridge. As we were about to cross I happened to cast my eyes to the other shore, where I saw a sight that made my blood turn cold with terror. On the opposite bank of the stream was a meadow, covered with beautiful flowers, and in the center a gallows upon which hung the body of a man! The face was turned toward us, and I could plainly distinguish the features, which, though black and distorted, showed unmistakable signs that death had come that very day.

I was upon the point of directing my companions' attention to the dreadful spectacle when a strange incident occurred: in the meadow appeared a young girl, with long golden hair, upon which rested a wreath of blossoms. She wore a bright-red dress, which seemed to me to light up the whole scene like a flame of fire. Nothing in her actions indicated fear of the corpse upon the gallows; on the contrary, she glided toward it barefooted through the grass, singing in a loud but sweet voice, and waving her arms to scare away the birds of prey that had gathered about it, uttering harsh cries and with a great buffeting of wings and snapping of beaks. At the girl's approach they all took flight, except one great vulture, which retained its perch upon the gallows and appeared to defy and threaten her. She ran close up to the obscene creature, jumping, dancing, screaming, until it, too, put out its wide wings and flapped heavily away. Then she ceased her dancing, and, taking a position at the gibbet's foot, calmly and thoughtfully looked up at the swinging body of the unfortunate man.

The maiden's singing had attracted the attention of my companions, and we all stood watching the lovely child and her strange surroundings with too much amazement to speak.

While gazing on the surprising scene, I felt a cold shiver run through my body. This is said to be a sure sign that someone has stepped upon the spot which is to be your grave. Strange to say, I felt this chill at the moment the maiden stepped under the gallows. But this only shows how the true beliefs of men are mixed up with foolish superstitions; for how could a sincere follower of Saint Franciscus possibly come to be buried beneath a gallows?

"Let us hasten," I said to my companions, "and pray for the soul of the dead."

We soon found our way to the spot, and, without raising our eyes, said prayers with great fervor; especially did I, for my heart was full of compassion for the poor sinner who hung above. I recalled the words of God, who said, "Vengeance is mine," and remembered that the dear Savior had pardoned the thief upon the cross at his side; and who knows that there were not mercy and forgiveness for this poor wretch who had died upon the gallows?

On our approach the maiden had retired a short distance, not knowing what to make of us and our prayers. Suddenly, however, in the midst of our devotions, I heard her sweet, bell-like tones exclaim, "The vulture! the vulture!" and her voice was agitated, as if she felt great fear. I looked up and saw a great gray bird above the pines, swooping downward. It showed no fear of us, our sacred calling and our pious rites. My brothers, however, were indignant at the interruption caused by the child's voice, and scolded her. But I said, "The girl is probably a relation of the dead man. Now think of it, brothers. This terrible bird comes to tear the flesh from his face and feed upon his hands and his body. It is only natural that she should cry out."

One of the brothers said, "Go to her, Ambrosius, and command her to be silent that we may pray in peace for the departed soul of this sinful man."

I walked among the fragrant flowers to where the girl stood with her eyes still fixed upon the vulture, which swung in ever narrowing circles about the gallows. Against a mass of silvery flowers on a bush by which she stood the maid's exquisite figure showed to advantage, as I wickedly permitted myself to observe. Perfectly erect and motionless, she watched my advance, though I marked a terrified look in her large, dark eyes, as if she feared that I would do her harm. Even when I was quite near her she made no movement to come forward, as women and children usually did, and kiss my hands.

"Who are you?" I said, "and what are you doing in this dreadful place all alone?"

She did not answer me, and made neither sign nor motion, so I repeated my question.

"Tell me, child, what are you doing here?"

"Scaring away the vultures," she replied, in a soft, musical voice, inexpressibly pleasing.

"Are you a relation of the dead man?" I asked.

She shook her head.

"You knew him?" I continued, "and you pity his unchristian death?"

But she was again silent, and I had to renew my questioning. "What was his name, and why was he put to death? What crime did he commit?"

"His name was Nathaniel Alfinger, and he killed a man for a woman," said the maiden, distinctly and in the most unconcerned manner that it is possible to conceive, as if murder and hanging were the commonest and most uninteresting of all events. I was astounded, and gazed at her sharply, but her look was passive and calm, denoting nothing unusual.

"Did you know Nathaniel Alfinger?"

"No."

"Yet you came here to protect his corpse from the fowls?"

"Yes."

"Why do you do that service to one whom you did not know?"

"I always do so."

"How—!"

"Always when anyone is hanged here I come and frighten away the birds and make them find other food. See—there is another vulture!"

She uttered a wild, high scream, threw her arms above her head, and ran across the meadow, so that I thought her mad. The big bird flew away, and the maiden came quietly back to me, and, pressing her sunburned hands upon her breast, sighed deeply, as from fatigue. With as much mildness as I could put into my voice, I asked her:

"What is your name?"

"Benedicta."

"And who are your parents?"

"My mother is dead."

"But your father—where is he?"

She was silent. Then I pressed her to tell me where she lived, for I wanted to take the poor child home and admonish her father to have better care of his daughter and not let her stray into such dreadful places again.

"Where do you live, Benedicta? I pray you tell me."

"Here."

"What! Here? Ah, my child, here is only the gallows."

She pointed toward the pines. Following the direction of her finger, I saw among the trees a wretched hut which looked like a habitation more fit for animals than human beings. Then I knew better than she could have told me whose child she was.

When I returned to my companions and they asked me who the girl was, I answered, "The hangman's daughter."

III

Having commended the soul of the dead man to the intercession of the Blessed Virgin and the holy saints, we left the accursed spot, but as we withdrew I looked back at the lovely child of the hangman. She stood where I had left her, looking

after us. Her fair white brow was still crowned with the
wreath of primroses, which gave an added charm to her wonderful beauty of feature and expression, and her large, dark
eyes shone like the stars of a winter midnight. My companions,
to whom the hangman's daughter was a most unchristian
object, reproved me for the interest that I manifested in her;
but it made me sad to think this sweet and beautiful child
was shunned and despised through no fault of her own. Why
should she be made to suffer blame because of her father's
dreadful calling? And was it not the purest Christian charity
which prompted this innocent maiden to keep the vultures
from the body of a fellow creature whom in life she had not
even known and who had been adjudged unworthy to live?
It seemed to me a more kindly act than that of any professed
Christian who bestows money upon the poor. Expressing these
feelings to my companions, I found, to my sorrow, that they
did not share them; on the contrary, I was called a dreamer
and a fool who wished to overthrow the ancient and wholesome
customs of the world. Everyone, they said, was bound to
execrate the class to which the hangman and his family belonged, for all who associated with such persons would surely
be contaminated. I had, however, the temerity to remain steadfast in my conviction, and with due humility questioned the
justice of treating such persons as criminals because they
were a part of the law's machinery by which criminals were
punished. Because in the church the hangman and his family
had a dark corner specially set apart for them, that could not
absolve us from our duty as servants of the Lord to preach
the gospel of justice and mercy and give an example of
Christian love and charity. But my brothers grew very angry
with me, and the wilderness rang with their loud vocifera-
tions, so that I began to feel as if I were very wicked, although
unable to perceive my error. I could do nothing but hope that
heaven would be more merciful to us all than we are to one
another. In thinking of the maiden it gave me comfort to know
that her name was Benedicta. Perhaps her parents had so
named her as a means of blessing one whom no one else would
ever bless.

But I must relate what a wonderful country it was into

which we were now arrived. Were we not assured that all the world is the Lord's, for he made it, we might be tempted to think such a wild region the kingdom of the Evil One.

Far down below our path the river roared and foamed between great cliffs, the gray points of which seemed to pierce the very sky. On our left, as we gradually rose out of this chasm, was a black forest of pines, frightful to see, and in front of us a most formidable peak. This mountain, despite its terrors, had a comical appearance, for it was white and pointed like a fool's cap, and looked as if someone had put a flour sack on the knave's head. After all, it was nothing but snow. Snow in the middle of the glorious month of May! Surely the works of God are wonderful and almost past belief! The thought came to me that if this old mountain should shake his head the whole region would be full of flying snow.

We were not a little surprised to find that in various places along our road the forest had been cleared away for a space large enough to build a hut and plant a garden. Some of these rude dwellings stood where one would have thought that only eagles would have been bold enough to build; but there is no place, it seems, free from the intrusion of man, who stretches out his hand for everything, even that which is in the air. When at last we arrived at our destination and beheld the temple and the house erected in this wilderness to the name and glory of our beloved saint, our hearts were thrilled with pious emotions. Upon the surface of a pine-covered rock was a cluster of huts and houses, the monastery in the midst, like a shepherd surrounded by his flock. The church and monastery were of hewn stone, of noble architecture, spacious and comfortable.

May the good God bless our entrance into this holy place.

IV

I have now been in this wilderness for a few weeks, but the Lord, too, is here, as everywhere. My health is good, and this house of our beloved saint is a stronghold of the faith, a house of peace, an asylum for those who flee from the wrath of the

Evil One, a rest for all who bear the burden of sorrow. Of myself, however, I cannot say so much. I am young, and although my mind is at peace, I have so little experience of the world and its ways that I feel myself peculiarly liable to error and accessible to sin. The course of my life is like a rivulet which draws its silver thread smoothly and silently through friendly fields and flowery meadows, yet knows that when the storms come and the rains fall it may become a raging torrent, defiled with earth and whirling away to the sea, the wreckage attesting the madness of its passion and its power.

Not sorrow nor despair drew me away from the world into the sacred retreat of the Church, but a sincere desire to serve the Lord. My only wish is to belong to my beloved saint, to obey the blessed mandates of the Church, and, as a servant of God, to be charitable to all mankind, whom I dearly love. The Church is, in truth, my beloved mother, for, my parents having died in my infancy, I, too, might have perished without care had she not taken pity on me, fed and clothed me and reared me as her own child. And, oh, what happiness there will be for me, poor monk, when I am ordained and receive holy orders as a priest of the Most High God! Always I think and dream of it and try to prepare my soul for that high and sacred gift. I know I can never be worthy of this great happiness, but I do hope to be an honest and sincere priest, serving God and man according to the light that is given from above. I often pray heaven to put me to the test of temptation, that I may pass through the fire unscathed and purified in mind and soul. As it is, I feel the sovereign peace which, in this solitude, lulls my spirit to sleep, and all life's temptations and trials seem far away, like perils of the sea to one who can but faintly hear the distant thunder of the waves upon the beach.

V

Our superior, Father Andreas, is a mild and pious gentleman. Our brothers live in peace and harmony. They are not idle, neither are they worldly nor arrogant. They are temperate, not indulging too much in the pleasures of the table—a praise-worthy moderation, for all this region, far and wide—the hills and the valleys, the river and forest, with all that they contain—belongs to the monastery. The woods are full of all kinds of game, of which the choicest is brought to our table, and we relish it exceedingly. In our monastery a drink is prepared from malt and barley—a strong, bitter drink, refreshing after fatigue, but not, to my taste, very good.

The most remarkable thing in this part of the country is the salt mining. I am told that the mountains are full of salt—how wonderful are the works of the Lord! In pursuit of this mineral man has penetrated deep into the bowels of the earth by means of shafts and tunnels, and brings forth the bitter marrow of the hills into the light of the sun. The salt I have myself seen in red, brown and yellow crystals. The works give employment to our peasants and their sons, with a few foreign laborers, all under the command of an overseer, who is known as the saltmaster. He is a stern man, exercising great power, but our superior and the brothers speak little good of him—not from any unchristian spirit, but because his actions are evil. The saltmaster has an only son. His name is Rochus, a handsome but wild and wicked youth.

VI

The people hereabout are a proud, stubborn race. I am told that in an old chronicle they are described as descendants of the Romans, who in their day drove many tunnels into these mountains to get out the precious salt, and some of these tunnels are still in existence. From the window of my cell I can see these giant hills and the black forests which at sunset burn like great firebrands along the crests against the sky.

The forefathers of these people (after the Romans) were, I am told, more stubborn still than they are, and continued in idolatry after all the neighboring peoples had accepted the cross of the Lord our Savior. Now, however, they bow their stiff necks to the sacred symbol and soften their hearts to receive the living truth. Powerful as they are in body, in spirit they are humble and obedient to the Word. Nowhere else did the people kiss my hand so fervently as here, although I am not a priest—an evidence of the power and victory of our glorious faith.

Physically they are strong and exceedingly handsome in face and figure, especially the young men; the elder men, too, walk as erect and proud as kings. The women have long golden hair, which they braid and twist about their heads very beautifully, and they love to adorn themselves with jewels. Some have eyes whose dark brilliancy rivals the luster of the rubies and garnets they wear about their white necks. I am told that the young men fight for the young women as stags for does. Ah, what wicked passions exist in the hearts of men! But since I know nothing of these things, nor shall ever feel such unholy emotions, I must not judge and condemn.

Lord, what a blessing is the peace with which thou hast filled the spirits of those who are thine own! Behold, there is no turmoil in my breast; all is calm there as in the soul of a babe which calls, "Abba," dear Father. And so may it ever be.

VII

I have again seen the hangman's beautiful daughter. As the bells were chiming for Mass I saw her in front of the monastery church. I had just come from the bedside of a sick man, and as my thoughts were gloomy the sight of her face was pleasant, and I should have liked to greet her, but her eyes were cast down. She did not notice me. The square in front of the church was filled with people, the men and youths on one side, on the other the women and maidens all clad in their high hats and adorned with their gold chains. They stood close together, but when the poor child approached all stepped aside, whispering and looking askance at her as if she were an accursed leper and they feared infection.

Compassion filled my breast, compelling me to follow the maiden, and, overtaking her, I said aloud, "God greet you, Benedicta."

She shrank away as if frightened, then, looking up, recognized me, seemed astonished, blushed again and again and finally hung her head in silence.

"Do you fear to speak to me?" I asked.

But she made no reply. Again I spoke to her. "Do good, obey the Lord, and fear no one. Then shall you be saved."

At this she drew a long sigh, and replied in a low voice, hardly more than a whisper, "I thank you, my lord."

"I am not a lord, Benedicta," I said, "but a poor servant of God, who is a gracious and kind Father to all his children, however lowly their estate. Pray to him when your heart is heavy, and he will be near you."

While I spoke she lifted her head and looked at me like a sad child that is being comforted by its mother. And, still speaking to her out of the great compassion in my heart, I led her into the church before all the people.

But do thou, O holy Franciscus, pardon the sin that I committed during that high sacrament! For while Father Andreas was reciting the solemn words of the Mass, my eyes constantly wandered to the spot where the poor child knelt in a dark corner set apart for her and her father, forsaken and alone. She seemed to pray with holy zeal, and surely thou didst grace her with a ray of thy favor, for it was through thy love of mankind that thou didst become a great saint, and didst bring before the Throne of Grace thy large heart, bleeding for the sins of all the world. Then shall not I, the humblest of thy followers, have enough of thy spirit to pity this poor outcast who suffers for no sin of her own? Nay, I feel for her a peculiar tenderness, which I cannot help accepting as a sign from heaven that I am charged with a special mandate to watch over her, to protect her, and finally to save her soul.

VIII

Our superior has sent for me and rebuked me. He told me I had caused great ill-feeling among the brothers and the people, and asked what devil had me in possession that I should walk into church with the daughter of the public hangman.

What could I say but that I pitied the poor maiden and could not do otherwise than as I did?

"Why did you pity her?" he asked.

"Because all the people shun her," I replied, "as if she were mortal sin itself, and because she is wholly blameless. It certainly is not her fault that her father is a hangman, nor his either, since, alas, hangmen must be."

Ah, beloved Franciscus, how the superior scolded thy poor servant for those bold words.

"And do you repent?" he demanded at the close of his reproof. But how could I repent of my compassion—incited, as I verily believe, by our beloved saint?

On learning my obduracy, the superior became very sad. He gave me a long lecture and put me under hard penance. I took my punishment meekly and in silence, and am now confined in my cell, fasting and chastising myself. Nor in this do I spare myself at all, for it is happiness to suffer for the sake of one so unjustly treated as the poor friendless child.

I stand at the grating of my cell, looking out at the high, mysterious mountains showing black against the evening sky. The weather being mild, I open the window behind the bars to admit the fresh air and better to hear the song of the stream below, which speaks to me with a divine companionship, gentle and consoling.

I know not if I have already mentioned that the monastery is built upon a rock high over the river. Directly under the windows of our cells are the rugged edges of great cliffs, which none can scale but at the peril of his life. Imagine, then, my astonishment when I saw a living figure lift itself up from the awful abyss by the strength of its hands, and, drawing itself across the edge, stand erect upon the very verge! In the dusk I could not make out what kind of creature it was. I thought it some evil spirit come to tempt me, so I crossed myself and said a prayer. Presently there is a movement of its arm, and something flies through the window, past my head, and lies upon the floor of my cell, shining like a white star. I bend and pick it up. It is a bunch of flowers such as I have never seen—leafless, white as snow, soft as velvet, and without fragrance. As I stand by the window, the better to see the wondrous flowers, my eyes turn again to the figure on the cliff, and I hear a sweet, low voice, which says, "I am Benedicta, and I thank you."

Ah, heaven! It was the child, who, that she might greet me in my loneliness and penance, had climbed the dreadful rocks, heedless of the danger. She knew, then, of my punishment—knew that it was for her. She knew even the very cell in which I was confined. O holy saint! Surely she could not have known all this but from thee, and I were worse than an infidel to doubt that the feeling which I have for her signifies that a command has been laid upon me to save her.

I saw her bending over the frightful precipice. She turned a moment and waved her hand to me and disappeared. I uttered an involuntary cry—had she fallen? I grasped the iron bars of my window and shook them with all my strength, but they did not yield. In my despair I threw myself upon the floor, crying and praying to all the saints to protect the dear child in her dangerous descent if still she lived, to intercede for her unshriven soul if she had fallen. I was still kneeling when Benedicta gave me a sign of her safe arrival below. It was such a shout as these mountaineers utter in their untamed enjoyment of life—only Benedicta's shout, coming from far below in the gorge, and mingled with its own strange echoes, sounded like nothing I had ever heard from any human throat, and so affected me that I wept, and the tears fell upon the wild flowers in my hand.

IX

As a follower of Saint Franciscus, I am not permitted to own anything dear to my heart, so I have disposed of my most precious treasure. I have presented to my beloved saint the beautiful flowers which were Benedicta's offering. They are so placed before his picture in the monastery church as to decorate the bleeding heart which he carries upon his breast as a symbol of his suffering for mankind.

I have learned the name of the flower: because of its color, and because it is finer than other flowers, it is called *edelweiss* —noble white. It grows in so rare perfection only upon the highest and wildest rocks—mostly upon cliffs, over abysses many hundred feet in depth, where one false step would be fatal to him who gathers it.

These beautiful flowers, then, are the real evil spirits of this wild region. They lure many mortals to a dreadful death. The brothers here have told me that never a year passes but some shepherd, some hunter or some bold youth, attracted by these wonderful blossoms, is lost in the attempt to get them.

May God be merciful to all their souls!

X

I must have turned pale when one of the brothers reported at the supper table that upon the picture of Saint Franciscus had been found a bunch of edelweiss of such rare beauty as grows nowhere else in the country but at the summit of a cliff which is more than a thousand feet high, and overhangs a dreadful lake. The brothers tell wondrous tales of the horrors of this lake—how wild its waters and how deep, and how the most hideous specters are seen along its shores or rising out of it.

Benedicta's edelweiss, therefore, has caused great commotion and wonder, for even among the boldest hunters there are few, indeed, who dare to climb that cliff by the haunted lake. And the tender child has accomplished this feat! She has gone quite alone to that horrible place, and has climbed the almost vertical wall of the mountain to the green spot where the flowers grow with which she was moved to greet me. I doubt not that heaven guarded her against mishap in order that I might have a visible sign and token that I am charged with the duty of her salvation.

Ah, thou poor sinless child, accursed in the eyes of the people, God hath signified his care of thee, and in my heart I feel already something of that adoration which shall be thy due when thy purity and holiness he shall bestow upon thy relics some signal mark of his favor, and the Church shall declare thee blessed!

I have learned another thing that I will chronicle here. In this country these flowers are the sign of a faithful love. The youth presents them to his sweetheart, and the maidens decorate the hats of their lovers with them. It is clear that, in expressing her gratitude to a humble servant of the Church, Benedicta was moved, perhaps without knowing it, to signify at the same time her love of the Church itself, although, alas, she has yet too little cause.

As I ramble about here, day after day, I am becoming familiar with every path in the forest, in the dark pass, and on the slopes of the mountains.

I am often sent to the homes of the peasants, the hunters and the shepherds, to carry either medicine to the sick or consolation to the sad. The most reverend superior has told me that as soon as I receive holy orders I shall have to carry the sacraments to the dying, for I am the youngest and the strongest of the brothers. In these high places it sometimes occurs that a hunter or a shepherd falls from the rocks, and after some days is found, still living. It is then the duty of the priest to perform the offices of our holy religion at the bedside of the sufferer, so that the blessed Savior may be there to receive the departing soul.

That I may be worthy of such grace, may our beloved saint keep my heart pure from every earthly passion and desire!

XI

The monastery has celebrated a great festival, and I will report all that occurred.

For many days before the event the brothers were busy preparing for it. Some decorated the church with sprays of pine and birch and with flowers.

They went with the other men and gathered the most beautiful Alpine roses they could find, and as it is midsummer they grow in great abundance. On the day before the festival the brothers sat in the garden, weaving garlands to adorn the church; even the most reverend superior and the fathers took pleasure in our merry task. They walked beneath the trees and chatted pleasantly while encouraging the brother butler to spend freely the contents of the cellars.

The next morning was the holy procession. It was very beautiful to see, and added to the glory of our holy Church. The superior walked under a purple silken canopy, surrounded by the worthy fathers, and bore in his hands the sacred emblem of the crucifixion of our Savior. We brothers followed, bearing burning candles and singing psalms. Behind us came a great crowd of the people, dressed in their finest attire.

The proudest of those in the procession were the mountaineers and the salt miners, the saltmaster at their head on a beautiful horse adorned with costly trappings. He was a proud-looking man, with his great sword at his side and a plumed hat upon his broad, high brow. Behind him rode Rochus, his son. When we had collected in front of the gate to form a line, I took special notice of that young man. I judge him to be self-willed and bold. He wore his hat on the side of his head and cast flaming glances upon the women and the maidens. He looked contemptuously upon us monks. I fear he is not a good Christian, but he is the most beautiful youth that I have ever seen: tall and slender like a young pine, with light-brown eyes and golden locks.

The saltmaster is as powerful in this region as our superior. He is appointed by the duke and has judicial powers in all affairs. He has even the power of life and death over those accused of murder or any other abominable crime. But the Lord has fortunately endowed him with good judgment and wisdom.

Through the village the procession moved out into the valley and down to the entrances of the great salt mines. In front of the principal mine an altar was erected, and there our superior read High Mass, while all the people knelt. I observed that the saltmaster and his son knelt and bent their heads with visible reluctance, and this made me very sad. After the service the procession moved toward the hill called Mount Calvary, which is still higher than the monastery, and from

the top of which one has a good view of the whole country below. There the reverend superior displayed the crucifix in order to banish the evil powers which abound in these terrible mountains; and he also said prayers and pronounced anathemas against all demons infesting the valley below. The bells chimed their praises to the Lord, and it seemed as if divine voices were ringing through the wilderness. It was all, indeed, most beautiful and good.

I looked about me to see if the child of the hangman were present, but I could not see her anywhere, and knew not whether to rejoice that she was out of reach of the insults of the people or to mourn because deprived of the spiritual strength that might have come to me from looking upon her heavenly beauty.

After the services came the feast. Upon a meadow sheltered by trees tables were spread, and the clergy and the people, the most reverend superior and the great saltmaster partook of the viands served by the young men. It was interesting to see the young men make big fires of pine and maple, put great pieces of beef upon wooden spits, turn them over the coals until they were brown, and then lay them before the fathers and the mountaineers. They also boiled mountain trout and carp in large kettles. The wheaten bread was brought in immense baskets, and as to drink, there was assuredly no scarcity of that, for the superior and the saltmaster had each given a mighty cask of beer. Both of these monstrous barrels lay on wooden stands under an ancient oak. The boys and the saltmaster's men drew from the cask which he had given, while that of the superior was served by the brother butler and a number of us younger monks. In honor of Saint Franciscus, I must say that the clerical barrel was of vastly greater size than that of the saltmaster.

Separate tables had been provided for the superior and the fathers, and for the saltmaster and the best of his people. The saltmaster and superior sat upon chairs which stood upon a beautiful carpet, and their seats were screened from the sun by a linen canopy. At the table, surrounded by their beautiful wives and daughters, sat many knights, who had come from their distant castles to share in the great festival. I helped at table. I handed the dishes and filled the goblets and was able to see how good an appetite the company had, and how they loved that brown and bitter drink. I could see also how amorously the saltmaster's son looked at the ladies, which provoked me very much, as he could not marry them all, especially those already married.

We had music, too. Some boys from the village, who practice on various instruments in their spare moments, were the performers. Ah, how they yelled, those flutes and pipes, and how the fiddle bows danced and chirped! I do not doubt the music was very good, but heaven has not seen fit to give me the right kind of ears.

I am sure our blessed saint must have derived great satisfaction from the sight of so many people eating and drinking their bellies full. Heavens! How they did eat—what unearthly quantities they did away with! But that was nothing to their drinking. I firmly believe that if every mountaineer had brought along a barrel of his own he would have emptied it, all by himself. But the women seemed to dislike the beer, especially the young girls. Usually before drinking a young man would hand his cup to one of the maids, who barely touched it with her lips, and, making a grimace, turned away her face. I am not sufficiently acquainted with the ways of woman to say with certainty if this proved that at other times they were so abstemious.

After eating, the young men played at various games which exhibited their agility and strength. Holy Franciscus! What legs they have, what arms and necks! They leapt, they wrestled with one another; it was like the fighting of bears. The mere sight of it caused me to feel great fear. It seemed as if they would crush one another. But the maidens looked on, feeling neither fear nor anxiety; they giggled and appeared well pleased. It was wonderful, too, to hear the voices of these young mountaineers; they threw back their heads and shouted till the echoes rang from the mountainsides and roared in the gorges, as if from the throats of a legion of demons.

Foremost among all was the saltmaster's son. He sprang like a deer, fought like a fiend, and bellowed like a wild bull. Among these mountaineers he was a king. I observed that many were jealous of his strength and beauty, and secretly hated him; yet all obeyed. It was beautiful to see how this young man bent his slender body while leaping and playing in the games—how he threw up his head like a stag at gaze, shook his golden locks and stood in the midst of his fellows with flaming cheeks and sparkling eyes. How sad to think that pride and passion should make their home in so lovely a body, which seems created for the habitation of a soul that would glorify its maker!

It was near dusk when the superior, the saltmaster, the fathers and all the distinguished guests parted and retired to their homes, leaving the others at drink and dance. My duties compelled me to remain with the brother butler to serve the debauching youths with beer from the great cask. Young Rochus remained, too. I do not know how it occurred, but suddenly he stood before me. His looks were dark and his manner proud.

"Are you," he said, "the monk who gave offense to the people the other day?"

I asked humbly—though beneath my monk's robe I felt a sinful anger—"What are you speaking of?"

"As if you did not know!" he said, haughtily. "Now bear in mind what I tell you. If you ever show any friendship toward that girl I shall teach you a lesson which you will not soon forget. You monks are likely to call your impertinence by the name of some virtue, but I know the trick, and will have none of it. Make a note of that, you young cowl-wearer, for your handsome face and big eyes will not save you."

With that he turned his back upon me and went away, but I heard his strong voice ringing out upon the night as he sang and shouted with the others. I was greatly alarmed to learn that this bold boy had cast his eyes upon the hangman's lovely daughter. His feeling for her was surely not honorable, or, instead of hating me for being kind to her, he would have been grateful and would have thanked me. I feared for the child, and again and again did I promise my blessed saint that I would watch over and protect her, in obedience to the miracle he has wrought in my breast regarding her. With that wondrous feeling to urge me on, I cannot be slack in my duty, and, Benedicta, thou shalt be saved—thy body and thy soul!

XII

Let me continue my report.

The boys threw dry brushwood into the fire so that the flames illuminated the whole meadow and shone red upon the trees. Then they laid hands upon the village maidens and began to turn and swing them round and round. Holy saints! How they stamped and turned and threw their hats 'in the air, kicked up their heels, and lifted the girls from the ground, as if the sturdy wenches were nothing but feather balls! They shouted and yelled as if all the evil spirits had them in possession, so that I wished a herd of swine might come, that the devils might leave these human brutes and go into the four-legged ones. The boys were quite full of the brown beer, which for its bitterness and strength is a beastly drink.

Before long the madness of intoxication broke out; they attacked one another with fists and knives, and it looked as if they would do murder. Suddenly the saltmaster's son, who had stood looking on, leaped among them, caught two of the combatants by the hair and knocked their heads together with such force that the blood started from their noses, and I thought surely their skulls had been crushed like eggshells; but they must have been very hard-headed, for on being released they seemed little the worse for their punishment. After much shouting and screaming, Rochus succeeded in making peace, which seemed to me, poor worm, quite heroic. The music set in again. The fiddles scraped and the pipes shrieked, while the boys, with torn clothes and scratched and bleeding faces, renewed the dance as if nothing had occurred. Truly this is a people that would gladden the heart of a Bramarbas or a Holofernes!

I had scarcely recovered from the fright which Rochus had given me, when I was made to feel a far greater one. Rochus was dancing with a tall and beautiful girl, who looked the very queen of this young king. They made such mighty leaps and dizzy turns, but at the same time so graceful, that all looked on with astonishment and pleasure. The girl had a sensuous smile on her lips and a bold look in her brown face, which seemed to say, "See! I am the mistress of his heart!" But suddenly he pushed her from him as in disgust, broke from the circle of dancers, and cried to his friends, "I am going to bring my own partner. Who will go with me?"

The tall girl, maddened by the insult, stood looking at him with the face of a demon, her black eyes burning like flames of hell! But her discomfiture amused the drunken youths, and they laughed aloud.

Snatching·a firebrand and swinging it about his head till the sparks flew in showers, Rochus cried again, "Who goes with me?" and walked rapidly away into the forest. The others, seizing firebrands also, ran after him, and soon their voices could be heard far away, ringing out upon the night, themselves no longer seen. I was still looking in the direction which they had taken, when the tall girl whom Rochus had insulted stepped to my side and hissed something into my ear. I felt her hot breath on my cheek.

"If you care for the hangman's daughter, then hasten and save her from the drunken wretch. No woman resists him!"

God! How the wild words of that woman horrified me! I did not doubt the girl's words, but in my anxiety for the poor child I asked, "How can I save her?"

"Run and warn her, monk," the wench replied. "She will listen to you."

"But they will find her sooner than I."

"They are drunk and will not go fast. Besides, I know a path leading to the hangman's hut by a shorter route."

"Then show me and be quick!" I cried.

She glided away, motioning me to follow. We were soon in the woods, where it was so dark I could hardly see the woman's figure; but she moved as fast and her step was as sure as in the light of day. Above us we could see the torches of the boys, which showed that they had taken the longer path along the mountainside. I heard their wild shouts, and trembled for the child. We had walked for some time in silence, having left the youths far behind, when the young woman began speaking to herself. At first I did not understand, but soon my ears caught every passionate word.

"He shall not have her! To the devil with the hangman's whelp! Everyone despises her and spits at the sight of her. It is just like him—he does not care for what people think or say. Because they hate he loves. Besides, she has a pretty face. I'll make it pretty for her. I'll mark it with blood! But if she were the daughter of the devil himself he would not rest until he had her. He shall not!"

She lifted her arms and laughed wildly—I shuddered to hear her! I thought of the dark powers that live in the human breast, though I know as little of them, thank God, as a child.

At length we reached the Galgenberg, where stands the hangman's hut, and a few moments' climb brought us near the door.

"There she lives," said the girl, pointing to the hut, through the windows of which shone the yellow light of a tallow candle. "Go warn her. The hangman is ill and unable to protect his daughter, even if he dared. You'd better take her away— take her to the Alpfeld on the Göll, where my father has a house. They will not look for her up there."

With that she left me and vanished in the darkness.

XIII

Looking in at the window of the hut, I saw the hangman sitting in a chair, with his daughter beside him, her hand upon his shoulder. I could hear him cough and groan, and knew that she was trying to soothe him in his pain. A world of love and sorrow was in her face, which was more beautiful than ever.

Nor did I fail to observe how clean and tidy were the room and all in it. The humble dwelling looked, indeed, like a place blessed by the peace of God. Yet these blameless persons are treated as accused and hated like mortal sin! What greatly pleased me was an image of the Blessed Virgin on the wall opposite the window at which I stood. The frame was decorated with flowers of the field, and the mantle of the Holy Mother festooned with edelweiss.

I knocked at the door, calling out at the same time, "Do not fear. It is I—Brother Ambrosius."

It seemed to me that, on hearing my voice and name, Benedicta showed a sudden joy in her face, but perhaps it was only surprise—may the saints preserve me from the sin of pride. She came to the window and opened it.

"Benedicta," said I, hastily, after returning her greeting, "wild and drunken boys are on their way hither to take you to the dance. Rochus is with them, and says that he will fetch you to dance with him. I have come before them to assist you to escape."

At the name of Rochus I saw the blood rise into her cheeks and suffuse her whole face with crimson. Alas, I perceived that my jealous guide was right: no woman could resist that beautiful boy, not even this pious and virtuous child. When her father comprehended what I said he rose to his feet and stretched out his feeble arms as if to shield her from harm, but, although his soul was strong, his body I knew, was powerless. I said to him, "Let me take her away. The boys are drunk and know not what they do. Your resistance would only make them angry, and they might harm you both. Ah, look! See their torches, hear their boisterous voices! Hasten, Benedicta —be quick, be quick!"

Benedicta sprang to the side of the now sobbing old man and tenderly embraced him. Then she hurried from the room, and after covering my hands with kisses ran away into the woods, disappearing in the night, at which I was greatly surprised. I waited for her to return, for a few minutes, then entered the cabin to protect her father from the wild youths, who, I thought, would visit their disappointment upon him.

But they did not come. I waited and listened in vain. All at once I heard shouts of joy and screams that made me tremble and pray to the blessed saint. But the sounds died away in the distance, and I knew that the boys had retraced their steps down the Galgenberg to the meadow of the fires. The sick man and I spoke of the miracle which had changed their hearts, and we were filled with gratitude and joy. Then I returned along the path by which I had come. As I arrived near the meadow, I could hear a wilder and madder uproar than ever, and could see through the trees the glare of greater fires, with the figures of the youths and a few maids dancing in the open, their heads uncovered, their hair streaming over their shoulders, their garments disordered by the fury of their movements. They circled about the fires, wound in and out among them, showing black or red according to how the light struck them, and looking altogether like demons of the pit commemorating some infernal anniversary or some new torment for the damned. And, holy Savior! there, in the midst of an illuminated space, upon which the others did not trespass, dancing by themselves and apparently forgetful of all else, were Rochus and Benedicta!

XIV

Holy Mother of God! What can be worse than the fall of an angel? I saw—I understood, then, that in leaving me and her father, Benedicta had gone willingly to meet the very fate from which I had striven to save her!

"The accursed wench has run into Rochus' arms," hissed someone at my side, and, turning, I saw the tall brown girl who had been my guide, her face distorted with hate. "I wish that I had killed her. Why did you suffer her to play us this trick, you fool of a monk?"

I pushed her aside and ran toward the couple without thinking what I did. But what could I do? Even at that instant, as though to prevent my interference, though really unconscious of my presence, the drunken youths formed a circle about them, bawling their admiration and clapping their hands to mark the time.

As these two beautiful figures danced they were a lovely picture. He, tall, slender and lithe, was like a god of the heathen Greeks, while Benedicta looked like a fairy. Seen through the slight mist upon the meadows, her delicate figure, moving swiftly and swaying from side to side, seemed veiled with a web of purple and gold. Her eyes were cast modestly upon the ground. Her motions, though agile, were easy and graceful. Her face glowed with excitement, and it seemed as if her whole soul were absorbed in the dance. Poor, sweet child! Her error made me weep, but I forgave her. Her life was so barren and joyless; why should she not love to dance? Heaven bless her! But Rochus—ah, God forgive him!

While I was looking on at all this, and thinking what it was my duty to do, the jealous girl—she is called Amula—had stood near me, cursing and blaspheming. When the boys applauded Benedicta's dancing Amula made as if she would spring forward and strangle her. But I held the furious creature back, and, stepping forward, called out, "Benedicta!"

She started at the sound of my voice, but though she hung her head a little lower, she continued dancing. Amula could control her rage no longer, and rushed forward with a savage cry, trying to break into the circle. But the drunken boys prevented. They jeered at her, which maddened her the more, and she made effort after effort to reach her victim. The boys drove her away with shouts, curses and laughter. Holy Franciscus, pray for us! When I saw the hatred in Amula's eyes a cold shudder ran through my body. God be with us! I believe the creature capable of killing the poor child with her own hands, and glorying in the deed!

I ought now to have gone home, but I remained. I thought of what might occur when the dance was over, for I had been told that the youths commonly accompanied their partners home, and I was horrified to think of Rochus and Benedicta alone together in the forest and the night.

Imagine my surprise when all at once Benedicta lifted her head, stopped dancing, and, looking kindly at Rochus, said in her sweet voice, so like the sound of silver bells:

"I thank you, sir, for having chosen me for your partner in the dance in such a knightly way."

Then bowing to the saltmaster's son, she slipped quickly through the circle, and, before any one could know what was occurring, disappeared in the black spaces of the forest. Rochus at first seemed stupefied with amazement, but when he realized that Benedicta was indeed gone he raved like a madman. He

shouted, "Benedicta!" He called her endearing names, but all
to no purpose—she had vanished. Then he hurried after her
and wanted to search the forest with torches, but the other
youths dissuaded him. Observing my presence, he turned his
wrath upon me. I think if he had dared he would have struck
me. He cried, "I'll make you smart for this, you miserable
cowl-wearer!"

But I do not fear him. Praise be to God! Benedicta is not
guilty, and I can respect her as before. Yet I tremble to think
of the many perils which beset her. She is defenseless against
the hate of Amula as well as against the lust of Rochus. Ah,
if I could be ever at her side to watch over and protect her!
But I commend her to thee, O Lord: the poor motherless child
shall surely not trust to thee in vain.

XV

Alas! my unhappy fate!—again punished and again unable
to find myself guilty.

It seems that Amula has talked about Benedicta and Rochus.
The brown wench strolled from house to house telling how
Rochus went to the gallows for his partner in the dance. And
she added that Benedicta had acted in the most shameless
manner with the drunken boys. When the people spoke to me
of this I enlightened them regarding the facts, as it seemed
to me my duty to do, and told all as it had occurred.

By this testimony in contradiction of one who broke the
Decalogue by bearing false witness against her neighbor I
have, it seems, offended the superior. I was summoned before
him and accused of defending the hangman's daughter against
the statements of an honest Christian girl. I asked, meekly,
what I should have done—whether I should have permitted
the innocent and defenseless to be calumniated.

"Of what interest," I was asked, "can the hangman's
daughter be to you? Moreover, it is a fact that she went of
her own will to associate with the drunken boys."

To this I replied, "She went out of love to her father, for if
the intoxicated youths had not found her they would have

maltreated him—and she loves the old man, who is ill and helpless. Thus it happened, and thus I have testified."

But his reverence insisted that I was wrong, and put me under severe penance. I willingly undergo it. I am glad to suffer for the sweet child. Nor will I murmur against the revered superior, for he is my master, against whom to rebel, even in thought, is sin. Is not obedience the foremost commandment of our great saint for all his disciples? Ah, how I long for the priestly ordination and the holy oil! Then I shall have peace and be able to serve heaven better and with greater acceptance.

I am troubled about Benedicta. If not confined to my cell I should go toward the Galgenberg: perhaps I should meet her. I grieve for her as if she were my sister.

Belonging to the Lord, I have no right to love anything but him who died upon the cross for our sins—all other love is evil. O blessed saints in heaven! What if it be that this feeling which I have accepted as a sign and token that I am charged with the salvation of Benedicta's soul is but an earthly love? Pray for me, O dear Franciscus, that I may have the light, lest I stray into that road which leads down to hell. Light and strength, beloved saint, that I may know the right path, and walk therein forever!

XVI

I stand at the window of my cell. The sun sinks and the shadows creep higher on the sides of the mountains beyond the abyss. The abyss itself is filled with a mist whose billowy surface looks like a great lake. I think how Benedicta climbed out of these awful depths to fling me the edelweiss. I listen for the sound of the stones displaced by her daring little feet and plunging into the chasm below. But night after night has passed. I hear the wind among the pines. I hear the water roaring in the deeps. I hear the distant song of the nightingale. But her voice I do not hear.

Every evening the mist rises from the abyss. It forms billows, then rings, then flakes, and these rise and grow and darken until they are great clouds. They cover the hill and the valley, the tall pines and the snow-pointed mountains. They extinguish the last remaining touches of sunlight on the higher peaks, and it is night. Alas, in my soul also there is night—dark, starless and without hope of dawn!

Today is Sunday. Benedicta was not in church—"the dark corner" remained vacant. I was unable to keep my mind upon the service, a sin for which I shall do voluntary penance.

Amula was among the other maidens, but I saw nothing of Rochus. It seemed to me that her watchful black eyes were a sufficient guard against any rival, and that in her jealousy Benedicta would find protection. God can make the basest passions serve the most worthy ends, and the reflection gave me pleasure, which, alas, was of short life.

The services being at an end, the fathers and friars left the church slowly in procession, moving through the vestry, while the people went out at the main entrance. From the long, covered gallery leading out of the vestry one has a full view of the public square of the village. As we friars, who were behind the fathers, were in the gallery, something occurred which I shall remember even to the day of my death as an unjust deed which heaven permitted for I know not what purpose. It seems that the fathers must have known what was coming, for they halted in the gallery, giving us all an opportunity to look out upon the square.

I heard a confused noise of voices. It came nearer, and the shouting and yelling sounded like the approach of all the fiends of hell. Being at the farther end of the gallery, I was unable to see what was going on in the square, so I asked a brother at a window nearby what it was all about.

"They are taking a woman to the pillory," he answered.

"Who is it?"

"A girl."

"What has she done?"

"You ask a foolish question. Whom are pillories and whipping posts for but fallen women?"

The howling mob passed farther into the square, so that I had a full view. In the front were boys, leaping, gesticulating and singing vile songs. They seemed mad with joy and made savage by the shame and pain of their fellow creature. Nor did the maids behave much better. "Fie upon the outcast!" they cried. "See what it is to be a sinner! Thank heaven, we are virtuous."

In the rear of these yelling boys, surrounded by this mob of screaming women and girls—O, God! how can I write it? How can I express the horror of it? In the midst of it all—she, the lovely, the sweet, the immaculate Benedicta!

O my Savior! How did I see all this, yet am still living to relate it? I must have come near to death. The gallery, the square, the people seemed whirling round and round; the earth sank beneath my feet, and, although I strained my eyes open to see, yet all was dark. But it must have been for but a short time. I recovered, and, looking down into the square, saw her again.

They had clothed her in a long gray cloak, fastened at the waist with a rope. Her head bore a wreath of straw, and on her breast, suspended by a string about the neck, was a black tablet bearing in chalk the word "Buhle"—harlot.

By the end of the rope about her waist a man led her. I looked at him closely, and—O most holy Son of God, what brutes and beasts thou didst come to save!—it was Benedicta's father! They had compelled the poor old man to perform one of the duties of his office by leading his own child to the pillory! I learned later that he had implored the superior on his knees not to lay this dreadful command upon him, but all in vain.

The memory of this scene can never leave me. The hangman did not remove his eyes from his daughter's face, and she frequently nodded at him and smiled. By the grace of God, the maiden smiled!

The mob insulted her, called her vile names and spat upon the ground in front of her feet. Nor was this all. Observing that she took no notice of them, they pelted her with dust and grass. This was more than the poor father could endure, and, with a faint, inarticulate moan, he fell to the ground in a swoon.

Oh, the pitiless wretches! They wanted to lift him up and make him finish his task, but Benedicta stretched out her arm in supplication, and with an expression of so ineffable tenderness upon her beautiful face that even the brutal mob felt her gentle power and recoiled from before her, leaving the unconscious man upon the ground. She knelt and took her father's head in her lap. She whispered in his ears words of love and comfort. She stroked his gray hair and kissed his pale lips until she had coaxed him into consciousness and he had opened his eyes. Benedicta, thrice-blessed Benedicta, thou surely art born to be a saint, for thou didst show a divine patience like that with which our Savior bore his cross and with it all the sins of the world!

She helped her father to rise, and smiled brightly in his face when he made out to stand. She shook the dust from his clothing, and then, still smiling and murmuring words of encouragement, handed him the rope. The boys yelled and sang, the women screamed, and the wretched old man led his innocent child to the place of shame.

XVII

When I was back again in my cell I threw myself upon the stones and cried aloud to God against the injustice and misery that I had witnessed, and against the still greater misery of which I had been spared the sight. I saw in my mind the father binding his child to the post. I saw the brutal populace dance about her with savage delight. I saw the vicious Amula spit in the pure one's face. I prayed long and earnestly that the poor child might be made strong to endure her great affliction.

Then I sat and waited. I waited for the setting of the sun, for at that time the sufferer is commonly released from the whipping post. The minutes seemed hours, the hours eternities. The sun did not move; the day of shame was denied a night.

It was in vain that I tried to understand it all. I was stunned and dazed. Why did Rochus permit Benedicta to be so disgraced? Does he think the deeper her shame the more easily he can win her? I know not, nor do I greatly care to search out his motive. But, God help me! I myself feel her disgrace, most keenly.

And, Lord, Lord, what a light has come into the understanding of thy servant! It has come to me like a revelation out of heaven that my feeling for Benedicta is more and less than what I thought it. It is an earthly love—the love of a man for a woman. As first this knowledge broke into my consciousness my breath came short, my heart beat quick and hard; it seemed to me that I should suffocate. Yet such was the hardness of my heart from witnessing so terrible an injustice tolerated by heaven that I was unable wholly to repent. In the sudden illumination I was blinded: I could not clearly see my degree of sin. The tumult of my emotions was not altogether disagreeable. I had to confess to myself that I would not willingly forego it, even if I knew it wicked. May the Mother of Mercy intercede for me!

Even now I cannot think that in supposing myself to have a divine mandate to save the soul of Benedicta, and prepare her for a life of sanctity, I was wholly in error. This other human desire—comes it not also of God? Is it not concerned for the good of its object? And what can be a greater good than salvation of the soul?—a holy life on earth, and in heaven eternal happiness and glory to reward it. Surely the spiritual and the carnal love are not so widely different as I have been taught to think them. They are, perhaps, not antagonistic, and are but expressions of the same will. O holy Franciscus, in this great light that has fallen about me, guide thou my steps. Show to my dazzled eyes the straight, right way to Benedicta's good!

At length the sun disappeared behind the cloister. The flakes and cloudlets gathered upon the horizon; the haze rose from the abyss and, beyond, the purple shadow climbed higher and higher the great slope of the mountain, extinguishing at last the gleam of light upon the summit. Thank God, O thank God, she is free!

XVIII

I have been very ill, but by the kind attention of the brothers am sufficiently recovered to leave my bed. It must be God's will that I live to serve him, for certainly I have done nothing to merit his great mercy in restoring me to health. Still, I feel a yearning in my soul for a complete dedication of my poor life to him and his service. To embrace him and be bound up in his love are now the only aspirations that I have. As soon as the holy oil is on my brow, these hopes, I am sure, will be fulfilled, and, purged of my hopeless earthy passion for Benedicta, I shall be lifted into a new and diviner life. And it may be that then I can, without offense to heaven or peril to my soul, watch over and protect her far better than I can now as a wretched monk.

I have been weak. My feet, like those of an infant, failed to support my body. The brothers carried me into the garden. With what gratitude I again looked upward into the blue of the sky! How rapturously I gazed upon the white peaks of the mountains and the black forests on their slopes! Every blade of grass seemed to me of special interest, and I greeted each passing insect as if it were an old acquaintance.

My eyes wander to the south, where the Galgenberg is, and I think unceasingly of the poor child of the hangman. What has become of her? Has she survived her terrible experience in the public square? What is she doing? Oh, that I were strong enough to walk to Galgenberg! But I am not permitted to leave the monastery, and there is none of whom I dare ask her fate. The friars look at me strangely; it is as if they no longer regarded me as one of them. Why is this so? I love them, and desire to live in harmony with them. They are kind and gentle, yet they seem to avoid me as much as they can. What does it all mean?

XIX

I have been in the presence of the most reverend superior, Father Andreas. "Your recovery was miraculous," said he. "I wish you to be worthy of such mercies, and to prepare your soul for the great blessing that awaits you. I have, therefore, my son, ordained that you leave us for a season, to dwell apart in the solitude of the mountains, for the double purpose of restoring your strength and affording you an insight into your own heart. Make a severe examination apart from any distractions, and you will perceive, I do not doubt, the gravity of your error. Pray that a divine light may be shed upon your path, that you may walk upright in the service of the Lord as a true priest and apostle, with immunity from all base passions and earthly desires."

I had not the presumption to reply. I submit to the will of his reverence without a murmur, for obedience is a rule of our order. Nor do I fear the wilderness, although I have heard that it is infested with wild beasts and evil spirits. Our superior is right: the time passed in solitude will be to me a season of probation, purification and healing, of which I am doubtless in sore need. So far I have progressed in sin only; for in confession I have kept back many things. Not from the fear of punishment, but because I could not mention the name of the maiden before any other than my holy and blessed Franciscus, who alone can understand. He looks kindly down upon me from the skies, listening to my sorrow; and whatever of guilt there may be in my compassion for the innocent and persecuted child he willingly overlooks for the sake of our blessed Redeemer, who also suffered injustice and was acquainted with grief.

In the mountains it will be my duty to dig certain roots and send them to the monastery. From such roots as I am instructed to gather the fathers distill a liquor which has become famous throughout the land, even as far, I have been told, as the great city of Munich. This liquor is so strong and so fiery with spices that after drinking it one feels a burning in his throat as if he had swallowed a flame from hell; yet it is held in high esteem everywhere by reason of its medicinal properties, it being a remedy for many kinds of ills and infirmities; and it is said to be good also for the health of the soul, though I should suppose a godly life might be equally efficacious in places where the liquor cannot be obtained. However this may be, from the sale of the liquor comes the chief revenue of the monastery.

The root from which it is chiefly made is that of an Alpine plant called *gentiana*, which grows in great abundance on the sides of the mountains. In the months of July and August the friars dig the roots and dry them by fire in the mountain cabins, and they are then packed and sent to the monastery. The fathers have the sole right to dig the root in this region, and the secret of manufacturing the liquor is jealously guarded.

As I am to live in the high country for some time, the superior has directed me to collect the root from time to time as I have the strength. A boy, a servant in the monastery, is to guide me to my solitary station, carrying up my provisions and returning immediately. He will come once a week to renew my supply of food and take away the roots that I shall have dug.

No time has been lost in dispatching me on my penitential errand. This very evening I have taken leave of the superior, and, retiring to my cell, have packed my holy books, the *Agnus* and the *Life of Saint Franciscus*, in a bag. Nor have I forgotten writing materials with which to continue my diary. These preparations made, I have fortified my soul with prayer, and am ready for any fate, even an encounter with the beasts and demons.

Beloved saint, forgive the pain I feel in going away without having seen Benedicta, or even knowing what has become of her since that dreadful day. Thou knowest, O glorious one, and humbly do I confess, that I long to hasten to the Galgenberg, if only to get one glimpse of the hut which holds the fairest and best of her sex. Take me not, holy one, too severely to task, I beseech thee, for the weakness of my erring human heart!

XX

As I left the monastery with my young guide all was quiet within its walls; the holy brotherhood slept the sleep of peace, which had so long been denied to me. It was early dawn, and the clouds in the east were beginning to show narrow edges of gold and crimson as we ascended the path leading to the mountain. My guide, with bag upon his shoulder, led, and I followed, with my robe fastened back and a stout stick in my hand. This had a sharp iron point which might be used against wild beasts.

My guide was a light-haired, blue-eyed young fellow with

a cheerful and amiable face. He evidently found a keen delight in climbing his native hills toward the high country whither we were bound. He seemed not to feel the weight of the burden that he bore; his gait was light and free, his footing sure. He sprang up the steep and rugged way like a mountain goat.

The boy was in high spirits. He told me strange tales of ghosts and goblins, witches and fairies. These last he seemed to be very well acquainted with. He said they appeared in shining garments, with bright hair and beautiful wings, and this description agrees very nearly with what is related of them in books by certain of the fathers. Anyone to whom they take a fancy, says the boy, they are able to keep under their spell, and no one can break the enchantment, not even the Holy Virgin. But I judge that this is true of only such as are in sin, and that the pure in heart have nothing to fear from them.

We traveled up hill and down, through forests and blooming meadows and across ravines. The mountain streams, hastening down to the valleys, full-banked and noisy, seemed to be relating the wonderful things that they had seen and the strange adventures they had met with on their way. Sometimes the hillsides and the woods resounded with nature's various voices, calling, whispering, sighing, chanting praises to the Lord of All. Now and again we passed a mountaineer's cabin, before which played children, yellow-haired and unkempt. On seeing strangers, they ran away. But the women came forward, with infants in their arms, and asked for benedictions. They offered us milk, butter, green cheese and black bread. We frequently found the men seated in front of their huts, carving wood, mostly images of our Savior upon the cross. These are sent to the city of Munich, where they are offered for sale, bringing, I am told, considerable money and much honor to their pious makers.

At last we arrived at the shore of a lake, but a dense fog prevented a clear view of it. A clumsy little boat was found moored to the bank; my guide bade me enter it, and presently it seemed as if we were gliding through the sky in the midst of the clouds. I had never before been on the water, and felt a terrible misgiving lest we should capsize and drown. We heard nothing but the sound of the ripples against the sides of the boat. Here and there, as we advanced, some dark object became dimly visible for a moment, then vanished as suddenly as it had appeared, and we seemed gliding again through empty space. As the mist at times lifted a little, I observed great black rocks protruding from the water, and not far from shore were lying giant trees half submerged, with huge limbs that looked like the bones of some monstrous skeleton. The scene was so full of horrors that even the joyous youth was silent now, his watchful eye ever seeking to penetrate the fog in search of new dangers.

By all these signs I knew that we were crossing that fearful lake which is haunted by ghosts and demons, and I therefore commended my soul to God. The power of the Lord overcomes all evil. Scarcely had I said my prayer against the spirits of darkness, when suddenly the veil of fog was rent asunder, and like a great rose of fire the sun shone out, clothing the world in garments of color and gold!

Before this glorious eye of God the darkness fled and was no more. The dense fog, which had changed to a thin, transparent mist, lingered a little on the mountainside, then vanished quite away. Except in the black clefts of the hills, no vestige of it stayed. The lake was as liquid silver; the mountains were gold, bearing forests that were like flames of fire. My heart was filled with wonder and gratitude.

As our boat crept on I observed that the lake filled a long, narrow basin. On our right the cliffs rose to a great height, their tops covered with pines, but to the left and in front lay a pleasant land, where stood a large building. This was Saint Bartholomae, the summer residence of his reverence, Superior Andreas.

This garden spot was of no great extent. It was shut in on all sides but that upon which the lake lay by cliffs that rose a thousand feet into the air. High in the front of this awful wall was set a green meadow, which seemed like a great jewel gleaming upon the gray cloak of the mountain. My guide pointed it out as the only place in all that region where the edelweiss grew. This, then, was the very place where Benedicta had culled the lovely flowers that she had brought to me during my penance. I gazed upward to that beautiful but terrible spot with feelings that I have no words to express. The youth, his mood sympathetic with the now joyous aspect of nature, shouted and sang, but I felt the hot tears rise into my eyes and flow down upon my cheeks, and concealed my face in my cowl.

XXI

After leaving the boat we climbed the mountain. Dear Lord, nothing comes from thy hand without a purpose and a use, but why thou shouldst have piled up these mountains, and why thou shouldst have covered them with so many stones, is a mystery to me, since I can see no purpose in stones, which are a blessing to neither man nor beast.

After hours of climbing we reached a spring, where I sat down, faint and footsore and out of breath. As I looked about me the scene fully justified all that I had been told of these high solitudes. Wherever I turned my eyes was nothing but gray, bare rocks streaked with red and yellow and brown. There were dreary wastes of stones where nothing grew— no single plant nor blade of grass—dreadful abysses filled with ice, and glittering snowfields sloping upward till they seemed to touch the sky.

Among the rocks I did, however, find a few flowers. It seemed as if the Creator of this wild and desolate region had himself found it too horrible, and, reaching down to the valleys, had gathered a handful of flowers and scattered them in the barren places. These flowers, so distinguished by the divine hand, have bloomed with a celestial beauty that none others know. The boy pointed out the plant whose root I am to dig, as well as several strong and wholesome herbs serviceable to man, among them the golden-flowered arnica.

After an hour we continued our journey, which we pursued until I was hardly able to drag my feet along the path. At last we reached a lonely spot surrounded by great black rocks. In the center was a miserable hut of stones, with a low opening in one side for an entrance, and this, the youth told me, was to be my habitation. We entered, and my heart sank to think of dwelling in such a place. There was no furniture of any kind. A wide bench, on which was some dry Alpine grass, was to be my bed. There was a fireplace, with some wood for fuel, and a few simple cooking utensils.

The boy took up a pan and ran away with it, and, throwing myself down in front of the hut, I was soon lost in contemplation of the wildness and terror of the place in which I was to prepare my soul for service of the Lord. The boy soon returned, bearing the pan in both hands, and on seeing me he gave a joyful shout, whose echoes sounded like a hundred voices babbling among the rocks on every side. After even so short a period of solitude I was so happy to see a human face that I came near answering his greeting with unbecoming joy. How, then, could I hope to sustain a week of isolation in that lonely spot?

When the boy placed the pan before me it was full of milk, and he brought forth from his clothing a pat of yellow butter, prettily adorned with Alpine flowers, and a cake of snow-white cheese wrapped in aromatic herbs. The sight delighted me, and I asked him, jokingly:

"Do butter and cheese, then, grow on stones up here, and have you found a spring of milk?"

"You might accomplish such a miracle," he replied, "but I prefer to hasten to the Black Lake and ask this food of the young women who live there."

He then got some flour from a kind of pantry in the hut, and, having kindled a fire on the hearth, proceeded to make a cake.

"Then we are not alone in this wilderness," I said. "Tell me where is that lake on the shore of which these generous people dwell?"

"The Black Lake," he replied, blinking his eyes, which were full of smoke, "is behind that *Kogel* yonder, and the dairy house stands on the edge of the cliff above the water. It is a bad place. The lake reaches clear down to hell, and you can hear, through the fissures of the rocks, the roaring and hissing of the flames and the groans of the souls. And in no other place in all this world are there so many fierce and evil spirits. Beware of it! You might fall ill there in spite of your sanctity.

Milk and butter and cheese can be obtained at the Green Lake lower down, but I will tell the women to send up what you require. They will be glad to oblige you, and if you will preach them a sermon every Sunday, they will fight the very devil for you!"

After our meal, which I thought the sweetest that I had ever eaten, the boy stretched himself in the sunshine and straightway fell asleep, snoring so loudly that, tired as I was, I could hardly follow his example.

XXII

When I awoke the sun was already behind the mountains, whose tops were fringed with fire. I felt as one in a dream, but was soon recalled to my senses, and made to feel that I was alone in the wilderness by shouts of the young man in the distance. Doubtless he had pitied my condition, for, instead of disturbing me, he had gone away without taking leave, being compelled to reach the dairy on the Green Lake before nightfall. Entering the cabin, I found a fire burning lustily and a quantity of fuel piled beside it. Nor had the thoughtful youth forgotten to prepare my supper of bread and milk. He had also shaken up the grass on my hard bed, and covered it with a woolen cloth, for which I was truly grateful to him.

Refreshed by my long sleep, I remained outside the cabin till late in the evening. I said my prayers in view of the gray rocks beneath the black sky, in which the stars blinked merrily. They seemed much more brilliant up here than when seen from the valley, and it was easy to imagine that, standing on the extreme summit, one might touch them with his hands.

Many hours of that night I passed under the sky and the stars, examining my conscience and questioning my heart. I felt as if in church, kneeling before the altar and feeling the awful presence of the Lord. And at last my soul was filled with a divine peace, and as an innocent child presses its mother's breast, even so I leaned my head upon thine, O Nature, mother of us all!

XXIII

I had not before seen a dawn so glorious! The mountains were rose-red, and seemed almost transparent. The atmosphere was of a silvery lucidity, and so fresh and pure that with every breath I seemed to be taking new life. The dew, heavy and white, clung to the scanty grass blades like rain and dripped from the sides of the rocks.

It was while engaged in my morning devotions that I involuntarily became acquainted with my neighbors. All night long the marmots had squealed, greatly to my dismay, and they were now capering to and fro like hares. Overhead the brown hawks sailed in circles with an eye to the birds flitting among the bushes and the wood mice racing along the rocks. Now and again a troop of chamois passed near, on their way to the feeding grounds on the cliffs, and high above all I saw a single eagle rising into the sky, higher and higher, as a soul flies heavenward when purged of sin.

I was still kneeling when the silence was broken by the sound of voices. I looked about, but, although I could distinctly hear the voices and catch snatches of song, I saw no one. The sounds seemed to come from the heart of the mountain and, remembering the malevolent powers that infest the place, I repeated a prayer against the Evil One and awaited the event.

Again the singing was heard, ascending from a deep chasm, and presently I saw rising out of it three female figures. As soon as they saw me they ceased singing and uttered shrill screams. By this sign I knew them to be daughters of the earth, and thought they might be Christians, and so waited for them to approach.

As they drew near I observed that they carried baskets on their heads, and that they were tall, good-looking lasses, light-haired, brown in complexion and black-eyed. Setting their baskets upon the ground, they greeted me humbly and kissed my hands, after which they opened the baskets and displayed the good things they had brought me—milk, cream, cheese, butter and cakes.

Seating themselves upon the ground, they told me they were from the Green Lake, and said they were glad to have a "mountain brother" again, especially so young and handsome a one; and in saying so there were merry twinkles in their dark eyes and smiles on their red lips, which pleased me exceedingly.

I inquired if they were not afraid to live in the wilderness, at which they laughed, showing their white teeth. They said they had a hunter's gun in their cabin to keep off bears, and knew several powerful sentences and anathemas against demons. Nor were they very lonely, they added, for every Saturday the boys from the valley came up to hunt wild beasts, and then all made merry. I learned from them that meadows and cabins were common among the rocks, where herdsmen and herdswomen lived during the whole summer. The finest meadows, they said, belonged to the monastery, and lay but a short distance away.

The pleasant chatting of the maidens greatly delighted me, and the solitude began to be less oppressive. Having received the benediction, they kissed my hand and went away as they had come, laughing, singing and shouting in the joy of youth and health. So much I have already observed: the people in the mountains lead a better and happier life than those in the damp, deep valleys below. Also, they seem purer in heart and mind, and that may be due to their living so much nearer to heaven, which some of the brothers say approaches more closely to the earth here than at any other place in the world excepting Rome.

XXIV

The maidens having gone, I stowed away the provisions which they had brought me, and, taking a short pointed spade and a bag, went in search of the gentiana roots. They grew in abundance, and my back soon began to ache from stooping and digging; but I continued the labor, for I desired to send a good quantity to the monastery to attest my zeal and obedience. I had gone a long distance from my cabin without observing the direction which I had taken, when suddenly I found myself on the brink of an abyss so deep and terrible that I recoiled with a cry of horror. At the bottom of this chasm, so far below my feet that I was giddy to look down, a small circular lake was visible, like the eye of a fiend. On the shore of it, near a cliff overhanging the water, stood a cabin, from the stone-weighted roof of which rose a thin column of blue smoke. About the cabin, in the narrow and sterile pasture, a few cows and sheep were grazing. What a dreadful place for a human habitation!

I was still gazing down with fear into this gulf when I was again startled: I heard a voice distinctly call a name! The sound came from behind me, and the name was uttered with so caressing sweetness that I hastened to cross myself as a protection from the wiles of the fairies with their spells and enchantments. Soon I heard the voice again, and this time it caused my heart to beat so that I was near suffocation, for it was Benedicta's! Benedicta in this wilderness, and I alone with her! Surely I now had need of thy guidance, blessed Franciscus, to keep my feet in the path of the divine purpose.

I turned about and saw her. She was now springing from rock to rock, looking backward and calling the name that was strange to me. When she saw that I looked at her she stood motionless. I walked to her, greeting her in the name of the Blessed Virgin, though, God forgive me! hardly able in the tumult of my emotions to articulate that holy title.

Ah, how changed the poor child was! The lovely face was as pale as marble; the large eyes were sunken and inexpressibly sad. Her beautiful hair alone was unaltered, flowing over her shoulders like threads of gold. We stood looking at each other, silent from surprise; then I again addressed her:

"Is it, then, you, Benedicta, who live in the cabin down there by the Black Lake—near the waters of Avernus? And is your father with you?"

She made no reply, but I observed a quivering about her delicate mouth, as when a child endeavors to refrain from weeping. I repeated my question, "Is your father with you?"

She answered faintly, in a tone that was hardly more than a sigh:

"My father is dead."

I felt a sudden pain in my heart, and was for some moments unable to speak further, quite overcome by compassion. Benedicta had turned away her face to hide her tears, and her fragile frame was shaken by her sobs. I could no longer restrain myself. Stepping up to her, I took her hand in mine, and, trying to crush back into my secret heart every human desire, and address her in words of religious consolation, said:

"My child—dear Benedicta—your father is gone from you, but another Father remains who will protect you every day of your life. And as far as may accord with his holy will I, too, good and beautiful maiden, will help you to endure your great affliction. He whom you mourn is not lost. He is gone to the mercy seat, and God will be gracious to him."

But my words seemed only to awaken her sleeping grief. She threw herself upon the ground and gave way to her tears, sobbing so violently that I was filled with alarm. O Mother of Mercy! How can I bear the memory of the anguish I suffered in seeing this beautiful and innocent child overwhelmed with so great a flood of grief? I bent over her, and my own tears fell upon her golden hair. My heart urged me to lift her from the earth, but my hands were powerless to move. At length she composed herself somewhat and spoke, but as if she were talking to herself rather than to me.

"Oh, my father, my poor, heartbroken father! Yes, he is dead—they killed him—he died long ago of grief. My beautiful mother, too, died of grief—of grief and remorse for some great sin, I know not what, which he had forgiven her. He could only be compassionate and merciful. His heart was too tender to let him kill a worm or a beetle, and he was compelled to kill men. His father and his father's father had lived and died in the Galgenberg. They were hangmen all, and the awful inheritance fell to him. There was no escape, for the terrible people held him to the trade. I have heard him say that he was often tempted to kill himself, and but for me I am sure he would have done so. He could not leave me to starve, though he had to see me reviled, and at last, O Holy Virgin! publicly disgraced for that of which I was not guilty."

As Benedicta made this reference to the great injustice that she had been made to suffer her white cheeks kindled to crimson with the recollection of the shame which for her father's sake she had, at the time of it, so differently endured.

During the narrative of her grief she had partly risen and had turned her beautiful face more and more toward me as her confidence had grown; but now she veiled it with her hair, and would have turned her back but that I gently prevented her and spoke some words of comfort, though God knows my own heart was near breaking through sympathy with hers. After a few moments she resumed.

"Alas, my poor father! he was unhappy every way. Not even the comfort of seeing his child baptized was granted him. I was a hangman's daughter, and my parents were forbidden to present me for baptism; nor could any priest be found who was willing to bless me in the name of the Holy Trinity. So they gave me the name Benedicta, and blessed me themselves, over and over again.

"I was only an infant when my beautiful mother died. They buried her in unconsecrated ground. She could not go to the Heavenly Father in the mansions above, but was thrust into the flames. While she was dying my father had hastened to the reverend superior, imploring him to send a priest with the sacrament. His prayer was denied. No priest came, and my poor father closed her eyes himself, while his own were blind with tears of anguish for her terrible fate.

"And all alone he had to dig her grave. He had no other place than near the gallows, where he had so often buried the hanged and the accursed. With his own hands he had to place her in that unholy ground, nor could any Masses be said for her suffering soul.

"I well remember how my dear father took me then to the image of the Holy Virgin and bade me kneel, and, joining my little hands, taught me to pray for my poor mother, who had stood undefended before the terrible Judge of the Dead. This I have done every morning and evening since that day, and now I pray for both; for my father also has died unshriven, and his soul is not with God, but burns in unceasing fire.

"When he was dying I ran to the superior, just as he had done for my dear mother. I besought him on my knees. I prayed and wept and embraced his feet, and would have kissed his hand but that he snatched it away. He commanded me to go."

As Benedicta proceeded with her narrative she gained courage. She rose to her feet and stood erect, threw back her beautiful head, and lifted her eyes to the heavens as if recounting her wrongs to God's high angels and ministers of doom. She stretched forth her bare arms in gestures of so natural force and grace that I was filled with astonishment, and her unstudied words came from her lips with an eloquence of which I had never before had any conception. I dare not think it inspiration, for, God forgive us all! every word was an unconscious arraignment of him and his holy church; yet surely no mortal with lips untouched by a live coal from the altar ever so spake before! In the presence of this strange and gifted being I so felt my own unworth that I had surely knelt, as before a blessed saint, but that she suddenly concluded, with a pathos that touched me to tears.

"The cruel people killed him," she said, with a sob in the heart of every word. "They laid hands upon me whom he loved. They charged me falsely with a foul crime. They attired me in a garment of dishonor, and put a crown of straw upon my head, and hung about my neck the black tablet of shame. They spat upon me and reviled me, and compelled him to lead me to the pillory, where I was bound and struck with whips and stones. That broke his great, good heart, and so he died, and I am alone."

XXV

When Benedicta had finished I remained silent, for in the presence of such a sorrow what could I say? For such wounds as hers religion has no balm. As I thought of the cruel wrongs of this humble and harmless family there came into my heart a feeling of wild rebellion against the world, against the Church, against God! They were brutally unjust, horribly, devilishly unjust!—God, the Church and the world.

Our very surroundings—the stark and soulless wilderness, perilous with precipices and bleak with everlasting snows—

seemed a visible embodiment of the woeful life to which the poor child had been condemned from birth; and truly this was more than fancy, for since her father's death had deprived her of even so humble a home as the hangman's hovel she had been driven to these eternal solitudes by the stress of want. But below us were pleasant villages, fertile fields, green gardens, and homes where peace and plenty abided all the year.

After a time, when Benedicta was somewhat composed, I asked her if she had anyone with her for protection.

"I have none" she replied. But observing my look of pain, she added, "I have always lived in lonely, accursed places. I am accustomed to that. Now that my father is dead, there is no one who cares even to speak to me, nor any whom I care to talk with—except you." After a pause she said, "True, there is one who cares to see me, but he—"

Here she broke off, and I did not press her to explain lest it should embarrass her. Presently she said:

"I knew yesterday that you were here. A boy came for some milk and butter for you. If you were not a holy man the boy would not have come to me for your food. As it is, you cannot be harmed by the evil which attaches to everything I have or do. Are you sure, though, that you made the sign of the cross over the food yesterday?"

"Had I known that it came from you, Benedicta, that precaution would have been omitted," I answered.

She looked at me with beaming eyes, and said:

"Oh, dear sir, dear Brother!"

And both the look and the words gave me the keenest delight—as, in truth, do all this saintly creature's words and ways.

I inquired what had brought her to the cliff-top, and who the person was that I had heard her calling.

"It is no person," she answered, smiling. "It is only my goat. She has strayed away, and I was searching for her among the rocks."

Then nodding to me as if about to say farewell, she turned to go, but I detained her, saying that I would assist her to look for the goat.

We soon discovered the animal in a crevice of rock, and so

glad was Benedicta to find her humble companion that she
knelt by its side, put her arms about its neck and called it by
many endearing names. I thought this very charming, and
could not help looking upon the group with obvious admiration.
Benedicta, observing it, said:

"Her mother fell from a cliff and broke her neck. I took the
little one and brought it up on milk, and she is very fond of me.
One who lives alone as I do values the love of a faithful
animal."

When the maiden was about to leave me I gained the courage to speak to her of what had been so long in my mind. I said, "It is true, is it not, Benedicta, that on the night of the festival you went to meet the drunken boys in order to save your father from harm?"

She looked at me in great astonishment. "For what other reason could you suppose I went?"

"I could not think of any other," I replied, in some confusion.

"And now, good-by, Brother," she said, moving away.

"Benedicta," I cried. She paused and turned her head.

"Next Sunday I shall preach to the dairy women' at the Green Lake. Will you come?"

"Oh, no, dear Brother," she replied, hesitating and in low tones.

"You will not come?"

"I should like to come, but my presence would frighten away the dairy women and others whom your goodness would bring there to hear you. Your charity to me would cause you trouble. I pray you, sir, accept my thanks, but I cannot come."

"Then I shall come to you."

"Beware, O, pray, beware!"

"I shall come."

XXVI

The boy had taught me how to prepare a cake. I knew all that went to the making of it, and the right proportions, yet when I tried to make it I could not. All that I was able to make was a smoky, greasy pap, more fit for the mouth of Satan than for a pious son of the Church and follower of Saint Franciscus. My failure greatly discouraged me, yet it did not destroy my appetite; so, taking some stale bread, I dipped it in sour milk and was about to make my stomach do penance for its many sins, when Benedicta came with a basketful of good things from her dairy. Ah, the dear child. I fear that it was not with my heart only that I greeted her that blessed morning.

Observing the smoky mass in the pan, she smiled, and quietly throwing it to the birds (which may heaven guard!), she cleansed the pan at the spring, and, returning, arranged the fire. She then prepared the material for a fresh cake. Taking two handfuls of flour, she put it into an earthen bowl, and upon the top of it poured a cup of cream. Adding a pinch of salt, she mixed the whole vigorously with her slender white hands until it became a soft, swelling dough. She next greased the pan with a piece of yellow butter, and, pouring the dough into it, placed it on the fire. When the heat had penetrated the dough, causing it to expand and rise above the sides of the pan, she deftly pierced it here and there that it should not burst, and when it was well browned she took it up and set it before me, all unworthy as I was. I invited her to share the meal with me, but she would not. She insisted, too, that I should cross myself before partaking of anything that she had brought me or prepared, lest some evil come to me because of the ban upon her; but this I would not consent to do. While I ate she culled flowers from among the rocks, and, making a wreath, hung it upon the cross in front of the cabin; after which, when I had finished, she employed herself in cleansing the dishes and arranging everything in order as it should be, so that I imagined myself far more comfortable than before, even in merely looking about me. When there was nothing more to be done, and my conscience would not permit me to invent reasons for detaining her, she went away, and O, my Savior! how dismal and dreary seemed the day when she was gone! Ah, Benedicta, Benedicta, what is this that thou hast done to me?—making that sole service of the Lord to which I am dedicated seem less happy and less holy than a herdsman's humble life here in the wilderness with thee!

XXVII

Life up here is less disagreeable than I thought. What seemed to me a dreary solitude seems now less dismal and desolate. This mountain wilderness, which at first filled me with awe, gradually reveals its benign character. It is marvelously beautiful in its grandeur, with a beauty which purifies and elevates the soul. One can read in it, as in a book, the praises of its

Creator. Daily, while digging gentiana roots, I do not fail to listen to the voice of the wilderness and to compose and chasten my soul more and more.

In these mountains are not feathered songsters. The birds here utter only shrill cries. The flowers, too, are without fragrance, but wondrously beautiful, shining with the fire and gold of stars. I have seen slopes and heights here which doubtless were never trodden by any human foot. They seem to me sacred, the touch of the Creator still visible upon them, as when they came from his hand.

Game is in great abundance. Chamois are sometimes seen in such droves that the very hillsides seem to move. There are steinboks, veritable monsters, but as yet, thank heaven, I have seen no bears. Marmots play about me like kittens, and eagles, the grandest creatures in this high world, nest in the cliffs to be as near the sky as they can get.

When fatigued I stretch myself on the Alpine grass, which is as fragrant as the most precious spices. I close my eyes and hear the wind whisper through the tall stems, and in my heart is peace. Blessed be the Lord!

XXVIII

Every morning the dairy women come to my cabin, their merry shouts ringing in the air and echoed from the hills. They bring fresh milk, butter and cheese, chat a little while, and go away. Each day they relate something new that has occurred in the mountains or been reported from the villages below. They are joyous and happy, and look forward with delight to Sunday, when there will be divine service in the morning and a dance in the evening.

Alas, these happy people are not free of the sin of bearing false witness against their neighbors. They have spoken to me of Benedicta—called her a disgraceful wench, a hangman's daughter and (my heart rebels against its utterance) the mistress of Rochus! The pillory, they said, was made for such as she.

Hearing these maidens talk so bitterly and falsely of one

whom they so little knew, it was with difficulty that I mastered my indignation. But in pity of their ignorance I reprimanded them gently and kindly. It was wrong, I said, to condemn a fellow being unheard. It was unchristian to speak ill of any one.

They do not understand. It surprises them that I defend a person like Benedicta—one who, as they truly say, has been publicly disgraced and has not a friend in the world.

XXIX

This morning I visited the Black Lake. It is indeed an awful and accursed place, fit for the habitation of the damned. And there lives the poor forsaken child! Approaching the cabin, I could see a fire burning on the hearth, and over it was suspended a kettle. Benedicta was seated on a low stool, looking into the flames. Her face was illuminated with a crimson glow, and I could observe heavy teardrops on her cheeks.

Not wishing to see her secret sorrow, I hastened to make known my presence, and addressed her as gently as I could. She was startled, but when she saw who it was, smiled and blushed. She rose and came to greet me, and I began speaking to her almost at random, in order that she might recover her composure. I spoke as a brother might speak to his sister, yet earnestly, for my heart was full of compassion.

"O, Benedicta," I said, "I know your heart, and it has more love for that wild youth Rochus than for our dear and blessed Savior. I know how willingly you bore infamy and disgrace, sustained by the thought that he knew you innocent. Far be it from me to condemn you, for what is holier or purer than a maiden's love? I would only warn and save you from the consequence of having given it to one so unworthy."

She listened with her head bowed, and said nothing, but I could hear her sighs. I saw, too, that she trembled. I continued:

"Benedicta, the passion which fills your heart may prove your destruction in this life and hereafter. Young Rochus is not one who will make you his wife in the sight of God and man. Why did he not stand forth and defend you when you were falsely accused?"

"He was not there," she said, lifting her eyes to mine. "He

and his father were at Salzburg. He knew nothing till they told him."

May God forgive me if at this I felt no joy in another's acquittal of the heavy sin with which I had charged him. I stood a moment irresolute, with my head bowed, silent.

"But, Benedicta," I resumed, "will he take for a wife one whose good name has been blackened in the sight of his family and his neighbors? No, he does not seek you with an honorable purpose. O, Benedicta, confide in me. Is it not as I say?"

But she remained silent, nor could I draw from her a single word. She would only sigh and tremble; she seemed unable to speak. I saw that she was too weak to resist the temptation to love young Rochus; nay, I saw that her whole heart was bound up in him, and my soul melted with pity and sorrow— pity for her and sorrow for myself, for I felt that my power was unequal to the command that had been laid upon me. My agony was so keen that I could hardly refrain from crying out.

I went from her cabin, but did not return to my own. I wandered about the haunted shore of the Black Lake for hours, without aim or purpose.

Reflecting bitterly upon my failure, and beseeching God for greater grace and strength, it was revealed to me that I was an unworthy disciple of the Lord and a faithless son of the Church. I became more keenly conscious than I ever had been before of the earthly nature of my love for Benedicta, and of its sinfulness. I felt that I had not given my whole heart to God, but was clinging to a temporal and human hope. It was plain to me that unless my love for the sweet child should be changed to a purely spiritual affection, purified from all the dross of passion, I could never receive holy orders, but should remain always a monk and always a sinner. These reflections caused me great torment, and in my despair I cast myself down upon the earth, calling aloud to my Savior. In this my greatest trial I clung to the Cross. "Save me, O Lord!" I cried. "I am engulfed in a great passion—save me, oh, save me, or I perish forever!"

All that night I struggled and prayed and fought against the evil spirits in my soul, with their suggestions of recreancy to the dear Church whose child I am.

"The Church," they whispered, "has servants enough. You

are not as yet irrevocably bound to celibacy. You can procure a dispensation from your monastic vows and remain here in the mountains, a layman. You can learn the craft of the hunter or the herdsman, and be ever near Benedicta to guard and guide her—perhaps in time to win her love from Rochus and take her for your wife."

To these temptations I opposed my feeble strength and such aid as the blessed saint gave me in my great trial. The contest was long and agonizing, and more than once, there in the darkness and the wilderness, which rang with my cries, I was near surrender; but at the dawning of the day I became more tranquil, and peace once more filled my heart, even as the golden light filled the great gorges of the mountain where but a few moments before were the darkness and the mist. I thought then of the suffering and death of our Savior, who died for the redemption of the world, and most fervently I prayed that heaven would grant me the great boon to die likewise, in a humbler way, even though it were for but one suffering being—Benedicta.

May the Lord hear my prayer!

XXX

The night before the Sunday on which I was to hold divine service great fires were kindled on the cliffs—a signal for the young men in the valley to come up to the mountain dairies. They came in great numbers, shouting and screaming, and were greeted with songs and shrill cries by the dairy maidens, who swung flaming torches that lit up the faces of the great rocks and sent gigantic shadows across them. It was a beautiful sight. These are indeed a happy people.

The monastery boy came in with the rest. He will remain over Sunday, and, returning, will take back the roots that I have dug. He gave me much news from the monastery. The reverend superior is living at Saint Bartholomae, fishing and hunting. Another thing—one which gives me great alarm—is that the saltmaster's son, young Rochus, is in the mountains not far from the Black Lake. It seems he has a hunting lodge on the upper cliff, and a path leads from it directly to the lake. The boy told me this, but did not observe how I trembled when hearing it. Would that an angel with a flaming sword might guard the path to the lake, and to Benedicta!

The shouting and singing continued during the whole night, and between this and the agitation in my soul I did not close my eyes. Early the next morning the boys and girls arrived in crowds from all directions. The maidens wore silken kerchiefs twisted prettily about their heads, and had decorated themselves and their escorts with flowers.

Not being an ordained priest, I was not permitted either to read Mass or to preach a sermon, but I prayed with them and spoke to them whatever my aching heart found to say. I spoke to them of our sinfulness and God's great mercy; of our harshness to one another and the Savior's love for us all; of his infinite compassion. As my words echoed from the abyss below and the heights above, I felt as if I were lifted out of this world of suffering and sin and borne away on angels' wings to the radiant spheres beyond the sky! It was a solemn service, and my little congregation was awed into devotion and seemed to feel as if it stood in the Holy of Holies.

The service being concluded, I blessed the people and they quietly went away. They had not been long gone before I heard the lads send forth ringing shouts, but this did not displease me. Why should they not rejoice? Is not cheerfulness the purest praise a human heart can give?

In the afternoon I went down to Benedicta's cabin and found her at the door, making a wreath of edelweiss for the image of the Blessed Virgin, intertwining the snowy flowers with a purple blossom that looked like blood.

Seating myself beside her, I looked on at her beautiful work in silence, but in my soul was a wild tumult of emotion and a voice that cried, "Benedicta, my love, my soul, I love you more than life! I love you above all things on earth and in heaven!"

XXXI

The superior sent for me, and with a strange foreboding I followed his messenger down the difficult way to the lake and embarked in the boat. Occupied with gloomy reflections and presentiments of impending evil, I hardly observed that we had left the shore before the sound of merry voices apprised me of our arrival at St. Bartholomae. On the beautiful meadow surrounding the dwelling of the superior were a great number of people—priests, friars, mountaineers and hunters. Many were there who had come from afar with large retinues of servants and boys. In the house was a great bustle—a confusion and a hurrying to and fro, as during a fair. The doors stood wide open, and people ran in and out, clamoring noisily. The dogs yelped and howled as loud as they could. On a stand under an oak was a great cask of beer, and many of the people were gathered about it, drinking. Inside the house, too, there seemed to be much drinking, for I saw many men near the windows with mighty cups in their hands.

On entering, I encountered throngs of servants carrying dishes of fish and game. I asked one of them when I could see the superior. He answered that his reverence would be down immediately after the meal, and I concluded to wait in the hall. The walls were hung with pictures of some large fish which had been caught in the lake. Below each picture the weight of the monster and the date of its capture, together with the name of the person taking it, were inscribed in large letters. I could not help interpreting these records—perhaps uncharitably—as intimations to all good Christians to pray for the souls of those whose names were inscribed.

After more than an hour the superior descended the stairs. I stepped forward, saluting him humbly, as became my position. He nodded, eyed my sharply, and directed me to go to his apartment immediately after supper. This I did.

"How about your soul, my son Ambrosius?" he asked me, solemnly. "Has the Lord shown you grace? Have you endured the probation?"

Humbly, with my head bowed, I answered:

"Most reverend Father, God in my solitude has given me knowledge."

"Of what? Of your guilt?"

This I affirmed.

"Praise be to God!" exclaimed the superior. "I knew, my son, that solitude would speak to your soul with the tongue of an angel. I have good tidings for you. I have written in your behalf to the bishop of Salzburg. He summons you to his palace. He will consecrate you and give you holy orders in person, and you will remain in his city. Prepare yourself, for in three days you are to leave us."

The superior looked sharply into my face again, but I did not permit him to see into my heart. I asked for his benediction, bowed and left him. Ah, then, it was for this that I was summoned! I am to go away forever. I must leave my very life behind me; I must renounce my care and protection of Benedicta. God help her and me!

XXXII

I am once more in my mountain home, but tomorrow I leave it forever. But why am I sad? Does not a great blessing await me? Have I not ever looked forward to the moment of my consecration with longing, believing it would bring me the supreme happiness of my life? And now that this great joy is almost within my grasp, I am sad beyond measure.

Can I approach the altar of the Lord with a lie on my lips? Can I receive the holy sacrament as an impostor? The holy oil upon my forehead would turn to fire and burn into my brain, and I should be forever damned.

I might fall upon my knees before the Bishop and say, "Expel me, for I do not seek after the love of Christ, nor after holy and heavenly things, but after the things of this world."

If I so spoke, I should be punished, but I could endure that without a murmur.

If only I were sinless and could rightly become a priest, I could be of great service to the poor child. I should be able to give her infinite blessings and consolations. I could be her confessor and absolve her from sin, and, if I should outlive her—which God forbid!—might by my prayers even redeem her soul from purgatory. I could read Masses for the souls of her poor dead parents, already in torment.

Above all, if I succeeded in preserving her from that one great and destructive sin for which she secretly longs; if I could take her with me and place her under thy protection, O Blessed Virgin, that would be happiness indeed.

But where is the sanctuary that would receive the hangman's daughter? I know it but too well: when I am gone from here, the Evil One, in the winning shape he has assumed, will prevail, and she will be lost in time and eternity.

XXXIII

I have been at Benedicta's cabin.

"Benedicta," I said, "I am going away from here—away from the mountains—away from you."

She grew pale, but said nothing. For a moment I was overcome with emotion; I seemed to choke, and could not continue. Presently I said, "Poor child, what will become of you? I know that your love for Rochus is strong, and love is like a torrent which nothing can stay. There is no safety for you in clinging to the cross of our Savior. Promise me that you will do so— do not let me go away in misery, Benedicta."

"Am I, then, so wicked?" she said, without lifting her eyes from the ground. "Can I not be trusted?"

"Ah, but, Benedicta, the enemy is strong, and you have a traitor to unbar the gates. Your own heart, poor child, will at last betray you."

"He will not harm me," she murmured. "You wrong him, sir, indeed you do."

But I knew that I did not, and was all the more concerned to judge that the wolf would use the arts of the fox. Before the sacred purity of this maiden the base passions of the youth had not dared to declare themselves. But nonetheless I knew that an hour would come when she would have need of all her strength, and it would fail her. I grasped her arm and demanded that she take an oath that she would throw herself into the waters of the Black Lake rather than into the arms of Rochus. But she would not reply. She remained silent, her eyes fixed upon mine with a look of sadness and reproach which filled my mind with the most melancholy thoughts, and, turning away, I left her.

XXXIV

Lord, Savior of my soul, whither hast thou led me? Here am I in the culprit's tower, a condemned murderer, and tomorrow at sunrise I shall be taken to the gallows and hanged! For whoso slays a fellow being, he shall be slain; that is the law of God and man.

On this the last day of my life I have asked that I be permitted to write, and my prayer is granted. In the name of God and in the truth I shall now set down all that occurred.

Leaving Benedicta, I returned to my cabin, and, having packed everything, waited for the boy. But he did not come. I should have to remain in the mountains another night. I grew restless. The cabin seemed too narrow to hold me, the air too heavy and hot to sustain life. Going outside, I lay upon a rock and looked up at the sky, dark and glittering with stars. But my soul was not in the heavens; it was at the cabin by the Black Lake.

Suddenly I heard a faint, distant cry, like a human voice. I sat upright and listened, but all was still. It may have been, I thought, the note of some night bird. I was about to lie down again, when the cry was repeated, but it seemed to come from another direction. It was the voice of Benedicta! It sounded again, and now it seemed to come from the air—from the sky above my head, and distinctly it called my name; but, O Mother of God, what anguish was in those tones!

I leaped from the rock. "Benedicta, Benedicta!" I cried aloud. There was no reply.

"Benedicta, I am coming to thee, child!"

I sprang away in the darkness, along the path to the Black Lake. I ran and leaped, stumbling and falling over rocks and stumps of trees. My limbs were bruised, my clothing was torn, but I gave no heed; Benedicta was in distress, and I alone could save and guard her. I rushed on until I reached the Black Lake. But at the cabin all was quiet. There was neither light nor sound; everything was as peaceful as a house of God.

After waiting a long time, I left. The voice that I had heard calling me could not have been Benedicta's, but must have been that of some evil spirit mocking me in my great sorrow. I meant to return to my cabin, but an invisibile hand directed my steps another way; and although it led me to my death, I know it to have been the hand of the Lord.

Walking on, hardly knowing whither, and unable to find the path by which I had descended, I found myself at the foot of a precipice. Here was a narrow path leading steeply upward along the face of the cliff, and I began ascending it. After I had gone up some distance I looked above, and saw outlined against the starry sky a cabin perched upon the very verge. It flashed through my mind that this was the hunting lodge of the saltmaster's son, and this the path by which he visited Benedicta. Merciful Father! he, Rochus, was certain to come this way; there could be no other. I would wait for him here.

I crouched in the shadow and waited, thinking what to say to him and imploring the Lord for inspiration to change his heart and turn him from his evil purpose.

Before long I heard him approaching from above. I heard the stones displaced by his foot roll down the steep slopes and leap into the lake far below. Then I prayed God that if I should be unable to soften the youth's heart he might miss his footing and fall, too, like the stones; for it would be better that he should meet a sudden and impenitent death, and his soul be lost, than that he should live to destroy the soul of an innocent girl.

Turning at an angle of the rock, he stood directly before me as, rising, I stepped into the faint light of the new moon. He knew me at once, and in a haughty tone asked me what I wanted.

I replied mildly, explaining why I had barred his way, and begging him to go back. He insulted and derided me.

"You miserable cowler," he said, "will you never cease

meddling in my affairs? Because the mountain maids are so foolish as to praise your white teeth and your big black eyes, must you fancy yourself a man, and not a monk? You are no more to women than a goat!"

I begged him to desist and to listen to me. I threw myself on my knees and implored him, however he might despise me and my humble though holy station, to respect Benedicta and spare her. But he pushed me from him with his foot upon my breast. No longer master of myself, I sprang erect, and called him an assassin and a villain.

At this he pulled a dagger from his belt, saying, "I will send you to hell!"

Quick as a flash of lightning my hand was upon his wrist. I wrested the knife from him and flung it behind me, crying, "Not with weapons, but unarmed and equal, we will fight to the death, and the Lord shall decide!"

We sprang upon each other with the fury of wild animals, and were instantly locked together with arms and hands. We struggled upward and downward along the path, with the great wall of rock on one side, and on the other the precipice, the abyss, the waters of the Black Lake! We writhed and strained for the advantage, but the Lord was against me, for he permitted my enemy to overcome me and throw me down on the edge of the precipice. I was in the grasp of a strong enemy, whose eyes glowed like coals of fire. His knee was on my breast and my head hung over the edge—my life was in his hands. I thought he would push me over, but he made no attempt to do so. He held me there between life and death for a dreadful time, then said in a low, hissing voice, "You see, monk, if I but move I can hurl you down the abyss like a stone. But I care not to take your life, for it is no impediment to me. The girl belongs to me, and to me you shall leave her. Do you understand?"

With that he rose and left me, going down the path toward the lake. His footfalls had long died away in the silent night before I was able to move hand or foot. Great God! I surely did not deserve such defeat, humiliation and pain. I had but wished to save a soul, yet heaven permitted me to be conquered by him who would destroy it!

Finally I was able to rise, although in great pain, for I was bruised by my fall, and could still feel the fierce youth's knee upon my breast and his fingers about my throat. I walked with difficulty back along the path, downward toward the lake. Wounded as I was, I would return to Benedicta's cabin and interpose my body between her and harm. But my progress was slow, and I had frequently to rest; yet it was near dawn before I gave up the effort, convinced that I should be too late to do the poor child the small service of yielding up my remnant of life in her defense.

At early dawn I heard Rochus returning, with a merry song upon his lips. I concealed myself behind a rock, though not in fear, and he passed without seeing me.

At this point there was a break in the wall of the cliff, the path crossing a great crevice that clove the mountain as by a sword stroke from the arm of a Titan. The bottom was strewn with loose boulders and overgrown with brambles and shrubs, through which trickled a slender stream of water fed by the melting snows above. Here I remained for three days and two nights. I heard the boy from the monastery calling my name as he traversed the path searching for me, but I made no answer. Not once did I quench my burning thirst at the brook nor appease my hunger with blackberries that grew abundantly on every side. Thus I mortified the sinful flesh, killed rebellious nature and subdued my spirit to the Lord until at last I felt myself delivered from all evil, freed from the bondage of an early love and prepared to devote my heart and soul and life to no woman but thee, O Blessed Virgin!

The Lord having wrought this miracle, my soul felt as light and free as if wings were lifting me to the skies. I praised the Lord in a loud voice, shouting and rejoicing till the rocks rang with the sound. I cried, "Hosanna! Hosanna!" I was now prepared to go before the altar and receive the holy oil upon my head. I was no longer myself. Ambrosius, the poor erring monk, was dead; I was an instrument in the right hand of God to execute his holy will. I prayed for the delivery of the soul of the beautiful maiden, and as I prayed, behold! there appeared to me in the splendor and glory of heaven the Lord himself, attended by innumerable angels, filling half the sky! A great rapture enthralled my senses; I was dumb with happiness. With a smile of ineffable benignity God spake to me:

"Because that thou hast been faithful to thy trust, and through all the trials that I have sent upon thee hast not faltered, the salvation of the sinless maiden's soul is now indeed given into thy hands."

"Thou, Lord, knowest," I replied, "that I am without the means to do this work, nor know I how it is to be done."

The Lord commanded me to rise and walk on, and, turning my face from the glorious Presence, which filled the heart of the cloven mountain with light, I obeyed, leaving the scene of my purgation and regaining the path that led up the face of the cliff. I began the ascent, walking on and on in the splendor of the sunset, reflected from crimson clouds.

Suddenly I felt impelled to stop and look down, and there at my feet, shining red in the cloudlight, as if stained with blood, lay the sharp knife of Rochus. Now I understood why the Lord had permitted that wicked youth to conquer me, yet had moved him to spare my life. I had been reserved for a more glorious purpose. And so was placed in my hands the means to that sacred end. My God, my God, how mysterious are thy ways!

XXXV

"You shall leave her to me." So had spoken the wicked youth while holding me between life and death at the precipice. He permitted me to live, not from Christian mercy, but because he despised my life, a trivial thing to him, not worth taking. He was sure of his prey; it did not matter if I were living or dead.

"You shall leave her to me." Oh, arrogant fool! Do you not know that the Lord holds his hand over the flowers of the field and the young birds in the nest? Leave Benedicta to you? Permit you to destroy her body and her soul? Ah, you shall see how the hand of God shall be spread above her to guard and save. There is yet time—that soul is still spotless and undefiled. Forward, then, to fulfill the command of the Most High God!

I knelt upon the spot where God had given into my hand the means of her deliverance. My soul was wholly absorbed in the mission entrusted to me. My heart was in ecstasy, and I saw plainly, as in a vision, the triumphant completion of the act which I had still to do.

I arose, and, concealing the knife in my robe, retraced my steps, going downward toward the Black Lake. The new moon looked like a divine wound in the sky, as if some hand had plunged a dagger into heaven's holy breast.

Benedicta's door was ajar, and I stood outside a long time, gazing upon the beautiful picture presented to my eyes. A bright fire on the hearth lit up the room. Opposite the fire sat Benedicta, combing her long golden hair. Unlike what it was the last time I had stood before her cabin and gazed upon it, her face was full of happiness and had a glory that I had never imagined in it. A sensuous smile played about her lips while she sang in a low, sweet voice the air of a love song of the people. Ah me! she was beautiful; she looked like a bride of heaven. But though her voice was as that of an angel, it angered me, and I called out to her:

"What are you doing, Benedicta, so late in the evening? You sing as if you expected your lover, and arrange your hair as for a dance. It is but three days since I, your brother and only friend, left you, in sorrow and despair. And now you are as happy as a bride."

She sprang up and manifested great joy at seeing me again, and hastened to kiss my hands. But she had no sooner glanced into my face than she uttered a scream of terror and recoiled from me as if I had been a fiend from hell!

But I approached her and asked, "Why do you adorn yourself so late in the night? Why are you so happy? Have the three days been long enough for you to fall? Are you the mistress of Rochus?"

She stood staring at me in horror. She asked, "Where have you been and why do you come? You look so ill! Sit, sir, I pray you, and rest. You are pale and you shake with cold. I will make you a warm drink and you will feel better."

She was silenced by my stern gaze. "I have not come to rest and be nursed by you," I said. "I am here because the Lord commands. Tell me why you sang."

She looked up at me with the innocent expression of a babe,

and replied, "Because I had for the moment forgotten that you were going away, and I was happy."

"Happy?"

"Yes—he has been here."

"Who? Rochus?"

She nodded. "He was so good," she said. "He will ask his father to consent to see me, and perhaps take me to his great house and persuade the reverend superior to remove the curse from my life. Would not that be fine? But then," she added, with a sudden change of voice and manner, lowering her eyes, "perhaps you would no longer care for me. It is because I am poor and friendless."

"What! He will persuade his father to befriend you? To take you to his home? You, the hangman's daughter? He, this reckless youth, at war with God and God's ministers, will move the Church! O, lie, lie, lie! O Benedicta—lost, betrayed Benedicta! By your smiles and by your tears I know that you believe the monstrous promises of this infamous villain."

"Yes," she said, inclining her head as if she were making a confession of faith before the altar of the Lord, "I believe him."

"Kneel, then," I cried, "and praise the Lord for sending one of his chosen to save your soul from temporal and eternal perdition!"

At these words she trembled as in great fear.

"What do you wish me to do?" she exclaimed.

"To pray that your sins may be forgiven."

A sudden rapturous impulse seized my soul. "I am a priest," I cried, "anointed and ordained by God himself, and in the name of the Father, and of the Son, and of the Holy Spirit, I forgive you your only sin, which is your love. I give you absolution without repentance. I free your soul from the taint of sin because you will atone for it with your blood and life."

With these words, I seized her and forced her down upon her knees. But she wanted to live; she cried and wailed. She clung to my knees and entreated and implored in the name of God and the Blessed Virgin. Then she sprang to her feet and attempted to run away. I seized her again, but she broke away from my grasp and ran to the open door, crying, "Rochus! Rochus! Help, O, help!"

Springing after her, I grasped her by the shoulder, turned her half-round and plunged the knife into her breast.

I held her in my arms, pressed her against my heart and felt her warm blood upon my body. She opened her eyes and fixed upon me a look of reproach, as if I had robbed her of a life of happiness. Then her eyes slowly closed, she gave a long, shuddering sigh, her little head turned upon her shoulder, and so she died.

I wrapped the beautiful body in a white sheet, leaving the face uncovered, and laid it upon the floor. But the blood tinged the linen, so I parted her long golden hair, spreading it over the crimson roses upon her breast. As I had made her a bride of heaven, I took from the image of the Virgin the wreath of edelweiss and placed it on Benedicta's brow; and now I remembered the edelweiss which she had once brought me to comfort me in my penance.

Then I stirred the fire, which cast upon the shrouded figure and the beautiful face a rich red light, as if God's glory had descended there to enfold her. It was caught and tangled in the golden tresses that lay upon her breast, so that they looked a mass of curling flame.

And so I left her.

XXXVI

I descended the mountain by precipitous paths, but the Lord guided my steps so that I neither stumbled nor fell into the abyss. At the dawning of the day I arrived at the monastery, rang the bell and waited until the gate was opened. The brother porter evidently thought me a fiend, for he raised a howl that aroused the whole monastery. I went straight to the room of the superior, stood before him in my bloodstained garments, and, telling him for what deed the Lord had chosen me, informed him that I was now an ordained priest. At this they seized me, put me into the tower, and, holding court upon me, condemned me to death as if I were a murderer. O, the fools, the poor demented fools!

One person has come to me today in my dungeon, who fell upon her knees before me, kissed my hands and adored me as God's chosen instrument—Amula, the brown maiden. She alone has discovered that I have done a great and glorious deed.

I have asked Amula to chase away the vultures from my body, for Benedicta is in heaven.

I shall soon be with her. Praise be to God! Hosanna! Amen.

[To this old manuscript are added the following lines in another hand: "On the fifteenth day of October, in the year of our Lord 1680, in this place, Brother Ambrosius was hanged, and on the following day his body was buried under the gallows, close to that of the girl Benedicta, whom he killed. This Benedicta, though called the hangman's daughter, was (as is now known through declarations of the youth Rochus) the bastard child of the saltmaster by the hangman's wife. It is also veritably attested by the same youth that the maiden cherished a secret and forbidden love for him who slew her in ignorance of her passion. In all else Brother Ambrosius was a faithful servant of the Lord. Pray for him, pray for him!"]

THE STORIES AND FABLES OF AMBROSE BIERCE

Designed by Susan Bishop

Composed in Century Expanded, with Cheltenham
Open display, by the Maryland Linotype Composition
Company, Baltimore, Maryland

Color separation by Graphic Technology, Fort
Lauderdale, Florida

Printed on 70-lb. Mead Moistrite Opaque Offset,
Regular Finish, by the John D. Lucas Printing
Company, Baltimore, Maryland

Bound in paper by the John D. Lucas Printing
Company, Baltimore, Maryland

Hardbound in Kivar Victoria Garnet and Kivar
Corinthian Gray by the Delmar Printing Company,
Charlotte, North Carolina